The Power of Rain

The Power of Rain

Gawain Barker

ISBN-13: 978-0-9876430-7-0

Cover design and imprint
bushbrother

website
thecolourofshadows.com

for

the old town

A Good Man

1975

She was a sweetie, the firelight turning her blonde hair into a nimbus of gold, the flicker of flames animating her young face with moving shadows. Among the big trees, up in the canopy high above them, a nightbird called out, and she paused and smiled.

Perky and intense, she'd been talking at speed. Seth was listening closely, pleased to be distracted, happy watching her hands help shape her rave, and desperate to be lost in her words. He didn't know much about colloidal silver, but he was right into it now.

With his heart pounding and his guts rolling, he looked at the others sitting on logs around the fire – three fellas and a chick, old mates by the sound of their laughter. Stay here by the fire with us, Seth silently pleaded. Please don't go anywhere.

A band was playing at the main house, someone handy on the drum kit, and the lead guitarist, a fella called Little Greg, was sending a solo soaring over the generators and the noise of a couple of hundred people.

As parties go, it was a big one – a double birthday for Babs and Moonie, two cool characters from the far north's non-straight community, the people who lived just ahead of the rules and close to their own terms. They liked drugs and music, souped-up cars, and fishing boats, and they dug the bush and the sea; everyone united in their general dislike for authority, especially the cops.

Some were mellow souls: hippies, artists, and greenies; others were tougher: revheads, fishermen, and labourers. There were some criminals and musicians too, and more than a few of this loosely affiliated mob grew and sold dope, with some groovers dealing acid, or other drugs.

Many made their own little version of Eden in the great emptiness of the far north, buying bush blocks with all the privacy they wanted – or needed. They built homes and worked out ways to live off their land. Others just needed somewhere to hide out when life had got too hot – a place to lick wounds, reload, and make better plans.

Moonie's property was remote, a clearing in the jungle an hour's drive from the nearest locality: a store with a fuel bowser. The closest neighbours were over in the next valley. Everything ran on generator, and there were no phones. If things got out of hand, nobody was calling the cops.

But things had got out of hand – way out of hand. Seth felt giddy, the horror of the moment upon him. He rallied, refocused on the young woman, and shit! – the blokes and the chick got up and began walking to the main house.

No, no, no, thought Seth. It was time to get up and take this chick down to the house. Struggling to find a reason, something that wasn't the truth, he tried on an apologetic smile as he looked for a good lie.

She began speaking again, but her eyes looked beyond him, and her brow furrowed. Through the trees came the approaching rumble of voices. He heard his brother Alex putting on a girlish voice, then the nasty guffaws of his mates the Macintyre brothers. The little blonde's eyes widened as the crunch of boots came up behind him. He felt a cuff to the head materialising out of the darkness.

Instead, a hand covered his face, acrid fingers wiping hard under his nose, and he twisted, nearly falling off the log. A punch caught the back of the head; not real hard, but still a good clout.

The little blonde chick yelled in surprise. Cruel laughter sounded as he regained his balance.

He felt total dread at what might happen now, but his brother and the Macs kept moving, walking right past.

Tall, lean, animal-fit; in cut-off shirts, jeans, and boots, firelight flickering on their biceps, grins, and knuckles, they looked like the hardest blokes on the planet.

The young woman stared up at them. "Hey!" she yelled at Alex.

"Hello, darling," he said, smiling at her in passing. "I wouldn't waste your time with him. He's a soft cock."

Malevolent laughter came from the Mac brothers, the bongs and rollies catching husky in Gordy's throat.

"You bastards! What's wrong with you?" Seething, she jumped to her feet.

"No, no, no," hissed Seth, fear ripping through him.

He couldn't stand aside again. He had to shut her up or there'd be proper violence; a cyclone of broken teeth, spilt blood, and broken bones; a storm that would crush him.

Liam Mac looked over his shoulder. Frantic now, Seth leapt to his feet, but Liam just sneered and kept going.

"Hey, I'm talking to you," yelled the little woman. Seth stepped in front of her, blocking her from view.

"Shoosh, shoosh," he crooned in terror.

"Shoosh yourself." She tried to move around him. His hand flew up to cover her mouth.

Eyes wide in shock, she angrily batted it away.

"What are you doing? He just punched you!"

Smiling in panic, he took her small shoulder in his big hand and forced her to turn back to the fire.

"What are you doing?" Disbelief and fear in her voice.

"Listen, please. Please shut up," said Seth. He began to push her back down onto the log seat.

Struggling, lashing her hair up at him, she tried to break free, her small body ducking and weaving. Firmly holding her, he kept pushing her down as he snatched a look over his shoulder. His brother and the Macs had disappeared into the darkness.

He let go and she stumbled away. Turning, she yelled at him, disappointment and anger huge on her face.

"You arsehole! I thought you were a good man!"

Z Force Commando Plan

1976

It wasn't just the M16 assault rifle the fella crawling towards the crop had with him that was freaking Seth out. It was also the dark blue overalls he was wearing with the word Police printed in white across the back.

Seth's scalp tingled with ice-cold electricity. He'd never seen a cop with a military weapon before. This was a raid, a deadly serious one.

The faint engine grumble that brought him to the ridge fifteen minutes ago must have been a police Land Cruiser bush-bashing in from Mt. Spurgeon Road or the logging track. It would be one of a few vehicles, that's for sure.

He let the binoculars fall against his chest. Their worst fears had been realised. He had to get back down pronto, sight unseen, and let his brother Alex, Lou, and the other two know that they were about to get done. With over seven hundred mature marijuana plants and a camp full of incriminating gear, it was going to be a balls-out race to avoid serious jailtime.

Nearly ten o'clock, it was already hot here at the edge of the Windsor Tablelands. The dividing range to the east was heavily forested, but these foothills were a landscape of dusty ridges, spear grass, and a million gum trees.

Seth eyed the fella with the gun for a few more seconds, then carefully scooted on his bum down the crest of the ridge. Out of sight of the cop, he jumped up and sprinted towards the long dry creek bed that led into the camp.

Holding the binoculars against his chest, he ran down the ridge onto flat ground and went all out. With boots pounding on the hard ground and sweat bursting from his armpits, he prayed like crazy that Alex, Pat, and Lenny were not going to get shot down in the crop.

After five minutes of running hard, the outcrop of rock and the stand of rose gums came into view. Near the camp, a lonely crow called. As its mournful cry evaporated in the hot air, Seth heard a percussive engine pulse in the eastern sky.

Pelting up to the camouflage netting of their tents, he saw Lou in shorts and sleeveless army shirt, staring up at the sky, looking for the helicopter heading their way.

Damn, damn, damn, thought Seth. What a cock-up. She shouldn't be here – not now, not in a raid.

"The cops are here!" he yelled. "They're real close. Grab what you need."

Lou responded instantly. That was good.

She'd been in Ballina for a month, and Alex had picked her up from the airport this morning. She'd been out to the crop once before, and it had been cool, but Alex should have left her at Digger Street as planned.

Trouble was, his brother's deck was stacked with wild cards, and he often did baffling things, never explaining his reasons. The silence between Lou and Alex when they arrived looked like they'd had a fight. Maybe bringing her up here was some sort of punishment. It was just what his brother would do.

Slipping the binoculars strap tight over his shoulder, he ran to the storage tent, grabbed the nickel-plated Acme Thunderer hanging there and gave it three ear-splitting blasts. Down at the crop they'd know what that meant. Out in the scrub, the cops would too. Everybody would start running like headless chooks now.

Alex's truck was getting its gearbox replaced, so he had borrowed Mick's Land Cruiser to go and get Lou, as well as picking up food supplies in Cairns. Mick, never happy loaning anything, had been glad to get his truck back but not pleased at seeing Lou. He'd been real polite to her, then, royally pissed off, he'd left, gruffly telling Alex he'd be back in a day or two.

That left the bikes. Just like the plan.

Leaving the whistle to swing, Seth grabbed bike keys and four small canvas haversacks, each one containing a torch, a rudimentary tool kit, and a two-litre canteen of water.

Alex had it all worked out. Revved up at meeting Seth's mate Les, who'd served in Southeast Asia, he'd devised a Z Force commando plan in case the crop ever got raided.

Mick would go into hiding; he'd found a quiet spot on the Tablelands and was prepared for days, if not weeks, of invisible camping. Everybody else would get the hell out of there, staying on trails in the scrub if they could, and using the Peninsula Development Road when they had to.

Eyes peeled for road blocks, he and Alex would leave the road at Mount Molloy and take the backroads to Black

Mountain Road. On the other side of the big forest there, they'd rendezvous in Kuranda, wait until nightfall, then slip back down to Cairns. Pat and Lenny would go north to mates on acreage near Cooktown, using hiding spots on the way to lay low if it got too hot.

The bikes, a Honda Elsinore, two Suzuki 185 Ag bikes, and a Yamaha DT 360, were tested off-road machines that had been used sparingly around here, as their two-stroke racket carried for miles. They all had plates from wrecked, dumped, or nicked bikes. When the dust cleared, the real licence plates would be reattached, and the bikes kept off-road for a while.

Seth put bags on seats, slotted keys into ignitions. Back at the storage tent, he grabbed helmets and goggles and ran them to the bikes.

Lou raced up. She had a shoulder bag and had changed into jeans – much better for riding pillion. Seth flashed on a change of clothes for when he got to the coast. If he got spotted up here, it just might save him from being busted.

He grabbed shorts and a t-shirt from his tent, ran back. Lou stood by the bikes, her breathing steady. Good girl. Seth smiled bravely. So did she.

"Okay," he said. "We're ready."

They looked towards the crop, hoping like hell to see the cut-off army shirts, green footy shorts, and suntanned faces of the boys coming through the scrub.

The scrub stared back. With no breeze, nothing moved. Insects shrilled mindlessly. The ground rippled with heat. It was like being inside a photograph. From the east, the drone of the chopper drew closer.

Seth looked at the Yamaha 360, Alex's bike customised with a seat instead of a utility rack, a solid exhaust shield, and pegs for riding pillion. He'd be using it if Alex didn't get his arse here soon. He stuffed the binoculars and his change of clothes into the bag on the bike's seat.

His heartbeat hammered, his arms tingled. The crow whinged again, bemoaning its hard life. Lou softly sighed, like she was watching a boring movie.

Sweat slid down Seth's neck. The hard mutter in the sky deepened; the chopper just a few kilometres away now. Indecision racked him.

Out in the scrub, maybe just coming into sight of the camp, were cops with automatic rifles. They were trained and everything, but with the heat and all the excitement, who knows how trigger-happy they might be? The chance of copping a bullet was growing by the second.

He ran a hand through his sweat-wet blonde hair. As intolerable as it was, he and Alex and the boys would get through a jail sentence in one piece. They were all pretty handy with their fists, and they'd look out for each other.

But Lou was beautiful, well-educated, and young. From a good family, she had a real future ahead of her.

She'd get smashed in jail. Steamrolled. He couldn't let that happen. Sorry, Alex, you're on your own.

"Seth?" said Lou. He turned to her.

She was holding a helmet out. "Let's go," she said.

"What about. . .?"

"I don't want to go to jail."

He felt a king-hit of relief. She'd called it.

Taking the helmet, he gave Lou the canvas bag, and she

pulled it on, then slung her own bag over her shoulder. He got on the Yamaha, turned the key, and kick-started it. The bike settled slightly as arms went around his waist, and a firm, warm shape pressed into his back.

For a long blissful moment, he wasn't there with the cops closing in and fear pumping through him. Lou had her arms around him, and it was perfect.

But the big, bad world roared back, and he checked her feet were on the pegs, then opened up the throttle and let rip. With the bike roaring between his thighs, and trees accelerating past, he felt a rousing rush of confidence.

Waiting just killed him; action made him come alive. Something in the physicality of *doing* mellowed him out, and his brain ran a step ahead of the action like the world had slowed down.

Riding away from the camp, they turned off the creek bed and into open eucalyptus forest. The hard, dry ground was scattered with clumps of kangaroo and spear grass. Dry dead tree trunks lurked in the grass tussocks; fists of hard rock too. With the gumtrees spaced widely apart, it was fast going, but those things hidden in the long grass could spill them off the bike and break bones.

Looking for the forestry road, Seth kept his bearings by checking on Mount Elephant, just visible over the next ridgeline. Riding hard, he weaved around ironbarks and yellow jackets, passing close to a purple spray of coral pea creeper devouring a tree.

Now Lou began to yell over the engine roar, her urgent tone directing him to look.

Snatching a glance to his left, he saw trees, red dirt, and

big tussocks of kangaroo grass. On his right, metres away and keeping up, was a cop in blue overalls on a Yamaha 250 with a holstered pistol on his belt.

For God's sake, thought Seth, a bloody motocross hero, the Gary Flood of the Queensland Police wanting to make me a feather in his cap. Seeing him looking, the copper signalled for him to pull over like they were cruising down Spence Street on a Sunday afternoon.

Yeah, right, thought Seth as the big, wide trunk of a white mahogany rapidly filled his vision. He went around one side, the cop around the other, and just metres past the tree the idiot put on speed, trying to cut him off, as though the hundred and fifty kilos of the Alex's bike wouldn't break his leg and send them all flying.

Seth braked hard, Lou flattening against him. He pulled the handlebars sideways, fighting to keep the bike up. As the fool flew by, he yelled some bullshit cop command.

Gunning the throttle, Seth took off at an angle, making for higher ground. Scrambling on the dirt, rocks jumped under the wheels as they rapidly ascended; Lou's extra weight just perfect for this.

Tacking across the slope, he rode smart and made good ground. Rocketing past fallen trees, he got to the top and looked back. In an explosion of dust, the cop was coming straight up the slope. Bucking and jerking like a fella on a rodeo bull, the stupid bastard was going to lose it.

Going hard, Seth rode down the other side of the hill. Down the bottom it didn't look real good – a dry creek bed filled with rocks and boulders. At the edge of this jumbled obstacle, he halted and pulled down his goggles.

Scanning the creek bed, he saw a spot that might work. It wasn't crash-hot, but it would have to do. He killed the engine, and without prompting, Lou hopped off. Looking around at the sky, he felt massive relief at not seeing or hearing the helicopter.

He wheeled the bike onto rocks, Lou jumping in to help. He didn't have to tell her to avoid touching the engine and exhaust pipe as they pushed and heaved the heavy bike. Timing her moves with his, she grunted in exertion, sweat running down her neck from under her helmet.

Metal scraped rock, rubber squealed, and with one last guts-effort push, they got the bike up onto the grass and dirt of the creek bank. Behind them, the yammering of the 250 came over the crest of the hill.

Frustration pummelled Seth. How bloody gung-ho was this bastard? Out here on his lonesome, chasing fugitives who might be armed, it was a sure bet he was aiming to star in a story he could retell for years. The silly prick was having the time of his life.

"You right?" he asked Lou. She quickly nodded, great, and they got back on the bike.

As he rode up the slope, Seth was relieved he didn't have a freaked-out chick to deal with. Lou was doing it right, clinging to him like a limpet, and moving as he did. That was good, because it was going to get hairy again.

The graded dirt road used by loggers going up onto the Windsor Tableland would be coming up soon. He'd take it to get onto the bitumen of the Peninsular Development Road. And that's where the bullymen would be – waiting with the road block.

With the sun as his guide, he rode in a more southerly direction, eyes straining through the goggles for the road.

Tall gums choked with rubber vine flashed by, and the landscape began to change: deep folds in the earth from ancient upheaval softened by erosion, the kangaroo grass everywhere on the uneven ground. Seth suddenly felt the bike's wheels slide along the edge of a washout.

He wrenched the handlebars, but the ground fell away. The back wheel swung out into space, and Lou clamped in hard as he tried to keep the front wheel on solid ground.

Dust and stones boiled up as rubber sawed into dirt. They teetered, the roaring bike on a seesaw, then the front wheel found purchase and Seth worked the throttle. With a surge of power, they became airborne for a few seconds. Thumping back down, he put on speed.

There was a flash of reflected light. The Yammie 250 materialised in the grass below them and came tearing up the slope. Swerving and jumping in his eagerness to get to them, the cop looked as if he might come off his bike.

With awful realisation, Seth saw that this bloke was a nutter – a young maverick with everything to prove to the old guard. He'd got across the rubble of the creek bed bloody quick, and he wasn't stopping till he ran out of gas.

This bastard's going to be like a tick, thought Seth, and dread intimation rose inside him. Someone could die out here today.

Super aware of Lou clinging to him, he knew he had to do something to stop this dangerous fool. Something decisive. Something stone-cold crazy.

Releasing the throttle, he slowed fast. The cop kept on

coming full tilt, and before he knew it, he was in the lead.

"Hold on!" yelled Seth, hoping Lou would understand. It seemed she did, the arms around his waist squeezing even tighter. Snapping back the throttle, he howled down the slope like a Mongol horseman.

Sunlight flashed on the cop's helmet as he looked over his shoulder. Seeing the approaching 360, he slowed right down. Nice one, thought Seth.

As he came alongside the 250, he jerked his knee up over his fuel tank and kicked out sideways – hard. The flat of his boot slammed into the cop. Shock ran through his leg, but the heavier bike with him and Lou on it wasn't going anywhere, and the 250 vanished.

He swerved back towards the ridgetop, his focus on the ground ahead. Praying hard that any rock or log under the grass was running for cover, he got to the top.

Looking back, he saw a small cloud of dust, but nothing moving. The cop must have stopped bouncing. Hopefully he wasn't too dinged up, but, shit, aye – you play with the bull, you get the horns.

Coming down the slope, moving through the trees, Seth saw that the ground ahead was levelling out. The forestry road couldn't be far off now. Then, just before the flat, the ground dropped away under the front wheel – another bloody washout hidden in the grass.

He went with it, Lou like an extension of his body, and they sailed out into space. When the bike hit the dirt again, they barrelled headlong towards trees.

Wildly correcting, Seth nearly hit a big turpentine, then rode into a fallen tree covered in coral pea. Its web of dead branches snapping and crackling on his arms, legs and helmet as they came to a halt. Among branches, Lou cried out. Seth dropped the revs to a grumble, twisted his head to look. "You right, Lou? You okay?" he yelled.

She banged his ribs, yelled, "Go, go!" and he did.

The grass thinned out and that meant more speed, and soon the logging road appeared through the trees. In a cloud of hot ochre, Seth roared out onto it.

The road ran parallel with the McLeod River, which lay just out of sight, and with the view ahead now clear, he gave the bike as much fuel as it wanted. It was time to see where the boys in blue were.

After long minutes of full throttle riding, the highway came into view, and thank Christ – there were no white four-wheel drives waiting on it.

Superfast on bitumen, they crossed the McLeod bridge, and Seth slowed right down, looking to get offroad. In the scrub to the right there was a maze of tracks. Fellas from the tungsten mine at Mount Carbine, and Curraghmore and Brooklyn Stations had been riding bikes and pig-shooting around here for years.

Shimmering in the heat, the mouth of a track appeared. Seth looked around, saw the highway was empty. Trying not to throw up dust, he motored slowly down the track, keen to get onto an intersecting track ahead. When he turned into it, he brought the speed back up again.

Using a network of tracks, he made for Mount Carbine, riding hard through an unfenced part of Brooklyn Station, as he roughly followed the highway. When a graded dirt road bisected the track, he turned onto it, going east.

Now the dust plumed behind them, time passing in the two-stroke engine roar. A long, bare hill topped with white boulders appeared, the rocks, stark against the blue sky, were like watching sentinels.

Five minutes later, he glimpsed through the trees, a clearing dotted with gravestones. Mount Carbine, on the highway, was real close. The mine workers there lived in demountable cabins and caravans, and they'd hear the 360 for sure. But it was the pricks in blue on the highway that worried Seth.

The road now curved towards the camp, and he left it. Much slower, he rode through the scrub and thick grass, uncomfortably aware of unseen snakes. Wending through gums and termite mounds, the strange rock-covered hill loomed up, filling the southern sky.

After another few kms, Seth reckoned they were past Mount Carbine and any roadblock there. The next danger zone was at the Mary River. The cops might be waiting on the bridge. If that were the case, he'd need to find a spot to ford the river. Otherwise, they'd have to just sit tight in the scrub and wait for the bastards to give up and leave.

Twenty minutes later, he saw the glint of water through the trees, and he stopped under some big shade trees and killed the engine. The hot bike ticked away in the booming silence. There was no sound of pursuit, no chopper, not even traffic on the nearby highway. For the first time since he'd seen the cop with the M16, Seth felt like he had a bit of breathing space.

He dropped the stand and they got off, Lou slipping the bags off her shoulder. Pulling off helmets and goggles, they looked at each other.

"You, alright?" said Seth. She nodded, but he saw blood on her arm. He had a look. The wound wasn't deep, but it wasn't nice. Taking a canteen, he sluiced water through torn flesh. Though she grimaced as he washed away bark and splinters, Lou looked pretty calm.

"Too small for stitches," she said. What a toughie.

Looking around, he saw a bloodwood and ran over to it. In the heat, thick red sap oozed from the trunk: it looked like somebody had been shot against it. He collected some of the antiseptic sap with his fingers. Back with Lou, he gently smeared the goo onto the gash, its deep, woody smell mingling with the tang of her sweat.

"Alright?" He stepped back, wiping his fingers on his pants. Lou nodded, grinned. "Thanks, doctor."

They drank water. He checked the Rolex Submariner on his wrist. He listened hard, looked to the west, and saw a wedgetail eagle circling in the sky.

"Wait here," he told Lou.

Grabbing the binoculars, he went through the scrub. At the river, staying in the cover of the trees, he moved closer to the bridge. Using the binoculars, he saw that there were no white cars or men in blue up there.

Sweating heavily, he jogged through the scrub to the highway. Peeping out, he saw no one waiting up the road. Great, they could use the bridge.

Back at the bike, Lou was sitting very still, staring at the ground. His shadow fell over her, but she didn't look up.

He'd known her for nearly a year, and he'd seen her go quiet like this before. But it wasn't the cowed silence of a chick in the face of the blokes, but more the calmness of a gun player surveying the state of play, her mind whirring, recalibrating, going over errors never to be made again.

Yeah, she was thinking about Alex.

Was he laying handcuffed in the dust at the crop? Or bouncing about in the back of a cop Land Cruiser heading towards Mareeba? With a bullet wound? Or even dead?

"Hey, Lou." She looked up.

"It's gonna be okay." He gave her his number-one smile, but to his dismay, a look of great loss swept her face.

"Oh, Seth, we had such a big fight this morning. I was in Ballina and I went and stayed with friends and ended up staying a week later than I said. We can't end like this."

End? He looked away, amazed that it could. If Alex had been caught, he wouldn't get bail. She'd only see him in court. He'd get real time, not just for the size of the crop, but also for the guns. Four, five, even eight years in Stuart Creek. Smart, gorgeous, almost twenty – Lou would move on.

She looked at him for long seconds, battling with hard misfortune. Then with an effort of will, she did a complete one-eighty degree turn, the anxiety and premature regret on her face suddenly gone. Wow, thought Seth.

"Yeah, it's going to work out," she said. "If anyone's going to get away, it's him."

He had to agree. Alex wouldn't go easy.

His legs prickled. Tiny spear grass seeds were stuck all over his pants; Lou was the same.

But there was blood around the seat of her jeans.

"Oh. Hey Lou, are you . . . okay?" He brusquely nodded

at the dark streak. She looked down.

"Oh, that. No prizes for beauty queens out here."

"But it looks like you've hurt yourself. I'll go behind a tree so you can check it out."

Lou's eyes glinted with amusement.

"It's my period, Seth. It came early."

He didn't know where to look.

An Inconsequential Blip

Ten kilometres along Black Mountain Road, he stopped and killed the engine. The forest stretched dark and dense around them, the hushed silence only broken by the sound of far-off birds.

Getting off the bike, they pulled off helmets and goggles and stretched their arms and legs. Seth wheeled the bike off the dirt road into the trees. Sitting down on the forest floor, he rubbed his face.

Christ almighty, what a total, bloody catastrophe. If he hadn't heard that engine or spotted that cop . . .

Alex's plan had been for everyone to get away from the crop as fast as they could, but Seth felt a real tickle of guilt about leaving him. Breathing slow and deep, he tried to ditch the feeling. Mate, you got her out, he told himself.

Lou sat down next to him. "You, okay?" she said.

"Yeah, I'm cool. Just a bit freaked out about having to shoot through like that."

"He would have done the same," said Lou.

Seth nodded, listened for a bike. From somewhere deep in the forest came the wild cries of cockatoos.

"Are we waiting for him here?" said Lou.

Hidden in the forest, it was tempting. Alex would surely come this way. But he needed to get Lou to a safe place as quick as he could.

"Nah, we'll go to Kuranda and wait for him at Ulysses' place. All part of Alex's Z Force commando plan."

Lou's laughter was welcome.

"Who's Ulysses?" she said.

"A mate of mine. Lives near Barron Falls. We'll wait there and when it gets dark, we'll go down the hill, come in through the back way at the Kamerunga bridge, then cruise into Digger Street. Easy peasey."

They fell silent and he flashed on them sitting like this, side by side, but somewhere nice.

The side of her fist thumped against his shoulder. "You did good, Seth."

She got up, went behind the bike, and changed back into her shorts, swapping her dust-caked army shirt for a clean white blouse.

Yeah, I did, didn't I? thought Seth.

They got going again, the forest going past in a shadowy blur, only slowing when two wild horses appeared on the dirt road. With wide-eyed alarm and great shakes of their manes, the horses wheeled and raced back into the trees.

Finally emerging out onto the Kennedy Highway, Seth shook off the temptation to just chance it and roar down the range to Digger Street.

He might make it, or he might draw the attention of the Cairns cops; the bastards fully alerted and keen to catch an outlaw dope grower. Or maybe shoot him right off his bike. No, he couldn't risk that with Lou again.

He turned right, and as they crossed the Barron River bridge, Lou squeezed him hard, and he felt laughter pass from her warm chest into his back.

They came into Kuranda, the Honey House Motel and old timber houses on the other side of the dusty park. At the service station, he quietly puttered down the jungle road behind it. Outside the Country Women's Association Hall, a gaggle of country women were chatting away, no one looking up as he turned onto Barron Falls Road.

Rattling across the timber bridge over Jumrum Creek, he powered up into the cutting, dry-season dust coating the bush alongside the road.

There were houses about, some near the road, but most were hinted at by mail boxes or long rutted driveways.

Riding along, sunlight tiger-striping the road, Seth kept his eyes peeled for Ulysses' place. Over the crest of the hill past Weir Road, he slowed down, cruising along until he saw the driveway. Turning into the dirt track, he whistled in loud relief, and felt Lou squeeze him. They'd made it.

Halfway down the drive, he pulled in under a big, shady cadagi and killed the engine. The silence was delicious.

They got off, dumped their helmets and goggles on the grass, stretched their arms and legs, and looked around at a landscape that wasn't rushing by.

At the end of the driveway was an old tin and timber shed with a brick chimney at one end. There were no cars or utes, so Ulysses must be out. But on the lawn by the shed, there was a small collection of tents and strung-up tarps, even a tepee. Ulysses appeared to have visitors, and sure enough, a mob of them now came out of the shed.

Everyone was sun-tanned and long-haired, dressed in shorts, sarongs, cheesecloth skirts, and floral blouses. In their late teens and early twenties, the boys were bare-chested, most of the girls too, and more than a few sported bead necklaces, bangles, and tropical ulcers.

"Oh, look – hippies," murmured Lou.

More kids from down south, thought Seth, drawn here by Kuranda's reputation as the hippie capital of Australia.

The hippies came up with a mix of curiosity and doubt on their faces; the doubt a result of the shit they copped from the world. Most people saw them as parasites, their work-shy lifestyle, filled with copious sex and drug use, to be despised – or maybe secretly envied.

The most senior hippie, by dint of his lush, full beard, looked well pleased to see some strangers.

"Hey, how ya doing?" His friendly tone encompassed the hospitality of the ages. Two fit lads with bumfluff on their chins, began 'oh wowing' around the bike.

"We're good, thanks, man," said Seth. "Ulysses about?"

Ulysses had been a drill-operator in W.A. who'd flown away from his previous life, changing his name to that of the brilliant blue tropical butterfly. The mention of his name replaced the doubt with smiles.

"Nah, he's down in Cairns getting supplies, and he's going fishing after that, so I can't say when he'll be back," said Fullbeard.

"Mmm, fresh fish," said a little chick in a tight sarong.

"Mind if we hang out here for a bit?" said Seth. "Got a mate coming by later, and then we'll head off."

"Yeah, yeah, that's cool," said Fullbeard. "The Weir is

good for a swim at the moment. Nice and clear, aye."

There was a happy babble of assent, a couple of sensual groans thrown in too.

"It's gorgeous," said a chick with a sun-burnt chest.

"What is it?" said a bumfluff boy, his hand on the bike's plain white plastic fuel tank.

"Yamaha 360," said Seth. "We put a bigger tank on it, a few other things."

"Man, it's perfect."

"You wanna cuppa?" said a bare-breasted girl to Lou.

"Love one," said Lou.

"Come on in," said Fullbeard. "Take a load off."

Seth and Lou thankfully took off their boots, then followed the smiling hippies over to the shed.

Inside, things had changed; Ulysses' functional space now full of hippie paraphernalia. Batik sarongs hung from beams. By an altar of crystals, seashells, and seed pods sat a chipped Buddha. On a school desk lay a Chinese-looking book with strange metal coins scattered across the cover, and a wooden easel held a painting in progress: a busty pink nude reclining under puce palm trees.

Everyone arranged themselves on grimy beanbags and stained cushions on the floor. Two comfy old chairs, likely refugees from a dairy farmer's lounge setting, were left for the guests.

Seth and Lou sat down. Everybody grinned expectantly at them. Seth had to breathe through his mouth; the reek of unwashed feet horrendous. No one was in a hurry to speak, and in the silence, the room's attention drifted to a chick crouching at the fireplace in the kitchen area.

Gorgeously wide-hipped, with a peach of a bottom, she was putting the billy on to boil. Everybody meditated on her earthmother curves, caught in a lovely spell between reverence and desire. Somebody sighed, and the room rocked with happy laughter, everybody cheerfully looking around at each other.

"What?" said the girl, aware she'd played some part in the merriment.

"You're beautiful, Rosie," said a chick, and everybody cheered. Rosie shook her hips and breasts proudly and pouted amiably. Everyone laughed some more and it was a nice vibe – affectionate not creepy, and out there in the open for everybody to acknowledge and enjoy.

Seth dug it; so bloody glad that things were changing. You didn't need to be a hippie to know it was better than what straight society foisted on you. This kind of vibe was unfakable and, well, healthy. Who'd have imagined it a few years ago? Or dope, or tripping on mushrooms and acid.

The laughter dissipated, and the hippies refocused on their visitors. Up here in these jungle hills, they must be a bit short on entertainment, thought Seth.

A young woman on the floor drew her legs up, and he tried not to look at the proud bush of hair now revealed.

Next to her was a young fella, also missing underwear. With his legs wide apart, his shorts barely concealed his masculinity. Any move to the left or right would make the dimensions of that masculinity clear.

Lou made a droll sound, and Seth saw she was enjoying this hippie attitude towards human anatomy. Just a year out of St. Monica's girls school, she could see that public nudity was a satisfyingly instant way of staking a claim to not being straight.

"So where have you come from?" said Fullbeard.

Seth resisted looking at Lou. From a full-on nightmare, he thought. The kind of freakout I wish none of you ever have to go through.

"Been visiting friends," said Lou. "Went for a ride, had a swim in a waterhole, and ended up staying the night."

"Oh, wow," said Bush Girl. "That sounds great."

Mr. Pythonpants leant back, his smooth biceps bulging, and his third eye peeked out. Lou made that noise again.

While the billy boiled, they shot the breeze, everyone keen to get the drum on swimming holes and places to camp. Seth was more than pleased to share what he knew; these young hippies a welcome distraction, but when talk turned to magical crystals, UFOs, and cosmic vibes, he gratefully accepted a cup of tea and zipped his lip.

As this nonsense burbled on, Seth saw how the packet of Capstan next to Fullbeard drew many eyes. When the bloke finally rolled himself one, there was an upheaval of relief, and one after another, the smokers got stuck in.

These kids are on the bones of their arses, he thought. Living rent-free in tents and under tarps, cooking on a fire and waiting for supplies to turn up. And by choice.

None of them wanted to cut cane, pick tobacco, or clean motel rooms. No one was getting a job in an office or shop, let alone taking on a degree or an apprenticeship.

It was a trade-off; living the carefree hippie life meant a serious lack of stuff – tobacco, grog, nice clothes, even essentials like vehicles or medicine. Yeah, bugger that.

No fan of jobs, offices, or physical work himself, Seth thought about what he'd chosen to do for a dollar. It was great. Until it fell on you like a bloody ton of bricks.

He counted the cost of this morning: Seven months of work flushed down the dunny. And Alex and the boys. What the hell had happened to them?

"Seth," murmured Lou. "You okay?"

He dug up a smile. "Yeah, yeah, I'm good."

Eventually the nutty chatter and stinky feet started to grate. Lou was looking a bit zapped now, so they went and sat in the shade of the cadagi tree.

Neither spoke, their thoughts weighing a ton. Putting her bag under her head, Lou fell asleep.

Changing into the footy shorts and t-shirt, Seth pulled spear grass seeds from his pants, one little needle after another, while in a foxtail palm above the lawn, a couple of drongos angrily went beak-to-beak.

Trousers finally de-seeded, he went to a water tank by the shed and refilled the two canteens. Inside, the hippies were playing a game they called Yee Ching, and it sure sounded like it: the metal coins jingling and rattling on the floor.

Back by the bike, Lou hadn't moved. Taking a peek, he saw that the bloodwood sap had dried, sealing the wound against flies and germs. Time inched by, Seth striving not to acknowledge the elephant in his head. Around three, curvy Rosie brought over a small hand of ladyfingers for them to eat, apologetic that there wasn't any else.

When she went back to the shed, Lou sat up and wiped the sleep from her eyes. She gave him a smile, but he could see the elephant had been knocking over the furniture in her head.

They ate the bananas and washed their hands, then Lou walked up to the road and stood there for a while. When she came back, he saw the tension in her face. She'd been a real trooper escaping the cops, but now she was doing it hard. Waiting around doing bugger-all didn't help one iota either.

He looked back at the shed. Everyone was inside doing hippie stuff.

"What do you reckon?" he said. "Go for a walk? Have a swim? Wash the dust off. We can be back in an hour."

Lou weighed it up. "Yeah, okay."

On Barron Falls Road it was hot and still. The air smelt of dust and the sky through the canopy of trees was more titanium than blue. With no houses from here on, and the Barron Falls dry at this time of the year, there was little chance of anyone driving past. Seth was cool with that. He didn't really want to be seen by anybody right now.

Maybe he was being paranoid, but he didn't want to go to the Weir either. It was the best swimming hole in these parts, but there could be someone there he knew.

They went further along the road, heading to where it forked – one way leading to the falls, the other to Wright's Lookout. From there, it wasn't far to the secluded pools of Surprise Creek. They'd be more than incognito there.

Walking in silence, their feet scuffed on fallen leaves, scaring sun-drowsy skinks. Creeper-covered trees formed towers alongside the road. Down in gullies, black-bodied tree ferns threw out great crowns of green leaves, the ones near the road dusted ochre brown.

A Ulysses butterfly, its colours acid trip sharp, jaunted through the foliage. A breeze rustled the tree tops, a wind coming up the Barron Gorge from the Coral Sea. Seth smiled, and for a moment, felt peace.

With no traffic or aircraft noise, no houses or chainsaws about, he felt right in the heart of country, and a big, wild sense of place took hold.

In his mind's eye he soared up above the hard sunlight and deep shadow of this midday jungle, seeing all detail with eagle-sharp eyes: every leaf delineated, every grain of quartz sand in every creek glinting with sunlight, every drop of water in the silent chasm of the gorge.

The feeling was overwhelming, timeless, atavistic, and the perfect antidote for the madness of today.

"Seth?" Lou was watching him with concern in her eyes. Seth smiled at her.

"I'm fine, Lou. I'm right *here*." He threw his arms out to encompass the forest around them, but she didn't get it. Knowing words would not suffice, he went for a laugh.

"It's those hippies – they got me feeling all cosmic."

No laugh came. Lou, expressionless, looked back at the road ahead, and Seth felt the dull dread in his guts again. The silence was anything but peaceful now.

At the fork in the road, they headed to the lookout, and now he remembered the creek that crossed the road up ahead. It had a pool, wide and deep enough to swim in, that looked down into the gorge. It was a good spot.

After a few bends, they came to the creek. It ran under the road through a big culvert. The sides were steep, but there were roots and branches to use as handholds.

"You okay getting down there?" said Seth.

Lou nodded and began climbing down. He watched for a moment, thinking how confident she was, and how tan and smoothly curved she looked. Down on the forest floor, he led her along the creek bank, ducking and weaving through vines and branches, squeezing past fallen trees.

Though dry-season low, the creek was running, its soft chuckle over rocks promising cool refreshment. Beams of sunlight hit drifts of sand on the bottom, and metallic blue dragonflies skittered and hovered over the moving water. It was idyllic in here – a tranquil sanctuary from the day's heat.

Approaching a pool, Seth saw something underwater in the shadows of the buttress roots of a big black bean tree. Crouching down, he pointed it out to Lou. "It's the biggest one I've seen."

Just under the surface, with the faintest movement of pectoral fins, was an eel, greenish brown and covered in dark leopard spots. "It must be very old," said Lou.

He dug the wonder in her voice.

Now came a flash of movement as a tiny finch landed for a drink. With manic hops, it came down to the water, its little head darting this way and that. The water next to it exploded. For a split-second, they saw the eel's head, then it was gone, taking the finch with it.

"Wow," said Lou, not looking the least bit perturbed, and he dug that, too.

They walked on, and a green tunnel of trees formed by the creek's passage took shape around them. Up ahead came the sound of falling water, and they came to where slabs and ledges of rock made a dog-leg turn in the creek, creating a steep little waterfall. The banks rose in jagged walls on either side, and they carefully moved down the moss and leaf-covered rocks to clamber around the bend.

A small hill appeared through the forest; a little clearing on its slope. Seth pointed it out. "An old gold miner camps there. He puts gold traps in the gullies. Pans the creeks."

He explained how after setting it all up, the old bloke would return after the wet to reap a harvest of spicks and specks of pure gold. Seth had met him once, but there was no tent there today.

As they passed close to the camp site, Lou bent down. Under decaying vegetation were small bottles that once held medicine. Lou picked one up; small, purple, and four sided, the dispensary name moulded in the glass. With a nod of appreciation, she popped it into her pocket.

The edge of the creek now looked almost man-made, the flat rocks riven with cracks like joins, and Seth flashed on Inca rock walls he'd seen in books.

They went along this strange road in silence, the stone a deep green, with little red and yellow leaves scattered about like feathers. Under the forest canopy, the light had a blue, granular feel. It was still and peaceful now, but in the wet this would all be covered by water roaring along the deep channel of the creek.

A small, steep gully came into view, rising above them. "For God's sake!" said Lou. "What's wrong with people?"

The narrow ravine was choked with green, brown, and clear glass – a great drift of beer, wine, and spirit bottles, many still intact, the heaped glass wedged in. Above it was a vegetative cover of creepers, fallen leaves, and branches.

"What – they came all the way out here to this beautiful place to dump their stupid rubbish?" Lou sounded pretty irate, and Seth didn't blame her.

"No, it's the blokes who built the railway," he explained. "There are terraces in the hillside up there where they had their camp. That's their bottle dump. Years worth."

"What a mob of polluters. We should clean it up."

"After ninety years, it's stuck tight, Lou. Be a real hassle to get it out. Plus we'd have to lug it back to the road."

Lou frowned and sighed with frustration. Seth looked glumly empathetic, then led them on.

Up ahead, a straight, dark line appeared spanning the creek – a small railway bridge on solid concrete supports. They'd come to the Atherton Tablelands line that ran parallel to the gorge. It came up three hundred metres from the coast, passing through tunnels and crossing high bridges on its way to Kuranda, Ravenshoe, and beyond.

At the bridge they crossed the track, and the gash in the rock grew deeper, the creek falling away through bush. In the jungle ahead, a patch of sunlight now appeared.

They climbed down rock terraces and little crags beside the creek, ever steeper, dodging logs caught fast in rocks, and squeezing around gnarly bushes anchored in cracks. The portal of light ahead of them began opening out, and Lou, now seeing where they'd come to, laughed with awe and delight.

The terminus of the creek was a small amphitheatre of rock carved out of the wall of the gorge by the torrents of ages. It looked out into bright space, the slabbed sides of grey-green rock painted with lichen constellations.

Through the gap in the canopy where the creek emptied out into the gorge, light flooded down onto a pool four or so metres wide. Tiny leaves floated on the surface; the water a deep green in the shadows. It was like a painting, every detail perfect in its pristine wildness.

On the gorge side of the pool, a flat slab of rock rose at an angle out of the water to make the edge. And what an edge it was. Beyond it was huge space: the other side a hundred metres away, the steep cliffs there topped with jungle, and the Barron River a hundred metres below.

Passing through streaming rays of sunlight, they used root and liana handholds to climb down to the little pool. At its edge, they sat down on a flat, moss-seamed rock.

There was a hush here that neither of them wanted to disturb, an ancient silence broken only by the trickle of unseen water and the cry of an eagle out over the gorge.

Sunlight lit the pool's edge, where a stream of water no more than a few centimetres wide fell out into space. In the light-saturated air something appeared, and they both gasped.

Right above the falling water, a tiny rainbow glittered and twisted like an ethereal jewel.

Lou's hand found Seth's hand and squeezed, and he felt wonderful connection with her. The rainbow scintillated, before turning to water, billowing in the air as spray that fell and faintly darkened the sheer rock edge.

The branches and leaves that framed the gorge moved. Leaves fluttered, spiralling past to tip-tap off rocks. A wind was blowing through the gorge.

Seth turned to Lou, and she was turning to him, and for one shocking moment he thought they were going to kiss.

But she bit her lip, delight in her eyes, let go of his hand, and slid forward. At the water's edge she slipped off her blouse, the tan of her back showing faint bikini lines.

She pulled her shorts and underpants off in one go and stood there, the muscles in her buttocks flexing as she kept her balance, one slender foot reaching out to test the slipperiness of the rock.

Seth reeled, a dozen day-dreams, and more than a few night-time fantasies right before his eyes.

Oh, man, he'd wanted her the moment they'd met. She hadn't been Alex's girl then. Fresh-faced, curvy, and just out of school, she was hotter than a pistol left out in the sun.

A bit straight, a bit stuck-up, she didn't take any shit. Other chicks liked her for this no-nonsense attitude, and blokes . . . well, the grubs soon gave up trying to dominate her, and the cool ones worked harder to win her heart.

She liked him, and it had been touch-and-go there for a bit, but Alex, as ever, had prevailed. He was just louder and funnier, bursting with the best bullshit. Savvy to her moods, he lifted her when she was down, brushing away any problem or mood in his imitable way.

Oh yeah, thought Seth – my brother. Full of explosive good cheer, he had that trickster's grasp of what made people tick. He could be anything for anybody, listening with empathy, even compassion, then stepping in boldly, usually overwhelmingly. It was a knack that Seth wished he had.

Still, he'd never had problems getting chicks. Mum was beautiful, her mother more so, and on Dad's side the men were all clean-cut, dapper blokes. He'd never call himself good-looking, but a lot of people did. Alex, of course, was more handsome than him.

Always grateful for how he was seen by women, Seth found it easier in the long run to avoid the full-on lookers and ambitious ones: they were too much work. Instead he tried to get with girls who were more down to earth, with big smiles, big curves, and lots of laughter.

But the laughter never lasted. So many times he'd find out that they were dealing with bad stuff: families, bastard ex- boyfriends, shit blokes in general, and he'd end up sort of nursing them, trying to help, even as he began to resent their unhappiness. Yep, he'd become real clever at finding reasons to move on.

Lou squatted down on her haunches, a fluff of pubes peeking out, and the curves of her were abruptly right there before him, elemental and divine. A thunderclap of lust cracked in his skull. A bolt of white lightning shot up from his groin.

She slid into the water, disappearing with a tiny splash.

Gob-smacked, and then some, he looked around. It was bloody ridiculous – there was no one there.

Lou surfaced, gasping with pleasure, the sound filling the space, claiming it all. In the crystal-clear water, her shape shimmered beneath the ripples.

Slicking the hair back from her face, she looked at him. Time slowed, froze. Her face, luminously pale against the dark water of the pool, drew him in. Everything around it faded to a meaningless blur.

Her expression was pure mystery. She'd never been an easy one to read, but her eyes now were more occult than anything he'd ever seen before.

And, Jesus, he was suddenly hard, and she'd easily see; him in his footy shorts, his knees akimbo. And before he could close his legs, Lou's eyes flicked down.

His stomach swooped, his heart roared like a V8 engine. Lou's eyes came back up to his, glittering with excitement, and a great bell went off inside him, its chime rocking him to the core.

There had been a good few chances, but Seth had never knowingly slipped it to another bloke's woman. Being the reason for some bloke's pain, or for a chick getting hit or ditched appalled him. It was a dog's act.

Dizzy, he stood, his shorts shamelessly distended. Lou's eyes widened, her breathing coming fast, and she nodded. As if in a dream, he pulled his shorts off. She laughed, soft and husky, and he slipped into the waiting pool.

This was more than wrong. This was taboo. This was the kind of mortal sin you'd go to hell for – but screaming with untold pleasure the whole damn way. The complete wrongness was an exquisite goad, a gorgeous thirst he'd never know.

He moved through cool water to her, and her face held precise new detail – every freckle, every strand of hair, perfectly drawn as if by the hand of a truly sensuous god.

She put out her hand, clasped his chin, made him stop. His feet touched rock, and he squatted and stared at her, buzzing right out of his fucking skin. She stared back, her look obliterating him. Then she slowly pulled his face to hers, her lips opening as her eyes closed.

They kissed, tiny tongues at first, and he felt the illicit demon fire spurting through him change, the urge to grab her and inhale her now transmuting into something softer and deeper.

Pulling his mouth from hers, he opened his eyes and was stunned by the unknowable look that she gave him. Filled with keening mystery, it was simultaneously vernal and ancient, both innocent and wise.

Then her fingers made a firm ring around the base of his old fella and squeezed. His gasp was huge, his eyes just about popping out of his head. As unbelievable sensation exploded up through him, Lou's eyes lit up with mischief, and she yelled with mad laughter.

Before he could do a thing, she let go, eyes ablaze with dead-set come-on. She turned and swam over to the edge. Mouth open, mind-blown, he watched her.

Throwing her tawny arms forwards, she pulled herself across the flat, angled rock, tummy-first, and looked out over the edge. Time unravelled, the infinite exposed, and Seth felt this moment engrave itself into his mind and stamp deep into his heart.

She looked like an angel, a hippy-trippy angel; feral and lush, spread there before him, just the sweetest thing he'd ever seen. With his old fella sticking out like a rudder, he swam over to her.

Wet-muscled, as lissom as a wild beast, he slid over her, water streaming onto her. She moulded up into him, her body firm and warm, his palms on the rock slab.

She gasped, turned blindly, open-mouthed, and they kissed deeply. Electric shudders of pleasure racked them, waves of sheer delight going from their toes to their giddy heads.

Squirming beneath him, Lou groaned into his mouth. She pulled away, panting, and faced the view. He put his cheek against hers, and they gazed over the precipice.

It was a stunning drop to the limpid green of the Barron River, its surface moving in tiny diamonds from the wind. On the other side of the gorge, the cliffs were visible for metres underwater before fading into the river's bronze gloom.

This abyss, primitive and massive, was hypnotising. It hummed with the spirit of place – gigantic and forever – and anything Seth could feel or think right now just paled into insignificance.

What they were doing here was an inconsequential blip compared with what the passage of time had wrought. This was just a joyous animal spasm, no different from the thousands of other natural things that happened right here every day.

Moving his hips, he pushed in gently, Lou raising hers in acquiescence. Mouth against her cheek, a groan slipped out, and she moaned in reply.

Lined up, they were like two slippery magnets about to click. Time unspooled, seconds spiralling into eternity, as neither of them made the final move.

Now a halo of blue, red, yellow, and green danced about their heads; the updraft-blown spray cool on their faces, running down their cheeks like tears.

In unison, they moved now, crying out, and a widening circle of ripples began rocking tiny red and yellow leaves.

Brothers

Out by the driveway, they sat by the Yamaha as though having a chat. But they were silent, with what they'd done reverberating loudly between them.

He wanted to do it again. And again. He'd wanted Lou since he'd first laid eyes on her, but now, with a giant, just about physical ache, he wanted her more.

He wanted to take off with her – leave Cairns, go down south, or north to Darwin to hop on a plane to Indonesia and the world. It was crazy, but he felt crazy.

Across the lawn, some hippies were at the tents and the tepee talking. From the shed came the smell of wood smoke and the light of kerosene lanterns. With no electric lights or TV, it felt like another era, a time of homespun settlers and bush pioneers. Except for the topless chicks.

Seth dragged his thoughts back to what the hell he and Lou were going to do now. Sunset had passed but Ulysses hadn't arrived. And neither had Alex. It wasn't good, but a quiet joy burned in his heart.

Okay, maybe he should go it alone when it got dark; go down the range fast and stash the bike at Digger Street. Lou could stay here, catch the Silver Bullet or a Whitecars to Cairns in the morning. It was probably safer.

Oh man, it was hard to look at Lou. Something magical had happened – more than just sex, as mind-blowing as it had been, it was something bigger, like destiny or fate, like they were meant to be.

The hippies began walking over to the shed. With dusk falling, the gloom under the cadagi tree was deep. When they'd gone inside, he slid next to Lou and took her hand. She looked at him with that mysterious expression again, and he felt emotion swell up in his chest.

Leaning in, he kissed her neck. She sighed. He stroked her hand, nuzzled the soft hair on her neck, and her shiver made his heart soar.

"Seth," she said. "This is crazy."

"It's a crazy day," he said. He put his arm around her, kissed her. She sighed again but didn't kiss him back, and they sat there listening to the insects singing in unison and the frogs going beep-beep-beep.

Kerosene lanterns now lit up the shed. Seth went to kiss Lou again and saw a pale face at the tepee's door – Curvy Rosie. He leaned back on his elbows, watched the hippie girl walk across the dark lawn to the shed.

"Oh, God, Seth." Lou sat up, ran her hands through her hair. "What on earth happened? Did they catch him? How would we know? I mean, if we go to the police station to ask, won't they arrest us too?"

Seth looked at the first stars and the glow of the rising moon behind the tree line, his bad thoughts making him feel good. I'll love you better than he can, he thought.

"Look, we don't know anything yet, Lou," he said.

In frustration, she shook a fist. "I just want to know."

He really felt for her. Things had certainly changed in the last couple of hours.

"He'll be fine," he said, looking at the illuminated face of his watch. He'd give it another half hour.

"Seth." Lou's voice soft and urgent. A two-stroke engine coming along Barron Falls Road, slowing right down. Now a beam of light flashed down the drive, and a trail bike grumbled up, illuminating them with its headlight.

Seth looked down at the bright grass. Lou cross-legged, didn't move. They were like kangaroos in a spotlight.

The engine and light died, the stand snapped down, and helmet straps rattled. In the dark, Seth tried to breathe slowly; that bad thought now a cross on his forehead.

"Thank Christ!" His brother sounded a bit drunk.

"Alex," said Lou, and she got up. Seth turned his head, listening hard, and in the faint glow of light thrown from the shed, he saw them embrace. Alex sighed gratefully, Lou murmured wordlessly.

"You okay, babe?" said Alex, Lou's reply too soft to hear.

Seth sat there, his heart racing as they came over. Alex had an arm around Lou, and most of a sixpack hanging from his free hand. With an affectionate noise, he kissed Lou's head, then, with a groan, sat down.

"How are you, mate?" Alex's voice, soft and husky, was full of compassion. Seth knew this so well, and gratitude flooded through him.

His brother was always real concerned about everyone when things went bad. He'd step in like a coach, squeezing arms and looking blokes in the eye, his voice soothing, his vibe reassuringly calm. He never got revved up or angry, remaining untouched by calamity really endeared him to blokes. It kept them onside, and they'd be keen to step up and have another go for him.

"Yeah, I'm alright," said Seth, trying, but failing, to keep the emotion out of his voice.

"Mate." His brother leaned in, bullet-proof, rock solid, and put a strong arm around him. Emotion welled up, but Seth fought it and won.

Alex squeezed him in, then released him. He pulled two beers from the plastic collar, gave one to Seth. They tore the ring-pulls off and drank deeply. Standing very still, Lou looked down at them.

Alex was silent. The frogs were going off and the smell of datura floated in on the still air.

"What a fuck up, aye?" said Seth, his voice catching. Alex made a sympathetic noise, but stayed silent, giving his little brother time to be cool again.

The moon cleared the trees, and with the light from the shed, Seth could see his brother's face now. A vision of Lou naked beneath him flashed through his head, and he nearly jumped out of his skin.

"You did real well, mate." Alex's approval was dead-set, even admiring.

"Getting Lou out of there was the right move. If she'd got done, I would never have forgiven myself."

Drinking beer, Seth tamped down an explosion of relief.

"Remember that helicopter we saw?" said Alex. "Like two months ago? I reckon that's when they spotted us. Clever pricks didn't come in, didn't make a pass. Didn't want to scare us off. But they saw us, alright."

"Yeah, right." Seth's scalp was tingling.

"Bastards had a roadblock at Mount Molloy," said Alex. "I spent four hours waiting in the scrub for them to piss off. That gave me a thirst, so I nipped in to Freddie Frog's place at Koah for a cold one. Had a few till it got dark."

A flash of rage burned through Seth. You arsehole, that wasn't the plan. We spent hours worrying about you.

"We must have sneaked through," he said. "We came out just before Mount Molloy, used the highway for a bit, then bush-bashed it again to Weatherby Station road."

His brother calculated it and growled happily.

"Yeah, of course. You're a smart bastard. And a fuckin' red-hot little rider, too. You did bloody well, mate."

"The police chased us on a trailbike," said Lou.

Alex twisted his head around, looking up at her, his face interrogative. Lou smiled but said nothing, and he turned back to Seth with an eager smile.

"Is that right? Sounds like fuckin' Steve McQueen."

Turning again, he grinned up at Lou. He slapped the ground beside him with his open hand. She sat down and he put an arm around her. Pulling her close, he fixed Seth with a story-time kid's eyes.

"This copper on a Yammie two-fifty chased us . . ." Seth began, but it wasn't easy remembering all the details. It had been a rampaging blur then; it seemed like a dream now. He'd remember a scene in a movie better than this.

"Yeah, he chased you, and –?"

The moon had cleared the jungle now, and Seth could see them both smiling at him. He gave his memory a few seconds to sharpen up, then began describing the chase.

He got into it easy, matter-of-fact casual at first, before chucking in some cheeky stuff that made them laugh. Stringing it out, he built it up as the chase developed. Then in mid-flow, he realised that he'd been at the white-hot centre of a top yarn – an absolute beauty of a tale that would be feted at pubs and parties for years to come.

Alex loved it, roaring with delight, his hand slapping the grass in delight, and they all laughed like family.

But Seth sensed that his brother's pleasure masked a measure of jealousy, that it wasn't him who'd outwitted the cop, and that he could never tell the story as his own.

Most blokes wouldn't want the law hot on their tail, but with Alex that sort of pressure was like fresh steak and icy-cold beer. Relishing risk, he dug a good dare, happy as the proverbial pig in it, if he was running along the edge.

In the perilous business of growing and selling dope, it sometimes felt like the money came second to the danger with him.

Their laughter subsiding, Lou took Alex's beer and had a swig. Alex popped out two fresh cans from the plastic and gave Seth one.

"I reckon Pat and Lenny got over the Desailly Range," said Alex. "They'll look for Mick. Give him the bad news."

Seth nodded and watched his brother swig beer.

"So, what have you two been doing all day?" said Alex. "I don't see Ulysses' truck. He's out, hey?"

"Yeah, but there's hippies here," said Lou. "We hung out with them a bit, then sat out here."

"Hippies? I'll need to check you both for nits!" Alex laughed loudly, the sound bursting up from his chest.

"They're alright," said Lou.

"They're a pack of bludgers. So, you stayed here," said Alex, a movement of his head taking in the property.

"Yeah, we did," said Lou. "Kept away from town."

Seth didn't close his eyes or look away.

Alex nodded, done with it. "So, where's Ulysses?"

Seth told him what Fullbeard had said. Alex got to his feet and stretched. Seth and Lou got up too. Alex began walking towards the shed.

"C'mon, Alex, let's go," said Seth. "He's not here."

Alex waved a dismissive hand. "Give us a minute."

They followed, Seth trying to see Lou's face in the dark. Coming into the light, she looked blankly composed.

Alex sauntered in like Bon Scott, faces turning to look. He gave them a royal smile, his eyes flicking around the room.

"Hey, this is my brother Alex," said Seth.

"Hello Alex," came a chorus of voices.

Alex smiled magnanimously, murmuring, "Nice," at the sight of the topless girls.

With a cheeky grin, he addressed Fullbeard, who was sitting in a lounge chair smoking a rollie.

"And here's the king of the hippies."

There was uncertain laughter. Alex winked at Fullbeard and pulled out a pack of Rothmans. Seeing eyes fasten on the packet, he held it out.

"Cigarette, anyone?"

The bumfluff boys and some girls gathered around, and Alex leaned in close to the girls' bare breasts, lighting each cigarette with a show of largesse. Seth knew it was a piss-take, but it was done with such sincerity that they all gave him heartfelt thanks.

"Alright?" said Alex, and he lit his own cigarette. Taking a deep drag, he stuffed the packet and lighter back in his pocket and addressed the room.

"Thanks for looking after these two."

"That's cool," said Curvy Rosie. "Your brother and his girlfriend are real sweeties."

Alex stared at her.

"I could tell they were uptight when they got here, but they loosened up after going for a swim. Lots of cuddling and kissing when they got back. The power of love, hey."

The Rothmans fell, lay smoking on the floor.

Like a king goanna, Alex's head swivelled to Seth.

"You little bastard," he said.

Seth blinked. He had close to three inches on Alex, but he'd always be a little bastard in his brother's eyes.

With a sudden squeak of boots, Alex threw himself at Seth, hooking an arm around his head and banging a big fist into it.

Fully smashed, Seth staggered, his brother holding him tight, and they knocked the hippie's nature altar flying, the crystals, shells, and seed pods rattling across the floor.

A chick screamed, blokes cried out, and Lou yelled like she was calling for a dog named Alex to heel. But the dog had a jaw-wrenching bicep around its sibling's head and was now driving hard knuckles into its ribs.

Using all of his power, Seth threw himself backwards, and with a metallic thunderclap, they slammed into a tin wall. A horrified wail rose up, the hippies all freaking out

47

at this sudden explosion of bestial violence. Something ancient and cursed was in the room – if not the original sin, then one not long after it.

Feet flat on the floor, Seth used a shitload of shoulder power to repeatedly drive his brother back, ramming him into framing studs. The noise was horrendous, drowning out the hippie screaming, and the crushing arm around his head fell away. He spun around, shaking his head like a mickey bull, and saw Alex against the wall, clutching an elbow with a grimace of pain.

Run for the bike on the drive, he told himself. But Alex would recover in seconds, give chase and knock him from the seat. And he couldn't leave Lou to the bastard's rage.

Moving fast, he stepped in and clubbed Alex square in the head with the side of his fist, unwilling to inflict any permanent damage. He felt somebody rush past him, and a bum-fluff boy jumped in, grabbing at Alex's arms and yelling, "Peace, man! Peace!" Alex put a forearm smash into the kid's head and he went down.

With horrified certainty, Seth saw he'd have to hurt his brother badly now. But he might avoid that by opening up cuts above Alex's eyes that would blind him with blood.

All that boxing in school, and all those melees as a hired defender of pub and club doors would be put to the test now. It was time to shake off a lifetime of fear, and this new guilt, and get scientific.

Throwing big sticks of gelignite punches, he attacked hard. Using swift footwork, he weaved around the return fire, landing some good hits into Alex's ribs, his knuckles going deep, detonating on bone.

His brother, in mid-swing, was stopped in his tracks, and his eyes went wide with pain.

Fullbeard, alarmed by the berserker vibe, now decided it was time to break it up. Throwing himself between the fighting men, he rammed a hefty shoulder into Alex, but at the last moment Alex hopped aside.

Grabbing the now completely off-balance Fullbeard by his hair and pants, he speared the poor bastard headfirst into the floor.

Demon quick, he came at Seth again, mashing muscle into bone with solid rock-hard punches. Under real pressure, Seth wildly deflected them with his arms and shoulders, grunting and gasping with pain. It was like being stoned with small boulders.

Behind Alex, Ulysses now appeared, his eyes wide at the shocker of a bashing going off in his house. Distracted, Seth leapt back, recovered, and aimed quick punches at his brother's eyebrows.

But the smart bastard knew what he was trying to do and, keeping his head back, he suddenly unleashed a flurry of brutal kicks.

Seth danced about trying to dodge the flying boots, but a kick connected and knocked him into the painting on the easel. His head tore through canvas as the easel fell, and he hit the deck hard, his head and shoulders tangling up in the painting.

Whack! A fist came through the canvas and crunched off his skull. Alex yelled in pain, then renewed his assault.

Lou screamed, "Alex! Alex! It's your brother!"

Ulysses shouted in anguished echo. "It's your brother!"

The Power of Rain

Under bone-thudding blows Seth tried to get to his feet, twisting about in the ripped and splintered painting.

Freeing his head, he looked up. It must be Alex, but he didn't recognise him. Amazed at the monstrous rage on the stranger's face, he was hammered into darkness.

Old Testament Prophet

1982

"Mate, I'm a career cop," said Chris Burns. "I left school wanting to be one, and I'll retire being one."

"That's admirable," said Seth, a Lee-Enfield jungle carbine slung across his back. The drug-squad detective walked ahead of him, a Savage rifle in both hands.

"Bugger admiration, I want respect," said the cop. "Not for the badge, but for what I achieve. Who I run down and lock away, the drugs, guns, and money I seize."

Walking along a track, the forest buzzing with insects, they passed through heavily overgrown clearings where the work of long-saws and axes had put edges up against the sky many moons ago. Running beside the track was a small creek, leaf-choked and stagnant, invisible creatures plopping into its murky water as they passed.

In the track's dried mud, Seth looked for the imprint of horseshoes – maybe a dairy farmer looking for a runaway cow, or kids out horseback riding. He also kept an eye out for the flash of spent shells – evidence of any hunters here before them.

But it was just an old pad, maybe used by an occasional bushwalker – and what looked like a shitload of pigs.

"Sus scrofa," said Burns, and he pointed at some double pockmarks hammered deep into the dried mud. "Look at the size of this bastard."

Among the jumble of pig tracks, they stood out. "That one's mine," he said, like he was joking.

"Big ones might not have tusks left," said Seth.

"Bullshit."

"Nope. And even if they did, it ain't relative to their size. Some smaller bastards have bigger tusks."

Puffing pissed-off air from his mouth, Burns looked a little cheated. He wanted trophies – big ones.

Seth hadn't been on a pig hunt for a while, a few years in fact, but Burns had just about begged him. Sure, they'd sort out their business later, when they camped for the night, but right now was the fun part of the day, walking around the ranges above Cairns looking for feral pigs to shoot. And why not?

Total vermin, probably a million strong, the bastards destroyed orchards, crops, and waterways, and ate baby animals alive. They were prolific breeders, crawling with disease, and boys and girls alike had razor-sharp tusks. Adults were sixty kilos of trouble, with some big chunks of wild pork weighing in at a hundred kilos or more.

There was a certain sort of bloke who hunted pigs with dogs and knives – no guns. But it was bloody messy, and Seth had lied that he didn't have mates who did that anymore. Burns had looked cheated about that too.

In silence, they resumed walking, passing through a forest, the track winding under the mass of branches. It smelt moist, with fallen trees covered in runs of fungus.

They moved quickly in the cool gloom, walking for a good few minutes. When they came out into more open ground, Burns started up with his yap again.

"Far north Queensland is the hot seat, mate. Number one priority in the state. Maybe the whole country. You'll see cops from all over up here. I'm just the start. Look, you know I smoke, and we know it'll be legal one day, so you know I'm no crusader. But where there's big drug profits, there's organised crime. That means firearms and people getting hurt or killed. I can't have that."

Burns laughed. "And I could really advance my career up here."

A nice little logical explanation, thought Seth, but the bottom line for this bloke is the thrills. Living undercover meant living on the edge in a life of electric risk and deceit. A double life full of danger became an addictive drug, Seth knew all about that, but one day you'd have to kick it, or you'd get rolled into a cell. Or into a hole in the ground.

Burns suddenly halted, made a hokey hand signal, and cocked his head like the bloke from Last of the Mohicans.

"What?" said Seth.

Burns shooshed him, and they listened to the same far-off birdcall they'd been hearing for the last ten minutes. Seth popped a fart.

"C'mon," hissed the cop. "Something's out there."

"Mate, there's always something out there, twenty-four hours a day. It's the bush!"

Working it, Burns stood poised like a hunting dog, his ears sucking in every sound. The bird yodelled again, and Burns turned and grinned like he'd been joking all along.

With an impatient hand, Seth shooed him forward.

He'd known the Brisbane drug-squad detective for five months, Gordy Mac introducing them one boozy night at The Outrigger in Cairns. Chris Burns had been Andy then, a potential grower wanting to get into the action that was exploding in far north Queensland.

And man, was it exploding.

When he'd first smoked a joint twelve years ago, pretty much no one had any idea what it was. Growing his first crop a year later, he'd given lots away, keen to turn people on to the herb superb.

He'd still ended up with five grand, and not only was that the most money he'd ever had, it also seemed like the most incredible thing: he'd cracked the great struggle of earning a living by growing weeds out in the scrub.

It was a piece of piss really; no study, no university, no need for ironed clothes and polished shoes. And no kow-towing to a bastard of a boss, or putting up with mongrel workmates. It was better than cool.

Now growing dope in the north had gone nuclear. Some joker on ABC radio had estimated that marijuana in north Queensland would soon be worth five hundred million dollars a year. Sweet Jesus in a hot rod.

But it wasn't until the punch-on with Burns in front of a mob of tourists in downtown Cairns, that Seth found out who the bastard really was.

Evenly matched, they'd dished up a biff buffet, fighting each other until the boys in blue had rocked up. Burns had produced his Queensland Police detective's badge and shown it to the Cairns cops, pissing them right off.

To top it off, Burns smoked dope, a habit he'd picked up working undercover, and he boasted of chatting with top brass at the Brisbane police headquarters bar while off his head. Yeah, that sounded about right.

Burns was a wildcard, but his smarts were impressive. Always on, he was awake to any possibility, ready to take good advantage of whatever he came across.

With the quick wit of a player, and a larrikin attitude to boot, he could be good fun – for a cop, and although pretty knowledgeable, he was willing to learn new things.

Like how to grow a dope crop. And for twenty thousand bucks, Seth was going to give him an education.

It was hot and nearly windless between the ridges, and they walked at a measured pace, not wanting to raise a sweat. Entering a large clearing choked chest-high with lantana slowed them even more. The thicket of prickle-covered bushes made impenetrable walls on either side of them, and in places, canes and tendrils grew over the track. Luckily, Seth had brought a pair of garden clippers.

Burns didn't want to relinquish the lead, and he scraped through the brightly flowered bushes, his rifle held up in front of him. Seth followed, snipping stems and branches, and a rotting citrus stink, chemical in its odour, began to taint the air.

He'd never given it a go – too much of a scratchy muck-around – but he'd heard of dope patches grown in the middle of lantana like this, the plants hidden from view, and defended by a hedge of infinite pain.

A flash of blue and black caught his eye. A second later, the indignant twitter of a fairy-wren assailed his ears, the speck of a bird jumping through the lantana, hell-bent on chewing him out. Seth grinned ear to ear.

It took long minutes to get through the thicket, and he didn't care for how close it all was. It was easy to see over, but impossible to look through. Pressing right in on them, it left no room to move.

They came out of the lantana and the ground began to rise, light coming through trees above them. Run-off from up there made the track squishy, and the dark earth was torn with pig tracks. Any sense of this being a path made by humans was now gone.

We're in the porky homelands, thought Seth, and sure enough, he got a big whiff of something musky and rank. Burns smelt it too, and he came to a halt, listening hard.

But there was nothing but the chitter of the fairy-wren back in the lantana. Then it stopped, and they listened to windless silence.

Burns shrugged and they continued walking, ascending the slope of a small hill. The muddy track grew wider and stinkier, their boots squelching as they walked to the top. Over Burns's shoulder, Seth saw a tree on the hill's crest, a dead jackwood that had been burnt black by lightning during some wild storm.

At the base of the jackwood was a big mud wallow filled with scummy brown water, the edges patterned with hoof prints. In the churned up mud, Seth saw a flash of colour – a scrap of blue tarp plastic.

"Jesus." Burns' voice was low. "It's the pig Hilton."

In the unmoving air, the place stunk of the animals.

"Let's go back," said Seth.

"What? No way, man. This is the spot. We can get off the track and wait for 'em."

"No, they're too smart for that. They'll smell us."

"You scared?"

More like smart, thought Seth, giving the detective a look of exasperation. Burns was like that cheeky kid at school who always double-dared you.

"Nah, I just don't fancy standing around here. It's like a busted septic," said Seth. But the silly bastard turned back to the wallow, eager for a dirty great boar to appear.

"We're better off lurking about back at the creek," said Seth. "It's warm and they'll want a drink soon enough."

A fat fly began dive-bombing Burn's sweaty head, and he turned with an easy smile. "You're the expert, mate."

Trudging back along the muddy trail, Seth leading now, he felt relief that Burns had been reasonable; his constant gung-ho got tiring.

As they re-entered the lantana thicket, clouds went over the sun. Trees vanished into deep shadow, and the great mass of thorny vines became dark and opaque.

Seth felt, more than heard, a faint drumming noise that came and went. Behind him, Burns coughed and spat. The drumming sound came again, closer now, and Seth felt the impact of hooves on the earth.

"What the fuck's that?" said Burns, like he didn't know.

The drumming sound grew louder, and Seth saw some metres away, the lantana begin to shake and bounce as though it was being hit from below.

With the jungle carbine still slung over his shoulder, he crouched down and immediately saw the big tunnels that had been bored through the lantana, pale light at the end of some, others just dark voids. Some of the tunnels were almost chest height.

"What are you doing?" said Burns.

The light at the end of one tunnel vanished. Something had come into it, and Seth knew it was rushing towards him. Drumming shook the ground, and from the midst of the crackling lantana came deep grunts of rage.

He jumped to his feet. A kinetic wake was travelling at speed right at him, the lantana jumping and shuddering.

"They're right here!" he yelled.

In frantic evasion, he sprung backwards, leaping up, and a massive pig barrelled past, its big shoulder hitting his legs. Flung against the springy lantana, he desperately tried not to fall to the ground. The carbine across his back stopped him getting stuck in the lantana, and he bounced back into the slot of the track and regained his balance.

"Holy fuckadoozie! That was huge!" yelled Burns, his rifle not only pointing the wrong way, but at gut level too.

"Watch your fucking gun!" shouted Seth.

The lantana began jumping down the side of the track, and he flashed on razor-sharp tusks at groin and femoral artery height. Hit bad and you'd quickly die.

In a thunder of hooves and gobs of mud, pigs burst across the track between the two men: a good-sized sow and piglets first, then others, none particularly small.

Unslinging his own rifle, Seth was more than pleased to see the cop lower his. Finger off his trigger, Seth held the carbine's barrel down. He didn't want to shoot in here. A wounded pig thrashing about would be more than iffy.

"Let's get out of this lantana!" he yelled.

He'd shot many pigs over the years, but hanging around here to get one more wasn't worth getting his balls ripped off.

But Burns had to let fly, shooting into the lantana. Seth yelled at him again, but Burns, now savvy to the tunnels, worked the rifle bolt, dropped to his knee, and aimed up one. Seth felt like shooting the stupid bastard.

Beyond the lantana now, the pigs crashed through the forest. But as the sound began to die away, he heard a new drumming resonating through the ground.

Quickly scanning the top of the thicket around them, he saw the lantana start jumping again, coming in on an angle right behind Burns.

Seth flashed on the big boar who'd led the charge: the cunning bastard had circled back for another go.

"Burns! Get up, man!"

The idiot paid no attention.

Seth threw the jungle carbine up, his arm thrusting through the canvas sling. It slammed onto his back as he ran forward. Grabbing Burns by his belt, he pulled hard. The Savage's barrel flew up, the rifle fired, and damn it to buggery – they fell backwards, Burns landing between his legs.

The king boar burst from the lantana. For a split second its evil eye regarded the two men, its massive head and shoulders right above them. Then it was gone, powering through the lantana like a hairy black tank.

Pushing Burns off him, Seth leapt to his feet and, with real anger, yelled at him, "Lesgetthefarkoutahia!"

With his rifle vertical against his chest and the cold fire of adrenaline pumping through his veins, he took off up the track. Whooping like a kid on firecracker night, Burns followed. Pelting through the lantana, with its stink and groin-high tunnels full of razored tusks, the cop's carry-on made Seth laugh.

Sprinting out of the thicket, he brought the carbine down, smacking the butt into his shoulder as he skidded to a halt. Burns rushed out, stopped and brought his gun up too, and the two rifle barrels swept back and forth, sightlines finally clear.

Breathing heavily, sweat popping from their foreheads, they listened like mice in a kitchen. From up on the ridge came the mocking cries of a cockatoo.

Seth shot Burns a look, saw the cop peering one-eyed down the iron sights of the Savage.

"What you gonna do if that boar charges at you from behind the tree there?" he said.

"You kidding? I'll put a bullet in its skull."

"No, you won't."

Burns side-eyed Seth. "The fuck I won't."

Seth laughed and lowered the Lee-Enfield.

"Pull the trigger."

With an obliging smile, Burns did. Nothing happened. He quickly worked the bolt, ejecting the empty shell and putting a fresh round in.

"You right there?" said Seth. "I'd have to save your sorry arse a second time."

Burns lowered the Savage, and shook with laughter.

"You're a funny bastard," he cackled.

It sure seemed that way, but Seth had seen the flash of white-hot resentment in his eyes.

Past the McLeod River, they turned off the Development Road onto the unsealed logging road that ran like a dusty vein up into the Windsor Tableland.

It was business time now – an inspection of the site as a real estate agent would say. Although they hadn't ended up shooting a pig, Burns was chipper at the wheel. When Seth directed him to go off-road into the scrub, he harooed jubilantly as they bumped across the stony ground.

Occasionally following creek lines, they threaded their way through an evenly spaced forest of yellowjackets and ironbarks baking in the sun, the spear grass hissing apart around the Land Cruiser, dead branches cracking under the wheels like stockwhips.

Taking his bearings from the dividing range on the right, Seth gave Burns directions. To get a better look at the terrain, he stuck his head out of the window from time to time, dodging the startled cicadas zipping up.

They backtracked once, Seth pretty spot-on in getting to the creek bed. As they followed it, a series of snap-shot memories played in his head, and the landscape became instantly familiar.

When he saw the rose gums and the rock outcrop, he directed Burns to drive there and stop. Wordlessly, he got out and went into the scrub. With an excited laugh, the detective followed.

Walking through the scrub, it was as if six years hadn't passed. He even recognised stands of trees. When they came out into the big overgrown clearing, he stopped and raised his arms like an Old Testament prophet. "You grow the crop here."

Burns made a soft sound of delight in his throat, and they briskly walked the length of the site, dodging through tussocks of grass and sapling gums; the rows of holes invisible in the ground beneath their feet.

At the edge of the clearing, Seth strode into the trees, Burns grinning like an idiot at his shoulder. They went up a slope towards a ridgeline nearly twenty metres away and stopped at the top.

At their feet, rocky as hell but glittering with water, was a small creek, a tributary of the McLeod.

"Water," intoned Seth.

Looking as pleased as a parrot, Burns laughed happily.

"So you made a bit of money here?" he said.

"Nah, we got raided by you blokes," said Seth, and he fielded an imaginary rifle.

"Coppers with M16s, a chopper, and one bloke chased me on a trail-bike. He tried to knock me off my bike, but I repaid him the favour and got away."

The detective stared at him, his mouth open, his eyes alive. This was what he'd been waiting to hear about.

Oh, yes, thought Seth. Camping out here on a dope plantation with guns, deceit, and danger, you're planning to have the crooked boy-scout adventure of your life.

"You know, I think I heard about that," laughed Burns. "You boys were public enemy number one for a while."

Looking impressed, he threw an arm around Seth, too genuine to be uncool. Reflexively hugging the nutter back,

Seth felt the memory of their fistfight in Cairns bounce along his ribs.

Camping by the rose gums that night, they ate steaks and drank rum, sealing their crooked boy-scout deal with a couple of joints.

Barrys

It was a funny thing – growing dope with the police. It seemed to bend the very laws of nature, like barracking for New South Wales at the footy. And it wasn't something you'd admit to either.

He'd lose a good few mates if they knew what he was about to do – propagating green gold with the cops. It was a crazy fool thing to do, but he'd let temptation tickle his winkle. Oh yeah, money was the heaviest voodoo around.

Burns had already paid him five grand, with another five due after planting. Once the dope had been harvested, dried, and packaged for sale, he'd get the remaining ten.

For his sting, the whole point of the exercise, Burns said he'd lined up some hard-nut crims from the Gold Coast to buy the whole crop. Knowing that locals weren't going to get busted made Seth feel a little easier.

And maybe those Gold Coast boys were bastards who sold smack and speed. Maybe they raped women and hurt people for fun and deserved to get done. Maybe.

The honest truth was: twenty grand was twenty grand. Demonising those blokes was nothing but a sop for his conscience, a balm made of bullshit. No, this was just too good an offer to pass up.

For ten or so days of work spread over seven months, it was money for green jam. And today was the first day on the job.

In the soft dawn light, he took his swag outside and put it by a twenty-litre water drum and a crate holding a small gas bottle and a bit of cooking gear. As he lugged an Esky out, the icebox full of food, a clean, white Land Cruiser, obviously governmental, pulled up out the front.

Seth had asked Burns what the go was with driving his own truck up to the crop, but the detective had vetoed it. Seth's chequered past might attract attention – maybe a tail, he said. Knocking out a serve of word salad, he also said that for optimum operational security, ingress and egress to the site had to be kept to a minimum.

Only a few vehicles were authorised to be there, anyone else was fair game for the local cops. So being with Burns was like having a get-out-of-jail-free card, and who could argue with that.

Burns gave him a hand to stow his gear amongst coils of polypipe, cartons of beer, and supermarket bags full of food.

Bright and affable, the cop drove with gusto. The road up the range to Kuranda featured a squashed python and a HR Holden down the side at Streets Creek. Burns frowned at the dead snake, and grinned at the wrecked car, and that was pretty cool.

They talked about cars they liked, different years and models, and Burns was pretty knowledgeable. He didn't say boo about where they were going, or who was going to be there, and Seth dug that too.

Black cockatoos swooped and called in the gums along the Barron River as they crossed the timber bridge into Mareeba. It was first thing quiet in town: a yawning bloke taking padlocks off the bowsers at a servo; a well-tanned farmer in overalls outside the post-office, engrossed in a handful of mail.

Out of town, the tobacco kilns and drying sheds were visible from the highway. Legal weed had been grown all around here for over fifty years. Some savvy farmers, with exactly the same gear and skills, had cottoned on to the other weed, and were making themselves big money.

Pelicans circled the swampland to the west. Early-bird drivers belted past them; veteran trucks driven by veteran farmers; semi-trailers hauling cargo west or up the Cape.

Mount Molloy was as ever dusty and decrepit, its glory days hinted at by the massive red brick, metal framed and strapped boiler, and the overgrown and rusty steam wheel still in place on the highway coming into town.

There was cattle near Mount Carbine, black, tan, and dusky bodies ambling on the road in the dusty sunlight. Coming to a standstill, Burns beep-beeped the horn. The curious cows shat indifferently, but cleared the way.

Ten minutes down the road, Seth pointed out a wedge-tail eagle soaring in the blue up ahead.

"One got shot in Tasmania that was nearly three metres across the wings," he said. "You'd keep little kids inside the house with something like that around, hey?"

"Wow." Looking thrilled, Burns craned his neck to look.

"I could never shoot anything like that," he said.

Good on ya, mate, thought Seth.

Past the McLeod River, they turned onto the logging road, and Burns gave it some gas, yahooing like a cow-cockie hitting town after months in the bush. Soon they got to the spot to leave the road, and began bush-bashing in towards the crop site.

Driving with assurance, Burns looked to have the route down pat now. Negotiating the rough ground, he grinned away as if thrilled at his luck at just being there.

Eventually, the tall rose gums came into view. With a toot of the horn, Burns drove up to a camp and parked.

From his seat, Seth checked it out: another government issue Land Cruiser and a 4x4 Ford XY ute parked close to the trees, not under them, and two big green canvas tarps rigged up with poles and ropes to some bloodwoods. And pitched to take advantage of any morning shade the tarps would throw: five sleeping tents of varying sizes.

Under one tarp was a row of twenty-litre water drums, big iceboxes, and some cooking gear, and on trestle tables, dry food, plates, and cutlery. Next to the tarp, a nine-litre gas bottle fed a burner and barbecue plate set up on a rusty steel frame. The other tarp sheltered the gear for growing the crop; everything heaped in stacks, boxes, and rolls, the smaller items crowding a trestle table.

It looked half-way professional, but most importantly, there was a nursery: a long shade-cloth-covered structure made of star-pickets, wire, and timber battens, its pristine condition free of leaves and dust suggesting it had just been erected. Beside it were stacks of six-inch pots, bulk bags of fertiliser, and a good heap of decent soil.

This boded well. Not only did it look like Burns had got

everything as specified and followed directions, but he was also looking like a good taskmaster as well.

They got out, and Seth stretched his back and casually eyed the four men sitting on camp chairs in the shade of the kitchen tarp. In shorts, polo shirts, and t-shirts, a couple with zinc cream on their noses, they looked like tourists.

"Well, fuck me, it's a north Queensland dope grower," said a bloke with a jaw like a slab of stubbled rock.

From the obedient tone of the ensuing laughter, Seth guessed that he outranked his mates.

A beefy young fella packed into tight shorts, wiped his blonde moustache, and drawled, "G'day, I'm Barry."

"I'm Barry, too," said Rockjaw.

A lanky fella raised a middle finger in greeting. "Barry." The fourth bloke, his face in a cloud of cigarette smoke, said nothing.

Burns found a camp chair, took a seat. Everyone stared at Seth, their smiles suddenly long gone.

"So, you must be Barry," said Rockjaw.

Blonde Mo, his hairy pink thighs like slabs of meat, was smoking a cigarette. Silent Smoker chained another off a butt. Packs of smokes, and tea mugs littered a card table in front of them.

Seth smiled amiably. He couldn't see the guns, but he knew they were there. In torrid silence, the bastards kept staring, trying to vibe him out.

Burns laughed. "Play nice, he's a good bloke."

"I don't think so," said Lanky.

Bugger standing here like a coolie boy being bagged by

the bwanas, thought Seth, and he went back to the Land Cruiser and began unloading it.

"He got a hole in the back to put batteries in?" Rockjaw got a dutiful laugh.

Leaving the Esky in the Land Cruiser, Seth took his gear to the rock outcrop. He'd set up here later. He unloaded the polypipe and took it to where the track to the crop began. Burns and the Barrys sat talking, the volume of their voices pitched to make their words intelligible.

Done unloading, Seth went and checked the gear: boxes of pipe fittings; splitters, joiners and taps, two hacksaws and plumber's tape. At one end, jerry cans of fuel, a small generator, and a Davy water pump sat on a wooden pallet. Outside the tarpaulin there was more polypipe stacked in head-high coils, plus many rolls of garden hose.

The tools were brand new. Shovels, mattocks, trowels, and wheelbarrow all sported a Tenni's Hardware sticker.

He's got everything, thought Seth. Even the red flagging tape. Grabbing the roll, he set out for the crop site, getting a half-arsed cheer from the sitting men. Burns got up and followed him.

"You're keen," he said.

"We're not here to root spiders," said Seth.

"Okay, what's first to do?"

"Are you serious, Burns? You clear the site."

The cop stopped as if to talk, but Seth kept going.

Down at the clearing, he walked the whole perimeter, tying off markers of red tape to saplings along the edges. When he'd marked it all, he walked back, pleased to now hear the thump of mattocks and the ring of shovels.

Working the first few rows, the Barrys were re-clearing, digging out saplings and tall clumps of grass and hurling them into the scrub. Rockjaw, Lanky and Blonde Mo were hard at it, sweating and grunting, but the chain smoker was making close to no effort, looking out at the scrub like his real gig was providing security. Balls-out bludging more like it.

Back in camp, Burns had sixteen different-sized bags of seeds, obviously garnered from raids, shakedowns, and evidence rooms, laid out on a trestle table to be looked at.

Using a couple of biscuit tin lids he'd brought, Seth took the detective through what constituted good seed. Hoping to see veiny brown seeds, waxy, glossy, and firm, the first bags were disappointing. Quickly checking them all, Seth found that three bags held corpses: hollow seeds expired in weevil dust. He chucked this rubbish in front of Burns.

"Yeah, yeah. I grabbed everything," said the cop. "Now, thanks to you, I know what not to take."

Fortunately, one bag turned out to be almost half full of vibrant, teardrop shaped seeds that looked right on the money. Better still, there were three to four hundred of them. This was a score – a reliable basis for the crop.

Burns went back to clearing the site while Seth looked through the rest of the seeds, sorting them into good and chuckum; the rejects immediately flicked to the ground.

Standing for a stretch, he peeked into the Eskys, curious to see what Barrys lived on. The first icebox was packed with large bottles of Fanta and Coke. Others were loaded with block ice and frozen veggies, porkchops, bacon, bulk sausages and cheap steak. Another held tomatoes, onions, and iceberg lettuce, salad cream, margarine, and tomato sauce. There were tins of beans and camp pie, and a milk crate full of loaves of sliced white bread. It was schoolboy food.

And filling the two biggest Eskys – beer, bloody Fourex, all carefully iced down like liquid gold. These kids were on holiday alright.

"You'll need more seeds," he said to Burns when they all came up for lunch.

Lanky and Blond Mo glared, their pink faces red, scalps swimming in sweat. Rockjaw spat out a laugh. "Is that fuckin' right?"

"Some won't come up. Some will die. You want to fill every gap in the clearing," said Seth. The Barrys stared at him, and he hoped they could visualise this.

"So, you know anyone with more seeds?" said Rockjaw.

"Nah," lied Seth. He'd gone through this with Burns.

"Reformed, but not really."

"Getting you seeds isn't what I'm here for," said Seth.

"We'll tell you what you're here for," said Rockjaw.

"Whoa, hold up . . . Barry," Burns said to him. "Barry here," he nodded at Seth, "will earn his keep, but he's got a legitimate job that comes with licences. He doesn't want to jeopardise any of that. Or what we're doing either."

The Barrys looked surprised, Rockjaw, Blonde Mo, and the Silent Smoker frowning at this unprecedented event – one of their own sticking up for a crim.

A little impressed himself, Seth nearly laughed in their dumb faces. Showing no acknowledgement of what Burns had said, he went to the Land Cruiser and made lunch.

With his Esky and its lid as a table, he stood in the Land Cruiser's shade, munching cabin crackers, cheddar, and carrots. In the luxury of their big tarp, the Barrys wolfed down marge and camp pie sangas.

It was hot, the sun cooking the air. With cuppas and ciggies, the boys lounged around under the tarp talking shit. Burns sat with Seth in the shade of the rocks and got the drill on germinating seeds, writing it all down in a red notebook.

Around two-thirty, bored brainless, the Barrys trooped back to the site and continued clearing. Not keen on being baked just yet, Seth went through the seeds again, rooting out more duds, before setting up his camp. After that he went to the clearing and wielded a mattock until dark.

That night, the Barrys drank beer and rum, whooping and boasting, just full of it. Out here, away from superiors, wives, and families, they were a mob of jive Jungle Jims, living out a naughty boy's own adventure.

Fortunately, Seth didn't hear too much of it. His camp, ten metres from theirs, was screened by the rock outcrop. Their voices were just audible, their delighted disgust and righteous laughter occasionally loud, but he didn't get any of the words, and that was just fine with him. Around boys like these, information was dangerous. With a big lump of rock between him and the loquacious Barrys, he'd sleep a lot easier.

Rockjaw came over and checked on it. Without greeting or acknowledgement, he stood there like it was his camp, listening to his dumb mates.

Satisfied, he looked down at Seth in his chair.

"You knew this place," he stated with a smile, obviously given the drum by Burns. Seth had to nod.

"Didn't do you much good, hey?"

"Not that time, no," said Seth. "But I'll make a bit now."

The cop showed his teeth. "If I had my way –"

Seth winked at him. Stonefish malignant now, Rockjaw stomped back to the Barrys.

Yeah, piss off, thought Seth.

With the sun now gone behind the Desailly Range in the west, Mount Spurgeon and Mount Windsor brooded in the dusk like the ramparts of an ancient city. It was time to eat before it got completely dark, and Seth cooked a nice feed on his gas bottle, then cleaned up.

Burns came over, and they talked, some of it about the crop, some not. Seth reckoned he was bored by the Barrys, but after an hour, the detective hopped up and went back over to his side of the fence.

Around ten o'clock, gunfire woke Seth – a shotgun and a pistol, the mindless noise echoing in the hills. He lay in his swag, listening to the brays of drunken laughter that followed. The kids were having fun.

The next morning, he was up at first light, the sound of snoring from the camp sullying the morning air. He made himself a cuppa and watched the sun slowly outline the main range.

As he made breakfast, he went over the coming day. After he'd shown them this next stage, they'd have enough to do for a while, and he could get out of here.

The Barrys were still farting in their tents and lighting up smokes when he began putting coils of pipe, boxes of irrigation gear, and a wooden pallet in the back of the XY ute. Burns, quickly tea and toasted, joined him, and they loaded in the irrigation gear.

The khaki-painted ute was a beauty. Before he got in, Seth crouched and checked out the suspension: front leaf spring mountings welded to the bodyshell, with high-lift springs and some top shockies raising the rear to match the front end. Very bloody nice.

"Where did you get this?" said Seth.

"Impounded," said Burns. "Some growers got busted. It was sitting there waiting to be sold."

"It's the duck's nuts. Two-hundred and fifty cubic inch straight-six. BorgWarner transmission. This is class."

Burns shrugged, pretending ignorance. "You rednecks love your bush chariots, hey?"

Seth gave him the finger. "I'll buy it off you," he said. "Part payment for my work here."

"Too late, mate, it's working for the law now."

Cutting down saplings in the way, they drove the ute to the slope near the creek. Locating the flat pad he had dug out years ago, Seth cleared away the accumulated dirt. They bedded the wooden pallet into the pad, and put the pump, the generator, and a jerrycan of fuel on it.

After joining sections of suction pipe together, they ran it from the pump up to the creek. Seth wired a bulb of wire mesh over the mouth of the pipe, weighed it with a lump of junk iron, and stuck it in the creek

It was proper hot now, and they all went back to the camp. Seth sat in the shade of the rocks by his camp and opened the book he'd started before Christmas last year.

It was set in seventeenth-century Japan, and things had got bad. The shipwrecked English navigator Blackthorne was mourning his squeeze, who'd been blown up by heavy *ninja* bastards. The book was very long and he wondered if he'd have it knocked over by next Christmas.

Half an hour later, the scuff of boots made him look up.

"Ooo, we've got ourselves a reader," grinned Burns.

"Well, unless you've got a portable TV that gets a signal out here, then this is it."

Burns ducked to see the cover. Seth held the book up.

"Ah-so, Japanese." He gave Seth a quizzical look.

"Know your enemy," said Seth.

Burns waited, then shrugged. "O-kay."

He nodded at the camp. "Let's get back into it, mate. It's hot but I want to get those seeds happening."

Bookmarking his page with a slender, blue kingfisher feather, Seth followed the big bwana back to work.

In the shade cloth nursery, Seth showed the Barrys how to plant seeds. He made a mix of fertiliser, sand, and soil, while Burns took notes. He filled a cardboard egg carton with the mix, brushing away any excess soil to expose the dozen openings. He stuck a twig into the first one, popped a seed into the resulting hole and put a pinch of the soil mix over it.

"See? Take a look. Don't pack it down. Keep it fluffy."

"Fluffy?" said Lanky. "What sort of poofy shit's that?"

"Fanny fluffy," said Burns. "The seed's roots need to slip right in."

Lanky frowned, not getting it. Burns laughed, a distinct undertone of 'you're a dumb bastard' in his voice.

Okay, thought Seth. Burns was the boss, but he seemed to see himself a cut above the Barrys – smarter for sure.

But did they know that their leader smoked dope? That he'd chatted to the brass while off his head? Probably not. It was just another level of deceit and thrills for Burns.

"Then you wet it down a bit." Seth used a spray bottle to dampen the soil. "You'll water them like this, too."

The Barrys stared at him like he was a housewife in a TV ad. But poofy or not, they got into it, sitting in the dirt in their shorts like the bad boys of kindy.

Seth and Burns went back to setting up the irrigation. Connecting large gauge polypipe to the pump, they ran it down the slope to the edge of the clearing. Seth fabricated a pipe splitter panel: a piece of plywood with a four-way pipe splitter screwed onto it, the splitter input attached to the pump pipe.

From a splitter, he ran polypipe along a cleared section, brushing away dirt and leaves to follow the line of holes hidden in the ground.

Attaching a tap fitting to a t-joiner, the thread tight with plumber's tape, he cut the polypipe and reconnected it with the joiner. Cutting off five metres of garden hose, he connected it to the tap, then put a spray nozzle on. Burns, watching all this, smiled and softly clapped his hands.

"You put in a tap every ten or so metres. The hose gives you a ten metre radius. You can reach six rows with each tap," said Seth.

"Clever." Burns nodded with real appreciation. "This your idea?"

Seth shook his head. "No, my brother's."

"Oh, where's he? Jail?"

Seth said nothing. Burns waited until he knew he wasn't getting an answer. "I can find out," he said.

Seth shrugged.

"Sounds a bit complicated." Burns' smile bored in.

"You're a bit complicated," said Seth.

Burns smiled at him with real affection.

Back at the camp, the Barrys were smoking and talking, pissing about doing nothing. There were rows of filled egg cartons, but the pile of seedling mix had been used.

Burns softly smiled. "Give us a hand," he said to Seth. As they made up the mix, Rockjaw watched them. When work resumed, Seth and Burns also planted seeds.

As they got to the last of them, Seth went and filled a bucket from a water drum. Back at his camp, he washed, soaping up and rinsing off. Though it was better feeling a little cleaner, the water was as warm as blood.

The Barrys went back to clearing the site, and Seth went to the nursery, now teeming with egg cartons. Toting a twenty-litre water drum, Burns joined him.

As they filled spray bottles and watered the egg cartons, Seth explained the process of getting the seedlings up and running. Then they got branches and rocks to hold down the shade cloth edges against any nocturnal creatures.

When the heat of the day finally started to back off, Burns came over to Seth's camp again, beer and notebook in hand. He asked more questions about dope seeds and germination and took more notes. He's like a pig dog running down a sucker, thought Seth.

The next morning, with everybody now aware of the drudgery of working in the heat, arses got themselves into gear early. Not long before seven, the Barrys, with bacon and eggs onboard, headed off, mattocks and shovels on their shoulders, with some joker whistling 'Hi-Ho, Hi-Ho, It's Off To Work We Go.'

While they chopped and dug, Seth and Burns continued setting up the irrigation system. Seth was pleased to see that Burns worked quickly with no mistakes – no mis-cuts, kinked or flattened polypipe, no stripped threads, or dirt-filled pipes and taps. He rolled out and positioned the polypipe deftly, and best of all, without any jibber jabber.

Working with a bloke usually provided a peek into their character, and Burns, for all the bullshit he spun at times, was showing himself to be solid where it mattered. Seth had to pay that.

When they got to the camp end of the clearing, Burns put the last tap on the row. "Nice one, mate," said Seth. "Only another ten rows to go now."

Grinning happily, Burns flicked sweat off his brow.

After lunch, Seth brought a mix of soil and fertiliser to the site in the wheelbarrow and showed the Barrys what all their clearing had revealed. Faintly raised rows had emerged. In them were the original holes from the crop. Seth re-dug a few, the earth coming out easily.

"Must have broken your heart when they all got ripped out and burnt," said Rockjaw. The Barrys grinned.

"Burnt? Is *that* what you blokes do with it?" said Seth.

"Fuck you," said Rockjaw.

Burns waved a calming hand, and Seth continued with

the lesson. He filled the holes with growing mix, making sure to leave a mound at the top, before using his heel to press the sides in tight.

"Each plant has to be raised to drain well. It might rain here into autumn, and that's good, but the plants can't sit in any sort of moisture. They'll rot and die."

The Barrys, sniffing and coughing and scratching their arses, appeared to understand.

"Just imagine if you'd put all this effort into growing something legal, like tobacco," said Rockjaw.

"Yeah, all that lung cancer, aye," said Seth, spearing the shovel into the earth-filled wheelbarrow. "Funny how it's legal to grow something that puts people in the ground."

Turning his back on the angry silence, he walked away. Yeah, think about that, you sanctimonious pricks.

When the day's work was over, Burns came and sat with Seth for his regulation hour, and they discussed the state of play. The clearing was nearly done, and the template for the irrigation system was laid out. Burns and the Barrys would continue with it until the site was covered.

And in the morning, Seth would demonstrate how to build the pest-roof fence to go around the clearing. They'd be well occupied while the seeds got going.

"So, a week to ten days to germinate," said Burns.

"And another ten before transplanting. You'll check 'em all to see," said Seth. "Just look for what I've told you."

"Yes, professor."

"We'll leave after my fencing demo tomorrow, yeah?" said Seth. "You can ring me in ten or so days' time."

A grin slit the cop's face. "Finding us hard going, mate?"

"That's actually the part you're paying for. The growing tips are thrown in for free."

Burns guffawed, just a bloke paying a joke, but his eyes were on the stubbie in his hand. When it came time to leave, he walked into the dusk, then turned.

"I was right about you, mate," he said. "I'm very pleased with how it's turning out. You're a pro."

That made Seth feel better than it should have.

As night swallowed the landscape, he cooked, ate, and cleaned up. Laying back on his swag, he went over what he'd overheard the last few days.

The Barrys had been pretty good at keeping it close to the chests, but here and there, Burns included, they'd let a few kittens out of the bag.

It looked like the Barrys would rotate through here as their normal day jobs allowed. Rockjaw was apparently in for the long haul, and it seemed that he and Burns wanted to get the crop in, and then enjoy a bit of pig-shooting, and maybe a beer or two in fabled Mareeba.

They were a mob of cocky pricks, that's for sure, but for all their yammer and bullshit, they were careful not to mention anything about who they were or what they did.

Seth decided to get it straight from the horse's mouth. Driving back the next morning, he put it on Burns.

"So, all of those blokes are cops?"

Burns laughed. "Mate, I'm saying zip. You don't know them, and you don't wanna know them. And vice fuckin' versa. They don't know who you are, and unless you really piss them off, they don't care."

"Just a mob of Barrys."

"Exactly. Operational security, man. I always run the game like this – and it always works."

"I've never seen any of them around Cairns."

Burns gave him a wink and a nod. "There you go."

"And what about you around Cairns?"

"I'm Andy, mate. You know that."

"But your boss in Brisbane knows about me, right?"

"Look, if things go wrong, which they won't, I'll have to tell him. I type fast. I'll knock up a profile. But, like I said, the operation is run by me. It's how it works."

"You got a file on me?" said Seth.

Burns chuckled. "Sorry, mate, but you don't rate one."

"So, I'm just a name and number in your notebook."

The cop tapped his head. "It's all in here. Operational security."

We Can't Let On

Back in Cairns, it was back to making a legitimate living again – the one he paid taxes on. Except you had to make some money first before you could pay tax. It hadn't been exactly crash-hot of late, and as sure as blokes drank beer, there was going to be a rates notice and a power bill in the mail box soon.

Three days without a proper wash had given Seth the itchy creepies. He took a good, long shower, then he rang his father to see if any work had materialised.

"Diddily squiddily squat," said Dad. "Nothing, nothing, and nothing. Sorry. Nobody in Cairns is missing or being adulterous. No one needs a background check or evidence for their day in court. There's close to a thousand dollars in the Kelly Investigations account, however."

Despite his disappointment, Seth smiled. Dad lived on the farm down near Edmonton, retired and growing fruit and veggies. He was also Seth's partner in the business.

Manning the phone, he winnowed out the time-wasters and weirdos, set up initial meetings, and took messages. With his university education and scientist's diction, he was the perfect public voice of Kelly Investigations. And come end of financial year, Dad did the books, keeping those beady-eyed bastards at the tax office at bay.

Seeing the Kelly name and the palm tree logo in the classified ads and on the business card was cool, but in hindsight, he could see that making a living as a private investigator in Cairns was no easy ride.

His ad, one-sixteenth of a page with two lines of bold, appeared in the Cairns Post and Tablelander on Fridays. It produced a reasonable number of serious enquiries, but the majority of people baulked at the open-ended nature of investigative work. The idea of paying seventy bucks a day for as long as it took was weird, even unscrupulous.

It was different with professionals and business people. They understood that things took time, and were used to paying for professional services. But in a place as small as Cairns, those sorts of clients were few and far between.

Bob Loftus, a solid-steel lawyer with a heart of gold, had given him some jobs; research and surveillance on behalf of clients, also preparing evidence for court. Perc Reed, an insurance claims honcho for SGIO also chucked a bit of work his way. They'd recommended him to other business people, and that had resulted in a few more jobs.

In the fourteen months since he'd got his licence, he now had a burgeoning rep as a diligent operative. It was nice, but it wasn't enough.

"I guess we'll have to put the Triumph convertible on hold," said Seth.

"And the hi-fi with the big speakers," said Dad.

"The Fiji cruise."

"The ocelots."

"The oce-whats?"

"Beautifully patterned felines, son. They're one of the largest small wild cats."

"Largest small?"

"We scientists like to be precise."

They laughed.

"Chin up, son," said Dad.

"Always, Dad," said Seth.

They'd been through living hell together, and nothing, especially not money, would keep them from smiling now.

It was a good thing he'd bought his house outright – a two-bedroom place on the beach on Cinderella Street at Machans Beach, close to the mouth of the Barron River. Without rent or mortgage payments, he just had food, power, and rates to think about. And beer and rum.

At least the weather was nice, and he went fishing with Johnny Pep and Maori George, staying a couple of nights on Snapper Island. Coming back, a mile or so off Rocky Point, Pep circled around, going on about a Yank Mitchell bomber that had crash-landed out here during the war.

The bottom wasn't even close to visible, and they had no tanks of air, so Pep, with a story for every bloody inch of the coast, told them about the plane going into the drink.

"Ran out of fuel. Circled the school at Rocky Point first, dropped a few flares to raise the alarm. Nobody's got hurt ditching and they're all rescued. On the beach over there, they fired off the rest of their flares for the school kids. The little tackers must have loved it."

"You're Mr. History, aren't you?" said Maori George.

"Mate, if we don't remember it, who will?"

A couple of times, Seth went next door and got on the grog with Rod Savage, who drove ore trucks on the mines out west. Home on a rostered fortnight off, and between girlfriends, he was happy to drink into the wee hours.

Although he smoked a pack or two of Winnie reds a day, Rod wasn't too keen on the wackos and bludgers smoking that mari-joo-ana. He must have smelt the smoke coming from Seth's place at times, but he never said a thing.

It's because I look straight, Seth reasoned. And work. To him, I'm a good citizen with my own home just playing the game. But it was as sad as a spilt bottle of rum: Rod, hammering his ciggies, didn't know what he was missing.

He also caught up with his cool and sexy friend, Stasia. But when they met at The Outrigger, with a table booked in the doozy of a restaurant, she wasn't feeling too good. Working bloody hard and dealing with that time of the month, the poor thing went home after one drink.

The Pig, his customised FJ55 Land Cruiser in two-tone pueblo brown and cygnus white, was running rough, and he took it over to Sabbo's new workshop. As well as a big hug, he got a free service, the result of getting his mate out of jail earlier in the year, and the bank balance liked that.

Then he got a job.

A Cairns builder was pretty sure an apprentice was stealing from him. The demountable site-office on one of his jobs was being rifled overnight. Over the last couple of weeks, a hundred bucks in petty cash, a new nail gun, and other valuable tools had vanished.

There were three keys to the demountable: one lived in

the builder's pocket, one in his desk drawer at home, the other with his head foreman, who'd been with him for ten years. The builder had spent fruitless nights watching, but he was flat out running three construction jobs and he needed his beauty sleep.

The suspect was a skinny kid who raced off after work to drink his body weight in beer at The Grand, his heart set on a shapely barmaid there. He'd put the word on her, getting smiles, even laughs, but nothing else. Then he'd cross the railway tracks to a share house off Scott Street, no doubt to dream of his cuddly, jug-pouring sweetheart.

Back at the building site, Seth sat in darkness listening to flying foxes squabble and shit. In the early hours of the fourth day, the lights of a car came down the next street. The car stopped, turned off its engine, and a few minutes later, a shadow flitted to the demountable's door, opened it and went inside. Torchlight flickered inside the office.

The thief didn't muck about. They were in and out in a minute, and Seth was soon tailing the car. With no traffic about he was cautious, even turning his lights off at times. Near the big mango trees at the reserve on Greenslopes Street, the car pulled in a driveway and the driver went into the house there.

Out of the Pig in seconds, Seth ran up the street to the house. Lights went on as he came up, and Seth saw a young fella in the kitchen. You little bastard, he thought.

When he described the thief, car, and address to the builder, it knocked him for six. Red-faced and mute, he'd counted out Seth's money with shaking hands.

Poor bastard. His shock was confirmation of what Seth

had thought. In the harsh neon of the kitchen light – the thief had looked like the builder's brother.

Over apple strudel and an iced chocolate at Mozart's, he reflected on the venal grubbiness inherent in man – that rotten urge to take what wasn't yours. And from your own brother too. What a shitshow that was going to be.

There was no use getting depressed about it. Not when you could have another slice of strudel or even a piece of Black Forest cake. And best of all, the building apprentice was in the clear, and who knows, maybe tonight he'd get to dive into a voluptuous ocean.

Belly and wallet full, Seth felt pretty good strolling over to the Commonwealth to bank the money.

A call from Burns that afternoon didn't make him feel quite the same way. Although the money was far better, the idea of spending time with those Neanderthals up at the crop tomorrow did not ice his cake. Fortunately, it was going to be a day trip this time.

Burns suggested they have a drink and dinner tonight. Seth weighed it up and decided on Tawny's. Down on the inlet, the restaurant was far enough away from the bars and pubs, and had prices that would put off most of his dope-smoking mates. A couple of hours there early on a Wednesday night should be fine.

Burns was in good form, wearing pressed jeans, a crisp white dress shirt, and into his second drink. They shot the breeze, no one much interested in talking about business, ditching the chat when the food arrived.

While Seth scarfed a peppery bowl of bisque, Burns ate a plate of cooked prawns with Tabasco. They had a dozen sizzling Kilpatrick each before hitting the mains: slabs of pan-fried snapper, grilled crayfish dripping with Pernod butter, perfect golden French fries, and an audibly crisp salad gleaming with the house dressing.

A few drinks after that, and Burns was telling stories about the other diners.

A big, fat fella eating alone had dodged a manslaughter charge – he'd rolled over and squashed his wife. The cool-looking American couple were professional gamblers taking a hard-earned break from the tables of Las Vegas, and the two well-dressed women laughing over a bottle of champers were cheating on their husbands – with each other.

It was pretty silly, but with the cop's non-stop, deadpan delivery, it was also funny. Even the waiter got a serve of bunkum, Burns telling him that he and Seth were in the market for an island. To set up a nudist resort.

A few more drinks later, they were sitting with the American couple, talking about blackjack and poker and why Cairns should have a casino. Burns and Seth were now the point men for a Sydney syndicate scouting out opportunities in the far north. With the international airport coming soon, the region was really going to take off.

But what Cairns was really crying out for, Burns told the wide-eyed couple, was a nudist resort. Stifling laughter, Seth had to look away.

It was all a bit of a giggle, but the next day at the crop, Burns looked as serious as a fella on a TV gardening show as he explained to Seth what had been happening.

New seeds he'd found had been planted, and he showed how the seedlings were ready for transplanting: the roots up against the carton walls and the first sets of true leaves evident.

Seth nodded along, but he was impressed. Burns had taken on board everything he'd been told.

The Barrys were all there, smoking and talking at the table under the kitchen tarp. There was a burst of filthy laughter as Seth and Burns came up, the culmination of some joke Blonde Mo had just told.

Seth was carrying a handful of butter knives he'd got at St. Vinnies in Cairns. "Look out," said Blonde Mo. "He's going to butter us up."

No one laughed. Rockjaw spat on the ground like it was Seth's grave.

"Okay, chaps," Burns used a Pommy officer's voice. "Let's move over to the demonstration area, shall we?"

Under the eyes of the Barrys, Seth made a mix of soil, sand, and fertiliser in the wheelbarrow. Loosely filling four of the six-inch pots with a trowel, he scraped them flat. With a butter knife, he made a good-sized hole in the dirt of the first pot.

From an egg carton, Seth gently released a seedling by running a butterknife around the cardboard. He lifted the plug of fragile soil with the blade under the seedling and his fingers around the soil, and landed it in the pot. Pretty much a perfect fit, it only needed small handful of soil sprinkled around the base of the seedling.

"Fluffy," he said. "Keep it fluffy."

"Fuckin' smart prick," said a Barry.

Repeating this process, he filled another three pots. It must surely be imprinted into their brains now.

"Watch them like hawks every day. Each one. Look for insects, rot, mould," he said. "Molly-coddle them."

"Ferfuck's sake," said Rockjaw.

"Listen to him," said Burns softly.

The imprinting seemed to have worked. Blonde Mo and Lanky filled pots, putting them out in rows in the nursery. Squatting and hopping about, Burns, Rockjaw, and Silent Smoker transplanted the seedlings into them.

"Careful, now," warned Burns. "Take it slowly."

This mother hen hoopla gave voice to Silent Smoker.

"Burns, just relax, willya?"

A twig bounced off a bonnet. Somewhere, a crow called.

The Barrys all concentrated on their work, everyone silently willing the slip-up away. Seth faked indifference, but once more he was amazed at the levels of deceit that Burns ran on.

Ten minutes went by. Burns got up, gestured at Seth.

"Let's go and look at the irrigation," he said.

No one looked up as they left.

As they walked, Burns gave him an update on the crop site. There'd been a few problems – some irrigation leaks and a mob of kangaroos sniffing around, but nothing that plumber's tape and a rifle couldn't fix.

Fully cleared and enclosed by a chicken wire fence, the site was ready to roll. Polypipe ran down every row, with all the taps in place and hoses attached. By the creek, the generator and pump platform had been shored up with big steel tent pegs. It's almost like it's legal, thought Seth.

With a captain's pride, Burns fired up the irrigation. The generator noise gave Seth a paranoid tickle. It might be a cop operation, but some things were ingrained.

Turning on a tap, Burns watered imaginary plants, a big dumb grin on his face, and Seth smiled at his nonsense.

"You need enough rain over the next six months to keep the creek from going dry," he said.

"It all hinges on that, hey?" said Burns.

"Sure does. Especially out here."

The seven hundred and eighty-two holes had all been dug out and were being filled with prepared soil.

"Seven hundred and eighty-two?" queried Seth.

In all his years of growing, nobody had ever thought to count the holes. Nobody counted plants either. What you counted was the weight of the product – and the money.

"Oh, yeah." Burns nodded seriously. "I counted 'em."

The next time Seth went up, nearly three weeks later, it was an overnighter. Burns was excited – the seedlings were ready to go into the ground.

In the clearing, the holes were all full, each one capped with a mound of dirt. Rockjaw in the Ford XY was busy ferrying plants down to the site.

"It's the same deal as the seedlings," said Seth when they'd gathered around. "But this time we use a trowel."

"Jesus, you're not doing much for your money," said Rockjaw.

With his eyes on Seth, Burns made a calming gesture with his hand.

As the first plant went into the ground, there was an

odd sense of significance. The Barrys watched in silence, looking almost contemplative. A snapshot of them would be a cool souvenir, thought Seth. Maybe even insurance.

Then everyone got into it, eager to get this crucial stage done. Bumping along from the nursery, Blonde Mo and Rockjaw brought more plants in the ute, leaving them at intervals throughout the site.

With the bit between their teeth, no one took more than an hour off for lunch, everyone pleased as piglets to be planting marijuana plants.

As the shadows lengthened, Seth inspected their work. Rockjaw looked up, his sunnies like big silver holes in his head. "Piss off, you fuckin' crim," he said.

Seth smiled and made whip-cracking noises.

By day's end, most of the plants were in the ground. Burns fired up the irrigation, and they all used the hoses to give them a light watering. When it was all done, the Barrys stood there, no one in a hurry it seemed, to get into a cold beer. Hands on hips, they gazed upon the expanse of green with a sort of reverential silence. Yeah, I should have brought a camera, thought Seth.

It was after sunset when Burns came to Seth's camp, his voice in the dark as he walked up already ladling it on.

"How's this? A crop is in! And all because of you. Top stuff, mate, top stuff."

Seth, trying not to let his pencil get pulled, said, "Well, that's great, because I'm gonna leave you to it for a while."

"Aww, you're making me sad," said Burns.

"Check them every day, keep them watered like I said. And make sure no animals get through the wire."

"Don't worry about that," said Burns. "A couple of the boys have got new rifles to break in."

"Sounds like you're looking forward to it."

"We've got to have some fun, too."

"Ring me if you have to, but I don't think you will."

In the half-light of the kero lanterns, Burns, looking cock-sure, nodded. Then he reached into his pocket.

"Aw, yeah, I nearly forgot."

He tossed an envelope to Seth. "Next instalment, mate."

The envelope was stuffed full of fifties. It looked like a hundred of them too. Very pleased to have the cash in his hand, Seth smiled. "Thanks, Chris. That's good of you."

He meant it, because when it came to illegal activity, with no recourse to the law, you hoped no one would be stupid. Trust became a currency in itself, sometimes more valuable than the dollars. Still, he counted the money in the envelope.

Smiling out at the night, Burns waited, listening to the raucous laughter coming from the Barrys' camp. Turning back, his smile had deepened.

"Mate, you know you can come sit with us," he said. "You'll get a bit of stick, but they'll settle down. So, what do you say? Let's go over and have a beer."

This bullshit pissed Seth off. A minute ago, there was a cool vibe; now Burns was playing up, acting like the bloke who held the roosters together to rev them up to fight.

"What?" Burns smirked. "You scared of them?"

With a pained smile, Seth gave a 'who-could-be-fucked' shrug. Why did this bloke have to be such a prick?

"You think you're better than them?" said Burns.

93

"You do," said Seth.

Burns chugged beer, his eyes back on the dark.

"Look," said Seth. "I don't care that they're cops. You're one, and we get along. You even smoke dope. But those blokes, they're . . . meatheads."

Burns laughed. "You're saying they lack intelligence?"

"More than that, they're . . ." Seth zipped his yap.

"What? They're what?"

I bet they've raped and bashed people, taken bribes, and stolen stuff, thought Seth. Maybe even knocked blokes.

Burns started laughing, his prankster eyes challenging Seth to say what he was thinking.

"They know you smoke dope?" said Seth. "With me?"

The cop's mouth was suddenly empty of sound, and he shut it. Juggling a smile, he nodded unconvincingly.

"Mate, I work undercover. It's fucking expected."

"So, it's cool to mention we've had a smoke together? I can light up a joint and hand it to you in front of them?"

Grinning like a dog, Burns stifled a nod. "Under normal circumstances, sure, but here and now, well . . . no."

"Normal circumstances? Like when we're all at a party, or doing the boogie at a blue light disco?"

With something between a smile and a snarl on his face, Burns kept his voice level. "We're setting up a major sting with a lot of marijuana as bait. That's cool. But these boys are a little old-fashioned about smoking it. We don't need to rub their noses in it, alright?"

Seth smirked at Burns.

"So they don't know you smoke dope."

The cop threw his empty stubble into the darkness, and

it smashed onto rock. Seth felt a stab of anger.

"Don't fuck with me," said Burns. He made a pistol shape with his hand and lazily aimed into the darkness.

Seth now flashed to earlier this year – *waiting alone in an interview room in the Cairns watchhouse. Hearing somebody come in behind him. It must be Sideburns back with a notepad. Then the metallic sound of a revolver cocking. The sense of something at the back of his head. Another click, the sound of brisk movement. Turning, looking up to see Burns grinning like a shark, his hand by his hip.*

Burns sighed. "Seth. Mate. Let's not be like this. We're a team. A bloody good one."

He arced up a winning smile.

"You're right, mate. We are smarter than them, but we can't let on, okay?"

Keen to prove himself as a bloke who could just get on with it, Burns didn't ring for a month. When he did, his voice was glowing with pride, even though all he said was that he'd be down on Tuesday to collect Seth. It seemed like the disciple was starting to feel like a master.

Unshaven, deeply suntanned, and wearing a creased Akubra hat, Burns looked cucumber cool when he picked Seth up. As they drove up to the crop, he said nothing about the crop, instead boasting about hiking the ridges shooting pigs and roos. The pub wildlife of Mareeba and Atherton got a mention too, with Burns much amused by what he called country customs.

In camp, Seth saw how the detective's vibe had rubbed

off on the Barrys like sweat from a horse. Blonde Mo and Lanky strutted about in cowdy hats, stinky and unshaven. Bare-chested and now fully bearded, Rockjaw diligently ignored Seth as he cleaned a scoped rifle, his eyes hidden behind his aviator sunnies.

Even Silent Smoker, probably the straightest-looking bastard there, had taken a few sartorial leaps and bounds of his own. Sitting with a Reader's Digest, smoking, he wore a pair of grotty Bombay Bloomers and a cut-off shirt that exposed his stick-thin arms. He had a blue bandanna around his neck and, looking real odd, cowboy boots on his feet. On the card table next to him was a large revolver in a holster. It was like a scene from a bad movie.

There was also a pile of beer cans and slaughtered spirit bottles. As they went to the crop, Seth asked Burns about the rubbish. Nodding reassuringly, the cop assured him it would all get taken to the tip in due course.

They took a good look at the plants, going down the rows and closely examining them. The heads, technically the flowers, were forming, and the majority of the plants had good height to them. As expected, some had been pulled for being runts. "Thirty-five, can you believe it?" said Burns.

"Another week or so, and you want to start trimming these shade leaves," said Seth, flicking a few. "Streamline each branch to let air and light in around the heads. Trim them every four or five days."

After another notebook entry, Burns surveyed the sea of pale green, a conquering smile on his face. In his dusty jeans and tight t-shirt, sunnies and desert boots, with the

Akubra sitting back on his head, he looked like the outlaw he always wanted to be.

The smiles continued driving back to Cairns. Burns was pleased with his progress, and pleased to show it off, and Seth was happy that he wouldn't be needed anytime soon.

The good feelings didn't last. Burns reneged on the full return trip, instead pulling up at the Whitecars stop in Mareeba. "You're kidding," said Seth.

"Mate, don't sweat. The last bus for the day is coming in twenty minutes. I checked, okay?"

Seth cranked up a smile, trying not to get steamed up. With ten grand chugging down the track towards him, an hour-long bus trip home was a small price to pay.

Burns nodded at the people waiting for the coach; a young woman, sweet-faced and country fresh, the focus of his attention.

"Look at that, mate. Might turn out a good move for you after all. Up the back. Bit of finger pie. Nice."

Steam whistled in Seth's ears.

"So, what the fuck would I've done if you'd got here late?" he said.

"Hitch?"

Seth yanked open the door. Burns grabbed his shoulder, too much concern on his face.

"Joke, mate, joke! Of course, I would have taken you back to your place. You know that."

Looking at him, Seth couldn't tell where the truth ended and the bullshit began.

Don't Mister Me

Against the green range of hills by Trinity Inlet, the De Havilland Beaver rose up into the blue sky. The noise of the floatplane bounced across the inlet to the back deck of the cabin cruiser, where Seth and Henry sat drinking tea.

"Unpressurised. Bloody noisy," said Henry, his eyes on the ascending aircraft.

"True?" said Seth. "You been on one?"

"Yep, that one. After a week of fishing, this Yank wanted a look at the outer reef. Took me with him."

Seth looked around, digging the boat. The *Maria* was a sweet Norman Wright cruiser that Henry had bought a few years ago. It was a thing of beauty, but it wasn't cheap to run or maintain.

It was a good job then that Henry was a gun fisherman who worked his ring off, his time divided between well-paid charters and the hard-yakka work of the marlin and barra seasons. Single at thirty, he saved his money too.

Sipping his tea, Seth wondered what was on his mate's mind. Henry, never one to rush unless it was something perilous on the water, leisurely scratched his forearm, his eyes still on the De Havilland.

Seth waited, happy to enjoy the view of town from here. It looked good – the way for a port to be seen. On the narrow coastal plain beside the Whitfield and Lamb Ranges, Cairns sat on the swampy, sandy shoreline of Trinity Inlet, where deep water provided safe anchorage.

There'd been over a hundred years of people checking out this view: the whitefellas, Chinamen, and Singhalese, and the Kanakas stolen from their island homes on the far side of the Coral Sea. And before them all, the indigenous Murri people, criss-crossing the inlet and catching tucker from bamboo rafts and log canoes.

The wharfs, jetties, pubs, hospital, and warehouses had come first, then the railway inland and a grid of houses spreading west and north – a tiny smudge of humanity surrounded by mangroves, swamps, and jungle hills.

For most of the town's history, the view hardly changed. In the 60s the gas tanks and the long bulk of the sugar terminal appeared, and over the last year, the apartments and the hotel looming above the fig trees along the Esplanade.

"There's this bloke who needs a hand," said Henry, his gaze now on a tanned couple on a yacht by the mangroves. Seth waited. Henry turned to him and softly smiled.

"An old skipper. Hit the salt back in the thirties and served in the war. After that he worked up to captain on Pacific line ships. In the sixties he got into cargo, salvage, timber, you name it. He went hard at it – then made his real money in property and business."

"His real money?" said Seth.

"Oh, he's not a poor man," said Henry.

"So what sort of a hand does he want?" said Seth.

"That private eye stuff you do," Henry grinned.

"Yep, that's what I do." Seth kept the exasperation from his voice, but his mate kept stirring.

"You still driving that old Land Cruiser, I see. You got nice shirts, but they always the same ones. You'd be better off being a bouncer again. Even cutting cane."

"Aw, cheers, mate, but I'm not dropping my rates."

"Mr. Exclusive."

"Damn right. It's a bloody bunfight going cut-price. You get the psycho neighbours and paranoid girlfriends."

"Sounds unattractive at any price."

Seth was tempted to skite, spinning the five grand from Burns as honest money made from a Kelly Investigations job. But that would be pretty weak.

"So, what's this bloke called?" he said.

"Hansen. Captain Jake Hansen. He's retired from the sea now. Lives in Lae, Cairns, Sydney, all over."

"How do you know him?"

"Crewed with him one time for a few months. Salvage job off the Wallis Islands. Early seventies . . . or maybe it was nineteen sixty-nine. Hard job anyway."

"So you kept in touch?"

"Nah, I was talking to a fella the other day who tells me Hansen's in town looking for a hand. I thought of you."

"Thanks, mate. So, what's he like?"

Henry smiled.

"Tough bastard. Didn't lose his temper much, but when he did – well, you'd want to watch out."

"Biff?"

"Probably. A couple of times he got stroppy, slapping backs, punching shoulders. I heard his stories about him fighting in big brawls back in the day. Rescuing his crew from waterfront pub brawls, then knocking them out back onboard when they gave him cheek."

"Whoa."

"Yeah, really."

"Any tips dealing with him?"

Henry cast his eyes to the north as he thought about it.

"I wouldn't muck around hiding something from him. Especially if it's right under his nose. Anything like that, even jokey stuff, and he'll go crook. You might see some biff then."

"No sense of humour?"

"Oh no, he likes a laugh, but not at him. The one time I saw him get proper mad, a bloke had made up a nickname for him, nothing serious, but when he got wind of it, he punched the bloke like he was joking, but *too* hard for a joke. Dropped him on the deck."

Seth nodded slowly. "Good tip."

"I know how he felt," said Henry. "When people run you down all clever. Putting you down, but not to your face."

Coming from the Torres Strait, Henry had copped his share of racial prejudice over the years.

"Do unto others what has been done to you," said Seth.

"Nah, that's not how it goes." Henry went to church.

"A tooth for a tooth," said Seth. "It's in the Bible."

"You sounding hard and bitter, man."

"Like a cabin cracker behind the freezer."

Henry snorted, his eyes back on the yachtie couple.

"So, you keen or what?" he said.

"Yeah," said Seth. "If it's money, I'm keen."

"He'll be at The Criterion tomorrow. From mid-day."

"The Criterion?" Seth pulled a face.

"Yeah. On the Barbary Coast where it's always been."

"That joint's a dump. I thought you said he's big money."

"I also said he's a tough bastard."

It sounded promising, and he needed all the promising he could get. Last month had netted him six hundred bucks – the builder, and a few days work for Bob Loftus doing a check on some blokes at a mining company.

Sure, he had the five grand from Burns stashed, but it was trouble money – only to be used in emergencies, like something bad happening with Dad's health.

So, the next day as he walked up to The Criterion, Seth was grateful that his mate had sent some work his way.

It wasn't yet midday but people here were drunk. A fella leaning against a post under the second-floor verandah looked ready to slide off it, and outside the front windows, a tiny, scruffy woman was shouting at someone inside, her words incomprehensible, probably even to herself.

As Seth went in, a rangy bloke stumbled backwards, his broken-knuckled hands hitching up stained jeans. Jesus, thought Seth, ducking around him, is this the Lost Patrol or what?

There were a slew of drinkers in the beery stink of the front bar, none fitting the description Henry had given him. In the back lounge, with sunlight streaming through high windows onto a cigarette-butt flecked lino floor, he saw two tables of Islander ladies drinking pots, purses, jugs of beer, ashtrays, and packets of Consulate crowding the table tops. Though they all kept on talking, everyone noted Seth's arrival. At the only other occupied table, he saw the man he was looking for.

Hansen was bear-sized, bearded, grey-haired and fat, his expensive watch looking too small for his wrist. His gaze was unfocused, and there was a scotch or brandy on ice by his hand. As Seth came over, he slowly looked up, his wrinkled, sun-beaten face impassive.

"Mr Hansen?" said Seth.

"Don't mister me. Sit down."

Seth did, feeling irked by the tone of command in the bloke's voice. He may have been skipper of many a ship, but this was dry land – and Seth wasn't on his crew yet.

"You drinking?" said Hansen, nodding at the bar hatch that serviced the lounge. Seth shook his head, and waited as the older man looked him over.

"You've known Henry long?" said Hansen.

"A few years," said Seth.

At the next table, a woman in a bright floral dress lit up and blew out smoke, the light in the room filtered with the haze of all the cigarettes of the last two hours. Hansen plucked his own cigarette from a pack of Benson & Hedges and lit it with a chunky gold lighter.

"Well, he's vouched for you," said Hansen. "And I take that very seriously. He better not be wrong."

Seth got up, the wrought-iron chair squeaking loudly on the lino floor. The voices in the room faded.

"What's got up your bum?" said Hansen.

Though Seth spoke softly, his voice was granite hard.

"You don't make anything even *close* to a threat about Henry. He's worth a dozen of you."

"You're right, he is," said Hansen. "He's a special bloke. A master sailor, a superlative fisherman, and a true family man. I'm more than honoured to know him."

"Is that right? So what's with this 'he better not be wrong' bullshit?"

As Seth asked the question, the answer hit him, and he sat back down. The laughter and talk of the ladies' lounge resumed. Hansen sat there placidly smoking his cigarette, his eyes once again looking at a place that wasn't here.

Seth let the anger flow off him like water from a banana leaf, almost smiling at the wink one of the Islander ladies gave him. He returned his attention to Hansen, and the bastard's eyes were now sharp and clear.

Even before the word came out of his mouth, Seth knew what it would be.

"Loyalty," said Hansen, "Can't buy it. You can rent it, but you're never really sure. And God help you if you run out of money. No, it's something that only true friendship can command. I see Henry has a true friend in you."

Seth didn't mind sitting a test, but he wanted to know what the hell for. But rapidly getting the measure of the man, he kept his mouth shut.

The tip of the Benson and Hedges crackled and glowed. Blowing smoke from his nostrils, Hansen looked like a gargoyle. He put the cigarette down in an ashtray bearing the evergreen legend of McWilliam's Cream Sherry.

"I'll pay you double your rate. I'm not sure how much

loyalty I'll get for that, but I'll expect some results."

"That's a hundred and forty dollars a day." Seth kept the surprise from his voice. Hansen nodded and went on.

"First up, I want you to look into two men involved with me. You do alright with that and I'll have more work for you. I'll put you on a weekly retainer."

That sounds cool, thought Seth, but something worried him. Being at sea could be life or death at times, with everyone on board subject to the skipper's orders.

"Look, Hansen," he said. "My discretion's guaranteed. But what exactly do you mean by loyalty?"

"That you won't jump ship on me."

"That's not a problem. I won't take on any other clients while I'm working for you."

"I don't mean another client."

Seth thought about that for a moment.

Hansen produced a piece of card, handed it over. On it was a name and two Cairns addresses. Seth saw that one was in town, the fella's workplace, the other in Stratford was obviously his home.

"Watch him, follow him," said Hansen.

"What will I be looking for?"

"Signs of money being spent. Gambling, other women."

"Other women?"

"He's married. Or boys. Any illegal activity."

"Illegal activity?"

"You know what that is, don't you?"

Seth nodded professionally.

"So, drugs too, yeah?" he said.

"All of it," said Hansen. "I want to know what rails he

might come off. We'll talk in a couple of days. Unless you find out something before then."

"What can you tell me about this bloke?"

Hansen shook his head.

"No, I want you looking at him with clear eyes. Mine are not so good lately."

"Expecting anything . . . rough from this bloke?"

"Rough?"

"Violence."

Hansen laughed, shook his head "As you'll soon find out, he's an accountant."

Seth got it now. This bloke might be siphoning off a bit of money for future reference.

Hansen watched him put the card in his wallet.

"Most accountants are good people like you and me," he said. "But when you're dealing with big sums of money, there's sometimes the temptation to forget whose it is. I'm hoping not to have to remind him."

"So, if I find something on him, will you need me as a witness in court? I'm familiar with that. You can hire me at my standard rate."

Hansen shook his head.

"No, just the investigative stuff."

I bet this old bastard dispenses justice himself, thought Seth. He certainly looks tough enough.

Now came a thump of feet on the floor, and cries of rage and alarm interrupted them. Seth turned to see the small drunk woman from outside being pursued into the room by an unshaven bastard with a bung leg and a gap-toothed frown. Grabbing an arm, he slammed her against the wall.

She cried out, and the ladies in the lounge began yelling at him.

For a moment, Seth was happy to let them break up the ruckus, but the woman, reeking, scruffy and intoxicated, her grimy feet in worn-out thongs, squealed in fear and pain as the bloke's fingers dug in hard, his other hand rising to deliver a punch or slap.

It was beyond pathetic, a perfect example of why Seth didn't drink around here. She was a down and out loser, and this scene would probably play out again and again in her life, but he couldn't stand by. Hopping up, he grabbed the bastard and pulled him off the woman.

"She's a fuckin' . . . she fuckin' did it, swear to God," gabbled the bloke through a stunning cloud of industrial-strength bad breath. Seth, head held back from the stink, propelled the grub towards the door in time-honoured bouncer style, kicking at his legs to hurry him up. The publican rushed up. "You right, mate? Wanna hand?"

"No, I'm good," said Seth. "Used to do this for a living."

With a look into the street for pedestrians, he propelled the bloke outside, where he stumbled to his knees. Hoots of laughter came from the people, who sat day and night, it seemed, under the trees on the median strip.

He checked his hands, relieved to see nothing yucky on them, and went back in.

The woman was now being ejected by the publican, and Seth moved to one side as they passed by, grateful for her complete unawareness of him standing there.

Back in the ladies' lounge, Hansen regarded him with heavy eyelids, something like a question in his eyes.

Seth shrugged. There was nothing to say. A woman was being hurt. Hansen gave him a nod, its meaning unclear. Seth stood there, not getting it.

But it felt like their business was done for now, so he nodded back. "Okay then – the accountant."

"That's right," said Hansen. "The accountant."

"So, how do I contact you?"

"The Pacific International Hotel. Suite two. If I'm not there, leave a message."

"The Pacific International?" said Seth.

The hotel was brand spanking new; it had been barely open a week.

"You don't think I'd lob into any of the fire-traps around here, do you?" said Hansen.

Seth smiled apologetically, feeling servile and hating it. Then – bugger it. "So why are you drinking here?"

Hansen's eyes narrowed.

"I drink all the twelve-year-old scotch I like, Thai snake wine, and hundred-year-old bottles of cognac too. I fart through fifty-dollar sheets and have girls with skin like milk and chocolate do whatever I want them to do to me, two or three at a time. I own twenty properties and nine businesses. But the moment I forget where I come from – I'm dead in the water."

Stay Professional

Pretty much since he was a teen, Seth had nursed a deep fear: the dread of being the married fella in suburbia with the wife and two kids who commuted to a deathly dull job like a clockwork toy each day, then sat in front of the telly at night worrying about the mortgage and what his in-laws really thought of him.

Though he didn't have the kids, Hansen's accountant, Dean Meadows, was that bloke. Bespectacled, pale, and weedy, he wore an ironed shirt, knee socks, and pressed tan shorts as he set off for work, lunchbox in hand. Back home, he scrubbed up real nice in ironed white shorts and a pastel polo-neck shirt.

The person doing the ironing and making up the lunch boxes, however, didn't look the slightest bit weedy.

Mrs. Meadows had serious curves, a good straight back, and glided most efficiently around the house. What spoilt this picture of homemaker perfection was the persistent frown on her lovely face.

With an effort, Seth pulled his gaze from her and looked around the quiet, dark street. Looking at people through their windows at night was a mucky thing to do, but it was part of the job.

Tonight, though, with Mrs. Meadows in the picture, he was feeling straight-up pervy – and some real concern.

An unhappy woman in the kitchen cooking up a storm was pretty bloody dismal. She had the bonny house with patio and garden, all the swish furnishings and mod-cons, even a flash double-door fridge. But it wasn't enough, and it hadn't taken long to see why.

Sitting in the lounge with his eyes intent on the TV, Meadows chain-smoked cigarettes and picked his nose, breaking up the fun with slugs of ice water from the jug next to him. Like an uptight insect, he looked the epitome of uncool.

It was a sure bet he wasn't getting into Rock Arena on a Tuesday night after smoking a joint. Any straighter, and you could have used him as a ruler.

Glenda – her name garnered from a Woman's Weekly re-subscription letter Seth had found in the mail box – came into the lounge three times, and each time hubby ignored her when she first spoke, before looking up with irritation at her interruption.

Back in the kitchen, Glenda glowered at the stove. Oh, baby, you're stuck with this drip, thought Seth. He must have seemed like a good prospect – a fella with a proper job paying proper money. And counting cash would never go out of fashion.

Her voice rose, loud and clear, frustration buried deep but there. Dinner was on the table, but Meadows still sat smoking, his glasses flickering blue, his mouth pursed in concentration at the cricket replay on the box.

Mrs. Meadows strode back into the kitchen. She looked

real dark, and an image flashed through Seth's head of a rail car full of dynamite, motionless under a full moon.

Jesus drunk in a scrum, he thought. A gorgeous woman cooking dinner? It didn't get much better than that. This fool should be jumping up and bestowing kisses on his kitchen goddess.

Instead, the goof sat mesmerised by the sight of Dennis Lillie repeatedly rubbing a cricket ball against his groin.

You're going to lose her, thought Seth. Truly vexed by this arrant nitwittery, he turned the key in the ignition. Under the streetlight, cane toads waited for dizzy moths to fall – but he was done.

On the third day of surveillance, Seth sat parked across the street from Meadow's second-floor office in Martyn Street, the morning slowly dragging its fingernails across the blackboard of his mind.

As lunchtime approached he found himself urging the bastard to do something dubious; something more than sitting in an air-conditioned office counting beans. It was a Friday, so maybe Meadows might take the rest of the day off, hitting the pub and meeting some dodgy-looking bloke in a creased suit. Or maybe he'd smoke a joint in an alley, or go and play the horses down at the TAB, blowing money that wasn't his.

But the drip didn't leave his office. He just stayed there, eating the lunch his considerate wife had made.

Seth sighed and thought about considerate wives, and marriage, and he remembered Alex and Lou's wedding at Palm Cove: a bar and two kegs set up on the verandah, the big buffet, her family up from Ballina, and Mum and Dad so proud of Alex.

And their mates and their ladies, most of them growers and dealers, all dressed up and behaving, with Seth the best man and Lou visibly pregnant. A lifetime ago.

He slouched back in the seat, wiggled his toes.

Marriage, aye. It was a big bloody word. It meant living with someone day in and day out, with the personal and the private mixing into one. He'd lived with women a few times, once for three months, and it had been alright.

Vibes grew, cool moments accumulated, and a shared appreciation of the world began to bloom. It took you out of yourself, widening your eyes and opening your mind. He liked that. Women usually had different ways of seeing things, and he liked that too.

Never lasted, though. And never the result of anything he'd done specifically – life had just barged in, tearing all those cosy little arrangements apart. He thought of Peggy. That could have been something, alright.

He rubbed the scar tissue on his ear, still tender from the craziness earlier in the year, and let Glenda Meadows sashay through his head again.

He liked the way she looked: her potent eyes, her bared arms in capable action, her serious walk. He liked how she looked down at Meadows watching TV; the expression on her face wilful and imperious. And very sexy.

But daydreaming about someone else's unhappy wife, a complete stranger, was a mug's game, and he corralled his thoughts elsewhere.

At five past five, Meadows went back to Casa Meadows,

and Seth settled in up the street. When it got dark, he'd park closer and see what was cooking tonight.

But when a freshly-showered Meadows hurried out and put a fold-up chair and sports bag in the boot of his car, Seth knew dinner wasn't on the menu. The tackle box and fishing rod that came out next confirmed it.

Meadows hopped into his silver four-door Cressida and drove off. Seth let him leave the street before he followed. Soon they were on Mulgrave Road, and when it turned into the Bruce Highway, Meadows drove at the maximum speed limit. There must be a real big fish calling his name, thought Seth.

Keeping this up for an hour, overtaking when he could, the accountant finally stopped at the Miriwinni Hotel, a cane farmers pub on the side of the highway.

Seth pulled over before the pub and watched Meadows go in. When he came back out, the accountant was clutching a six-pack of beer and two foil-topped bottles of bubbly.

Back on the highway, Meadows took the first left: the road to Bramston Beach. Seth kept back a fair way, the silver flash of the Cressida not hard to see against the cane fields.

The dusk softened the coastal range ahead, turning the jungle dark green. Out over some remnant swampland, a string of white ibis flew above stands of feather palms.

The road was narrow, unsealed in parts, and crossed a number of one-lane bridges, their loose timbers thumping and rattling under the nearly two ton weight of the Pig.

There were farms and sheds scattered amongst the cane

fields and banana plantations, and cow paddocks, too. With his eyes on the silver car ahead, Seth kept alert for stray cows and late tractors.

In his rear-view mirror, the state's highest mountain reared up, an indigo chunk of forever against the pink and orange of the western sky. If I wasn't working, he thought, I'd stop and just dig the view.

The coastal range now loomed dark and close, the road growing steeper. On the crest, he took a last look back at the mountain before flicking on his lights and descending through the jungle. Ahead, disappearing and reappearing around the curves, were the lights of the Cressida.

Coming down onto the coast, walls of guinea grass lined the road. An incongruous surfboard sign appeared in the gloom, proclaiming Bramston Beach.

The best fishing was north on Sassafras Street, where mangrove creeks fed into a tidal lagoon before hitting the sea. But Meadows, with his bottles of bubbly, didn't turn off. Continuing on, he passed the motel and slowed at the caravan park and camping ground by the beach.

A few overhead lights up on palm trees and the electric and kerosene lanterns of campers showed that the place wasn't even close to half-full. Shadows and silhouettes bobbed and moved as people made dinner.

Meadows turned onto the street that ran parallel to the beach. Houses lined the sides, each surrounded by a patch of nicely-mown lawn. These tin-roofed beach shacks had a bedroom or two and a front porch. Many had clamshells and coral by the steps, some with those poxy whitewashed rocks around the garden beds and lining the driveway.

Halfway along the street was a little store with a petrol bowser. Closed now, its bare outside light was already attracting a swirling halo of insects.

Bramston was a classic getaway place: small, sleepy, and off the beaten track. Besides the shop, caravan-park, and motel with its dodgy restaurant, there was the resort down the southern end. Near the resort, in the lee of a hill, was a boat ramp and anchorage.

He and Johnny Pep used to hit the resort back in the day when game fishing events were on. There'd be Sydney and Melbourne TV and entertainment people, other rich southerners, and local groovers. With live music, a resort licence, and buffet food, the parties would go till sunrise.

City slickers and locals alike, everybody let their hair down, and then some; more than a few smoking dope for the first time. In the darkness up the beach, Seth had let smart, fancy ladies off their heads ride him like cowgirls.

Now Meadows slowed and turned into the driveway of a bungalow. There were lights on inside, someone coming to the open door, and Seth didn't look as he drove by.

Two hundred metres down the road, he turned into the resort entrance. Seeing no traffic on the drive, he killed his lights, turned around, and parked along the road a bit. From here he could watch the street.

The resort had been the first coconut plantation in the north and many trees remained. Through the columns of palms, Polynesian torches were fluttering in an inshore breeze. Over by the beach, a crew of curlews started up, screaming like women being attacked.

When he was sure Meadows wasn't leaving, he slowly

drove back, looking on the bungalow side of the street for an unlit house without a vehicle in the car port. Finding one, he pulled over and parked.

There were no streetlights, and no one about. He got his pair of Tasco binoculars and quietly locked up. Flitting up the side of the vacant house, he went around the back to where the melaleuca swamp began. Something thumped across the grass – a wallaby foraging for its dinner. Sorry, mate, he thought, I've got some perving to do.

Walking parallel to the swamp, he went through back yards. With no fences between the houses, he was soon behind the bungalow.

A strip light lit the front room; in a back room a smaller light glowed. He stopped, listened, and heard two voices coming from the back room, both pitched in urgent tones.

He focused in through an open window and saw a wall jerking with shadows, and something happening on a bed. The voices carried in the still air: a female voice filled with filthy exhortation, and a bloke sounding like his cork was slowly being pulled.

Seth moved closer, raised the Tascos again. Meadows, knees apart and hard at work, was fully starkers. So was the woman kneeling, head down, bum up, on the bed. She looked nothing like Glenda Meadows – not even close. Skinny and gangly, with her hair pulled back from her flushed and spotty face, she was barely eighteen.

Eyes glittering with manic glee, she reached up between her legs and caught hold of the swinging part of Meadows not inside her. Like a freaky Looney Tunes character, his eyes rolled back and his tongue flopped out.

Okay, stay professional here, mate, Seth told himself, and he scanned the room looking for . . . for evidence to put in his report. The bedroom door was open, and out in the front room he saw the sweating bottles of bubbly on a table. The labels said Gala Spumante.

Dawn light woke him; the sea flat, a few clouds breezing past the Frankland Islands. He went for a run on the long, empty beach, leaving the first footprints for the day. Overhead, flights of imperial pigeons, ten, fifteen at a time, commuted in from the islands for the day's foraging on the mainland.

After the run, he had a nice, cold shower in the caravan park's little toilet block. The first jet of water startled a big huntsman spider, and it took cover in the creeper peeking in under the corrugated iron roof.

As he shaved in a wall mirror with its silvering mottled away at the edges, there came the scuff of sandy feet. A tight brown barrel of a bloke materialised in the mirror. Peppered with sunspots and cross-hatched with a lifetime of wrinkles, he held a threadbare towel. They exchanged grunts, Seth guessing he was a long-term resident here.

Ablutions over, he made a cuppa on his gas bottle and went down onto the beach. Sitting on the white powder sand, he drank sweet black tea, happily mindless in these opening hours of the day.

Two trawlers were anchored a kilometre out, the sea glittering crystalline around them. By his feet, motionless amongst the pink pompoms of Queen of the Sea flowers, a pinstriped skink soaked up its first sunshine of the day.

Last night, feeling nauseated by the manic copulating he'd unexpectedly witnessed, but knowing Hansen would want more, he'd booked in at the van park. The manager gave him the bad news: The resort wasn't doing food right now as the chef was in jail.

At the motel restaurant, he managed to chew down a steak from the Jurassic period. Spawned from a tin, the mushroom sauce was saltier than the sea, a few arbitrary fungal fragments floating in it, and the baked potato had the texture and taste of yesterday. Hungry as, he ate the worn-out salad too.

When the waitress, a chatty older lady who didn't need the make-up she wore, asked him how it all was, he lied, reluctant to spoil her genuine smile.

After a consoling beer, he went back to the love shack. The street was dead, and he'd snuck right up to the house and listened as Meadows and his young chickee babe sat on the porch drinking and talking.

Except it wasn't Meadows anymore, it was Rick, and the accountant didn't just have a new name; he had a whole new persona. He was a customs officer who spent his time on the high seas stopping and boarding ships, uncovering contraband, and confiscating drugs, guns, and salvage.

Slick Rick chucked in lots of details that had the ring of truth about them. The smart bastard was using someone else's maritime experience – Hansen's.

It was grubby, alright. Meadows had concocted a life of seamy subterfuge for himself, and it was where he really lived, in exultant fantasy, his straight life with Glenda in their suburban dreamhouse just cover.

But it was the home improvements that Meadows had in mind for the bungalow that had really caught Seth's ear: a master bedroom with an en-suite, a long verandah, and a walled garden complete with swimming pool. It had all sounded bloody expensive.

Careful not to startle the skink, he chucked the dregs of his cuppa onto the sand. Wandering back to the Pig, he slowly packed up his swag and put on a shirt. He took his time motoring out of Bramston over the coastal range, and in the morning sun, Bartle Frere looked fantastic.

He stopped, got out and filled up on country. Lost in the mountain, minutes passed. He could feel the massif as a self-evident truth, unnameable and essential, its strength and solace enormous. Bugger religion, he thought. This is the real deal, something no cathedral could ever rival.

On the Bruce Highway going south, traffic was light, with a few semi-trailers and early morning utes appearing and disappearing amongst the endless sugarcane. Soon he was crossing the jungle-fringed North Johnstone River and coming into Goondi Bend.

In town, he parked across from the Blue Bird Café, the building looking like a set from an old European movie. Dad had told him that swing bands used to play there, but it wasn't dancing he was after this morning.

A Greek family had the cafe, and for what seemed like forever, they'd made the best pies and pastries in their basement bakery. He could sure rumble one or two of them now.

A trim young lady served him, looking as fresh as the orange juice she squeezed for him. This long, cool quaff of sunshine washed down two spinach and cheese pastries, a you-beaut beef pie, and two slices of that Greek yoghurt cake, the one with all the syrup.

Man, he almost licked the plate clean, but the sweetie at the counter was watching, so he sucked a finger instead.

Sated, he walked up the street. Town was busying up now, with shops and offices opening doors. On the corner of Edith Street, he stopped outside the Court House.

Its big curved front and Roman columns really nailed the halls of justice look, but on principle, he avoided court houses. Fortunately, the ground floor was where the shire Land Titles Office was. Checking the Submariner on his wrist, he was pleased to see that it had just opened.

It didn't take him long to find out what he wanted. Soon he was heading back north on the Bruce, listening to Empty Glass on the Marantz car stereo, Townsend's voice growing on him. After that, he put on a mixed cassette he'd made, turning up Frijid Pink's Miss Evil as he came off Mulgrave Road into town.

At home, he rang an old mate, now a real estate agent, who added to what he knew. Then he rang Hansen.

"I got a result," he said.

"Get your arse over here," said Hansen.

Many a Rough Saint

Twenty-five minutes later, Seth stood on the Esplanade by Fogarty Park, looking up at the future. Twelve million bucks of world-class luxury with sweeping ocean views, the ads said. Ten stories of five-star bliss, with a big blue letter P painted up the top. Though not officially open yet, guests were already sipping cocktails and rolling about on king-sized beds.

The Pacific International. It felt weird saying the name. Standing there with the mudflats stink on the breeze, Seth let memories fill his head.

Two classic hotels had once stood there: The Strand, where famous travellers had stayed, with its restaurant, swimming pool, and afternoon teas. And next to it, The Pacific, with its fabulous red cedar staircase, a front bar on the waterfront, and a beloved concert room that had hosted many shows, even rock'n'roll, over the decades. Lifetimes had been lived in those old joints.

Now the future was here, a tall chunk of glass, steel, and concrete – with sweeping ocean views. The hotel looked like it belonged in Honolulu or the Gold Coast, not Cairns.

He crossed the Esplanade to the hotel, its pavement landscaping lush, the head-height concrete planter boxes on the corner bursting with greenery. Everything looked fresher than fresh. Some of the palms at the front hadn't been there a week ago. He went up the front steps, the awning overhead ten or twelve metres high, and saw a glittering lobby behind the big glass frontage.

Inside, a two-story atrium schmicked up with marble floors, square columns, and glittering chandeliers grandly welcomed him. It was hard to believe it was Cairns.

You could imagine some old bloke living on a battered wreck of a boat on the inlet accidentally wandering in here and getting the shock of his life.

And here was a curious local right now, with grass in his hair and no shoes on his feet, looking like he slept rough – probably in Anzac Park right across the street. Letting the glass door close behind him, the bearded man looked around with vague interest at this flashy new addition to downtown Cairns.

A receptionist, a young fella with a sharp blonde hairdo, zipped over. He wore a calm smile, kept his voice low, and coming in close to the park-dweller, his hand came out as if to help with a bag. With complete attention, he listened politely as the bearded bloke said his piece.

With an apologetic smile, he indicated the man's bare feet. The man looked down as if surprised and nodded sagely. He knew the score: no shoes, no service, and with a rocky smile, he made a dignified exit.

Nice work, thought Seth, walking to reception. Front of house, like the door of a club or a pub, was the first point of contact. You had to get people onside from the drop – so you could direct them later if need be.

The receptionist casually raced him to the front desk, won, and with an appreciative glint in his eye greeted him.

"Good morning. How can I help you?" Blondie checked Seth out, eyes lingering a tad too long on his broad chest and muscled arms.

Seth read his name tag. "Yeah, g'day Simon, I'm here to see Captain Hansen. He's expecting me."

"Yes, he's in suite two, Mr –?"

"Just call me Seth, mate."

"Oooo, that's unusual," said Simon. "Egyptian?"

Seth shook his head. The receptionist waited a beat, his eyes coolly intent. "Are you industry, Seth?"

"Industry?"

"Hospitality?"

"Yeah, sorta. I used to be."

"Security?"

Seth nodded. The receptionist stared for a couple more seconds, then pointed a manicured finger upward.

"Captain Hansen, I can tell you, is enjoying the luxury of his suite. It's got a faaabulous view of Trinity Inlet. Not quite as well-appointed as the Lee Marvin Suite, but gorgeous nonetheless."

With a cheeky twinkle of his baby blues, Simon added, "Mr. Marvin is quite the man, you know."

Seth grinned at this guff, and got a smile back.

"Thanks, mate." As he went over to the lifts, he had a feeling the cheeky bugger was looking at his arse. At the lift doors, he turned. Simon was watching him.

Seth wagged a finger, and the 'who me?' expression on the receptionist's face made him laugh.

Simon laughed too, and something flashed across the foyer – a recognition that they were simpatico, two cool players who knew the score. Seth raised a hand in salute, pleased to have a sharp ally in this new hotel.

Inside the mirrored box, he pressed the button for the first floor of accommodation and checked his reflection. He was no peacock, but he liked to present well for clients. Maybe Hansen didn't give two tenths of a damn, but it was important to maintain a good look. And who knows? A potential client, even a nice lady, might get in on the next floor.

But the lift ascended uninterrupted two floors, and he walked alone down the hallway, everything smelling fresh and synthetic, the walls gleaming from all the new paint.

Some light knuckle-work on the door of number two produced a ship captain's bark of acknowledgement, but nearly a minute passed before Hansen opened the door.

His white cotton shirt was open, exposing grey chest hair, his gut slumped over the waistband of his pants. He nodded brusquely and lumbered barefoot back into the room. Seth went in, the door closing silently behind him.

The suite was what you'd expect: plush carpet and cane furniture, tropical print cushions and curtains. There was a large main room with a dining table and a bar, a lounge area with a plump lounge suite and a bloody big TV, and doorways leading to bathrooms and bedrooms.

There was a smell of women's perfume, and Seth flashed on the old skipper's boasting at The Criterion.

Hansen went out to the balcony. Seth followed, looking at the dining table. One half of it was covered with ledgers, folders and ring-binders, and like gold bricks, half a dozen cartons of Benson & Hedges cigarettes. An electric adding machine plugged into the wall sat ready to go.

The balcony had outdoor furniture. On the table were more folders, a telephone on an extension cord, and a full ashtray. Hansen sat, his massive haunches straining his slacks. Seth went to the rail and looked out for the first time at a quintessential Cairns view.

Big figs stretching along the Esplanade, Fogarty Park below; The Harbour Board in the middle of the car park; Tawny's, the boat ramps and jetties by the water's edge, and beyond it all, the inlet dotted with yachts and boats, with Cape Grafton pointing out to the Coral Sea.

A lighter schnicked, he turned around. Hansen blew out smoke, gestured for him to sit. Seth took a chair, dug out his notebook and laid out what he'd found.

"Okay, as well as his home in Cairns, your accountant has a two-bedroom bungalow down at Bramston Beach. After a search at the Innisfail Lands Office, I can confirm that the title is in the name of Dean Meadows. He bought it seven months ago for fifteen thousand eight hundred dollars. He's planning substantial renovations on it."

Hansen smoked reflectively. Seth waited.

"And?"

"There's a girlfriend."

"Girlfriend? How do you know that?"

"I saw them having sex."

"Is that right? Get you all hot and bothered?"

Seth shook his head.

"A looker?" said Hansen.

"I preferred his wife."

The old skipper raised grey eyebrows.

"She looked to have a bit more personality," said Seth.

"Personality? That sort of thing will get you into strife. Learnt that from my second wife. Combine personality with a good lawyer, and it's a thousand dollars a week for the rest of your days."

Hansen dragged hard on his smoke.

"And?"

"I heard him talking to the girl."

"She young?"

"Just on the right side of jailbait."

Something flickered in Hansen's eyes. "And?"

"He was pretending to be somebody else, a bloke who knew the sea well. He had all the jargon, all the stories. Sounded like he'd spent a lifetime at sea. He told her he was a marine customs agent called Rick."

Hansen snorted. "Pretending, hey? Don't we all? It's rare to meet a man who really knows who he is."

Seth nodded solemnly.

"You that sort of man, Kelly?"

"Yeah, I reckon I am."

"Bullshit." Hansen's hooded eyes were combative.

"Look, I'm just here to do my job," said Seth.

Hansen laughed, hoisted himself to his feet. Seth kept a neutral expression on his face.

"Do your job, hey? Okay, I want you to look through some records for me," said Hansen, and he went inside.

Feeling nonplussed, Seth put his notebook away and joined the old skipper at the dining table.

"Those," said Hansen, indicating a stack of box folders. Seth stared down at them. You're kidding, he thought. Documents were no natural friend of his. But money was.

"You *can* read?"

Seth nodded at the jibe. Hansen put a pad and pen next to the marbled folders. "Go on, they won't bite."

Stony-faced, Seth sat down. He opened the top folder and saw financial records. Despondency gripped him like a python. Hansen stood over him, the smell of cigarettes strong.

"Okay, these are from when Meadows first started with me five years ago. My houses and commercial properties in Queensland. You look for any outgoings over a hundred dollars that aren't body corporate fees, rates, repairs, or property maintenance – that sort of thing. Odd sums. Anomalies. You understand?"

Feeling bushwhacked, Seth nodded, his eyes flinching from the howling wilderness of numbers before him. Man, this was straight-up paper grubbing. And it looked endless.

Hansen, picking up on his dismay, let out a chuckle.

"Easy money, hey? Sitting on your arse in a comfy chair, air conditioning, beautiful view. When I started out, it was salt rash and smashed knuckles, squashed cockroaches in sweaty hammocks and filthy old bosuns. Go on, take your shoes off. We'll take a break for lunch."

Seth nodded, took a deep breath, then applied himself. It took a few minutes to understand exactly how the pages were set out. Finally getting a rhythm, he tried to keep his eyes on the ledger pages and not on his watch.

Still it was dire, and the hours crawled by. Hansen read paperwork out on the balcony with his smokes, and they didn't speak. Seth wished there was music playing, but he had a fair idea the old bastard wouldn't go for that.

He was bloody grateful when at eight minutes past one, Hansen ordered them up lunch: steak sandwiches with fried onions, two sandwiches each, and French fries. They ate them with an icy cold Crown Lager apiece.

At fifty-one minutes past four, Hansen started a phone conversation on the balcony. He became angry, the rising growl of his voice culminating in brutal threat, and Seth heard the voice of a man who'd forced blokes to do things.

But from its tone, Seth could tell it wasn't the person on the other end of the line he was getting mad with. No, this was a warning to be passed on.

Back inside, Hansen marched over to the bar. Seth, his eyes on the papers of torture, heard ice in a glass, the crack of a bottle cap, and a few seconds later, a grunt of satisfaction. Hansen padded over, a scotch on the rocks in his paw. "How you going?" he said.

Seth shrugged, turned his note pad side-on, chary of his client's reaction. Hansen looked down at the three items listed; they totalled nearly seven hundred dollars.

"Well, well, well," he said. "A rat in the stores."

Seth waited, surprised when Hansen said, "You wanna get yourself a drink?"

He sure did. There were Crownies in the bar fridge and he opened one. Sucking down that first icy draught of mouth-numbing delight felt like a real reward.

"Let's call it a day," said Hansen. He went out onto the

balcony and Seth joined him. They sat in silence for a bit, drinking and looking at the view.

Across the inlet, the hills were turning purple, gold and green, the last sunlight streaming through the gap in the Lamb Range. At the Green Island jetty, the new Hayles catamaran was disgorging day-trippers. Crossing the inlet in tinnies, yachties were returning home with supplies.

"Half the room tariff is for the view." Hansen waved a hand at the vista. "You can see the same bloody thing from the bridge of a ship at the wharfs."

With the ball rolling now, Hansen began talking about hotels. He'd stayed in dozens; Suva's Grand Pacific, Aggie Greys in Apia, The Cecil in Port Moresby, and The Strand in Cairns being favourites. And of course, The Tradewinds up the road, owned by the Kamslers, who'd just built the Pacific International. "I've known them for years," said Hansen. "I booked a room here before it was built."

A good hotel, he said, was like a home away from home where the owners and staff treated you like family. It was the old way: the acme of hospitality, where requests were accommodated, and certain indiscretions too.

Nodding politely, drinking another, and then another beer, Seth found himself being thoroughly entertained. Hansen spun a yarn with a raconteur's dexterity, painting vivid pictures of times and places and populating them with a cast of characters, many a rough saint and smooth rascal among them.

Like a good actor, he weighted phrases and lines with humour and emotion, building up drama and chucking in the twists. It felt practised, but ad-libbed too. Watching

Seth's reactions, Hansen artfully chose what to leave in or take out, and this gift for tailoring the tale kept him in total command of the conversation.

As dusk fell like a cool blue veil, the wind dropping fast, Hansen brought the Johnnie Black out to the table, and they drank on. The old skipper was in full flow, and the only silence came when Seth went to get a fresh beer.

Maybe it was the grog, but he was beginning to feel that Hansen was warming to him. With his prompt unearthing of Meadows, not to mention his trawl through the books today, it felt like a door had been edged open.

Hansen's demeanour towards him seemed to hold gruff approval, and buried deep – relief, as though there'd been a gap that this new boy looked most capable of filling.

Seth quaffed his icy-cold Crownie, feeling pretty damn cool. Yep, things were looking up for the both of them.

Around eight, Hansen got on the phone and ordered up room service: grilled barramundi, buttered asparagus, and dauphin potatoes, plus a cheeseboard and some kind of gateau cake topped with liquor-soaked strawberries and a good whack of whipped cream.

It was all laid out on the dining table by a quick young fella in spotless black and white. He also put six Crown Lagers in the fridge, a bottle of Glenfiddich on the kitchen counter, and topped up the ice. Hansen stuck a ten in his hand as he left.

It felt a bit odd eating a proper dinner in a hotel room, but it wasn't bad either. Hansen stopped talking, and they demolished the food down to the last cherry. Then they went out to the balcony and drank some more.

After a harrowing story about eating hot, raw fish in a drifting rowboat, Hansen launched into a rave about the transforming nature of ocean-going, and how through the millennia ships had repeatedly changed the world.

He also believed that sea travel was an opportunity for anyone, rich or poor, to completely change their life.

"A man with the will to work and learn, can step off a dock onto a ship, then step off it onto another dock on the far side of the world. A lascar from Calcutta, a New Britain man with a sandalwood comb in his hair, even a kid from Woolloomooloo."

"That you?" said Seth. Hansen nodded.

"I grew up watching wool ships load at Finger Wharf. Saw 'em bleeding or dead on the McElhone stairs. Dulcie Markham gave me a ten bob once to watch for some fella aiming to give her grief. And always – sailors, salts, and pussers, grogging on, raising hell, then sleeping like babes on cold front steps, or snoring like pigs in a whore's bed."

Hansen paused, eyes distant, his fingers automatically feeling for a cigarette. Taking one, he grimly smiled.

"But really, it was a hard, dirty place."

Seth nodded, and waited while the old skipper lit up, thinking how bloody lucky he'd been growing up in the far north. Hansen had a few drags and began talking again.

"I stepped off the wharf in Woolloomooloo and never went back. When I got north of Capricorn I stayed there. The warmth, the people, the freedom to live your life, and make a quid.

"See, my father was navy. Served three countries. He was there at the Battle of Jutland. Seventeen years old, ten thousand dead. I never saw much of him, maybe two or three times a year if I was lucky. For a fortnight or so, I'd have all the lollies I wanted, handfuls of shillings, and I'd get to hear his stories."

Looking at Seth, Hansen smiled, the excitement of a kid gleaming in his eyes.

"And what stories they were. Extraordinary stuff, the likes of which beyond the imaginings of the average man, let alone a kid. Stories of voyages, storms, and oceans, and of incredible places and astonishing people. Early in the morning drinking mugs of bitter cocoa together, or late at night when he was three sheets to the wind – he told me stories."

Hansen inhaled smoke, slow and deep.

"You could say he made me twice. Once in my mother's belly, then again in those boarding houses along Dowling Street as I waited for him to come through the door and tell me all about where he'd been and what he'd seen. I began dreaming of the sea. I became a sailor."

"And your mum?"

Hansen's eyes drifted up to the stars over the inlet.

"Ahhh, she did her best, but the sailors and fellas who came to Woolloomooloo didn't have much money. I ate most days. I had shoes."

Hansen smoked, his face tinged with melancholy. Seth thought of his own mother, and memory shadowed his heart. It was time to go.

"So, what's on for tomorrow? More accountancy?"

Hansen sighed as if released from a burden. He blew out smoke. Down in Anzac Park, some bloke was yelling.

"I don't know," he said. "You're a bit bloody slow."

That made them smile.

Hansen tore off a piece of paper from a pad, wrote down an address, and passed it over.

"He's an older bloke, so I reckon he'll be at home most of the time. I want a detailed description of *everyone* who visits him. You're to ring me twice a day, at ten and six, to report."

"Anything I should know about him?"

Hansen shook his head.

Seth put the address in his wallet.

It was great to have a new task, but a question niggled at him. If he hadn't been drinking with Hansen over the last few hours, he probably wouldn't have asked.

"So . . . Meadows?"

"What about him?"

"Looks like he's stolen from you."

"And?" The concord of the last few hours was entirely absent now; Hansen's face a mask.

"What are you planning to do about him?"

"What do you care?"

Seth, lagered up, pressed on.

"You said you wouldn't take him to court, so . . .?"

"Jesus, Kelly, you're sounding like a virgin bride. What are you trying to say, man?"

"You going to punish him?"

Hansen said nothing, but his eyes zeroed in, brimming with encouragement. Not liking the implications of this predatory look, Seth finished his beer and stood up.

They'd eaten well, drunk a skinful, and talked for hours,

and although Hansen had been real good fun, the bastard was now looking like he wanted to be asked a question he couldn't wait to answer.

Too bad, *Mister* Hansen, thought Seth, I don't do that.

Number Ten

The address was for a house in McKenzie Street where it crossed the top end of Lake Street, an area where pillars of Cairns society like Boland and Lennon had once lived.

Many of the houses around here were classic old timber Queenslanders, built for tropical conditions with floors raised for air circulation, and big lattice-work screened verandahs providing shade and optimum breeze.

Seth parked on the wide strip of gravel and grass next to the street; the big verge dating from when the bullock teams needed space to turn. From the mottled shade of a flame tree, he made a first visual recce of the joint.

Behind a fence of wooden pickets in good repair, the house at number ten was screened by lush vegetation. He glimpsed a small lawn, framed by two big trees; a fig and a mango. In the smooth limbs of the fig, epiphytes and orchids had been encouraged to grow.

From the bits he could see – the tin hipped roofing, the long shadows of an encircling verandah, and a wizard's wand of a finial – he reckoned the house had been built back in the day, and at some cost.

It even sported a lychgate on the street, its peaked roof smothered with flowering jade vine, the blooms looking like hundreds of turquoise fish hooks.

Going on Hansen's nearly non-existent description of the house's inhabitant, Seth surmised the bloke must be from old money, a scion of the wealth produced by tireless enterprise. And some old-fashioned exploitation. Fortune favoured not just the brave but the ruthless as well. He'd certainly seen some of that before.

What Hansen wanted with the bloke here was anyone's guess, the only clue being that they both had money.

Recce done, he went and parked twenty metres away on the Esplanade, placing the Tascos on the passenger seat. From here, he could see clearly down McKenzie Street to number ten. It was a pleasant spot, and with the sea a few metres away, his presence here could be explained as a waterside stroll, maybe even cast-netting for prawns.

When it got dark, per his surveillance modus operandi, he'd move in and park close to the house.

Over the next two days, nobody came or went. He used a phone box on Sheridan Street to update Hansen on this inactivity. The calls lasted ten seconds, if that, with the old bastard hanging up without a word.

On the third day, not long after he'd parked up on the Esplanade, a fit Islander-looking bloke pulled up in a battered ute. Seth snatched up the binoculars, but his excitement withered as the fella got gardening tools out of the ute's tray and took them through the lychgate. Though he didn't much go for manual work, Seth envied the bloke having something to do.

After his morning phone call to Hansen, the mention of the gardener getting no response, he rang Stasia at her work. It was a bit cheeky, but seeing as she lived in a tiny flat at the office, it was the only place he could ring her.

Sure enough, she was under the pump, distracted but thankfully not irritated. She wasn't up for dinner tonight and was doing stuff with her brother's kids on Saturday, so she'd give him a ring Sunday if she wasn't going over to a mate's place who'd been having a rough time of it lately. No worries, said Seth as cheerfully as he could, but he felt relegated to the bench.

The day oozed by like sump oil, and the sunset set the sky on fire. When it got dark, he parked outside the house.

At seven, with the volume low, he listened to ABC News. The Queensland premier was trying to stop a group of Murri stockmen from buying a cattle station up at Archer River because . . . they were Murris. With the Supreme Court deliberating the case, Seth bloody well hoped those white-wigged bastards down in Canberra would act like decent human beings and give the peanut-brained prick of a premier a kick up the coit.

After the news, he sat scheming on how to generate business for Kelly Investigations. He could expand his advertising budget to Innisfail and Townsville, and he'd definitely spend time and petrol on a fresh round of the pubs and motels. Handing out business cards had got him a bit of work in the past. But he'd met so many drop-kicks in pubs along the coast and on the Atherton Tablelands. He sighed. Yep, a proper brainstorm with Dad about this was on the cards.

Something moved in the garden of number ten. Gently sliding down in his seat, Seth kept very still, his eyes just above the level of the dashboard. It wasn't just a hunter's sense of not scaring the quarry – it felt like there was something equally predatory in there.

Whatever it was didn't move again, and he dismissed the kinetic shadow as a cat, or maybe a frogmouth. But he stayed slumped there, listening to an illogical bell ringing in his head, the sort of silly shit you scared yourself with as a kid lying under the mosquito net on a hot, gusty night.

Another minute passed. Then spooky electricity zapped through him. In the darkness down the next street, he saw for an instant what looked like a face – the glint of eyes, a flash of teeth, the line of a jaw. It was freaky, and it was also very Cairns.

He didn't bother reporting this non-sighting to Hansen the next morning, but less than an hour after he'd made the call, a tallish figure came out from beneath the flower covered lychgate. Grabbing the Tascos, Seth focused in.

An old bloke: stringy, tanned, balding, a couple of cloth shopping bags hanging limp from a bony hand. With a forceful gait he walked out onto the wide grass verge and waited.

Seth glassed him properly, seeing an alert face lined by an outdoor life, a decent looking watch, and venerable but shiny shoes. With his well-pressed pants, the lines of his singlet visible under his shirt, and what was left of his hair in a neat comb over, he didn't look like a derelict wastrel rotting away in the ancestral home.

A squeal of brakes came from Sheridan Street and a taxi drove up. The old bloke got in and Seth tailed the cab to town where it pulled up outside Woolworths. Cruising by, he saw the bloke go into the supermarket.

The parking fairy was on duty today and he gratefully snared a spot outside the House of Ten Thousand Shells. Crossing the road, he nodded at the old blokes sitting on the benches under the shade trees in the meridian strip.

Near the entrance to the supermarket, he loitered about, faintly revolted by the young hippie fella with incredibly filthy feet, playing, if that was the word for it, a digeridoo, his grubby hat laid out to bludge for change.

After ten grinding minutes of this audio massacre, Seth began praying for a Murri bloke to come along and spear the bastard. As he contemplated giving the deluded kid a buck to shut up, the old bloke came out, his shopping bags bulging.

There was a queue at the taxi rank, so the old bloke went up the street, his head swivelling back and forth in search of a cab. A few minutes later he got one, and Seth went back to the Pig. When he got to McKenzie Street, the taxi was pulling away. Stopping on the verge up the street, he watched his target get his shopping through the gate. So we know he eats, he thought.

Pretty much close to nothing happened for the rest of the day. As it got dark, he went home. Outside of breakfast, he'd had nothing but a Frangipani's pie all day, and he needed some energy.

He also needed to make a couple of calls. First he rang Hansen, the old skipper indifferent at his report on the shopping expedition. Then before the surly bastard could hang up, Seth reminded him it had been a week since he'd started working for him.

Hansen told him to come over and get his money.

He rang Dad next. His father was impressed with news of this great new client, even more so with the double rate of pay. I'll never get tired of impressing him, thought Seth.

Though of similar vintage, Dad had never heard of the ex-skipper, but he was intrigued to hear about this tough old sea dog in his luxury suite at the Pacific International. When Dad asked him if he'd visited Uncle Don lately, Seth was ashamed to say he hadn't.

Uncle Don was one of the family's oldest friends, not an uncle by blood, but as good as. Nearly two years ago, he'd retired after nearly thirty years as a cop, embittered and angry at the corruption in the Queensland Police Force.

"He's drinking," said Dad. "Though she doesn't let on, Mary is worried sick. We have a chat with him, he comes good, then the next week he's out causing a stink again."

Seth said he'd go visit, and he also suggested taking him on a fishing trip. Dad cheerfully agreed, but there was something in his tone of voice that wasn't so good to hear.

When the call was done, Seth fired up the barbecue on the back porch. He made up two beef patties with some of Marsh's topside mince, half a finely chopped onion, a glug of Worcestershire sauce, salt, pepper, and a good pinch of the garlic powder he got from the Chinese shop.

With cupped hands, he repeatedly smacked the patties, compressing the mince so that it wouldn't fall apart on the grill plate.

Then he washed the fat off his hands and made up the salad; lettuce folded over – not sliced to buggery, slices of tomato and red onion, and the pièce de résistance: Golden Circle beetroot slices. And nothing else.

Because, fair dinkum, a burger didn't need cucumber or pickles, or, God forbid, pineapple. Bacon and egg were for breakfast, and cheese was for sandwiches. It wasn't rocket science.

The barbie now hot, he cooked the patties, toasting two sliced, buttered baps beside them on the grill plate. When they were done, he assembled the burgers, crowning the meat with a squirt of tomato sauce. Sitting outside with a cold beer, he got stuck in, and man, they were good.

He thought about Hansen as he drove in. The bloke was a tough old bastard, taking no prisoners, but he was also bloody entertaining, his gift for the gab grounded in real-life experience. Seth had met enough bullshit artists and real hard nuts to know the difference.

Realising that he was looking forward to seeing him, Seth laughed, half in embarrassment, half in excitement. It wasn't just the drinking, eating, and yarning, stuff he didn't do with clients; it was something more – a sense of the ante being upped, with an intimation of more to come.

He was being tested; he knew that, Hansen looking for his weaknesses and limits. He just had to keep passing the tests to find out what would happen next.

When he got out at Fogarty Park, he cast a long look across the grass at the flood-lit fountain, then checked the shadows under the fig trees along the Esplanade.

A woman had been raped in the park last year by four excuses for men, and not so late at night either.

I'd have straight-up killed them, he thought. Broken their fucking necks. But aside from a pair of statue-still stone curlews near the street, the park was empty.

Near the corner, he saw two fellas come down the stairs of the new bar at the front of the Pacific International. Reasonably dressed and talking loudly, they looked like a couple of white-collar workmates.

A little further up, a woman got out of a shiny white Statesman de Ville, and it drove off. Small, slim, and dark-skinned, she wore a tight blue dress that left her shoulders bare. As she came in under the lights at the bar's entrance, Seth saw her makeup and styled hair. And her youth. She looked maybe twenty.

The office boys saw her, and their yammering stopped. One bloke called out to her, and they moved into her path. Checking for cars, Seth crossed the Esplanade at a run. As he got to the pavement, he saw one of the men, a young prick with a fat face, reach out to grab the woman's arm.

Still moving, she leant at the hips, dodging the hand, but the other bastard, laughing unpleasantly, quickly cut her off.

"Hey! Leave her alone!" yelled Seth, sprinting now.

The blokes spun around in slack-mouthed surprise, the grog they'd sunk suddenly heavy on their faces. Seth could just about hear their thoughts – Jesus, a big blonde bastard coming out of nowhere! Hard-looking and bloody fit, with big-knuckled hands already shaped into fists, and killer glee on his face.

As he knew it would, the monstering did its job, and the gronks jumped away from the young woman. Frozen in the sidewalk light, she watched Seth come to a halt right by her. He smiled down in reassurance, quickly directing her with his hand to keep going.

She looked up as she passed, no fear or thanks in her eyes, and Seth saw real hardness there.

A working girl, he thought. Young, upmarket, dropped off in a smart car, but a working girl nonetheless.

He turned back to the boys cringing against the planter boxes. Neither looked interested in getting physical. One bloke wrestled a shit-eating smile onto his face. "Mate," he said hopefully. The other looked like he might cry.

With cold steel eyes, Seth gestured at the bar's entrance. "Why don't you fellas go and have another drink?"

Jostling each other taking this advice, they clattered up the tiled steps. Seth turned, looked up the pavement. The young woman, fleet of foot, was nearly at Spence Street. Good on you, girl, he thought.

Turning back, he waited a moment, just in case those bastards came back out to rush him from behind, maybe with a glass or bottle grabbed off a table.

That had happened to him – once. At a sports club in Darwin an empty longneck had been smashed into the back of his head courtesy of a drunk he'd just chucked out. He'd turned his back too soon. The blood had ruined his white shirt. The other bouncers had ruined the bloke.

But only the clink of glass and the hum of conversation came back down the steps, and he walked up to the corner thinking about his money.

Inside the hotel, blondie Simon wasn't on. There was another fella with annoyingly inquiring eyes. Politeness personified, Seth went over and explained that Captain Hansen in suite two was expecting him. Then, seeing the bloke's close shave, he asked if he was a Gillette man.

Under his professional smile, the bloke looked pleased. No, he'd gone electric, and Seth got the run-down on the Braun Micron Plus with its radical hard/soft body. In the mirrored lift, he winked at himself. Always get 'em onside.

As the lift smoothly ascended, he felt this new hotel vibe growing on him. Sniffing the cold air, he dug the scent of a woman's perfume, and it made him wonder who might be staying here: not just the businessmen and tourists, but the globetrotting groovers and cool single women.

There was something familiar about the fragrance, but wasn't that the trick with perfume – that it smelt like memories?

When Hansen opened the door, barefoot, scotch glass in hand, Seth smelt the perfume again, and he now remembered it from his last visit. Hansen had company.

Inside the suite, Seth saw the wearer of the perfume standing by the TV. It was the young working girl in the blue dress.

"Drink?" said Hansen. Seth nodded.

"You know where it is."

At the bar, he got a Crown. Pouring it into a chilled beer glass, he was aware of Hansen watching him, like he was expecting to be given stick for having a young hooker in his suite.

"Oh! That's him, Hansen. The one I told you about."

The young woman's voice was uneducated, direct; her accent far north Queensland through and through.

She was looking at Seth, a small finger pointing at him. Suddenly aware of this, she snapped her hand to her hip.

Hansen laughed grandly.

"Well, of course, sweetie. Kelly works for me."

She looked at Hansen, and Seth saw the quick flash of gratitude, and pride, the bastard had put in her eyes. Her gaze returned to the television, Seth apparently dismissed as a minion. But as he turned to Hansen, she said, "Thank you, Kelly."

"Nice work." Hansen toasted him, his eyes bland, but the invitation for Seth to correct him there.

Seth didn't return the toast. He drank his beer and gave the old bastard an inimical look over the glass.

Grinning now, Hansen gestured for Seth to take a seat. They sat at the dining table and Hansen slid an envelope across to him.

It's all nice and upmarket here, the Crown Lager frosty, and Hansen shaping up as a repeat client, thought Seth. He should just put the unopened envelope in his pocket, but he knew what this test required. It wasn't about trust; it was about attitude, and like a Woolloomooloo street kid, he counted his money.

The bills were all fifties, so he'd got a twenty-dollar tip, but instead of twenty notes, there were twenty-six. Seth looked up. "What's the three hundred for?"

Hansen nodded at the young woman across the room. Watching TV on the lounge, she had her shoes off and was massaging her feet.

"For looking out for Evelyn."

Seth drank beer, eyeing Hansen. The old bastard made a dismissive gesture that said this particular conversation was over, and that any attempt to prolong it would result in irritation and probably anger.

Seeing the innate foolishness of rejecting a bonus, Seth put the envelope in his pocket, and nodded thanks.

Hansen pushed a small chamois bag across the table.

"Have a look at these."

Seth felt a thrill go through him. This was uncharted waters and he liked it. Putting his beer down, he picked up the soft bag. Inside it, things like hard plastic clicked. Opening the drawstring, he saw little translucent boxes, an electric fire glittering in each one.

He carefully emptied the bag's contents onto the table and removed the lids of the five gem boxes to fully reveal the stones they contained.

Constellations, fireworks, and rainbows made the hair stand up on his neck.

"Know what they are?" said Hansen.

"Opals."

"Turn 'em in the light."

As directed, he held up each stone and slowly turned it. Perfectly cut and polished, the opals vibrated with colours he didn't have names for – colours that hovered beyond the physical stone like a hologrammatic aura.

Chunks of time and light, the opals gave him flashes of that old cosmic freakery, the mystical hoodoo voodoo the hippie trippers went on about. But this magic was real – solid and cool between his fingers.

"Wow," he said eventually.

"Wow, indeed," said Hansen.

Replacing the opals in the gem boxes, Seth put them back in the bag and pushed it across the table.

"Know what they're worth?" said Hansen.

Seth knew just enough about opals to recognise that the stones were something else. "A fortune?"

"And then some."

"A hundred thousand?"

"Quadruple it at least."

Seth swallowed cold beer to hide his shock.

Hansen hit his own drink, eyes lit with amusement.

Seth shot a look at the young woman on the lounge. Out of earshot, she was engrossed in TV.

Looking back, he saw Hansen's mirth now replaced by a look of cold enquiry, his eyes daring him to say it.

I'm not working as his security, thought Seth, so it's none of my business. But at his age, he must have worked out that working girls could be light-fingered.

Hansen watched him as he lit a smoke.

"You know what Meadows's problem was?" he said.

Seth shook his head.

"He looked at me, and because I have a lot, he thought he didn't have enough. He's got the wife, the house, a good living – even a respectable place in society. But he wanted what I've got. He wanted to be me."

Hansen's eyes were like shark hooks.

"You feel like that, Kelly? You want to be me?"

With a careful smile, Seth shook his head. Bugger you, he thought. I'm me. And I'm good at it.

The old skipper took that in, then nodded at Evelyn.

"When you grow up with nothing, you learn to make do. You learn to make *yourself*. It's wonderful to have things, but you don't need them to get by. She knows that. She's got her own. God bless her."

"I can dig that," said Seth.

"She trusts *me*," said Hansen. "It's a two-way street."

Seth nodded reflectively. Hansen, with a cheery wave of his hand, dismissed him. "Okay, you're paid, now piss off."

With a brisk smile, Seth got to his feet.

"Oh yeah," said Hansen. "Take tomorrow off."

Seth cocked his head. "Yeah?"

"Yeah. Get on the grog. Get stuck into your girlfriend."

A Lover and a Fighter

Be-ringed fingers, crimson-tipped, pinched his nipple. Electric sparks of sensation squirted from his nuts to his knees. With her breasts warm in his face and her hips in his hands, they moved in divine rhythm, groaning like filthy angels fallen to earth.

Seth went all in, each fluent stroke of his met by a top-spin of pelvic return. Waves of euphoria broke over him, the ocean roaring in his ears, the beach warm beneath the towel. He looked up – into those eyes.

Arcane, almost black, they shone with bold sapience, savage wit, and off-the-dial lust. There was nothing better, there was no one better, and she saw that in his eyes, and he saw it in hers, and it popped their corks.

Wordlessly loud, they stormed heaven. Eyes fabulously locked, toes spread, their bodies shook in galvanic climax.

A great wave of bliss swept them away, and they weren't *they* anymore. They were one – two souls indelibly fused together, just buzzing away on a beach towel with every molecule of their beings going 'wowwee-fuckin'-zowwee!'

Wallowing in endorphins, somewhere between dream and reality, Seth sucked down air, the taste of marijuana verdant and medicinal in his mouth. He was off his head.

With her long thighs gripping his hips, Stasia beamed down at him, her hair a pirate halo, her face glowing with euphoria. Seth glowed back at her. Beyond the fantastic sex, she was one of the coolest people he'd ever known.

He'd met her at a party six years ago, attracted by her rebellious look: an inspired mix of hippie-gypsy witchery and revhead rock and roll that made a lot of fella's heads spin. But when they started talking, immediately laughing at the same things, he'd really begun to dig her.

Sharp as a tack, very bloody funny, and truly devil-may-care, she had a dissolute sangfroid that either scared the shit out of blokes, or turned their brains into supplicating mush. He'd felt neither, and she'd dug that.

It had been no contest, with no battle of the sexes to be fought; they had too much fun having fun to worry about that bullshit.

Savvy, compassionate, Stasia was like an earth mother and bush lawyer to a fair few of the groovier women in Cairns, many a sweet hippie and rock'n'roll party monster among them. She provided counsel and help, sometimes financial, to a large network of friends from the Northern Rivers to Darwin.

Although they'd got it on over the years, he and Stasia firmly resisted the boyfriend-girlfriend thing, connecting when they did. Neither wanted to be caught by something that might spoil the vibe between them. Unspoken, it felt immeasurably cool and adult, and a real testament to the depth of their friendship.

Coming to their senses, they raced down to the ocean, eyes peeled for stingrays, and washed the sex off. Back at their towels, squatting on the hot sand sharing the water canteen, Stasia's eyes ran over him, something pleasingly proprietorial in their obsidian gleam.

Staring back, he enjoyed the look of her – sun-browned and dark-haired all over. She was a magnificent beast, and he said so. She narrowed her eyes, pushed him back on his arse, and sunk playful teeth into his stomach.

After some tomfoolery that nearly went funky monkey, they settled down and had something to eat. Seth cut up the wedge of watermelon he'd brought and they blissfully guzzled their treat, drops of juice making little plop marks in the sand.

"Why did we stop doing this?" said Stasia.

"Lorenz? Lorenzo? What was his name?" said Seth.

"Lawrence. That finished over a year ago now."

"He was from Spain, yeah? Somewhere cool."

"Melbourne." She sucked a mango skin clean, whirled it into the bushes.

"And you were with that gorgeous young thing, Debbie. How old was she? Eighteen?" she said.

"Nearly twenty."

Stasia sucked her fingers clean.

"You miss it?" she said. "Sydney?"

A couple of years ago, Seth had been living in the city, working security for rock bands, and Stasia had come and stayed for five months. It had been real busy as he also worked as an armoured car guard by day, but they'd had some very cool times together.

"Yeah, sometimes."

"You thinking of going back?" said Stasia.

"Nah, I'm pretty happy here," said Seth.

"How's the investigating going?"

"Ah yeah. I don't know if I'll ever make a packet, but I'm pretty good at it. I get results."

Stasia reached in schoolyard quick, pinched his nipple.

"I can vouch for that."

Seth batted her hand away. "What about you?"

She shook her head. "I'm not going anywhere right now. It's got really busy. My brother wasn't silly moving up here to start a concrete business. Perfect bloody timing."

"You must be making a bit. You're doing the hours."

"I'm seriously coining it, Seth. Dougie pays me a salary *and* a percentage of profits. The Charger, leather jackets, jewellery, the best liquor – I see it, I buy it. And check this. I've started saving for my own place. A few more months, and I'll be out of that shit box flat and paying the mortgage on a nice Queenslander with a big garden."

"You're one sharp chick, hey."

"Don't you forget it, boy."

She rummaged in her bag, produced a second joint.

"Wanna smoke this?"

He blew air through pursed lips, shook his head. Stasia raised her wicked eyebrows in disbelief.

"What's wrong with you? We've both got a day off. This is it. Live here now, babe."

Seth kept shaking his head. The first joint had been real strong. "Nah, that herb's like . . . Kunkamunchie Green."

Stasia yelled with laughter. "What? Kunkawhat?"

"Ah, I don't know." Seth waved his hand about. "It's just really strong, like bloody feral bush weed from out there, you know – Kunkamunchie."

On the long sweep of empty beach, they laughed like fools, and it was better than wonderful.

Walking back along the sand to the car, Seth lugging the cloth bag, they both smelt wood smoke and meat cooking. In the grove of trees where the rutted track down to the beach ended, they saw three parked vehicles; a black HT Belmont panel van and a nice mako-blue Torana, both in reasonable nick, and a two-door Corolla that looked well thrashed.

Next to the Belmont was a fire with some cooking going on. Around it were three men and two women, everyone wearing black or blue jeans, black t-shirts, and cut-off blue and red flannel shirts.

It was pretty much a certainty they were of the outlaw breed – road-running crims come up the coast from down south, likely on the run from cops or rivals, or maybe just craving a bit of Queensland sunshine.

There were two other blokes, leaning against Stasia's car like they owned the damn thing.

"Oh, for fuck's sake," murmured Stasia.

One of the mob by the fire saw them – a young bearded bloke, slim but muscled– and he calmly alerted his mates. Seth marked him as dangerous straight away.

The oldest bloke, a touch of grey in his beard, looked over his shoulder, then kept sipping from an enamel mug. Probably the top dog of the pack. One of the women, small and hatchet-faced, looked old enough to be his missus.

The other woman was tall, overweight, and young. She

wore big biker boots and looked to have some real muscle under the chub. She exuded trainee hard-nut vibes, her fierce stare showing her as someone with a lot to prove. Seth marked her as well.

The third fella, skinny-arsed and bare-chested, barely looked up. He was busy wrangling a cast-iron frying pan filled with what looked like sausages.

Seth nodded politely at them, the cloth bag printed with prancing cats feeling a tad incongruous. Nobody nodded back.

The blokes leaning on the bonnet of Stasia's car, clued in by the crew by the fire, turned. Seeing Seth and Stasia, they straightened up but didn't shift their arses off the car.

Okay, thought Seth, these two are going to start it.

It wasn't good odds, two first up, then five more. Stasia, though no scaredy-cat, was a lover not a fighter.

Far north Queensland, hey. Paradise one minute, crazy-arse bullshit the next. Was this lovely morning now going to end in bashing and rape?

There was still time to turn and run, but they'd lose the car, a sweet bronze and white, two-door Valiant Charger, powered by a serious engine courtesy of Sabbo, his master mechanic of a mate. Those two pricks would hot-wire it.

"You wanna go back up the beach for a bit?" said Seth.

"Look at the rego on that shit-box Corolla," said Stasia. "Western Australia. New South Wales plates on the other cars. Wonder how long these two sandgropers have been with this lot."

"Is that a yes or a no?"

"Ah shit. I like my car, Seth."

"Okay, but be ready to run up into headland if it all goes arse-up. I'll cop a bashing if I have to, but I don't want you getting raped."

"You've got no argument there."

They walked up to the Charger, and the two bumnuts grinned at Stasia in her shorts, braless in an over-sized man's shirt. With calculated insult, they ignored Seth.

"Ooo, hello darling," said the first bumnut to Stasia's breasts. Seth now saw that the other bumnut, a raddled ginger smear of a man, was holding a knife against his leg.

The paring knife in the cloth bag was sharp enough, but Seth knew that when it happened, he wouldn't need it. Besides, if you pulled a knife, you had to be prepared to use it, and he wasn't sure he wanted to kill anyone today.

Hopping up, the two bumnuts came down the side of the car to block the driver's door. Seth looked at the crims by the fire. Nobody looked interested . . . yet.

Stasia pulled a joint from the pocket of the voluminous shirt, sniffed it with a connoisseur's relish, then flipped it at Ginger Bumnut. He threw up a hand to catch, missed, and with magpie speed, his scurvy-looking mate snatched the joint up off the sand.

"Heheheh," he cackled, showing stubby teeth the colour of old piss. "You're a good little chick, aren't ya?"

Ginger Bumnut gave Seth a blank, unconcerned stare, but blew it by darting a look at the mob at the fire. Seth followed his gaze and saw that the two young ones he'd marked were watching. It would take them ten seconds to get over here. Ginger Bumnut gave them a tight nod. No one nodded back.

With a tiny sound of approval, Stasia stepped back. She was grinning her head off. Scurvy Bumnut grinning back, stuck the joint in his mouth. He pulled out a red Bic and lit up, his mate watching as he took a few luxurious drags. Rubbing the scar on his ear, Seth drifted in a pace or two.

Blowing smoke out of his nose, Scurvy Bumnut looked Stasia up and down again. Without taking his eyes off her, he held the joint out to his mate, who grabbed it and got stuck in.

"So, you like to party, hey?" he said. "Well, lady, you've met the right fella."

"Fellas," snuffled his mate.

Stasia laughed, a voluptuous sound, and her eyes flared with promise. Scurvy Bumnut made a sound like a toddler gurgling, and his eyes brimmed at his stupendous luck. Stasia ran a hand through her hair, and stretched out her neck.

"Oooo," said Scurvy Bumnut, and he gestured for the joint. He drew on hastily, quickly passed it back. Blowing out smoke, he said, "Whaaaaah."

Stasia smiled at Ginger Bumnut as he smoked, his eyes on her body. Seth moved in another step. Scurvy Bumnut rubbed an eye with a fist. The sunshine pouring off the bronze skin of the Charger was making him sweat. Ginger Bumnut blew out a cloud of smoke, passed the joint to his mate, then gestured at Seth with the knife. "I'm getting the feeling you're over blondie here."

The youngsters by the fire began to stir. Stasia stared at Ginger Bumnut with big dolly-bird eyes. Scurvy Bumnut busied himself with the roach, keen to get it done.

Seth made a loud exhalation of breath like a cough. The bumnuts looked at him. Scurvy Bumnut dropped the roach. Ginger Bumnut changed his grip on the knife.

"This yours, darling?" Stasia's voice was breezy.

Everyone looked at the red crimped shotgun shell in her hand. She flipped it at Seth and he grabbed it out of the air. The bumnuts' heads turned in unison, following the sudden play.

As they stared at Seth, Stasia jingled the Charger's keys and said, "Do you want the rest of it?"

The crims' idiot heads snapped back to her. Seth moved closer. Stasia's big shirt belonged to her brother. He went shooting when he could, but these idiots didn't know that.

Mongrel paranoia fogged their faces, and they stepped away from the car as if expecting a shotgun to suddenly appear in someone's hands.

Seth shaped the coming seconds in his head, and how he'd dodge the knife. If he could give Stasia ten seconds, she'd have enough time to get in the Charger and start it.

But what happened then, when the two young crims ran up, would be in the hands of the gods, the gods of biff.

By the ripped look of the bumnuts now, it was a sure bet the Kunkamunchie Green was making hangi pits of their heads. But the car keys had brought Ginger Bumnut back to earth. He stepped forward.

"I reckon it's time we go for a ride," he said.

Scurvy Bumnut's face went pale. The breeze blew the smell of sausages in. Ginger Bumnut's stomach grumbled.

"Little lady," he said to Stasia. "I reckon I'm gonna have a ride of you, too."

The muscles in the bastard's legs began to tense. Seth saw how he was going to rush Stasia, put the knife to her throat, and make her a hostage. Stasia flashed Seth a look, and like ES bloody P, they moved at the same time.

The stoned knife man was just too slow, his reactions further slowed by dealing with two moving figures.

Seth hopped, skipped, jumped, ducked the flash of the blade, and put a big punch into the side of the prick's head that dropped him. The youngsters by the fire broke into a run.

Scurvy Bumnut leapt at Stasia, who turned to flee. If he got an arm around her throat, he could – ow! Stasia drove an elbow back into his eye. Sidestepping the falling ginger bastard, Seth punched his head again. Blood flicked onto hot sand.

Spinning around, one eye shut in pain, Scurvy Bumnut faced Seth. He didn't look too confident, but he soaked up Seth's first punches with his arms and shoulders. Then dropped his head, hoping to hear knuckles break on it.

But this was a trick that Seth, with his own granite-hard cranium, used, and it took him a second of fancy footwork to line up a hard left into the prick's ear. Scurvy Bumnut pulled a lizard wriggle and dodged the blow. With fists held high he just goggled gormlessly at Seth. Behind him, Stasia stopped and turned, eyes going wide in alarm.

The young bloke was here now. Seth spun to face him and got a shock. He was just standing there! He'd come to watch.

A handsome cove, early twenties; his thick black hair looked oiled; his buccaneer beard and moustache shaped into points. He effortlessly oozed rockstar elan, but rough as, with acne-pitted cheeks, split and nicked eyebrows, and a deeply scarred bicep. His long fingers had rings to fracture jaws and mash lips, and something filled the front pocket of his jeans – a glimpse of metallic silver like a palm knife or .32 calibre pistol. Young, hard, and totally on, he looked the veteran crim.

Relaxed, he gave Seth a genuine smile, his eyes soft in mock deference. Then he looked at Stasia. Seth saw the buzz between them, and for a shitty second, saw them together; their gypsy motorhead looks so complimentary.

A shard of jealous poison pierced him, regret, too, that he looked so straight and always had. He felt old.

Now the big girl was there, her cold eyes eager. Scurvy Bumnut, seeing reinforcements, roared in triumph and charged in, swinging big blows.

Seth backpedalled, drawing him from the car, parrying his frenzied attack. While the big woman closely followed them like a referee at a boxing match, the young crim put his hands on his hips and watched.

That shocked the shit out of Scurvy Bumnut. No one was going the big blonde bastard! Real doubt and a wave of the old Kunkamunchie Green blunted his attack.

Oh, mate, thought Seth. You should be lying on the couch eating Twisties and watching Aunty Jack repeats, not making a bad show of it in front of real hard nuts who didn't think you were much chop in the first place.

With the sand soft beneath his feet, Seth floated in and audibly broke the bastard's jaw. At his shoulder, the big lass grunted with pleasure.

Really digging the look the young pirate now gave him, Seth threw up his hands and gave himself a round of applause. The young bloke's eyebrows shot up, his mouth an O of delight. The big girl growled, her scary eyes raking Seth's chest and groin.

Scurvy Bumnut started up, but his stuck-pig screaming was quickly deafened by the Charger's Hemi 265 roaring into life.

Sunshine Will Kill You

"Good day off?" Hansen wasn't interested in an answer. "Get back to McKenzie Street, then you ring me at eight sharp tonight."

Seth looked at his watch. Six fifty-one. He hadn't even had his morning cuppa.

"You got that, Kelly?"

"Yep, roger that."

"Roger my arse," said Hansen, hanging up.

After breakfast, a red pawpaw, poached eggs, and a few toasted slices of Mozart's rye, Seth showered, shaved, and set off for another day of the deadly dulls.

It was nice enough out, a cool breeze stirring the palms along the seawall, but the waiting was sure to sour the day. He'd brought a secret weapon, but he'd try to hold it back for as long as he could.

Watching the house, he thought about yesterday. Those young crims, boot girl and pirate boy, had looked almost sad to see them go.

And how was Stasia? Smart move with the joint, then chucking that errant shotgun shell about. And jamming her elbow in that prick's eye. Bloody touché, aye. What a woman – a lover *and* a fighter.

She'd be in her little air-conditioned office at Northern Concrete by now; comptroller, receptionist, and secretary rolled into one, already going hard, because come eight-thirty, the phone calls would start for the day.

A tsunami wave of development was flooding into the far north. Any tradie or labourer in any front bar in Cairns could tell you that. There was a chance here for Stasia to get ahead, and her big brother Dougie, with ten years of concreting under his belt, was the perfect person to go hard with. She seemed to dig it too, getting a real kick out of putting the jobs together, organising the money, men, and equipment.

But she knew as much about herbs as any naturopath, and the names of the trees and plants. She loved the bush, easily sleeping outside in a swag. She could look up at the night sky and read the stars, and hear the whisper of nature spirits on the breeze. Now she was selling concrete.

Seth scratched his head, slipped his shoes off and scratched his right foot. Down the street at number ten, nothing kept happening.

Not so hungry, he took a quick lunch break – a mango Weis bar from the corner store on Minnie Street.

Back on the Esplanade, he sat on the grass in the shade of a flame tree and nearly nodded off. He got into the Pig and drank some water. Another hour crawled by.

There was movement in a big tree on the corner, and he used the Tascos to locate a white heron. He watched the big, bright bird do bugger-all for a bit before chucking the binoculars back onto the seat. It was time for Shogun.

He hefted the book, all one thousand, one hundred and

fifty pages. You could knock out a bouncer on the Barbary Coast with it, but he'd hung in there, now hooked, and he opened it to page seven hundred and sixty and removed the feather. Not wanting to miss anything at number ten, he made sure to look up every few paragraphs.

Around five thirty, at page seven hundred and ninety-nine, he moved the Pig into McKenzie Street. Swapping the book for a Gregory's, he put the street directory on the seat next to him, ready as an alibi in case the fella in the house suddenly came out.

Of course, the scrawny old bugger didn't appear, and as it got dark, Seth put the directory back in the door pocket.

Just before seven, with no sign of nobody, he chucked it in. The bloke in there must watch a lot of telly – or be reading Shogun. With a numb arse and grumbling guts, Seth went home.

When he rang Hansen at eight, the old skipper sounded like a bull in a paddock full of flies. "Pick me up now."

Hansen was waiting when he pulled in under the high porte-cochère of the Pacific International. Grimacing, the old skipper got in, wedging himself onto the bench seat, his knees hard up against the dash. "You're a real bushie with your Toyota truck, hey?" he said.

Seth smiled nice, thinking of the upgraded upholstery, air-con control panel, and top-of-the-line Marantz stereo staring the bastard in the face.

"I need a drink," growled Hansen, absently patting the smokes in his shirt pocket. Seth waited until he was sure the old skipper wasn't going to use his seatbelt.

"Hansen, you need to . . ." Seth indicated the belt.

"Fuck's sake! Do they think we're children?"

"Apparently so."

Ripping the seatbelt out around his great girth, Hansen impotently stabbed the latch at the catch, the bulk of him obscuring the target. Seth took the latch from his fingers and clicked it home.

"So, where to?" he said.

Hansen gazed through the windscreen.

"Hides, the Marlin Bar, I don't care."

"Not the Criterion?"

"Just bloody drive."

In the lounge at Hides, they got drinks and went and sat at a table. The vibe in the place was upbeat, with lots of laughter and sun-tanned legs. Even the peace lilies in big pots looked spry.

Patrons were getting well-watered too: some local boys planning a night's mischief, a loud group of older tourist couples, even a table of office girls sharing the seafood platter while they charged up on cocktails in readiness for the dance floor at The Central.

Uninterested in mortal life, Hansen smoked and slowly drank, his eyes inward. Seth sipped his rum and coke as he checked out the room, his ex-bouncer's eyes picking out the beauties and the beasts.

A grunt brought him back to his charge. Hansen had finished his drink and was staring at him. Seth raised his eyebrows in query, fully aggravated when Hansen nodded at his empty glass on the table.

They stared at each other until the hundred and forty a

day won. With a blank smile, Seth got up. Hansen, looking nothing close to victorious, lit another cigarette.

Two drinks later, the old bastard came out of his reverie and fixed Seth with hard grey eyes.

"So, what did you do before the investigating?"

"Security work down in Sydney. Armoured cars by day, rock'n'roll bands by night."

"Is that right?" Hansen looked almost impressed as he worked his scotch. Seth now had an inkling of what was coming.

"Henry said you worked as a doorman and bouncer."

"What do you want, Hansen?"

"I need a hand. A strong one."

"You mean a fist?"

"Yeah, if it goes that way. But a slap might suffice."

"I don't do that, and even if I did, I'm an investigator with a licence. First sniff of trouble and the cops will revoke it."

"If it's just the licence you're worried about, that should be fixable if it becomes a problem."

"It's not just the licence."

Hansen nodded like he got it. But he hadn't.

"So, a hundred and forty a day gets me table service. What gets me muscle?"

"Look, I'll spell it out. I don't hurt people for money."

His voice had risen. A woman at the next table turned to look, her eyes and mouth wide. Hansen looked almost cheerful.

"So, what *do* you hurt them for?" he said.

Seth took an ice cube from his glass and crunched it to

pieces between his teeth. Hansen broke out a smile. Seth gave him a wet middle finger. Hansen laughed.

"No, I'm serious, Kelly. What does it take for you to give your knuckles a spin?"

"You'll never know."

Seth would always help out a mate in need, but Hansen was a client. Big bloody difference.

Hansen shrugged. "Your loss."

Seth finished his drink.

"So, was that it? That's what you rang me for?"

Hansen shook his head, lumbered to his feet.

"Let's go to McKenzie Street."

Yes sir, thought Seth.

When they got there, Hansen gestured redundantly to park outside the house. Seth parked and killed the engine. Some metres away, in a street light's radiance, two women were talking next to a two-door hatchback. Hansen undid his seatbelt and listlessly watched them.

Seth waited, unwilling yet to ask the bastard what they were doing here, and he soon worked out what the dicky little hatchback was – a Nissan Stanza, the sort of vehicle that wouldn't last too long on any road outside of town.

The sound of a lighter made him turn, its flare lighting Hansen's moribund face. Blowing smoke out the window, the old skipper stared at the lush garden of number ten.

I wonder how many smokes he's sucked down over the years, thought Seth. Thirty a day? Probably started on the streets when he was a teenager; he's in his mid-sixties now, so thirty times seven times –

"Must drive you crazy," said Hansen.

"What drives me crazy?" said Seth. The two women were saying their farewells.

"Sitting around hour after hour just watching."

Seth softly chuckled. If only he knew.

"Taking watch is like that," said Hansen as the Stanza drove off. "Hour after hour after hour, wave after wave after wave. And at night, you see nothing. Maybe the stars or moon if it's clear."

"But only for four hours at a time, right?"

Hansen snapped him a sour look.

"I've been doing long days and nights here," said Seth. "You're getting your money's worth."

"When you're skipper, you're on every hour of the day," snapped Hansen. He took a big drag on his cigarette, and blew out smoke into the Pig's cabin. Seth pulled his head back in disgust.

"Jesus, Hansen! Can you not do that? I'm making an exception for you as it is."

The bastard gave him the stink eye, flicked the cigarette out the window. "Let's go," he growled.

They got out. The conversation at Hides began to replay in Seth's head. The lychgate squeaked open and Hansen's shoes scuffed up the moonlit path.

In the garden, shadows pooled under the fig and mango trees. The air was filled with the scent of flowers. There was a light on somewhere inside, but the house was still.

Hansen stopped at the bottom of the front steps, looked up at the closed verandah doors, and said, "Wait here."

He went up, planks creaking under his weight. Above the doors a rising sun fretwork pediment gleamed in the moonlight. Hansen opened the doors. Beyond him, faint light shone from the open front door. He crossed the verandah, and without knocking or calling out, went into the house.

Perturbed, Seth stood there like a spare wheel. In the street, a 90cc motor bike puttered by. Above him, the mango tree sighed, its dark crown rustling with a breeze come in off the Coral Sea. Stepping into its shadow, he had a proper look at the house.

A long hip-roof with the rocket-ship shaped galvanised-tin air ventilators poking up. A wide, encircling verandah framed with dowel balustrades. Wonderful timber details on the verandah post brackets. It was a beauty.

Proportions perfect, it was the work of a real builder. Though it was undeniably grand, nothing felt overdone, the details all integrated into the lines and feel of the house.

Moving out onto the lawn, he looked up at the casement windows. Amber light came from an interior doorway, but the verandah was too deep to see anything inside.

A scent hit his nostrils – datura. On the other side of the fig tree, he saw the bush by the house, its trumpet-shaped flowers pale in the moonlight.

Voices came from inside the house, masculine, quickly rising – then silence. Listening hard, Seth slipped over to the steps and put a hand on the long, cool rail.

A car came gunning along the Esplanade. Under the cover of this noise, he ghosted up the steps onto the verandah, and stood by the front door. When the car had gone, he stuck his head inside the house.

The ambient sound of the outside world vanished, the

still air inside muffled and dampened by picture-covered timber walls, cane and timber furniture, antique rugs, and woven mats.

It felt simultaneously airy and cosy in there: the house soaked in history, but eminently ready for more plans and adventure. It was like a doorway in the continuum. This sensation of lives lived here, and of times to come, was heady and irresistible, and Seth just stood there.

The house smelt wonderful, too: an olfactory patina of old timber, coconut oil and furniture wax, sandalwood, woven mats, jasmine and frangipani.

Stepping over the threshold, he walked a few paces into the hallway, his eyes drawn to a massive turtle shell mounted on a far wall. As he opened his mouth to call out, something in the house fell and rattled on the floor. The sound was quickly followed by a double thump that ran through the floorboards.

Sweat pin-pricked his scalp; his ears out on stalks now. Heading to where the light was, he went through the hall and out into the strip-light brightness of a kitchen. He stopped and listened keenly. Somewhere a pipe gurgled.

From the kitchen he went into a dark passage. One side was shelving; the other all louvres and curtains. From not far away came the gurgling noise again, then the sudden, loud shuffle of weight moving on the timber floor.

With the light behind him, Seth's eyes went scotopic, his pupils enlarging, and in the dark end of the passage he saw Hansen kneeling over someone. It was the skinny old occupant of the house – being choked to death.

Running over, he grabbed Hansen's wrists and tried to

pull them from the old bloke's throat. The floor was highly polished, and as he pulled hard, the two combatants slid towards the light.

His foot stood on something. Snatching a look, he saw pointed silver – a stiletto knife. With his client snarling like a feral dog interrupted at a feed, Seth kicked the evil thing under the shelves along the wall.

Biceps bulging with effort, he pulled the two men into the light. Getting Hansen off his victim and trapping his arms wasn't easy, but with brute force he did it, and he began hauling the old skipper backwards.

Hansen resisted, twisting to look back at the fella on the floor, then suddenly relaxed. Without releasing him, Seth turned so Hansen could look at his victim.

The stringy bloke's eyes opened. Hansen stamped a foot on the floor to get his attention. In the kitchen, some china clattered on a draining rack.

"You Judas!" shouted Hansen. "You sold me out."

The bloke on the floor looked fully compos now.

"I'm getting the police here now," said Hansen. "They'll throw you out on the street where you belong. Pack your fucking duffel now!"

The old bloke sat up, coughed. Seth studied him over Hansen's shoulder. He wasn't looking too worse for wear, rubbing his throat while his eyes darted about looking for his weapon.

Not seeing it, he looked up and saw Seth with his arms around Hansen. Contempt filled his eyes, and he spoke to Seth in a smart-arse voice.

"You're finished, Harry!" roared Hansen, now pressing

forward. "Twenty-seven years, and you do this to me?"

Feeling like a buck gorilla taking on the old silverback, Seth wrangled Hansen back through the kitchen, their erratic footfalls violently loud in the old house.

In the front hallway, Hansen now went forward on his own volition towards the door, and Seth relinquished his hold. But with a doorman's distrust, he kept one hand on the skipper's wrist, the other gripping his shoulder.

Breathing through his nose like a winded bear, Hansen stamped across the verandah. Seth let go, and the crazy bastard pounded down the stairs and strode up the path.

Heartbeat de-accelerating, Seth followed. On the other side of the lychgate, Hansen pulled out his smokes.

Seth went out onto the grass verge and closed the gate, the latch loud in the empty street. Hansen lit a cigarette, standing in the moonlight like a walrus blowing steam.

What in God's name had just happened? Two old blokes in a beautiful house on a quiet night-time street – both set on killing each other. Oh man, thought Seth. This town never ceases to amaze me.

If he hadn't been there, Hansen would have crushed the fella's windpipe like a Pringles can. Or maybe the old bird might have slipped his blade up under Hansen's ribs and given his heart a tickle. And they reckoned the young blokes today were out of control.

But the thing that had really got him was the look the old bastard on the floor had given him, as though Seth was a ring-in, and a poor one at that. And the contempt in his voice when he said, "Sunshine will kill you."

Mates

A week passed before Hansen rang. Making no mention of the rumpus at McKenzie Street, he was after Seth's banking details. It was to put him on the books, and that was fair enough. The thirteen hundred in cash had been a pleasing bonus, but with Dad doing the tax, any Kelly Investigations income had to be squeaky clean.

When he asked Hansen what he had for him next, the old bastard grunted noncommittally and hung up.

Pissed off, Seth nearly rang him back. But he thought about the bastard's deep pockets and saw the wisdom of playing it cool for the time being.

Sure enough, when he looked at the business account five days later, he saw that Hansen had put three hundred bucks into it. He grinned like a chimp. Like something in a movie, he was now on a retainer. It was another level alright, and he didn't mind it at all.

Coming home down Cinderella Street, a new shirt from Blokes Up North and a bottle of Captain Morgan Black on the seat next to him, he saw a glittering vehicle parked out the front of his house. Unease eddied through him. He didn't have too many mates with brand-new cars.

He pulled into his carport. Killing the engine, he heard blokes laughter coming from his back porch. Then Robbie the Bomb's face popped up over the canna lily hedge, a smile on his mug and a beer in his hand. The boys from Upper Barron had dropped in.

Seth got out, grinning at his old mate. Robbie, all six foot something of him, ran out to the driveway, a tailor-made in his mouth. Throwing a hard, lean arm around Seth's shoulder, he led him out to the vehicle on the street.

"She a sweet beast, or what?" he said proudly.

Seth looked at the F60 Land Cruiser glistening with its showroom-fresh, cocoa brown paint job, and its spotless black tyres looking capable of taking it anywhere. She did look sweet.

"Hope they're making them a bit more rust-proof," he said, running his fingers over the truck's pristine skin. It was a constant battle keeping the metal cancer off the Pig.

"You live fifteen metres from the next king tide, mate," said Robbie. "Up on the tablelands we get our salt from the shop."

He drew on his cigarette, happily blew out smoke.

"She's got air-con, power steering, power winch, and seats as comfy as a dairy farmer's daughter. You should get one, mate. Leave yours for dead."

Seth nodded reflexively. He'd had the Pig for less than three years, and although a seventy-six model, she looked fine and was still going well.

But seeing a spanking new truck was to fall in love with an impeccable machine: its paintwork virginal, its engine devoid of grease and dust, the hub-caps clean enough to eat your dinner off. It gave you a real thrill to see such automotive perfection in its pristine state, knowing it was new, that nobody had even farted in it, and that it was the latest and therefore the best. Yep, a mint ride could really touch a bloke.

But looking at someone else's mint ride could also get you all green-eyed, and feeling like you were outdated and lagging behind, like you were a bit of a loser.

Settle down, he told himself. The Pig might be getting older, but she's fine. And besides, wasn't it one of the ten commandments – thou shalt not covert thy mate's truck?

"Seven grand," said Robbie. "Not bad, hey?"

That was pretty much what the average bloke made in a year. Repayments would take a bite out of Mr. Average's income each month, and he'd be thinking twice about buying nice shirts and bottles of top-shelf rum. But living on a budget had never worried Robbie the Bomb.

Along with his lieutenants, Evil Simon and Ray, Robbie headed a mob of dope growers. They were good at it, and being savvy lads, they disguised most of their naughty money buying acreage, and farms with legitimate crops.

Three intermarried families formed the nucleus of the gang, with a dozen or so other Tablelanders in tight-knit affiliation. They owned properties all over, even up on the Cape, with the titles often in the names of wives, mums, and grandparents.

As a founder member of the gang, Robbie was never short of cash. If he wanted to, he could buy a fleet of FJ60 Land Cruisers – and chuck one in for Seth.

Tearing his eyes away from his truck, Robbie puffed on his smoke and grinned at Seth.

"So, how's it going with your investigating?" he said.

"Not bad at the moment," said Seth, pleased to be able to say it. "Got a steady client. Real interesting bloke, too."

"Steady? What, are you stringing him along, going half-arsed so you keep getting paid?"

"Nah, he keeps giving me things to do."

"Yeah? Like what?"

"Like looking at land titles and going through accounts looking for fiscal discrepancies, and a lot of surveillance work, and . . . what?"

Robbie was grinning at him.

"Jesus, Seth. Accounts? Surveillance? You enjoy that?"

Seth offered up a smile.

"It's the job, mate."

Raising his eyebrows, Robbie finished his smoke, both of them looking at the gleaming Land Cruiser again.

"I'd never bag a bloke's choice of work, you know that," said Robbie. "But don't you ever want a bit more? Some real excitement? Like the old days?"

Back in the beginning of the whole damn thing, Seth and Robbie had pulled off some good scores growing and selling dope, their mutual trust established from day one.

Out riding his Vincent Black Shadow one afternoon, he'd met Robbie at the Peeramon pub. The tough-looking Tablelander rode a BSA Spitfire Scrambler, and was into rock'n'roll, motorbikes – and marijuana.

Over a few beers and a joint in the car park when it got dark, they'd clicked, each as quick as the other at getting the gist. Soon they were on the same team, growing and selling dope. They'd had some of the best times together, making money, partying, and chasing chicks.

"Yeah, sure," said Seth. "Everyone likes a bit of a buzz."

Robbie watched him with shrewd eyes, his stubble dark on his sun-browned skin. Seth nodded reflectively.

"But nothing could beat the buzz back then," he said. We blazed a trail, man. It was all new, and nobody knew anything. We turned people on. We changed things."

"Mate." Robbie the Bomb smiled in gentle reproof. "I'm *still* getting a buzz."

He gestured at the FJ 60. "Felt bloody great picking that up today. And last weekend I got more than friendly with a couple of lovely girls who'd heard a bit about me and how I look after people. Twins, mate. Twins. How about that, aye? Now that's a buzz!"

Seth chuckled, shook his head in admiration. Robbie smiled at him, but his eyes were serious. "There's always an opening with us. You know that."

"Thanks, mate," said Seth. "So, a beer?"

Thinking of the two or three bottles of NQ lager in the fridge, he made for the house. Robbie walked beside him, and as they went past the cannas, Seth felt his silence. Glancing around, he saw his mate looking at him.

"You're a bloke who needs a bit of excitement from time to time," said Robbie. "True story."

Over the next few days, it niggled at him – Robbie big-noting himself and just about looking down his nose at Seth for trying to carve out a lawful living, the intimation being that he'd become just another straight stiff.

But he couldn't tell his mate about Burns; he'd be better off admitting to rooting a billy goat. And punching out a couple of crims at the beach and stopping two old blokes from killing each other wouldn't impress him either.

Hansen's retainer now felt like chicken feed.

Sure, he liked a bit of excitement, but it had to turn a buck. He was getting on, turning thirty-two this year, and though he'd never completely cool the outlaw blood in his veins, it was time to play the game and get ahead.

The ten grand coming from Burns would give him space to consider his future. If investigating really wasn't worth it, he'd find something else that was.

Though it would be a lot of fun and bloody lucrative too, he didn't want to join Robbie's mob. He had to let the world of dope, cops, and crims fade into memory. After he was done with Burns, he'd hit the straight and narrow.

And as if in serendipitous affirmation of this move from dodgy bloke to law-abiding citizen, he got a call after tea from a mate who'd done just that.

Jeffyman, by dint of being Murri, knew all about the law. He knew what a twisted piece of shit it was when your skin convicted you, and he'd trodden a super-savvy path through his teens and twenties avoiding jail and bullyman bashings, even as he'd lived a life of crime.

He'd been a dope grower, one time producing a beauty of a crop with Seth that made them good money. Jeffyman had also sold dope, and over the years, a few hot cars and utes had passed through his hands.

Then, two years ago, he'd gone straight, completing an apprenticeship in Brisbane, confounding the naysayers in his big family and his party-happy mates. Back in Cairns as a qualified electrician, he was keen to stack legit coin.

Jeffyman could be full-on at times, but Seth loved the bloke: a staunch mate and the perfect person to spend a few months crop-sitting with. Since they'd met, cutting cane twelve years ago, they'd done a bit of fishing and camping, smoked many joints, and drunk a lot of beer.

"Okay listen. We'll have a nice feed tomorrow night." Jeffyman had it all worked out. "Seafood. Prawns, alright. Then we'll go and check out The Central. Have a dance."

Seth agreed, though only one of the two things appealed to him.

When he went to collect Jeffyman from Uncle Owen's place in Manunda the following night, he wove through the usual mob of yelling kids, taking feisty punches on his hands, and a couple of sneaky ones to his legs and bum.

Out the back under a moth-infested light, Jeffyman was sitting with his uncle; the fifty something railway worker relaxing in a deckchair, fully muscled up under his t-shirt, with a perspiring longneck of Cairns Draught in one big fist. Seth said hello to him and got a brisk nod in reply.

Jeffyman was looking smooth in gleaming oxblood leather R.M Williams boots, tan-coloured slacks, and a nice cream-coloured, long-sleeved shirt. He'd never been a slouch when it came to clothes.

Seth had some nice gear on too, and like Jeffyman, his shoes were buffed up nice and shiny. Uncle Owen sniffed the air, taking in the massed cologne and aftershave.

"Huh," he said. "If you boys don't get yourself a woman tonight, you've always got each other."

"Yeah, it's a long way from coconut oil, Johnson's baby powder, and ironed shorts, Uncle," said Jeffyman. "They even play guitars through speakers now, so the old men can hear it down the back."

Uncle Owen ignored the insult, took a swig of his beer. He'd had his wild times back in the day when things *were* wild. Married with kids now, he worked his arse off on the railway, chucking about ten-pound sledgehammers in the Capricornia sun. He was happy having a beer at home.

About the closest thing he came to letting his hair down nowadays, was when the boxing troupes came to town. He'd have a shot or three of rum, then knock out blokes half his age.

With kids, Uncle Owen had a kind face; with his missus, a twinkle in his eye, but if you were a bloke you'd always be judged on your physicality and stamina. When it came down to the good old-fashioned values of hard work and biff, Uncle Owen had written the book.

"You drinking tonight?" he said to Seth.

"Nah, just a few I reckon," said Seth.

Uncle Owen nodded, took a swig of beer. Seth waited.

"Remember, there's a lot of breathalyser around," he said. "A taxi is cheaper than a fine."

"Awww, c'mon, Uncle," cried Jeffyman. "Seth's a big boy. He doesn't need a lecture."

"You look out for each other," said Uncle Owen as they left. "And not just for the bullymen. Cairns has always been a fighting town. You boys know that."

Parking near The Central in town, they had a few drinks in the Manana Lounge to kick off, then got on the outside of pan-fried prawns up the street at The Porthole.

Jeffyman was in good form, making the waitress laugh, and he gave Seth the drum on the two-week job he had on across the inlet in Yarrabah.

"Some of the Murri fellas there don't like it in town there. They got beach camps around the cape. They living traditional. No grog, just fully fishing every day. I'm up in stinking hot roofs putting in electrical cable, and those boys are swimming around catching big fat crayfish!"

Seth could sure dig that. Cape Grafton was sixty square kilometres of forested coastal headland, edged by inshore reefs, and castaway beaches.

At The Marlin Bar, they had a couple more, Jeffyman moving from beer to rum, Seth sticking with NQ Lager.

There was a nice little crowd in there, everyone having fun. Bonnie was tickling the ivories, and at the bar, two working girls were warming up on an older bloke a few drinks in. At one well-sauced table, a tall, camp bloke was playing up for a coterie of male and female admirers, their antics stirring wicked laughter.

After talking about a couple of mutual mates, Jeffyman began ruminating on his love life, and Seth drank and listened, happy that his mate confided in him.

"See, I'm just a normal fella. You know what it's like. I love the ladies, but if I want to be with Evie, she says there's no halfway. It's all or nothing with her."

Evie was the woman with Jeffyman's heart on a chain. Seth hadn't met her, but she lived up in Kuranda, from where she either tormented or delighted Jeffyman. She'd play hard to get, then play hard; her love-struck beau like a yo-yo on her little finger.

Jeffyman knew what would maintain some equilibrium – moving in together. But he wanted to save some money first, and make his name as a spot-on sparky. That's when he'd buy his own place.

Evie, impatient, said he was scared of committing, but Jeffyman knew she was secretly proud of his long-term planning. Oh man, if she could just focus on that, and not pipe up with the other nonsense.

"How long you been seeing her?" said Seth.

"Nearly two years."

"Wow. Big investment of time. Emotions too, aye."

"Investment? Sounds like a business."

"You know what I mean."

With a quick shake of his head, Jeffyman looked around at the other drinkers, the topic of conversation done.

As they fitted in another round, the Marlin Bar filled up: older mamas in mumus and blue eyeshadow; blokes on the make, clean-shaven and dirty-minded; sweet young things demolishing the drinks and cigarettes; sun-brown fishermen in nearly clean trousers, everyone roaring away in a cloud of booze, ciggie smoke, and perfume.

It was just another night at the Marlin Bar – upbeat but not over the top. Seth saw several people he knew, and it wouldn't be much of a surprise if a mate like Johnny Pep or Maori George walked in. He was happy to just hang here all night. But Jeffyman wanted a dance.

At The Central, they joined the boisterous queue, the clown of a doorman frowning down the line at Jeffyman until he saw that Seth was with him.

You racist prick, thought Seth.

Upstairs, it was steaming, too loud to talk; the bass-bins thumping like a stamp mill crushing ore. Seth got drinks from the packed bar, patient in the crush as he ducked hips, tits, and elbows.

Drinks sorted, he stood blinking in the strobes next to a gyrating Jeffyman. On the dance floor, sweating dancers were getting down to DJ Whatsit's selection of the latest and greatest, the smell of hot bodies strong. None of the music tickled any bit of Seth, but like cattle-dips, he knew discos had a place in the world.

Out at night, Jeffyman usually wanted a dance. Not only did he like the physicality of it, 'relaxation on your feet' he called it, he also liked an audience.

Most of all, he liked the dancing queens shaking their groove thangs, the boogie mamas who could do the funk fandango as good as he could. And these dancefloor divas, he swore, were honeysweet dynamite in the sack.

Discarding his empty glass on a table, Jeffyman joined the fray. On the one, he hit the rhythm straight up, and was immediately the coolest bloke on the dancefloor.

This prowess usually got the girls speculating on what he could do off the dancefloor, and within minutes there were three girls dancing with him. Seth would put money on it that one of them would want to take Jeffyman home.

Finishing his drink, Seth went and took a slash, waiting his turn among the crush of loud and perspiring men.

Back in the disco inferno, the heat drove him outside to the balcony above Lake Street. He went over to the rail and looked down at the mobs of carousing people in the street. Not yet ten o'clock, people looked really drunk.

Turning back, he saw some surreptitious hand action as a drug deal went down next to him. One of the blokes gave him the eye. Seth gave him a who-gives-a-shit shrug.

After fifteen minutes he went back in, and sure enough, Jeffyman had hooked one of the dancing women; a cutie in red jeans, all big eyes and pearly-white laughter. Seth watched them dance for a bit, then break off to get a drink.

At the bar, Jeffyman leaned in to hear what the woman was saying, his hand cupping the small of her back. When they'd secured drinks, Seth caught Jeffyman's questing eye and gestured for them to come out to the balcony.

Her name was Lisa, up from Sydney on holiday with her friends, and wasn't Jeffery the best dancer! She cuddled in to Jeffyman, who cuddled right back.

Okay, thought Seth, we don't need a pack of Tarot cards to know where this is going. Jeffyman caught his vibe.

"Hey Lisa, tell your friends to come out here," he said. "Seth's a single man."

"No, no, I'm fine," said Seth.

"Nah, he's just saying that," said Jeffyman.

Seth put up a hand. "No, honestly, I'm fine."

Laughing, Jeffyman pushed his hand back down.

"No, grab 'em, Lisa. He's acting shy, but he's up for it."

With a knowing wink, Lisa darted back inside.

Vexation claimed Seth. He sighed, sadly shook his head.

"What?" said Jeffyman. "What's eating your biscuit?"

"I dunno, man. You just told me about Evie, how you're going to buy a house and live with her, and now you're lining up a girl from Sydney you've just boogied onto."

"Aye? Are you serious?"

"More to the point, are you?"

Jeffyman stared at Seth.

"If you're just making conversation, let's talk about the footy. Something with actual facts," said Seth.

"Who the hell do you think you are – my mother?"

Okay, time to back off, thought Seth. He gets a bee in his bonnet and next thing the whole swarm's up his arse.

Laughing, he reached out, but Jeffyman shook his hand off. "Nah, bugger you. Bloody well preaching at me."

"Yep, that's me, Preacher Kelly."

He said it silly, trying to defuse the vibe, but Jeffyman turned on his heel and strode inside.

Seth stared down at his shiny shoes. Okay, he wasn't hanging out with his mate tonight. But at least he didn't have to chat up Lisa from Sydney's girlfriends now.

With the inane disco thump, thump, thump, whacking him over the head, he got the hell out of there.

In the street, flying foxes filled the sky, making for the big fig trees by the council chambers. Groups of drunken people moved along the pavement like migrating animals; the less hardy ones already slumped against shopfronts and fig tree roots.

There was a paddy wagon out the front of the Cinema Capri, the cops manhandling two fellas into the back, one shouting lad's shirt hanging in shreds from his waist. Oh yeah, Cairns was rocking tonight.

Seeking succour, he ducked past the bosoms, big hair, and filthy mouths of a hen's night, and zipped up the flight of stairs to Dukes. Opening the door, he let the air-con and music welcome him in.

A smooth bloke on the grand piano, and a young blonde woman singing, were holding the attention of the crowd, their talent and appreciation for the music obvious.

Moving unobtrusively over to the bar, Seth got a drink, nodding at the Pommy owner. Sipping his rum and coke, he checked out the room. There were all sorts: couples, singles, tables of groovers, freshly knocked-off restaurant staff, pale nightbirds, sin sisters, and players with a bit of class – everyone with a yen for a good drink and some jazz.

As usual, Seth wasn't just looking at people out for the night; he was also looking for potential strife. It was damn near automatic with him. Looking at body language and faces, it didn't take long to see there was no trouble here.

There were certainly some dodgy types, but they wore nice watches and sleek smiles, fellas unlikely to shit in the nest they were having a good time in.

But Seth knew that under the right combination of grog and circumstance, average, usually law-abiding citizens could cause the most horrendous damage.

Heads split open on tables and tiled floors; limbs and faces flayed by plate glass; brain bleeds, comas, even death. It would be pathetic if it wasn't so awful.

The stupid bastards usually became dumbstruck with horror, going from full raging bull to complete remorse in seconds flat. And outside of the court cases and jail time, the pain and injury these fools so quickly inflicted lasted months, years, or lifetimes. They never showed that in the movies.

You didn't have to be Nostradamus to know that this kind of havoc would go down in town tonight. But here in the bosom of Dukes, the odds of it happening were close to nil. Enjoying his drink, Seth let the music wash away nearly a decade's worth of habit.

The singer and the pianist spun out the song, everybody in hushed appreciation; languid hands holding glasses and cigarettes; jewellery and wineglasses glinting in the soft light; perfume and aftershave floating on the chill air.

Though he'd be a little pressed spelling it, Seth knew what sophistication was, and right now, he could feel it all the way to his toes.

The song ended, and when the applause died down, the singer conferred with the pianist, and they laid out an immaculate take on Body and Soul that re-enthralled the crowd. Wow, thought Seth. These two are on a roll.

Time slowed, the singer's delivery haunting every heart in the place. With reverence, Seth slowly shook his head. She looked all of twenty. How could somebody so young get so much out of the words?

Heads now began turning, women at first, their faces looking towards the door. Casually, he took a peek. Like the young Queen of Sheba and old Abraham himself, Evelyn and Hansen had come into the room.

Real Trouble

Evelyn should have been ill-equipped to be there, but she looked better than most women in the place. Glowing with youth and beauty, and what looked like diamond earrings, she looked both demure and born to rule.

Hansen loomed behind her, his bulk diminished by her star, looking like a sculptor admiring his creation, grateful at the gift he'd given the world.

Expertly taking in the room, Evelyn saw Seth, and she smiled as if she'd been expecting him. He went over and they found a table, Evelyn's guiding hand on Hansen's shoulder as he hoisted himself down.

Not wanting to talk over the song, Seth made a 'you want a drink?' gesture. Evelyn nodded, Hansen grinned. He went to the bar and got a Coke, a double Johnnie Black on the rocks, and another rum and coke for himself.

He brought the drinks over, sat down. Hansen gave him a nod as he picked up his scotch. Evelyn leant across the table, lightly touched Seth's hand in greeting, her eyes effervescent, then gave her full attention to the singer.

Happy to do the same, he shot Hansen a covert glance, not wanting to catch his eye. Getting caught in talk or a long story, with the bastard's big voice breaking the spell, wasn't something he wanted to instigate.

With his glass held to his mouth, Hansen was staring at the singer, his grizzled face slack with contemplation. He must really dig jazz, thought Seth.

A few minutes later, he snuck another peek. Hansen, chin on fist, was now watching Evelyn as she avidly took in the singer's performance.

A minute later, there was a sudden rattle and thump on the table. Seth turned to see Hansen recovering from a slip; his chin had come off his hand. Okay, thought Seth, I'm going to be earning some of that retainer tonight.

When Hansen signalled for another drink, Seth drank water at the bar. Back at the table, Evelyn caught his eye. He answered her wordless query with a nod, and gratitude shone from her eyes.

From the McKenzie Street tussle the other night, Seth had a good idea of Hansen's weight. He was pretty sure he could get him down the stairs and into a cab. It was just a question of when.

In the short gaps between songs, Hansen was silent, his eyes on the table. When a song started, his gaze returned to Evelyn and the singer, something beatific lurking in his face.

Through the blue sheen of cigarette smoke, a bloke went past the table. He looked like a player, and he gave Seth a nod in acknowledgement of what he saw – the big blonde guy the muscle, the fat old bloke the boss, and the flash little chick the boss's moll. Seth nearly smiled. They were indeed the perfect little crim nuclear family.

When Hansen's head began to sag, his cigarette falling from his fingers, Seth went and asked the owner to ring a cab. Going down the staircase, Seth fought to support the old skipper against his shoulder, Hansen chuckling in his ear about having the coxswain on his arse again.

Out on the street, Hansen started flagging, and Evelyn stretched up and slapped his face. Faces snapped around in shock. Two blokes stared. Seth stared right back.

It was a new test of his muscles getting Hansen in the cab. At the hotel, Evelyn paid the driver as he got Hansen out, the scuffle of their shoes echoing off the high porte cochere roof above them. Across the street, some park people shouted encouragement.

"I'm right," burbled Hansen. "Just a swell."

Seth grabbed his belt, not giving a damn about decorum now. Evelyn wedged in on the other side, as though her slight frame might be of help.

Blinking at her, Hansen said, "You look lovely, darling," and she smiled like it was the first time anyone had ever told her that.

Going hard, Seth pulled the old bastard up the steps. Oh man, he thought, I better have the strength to stop him from falling and cracking his skull if his legs give out.

The yelling from the park reached a crescendo as they summited. Seth and Evelyn held Hansen as he shook with a gargantuan cough. When it had subsided, he said softly, "You're good kids."

At the big double doors, Evelyn pushed one open, and Seth wrangled Hansen in. Fortunately, the front desk was unmanned, and he leaned right into Hansen, moving him quickly to the lifts. Evelyn, savvy to what a bad look this was, rushed ahead to work the lift buttons.

Turning, she watched the front desk. Muscles pumped, Seth held Hansen by the lift door.

"Someone there now," said Evelyn. A beautiful smile lit her face, and she gave a goodnight wave. The lift dinged, opened. Seth casually bulldozed Hansen in, and used his weight to prop him up. Looking out at reception, he saw Braun Micro Plus man, and they exchanged waves.

Up at the suite's doorway, Hansen thumped against the wall. Seth held him as Evelyn opened the door. As he got the old bugger in, he heard the door across the hall open. Damn it, they'd woken a guest.

He kept Hansen moving into the master bedroom and plonked him down to sit upright on the bed. Eyes closed and breathing loudly, Hansen sat patiently while Evelyn got his shoes and socks off.

"Get some water," she said to Seth. He went into the en-suite and filled a tumbler. On the marble counter was the usual stuff: shaving brush, steel safety razor, cologne and talc, and something he'd never seen before: foil-backed sheets of individually sealed pills.

In the bedroom, Evelyn took the tumbler, and he saw white pills in her hand. She turned to the sitting man.

"Hansen," she said. He looked like he'd fallen asleep. She touched his face, and Seth left the room.

Rotating an arm, a bit strained from the effort of the last fifteen minutes, he went to the second bedroom, Evelyn's room, and looked inside.

A pop music magazine lay on the bed; everything else was squared away. No dropped shoes or clothes on the floor; no perfume bottles or sweet wrappers on the desk.

A room key was lined up with the edge of the blotter, and Seth sensed a respect for order here – a manifestation of the young woman's will.

Taking a seat at the dining table, he looked at the files and folders of Hansen's life, and saw an ocean of living distilled into paper.

It seemed to be where the world was headed these days: less action and real experience, more numbers and words. Wisdom received from television and magazines; systems making rules and decreeing permissions, with everything proclaimed in ever-impenetrable officialese.

The electric glare of the television suddenly bathed the end of the room. Seth turned. The master bedroom door was closed. Evelyn sat on the lounge with her eyes on the screen, diamonds glittering in her ears. She picked up a button-studded control box and used it to change the channel. Huh, thought Seth, that's a cool thing.

Cat-like whoops came from the screen as Bruce Lee hammered a high kick into a goon's head. Seth wandered over, trying to guess the movie. Evelyn looked up at him.

"You like fighting?" she said.

Seth grinned sheepishly, shrugged.

"I used to, hey. When I was younger."

"A fighting man is not always a good man."

"You're not wrong," he said. "Goes with the territory."

She regarded him, waiting for further qualification of where her sugar-daddy's muscle placed himself on the scale of good and bad men.

Bloody hell, thought Seth, she's like somebody's hard-nut granny.

He shrugged again. On the screen, Bruce Lee cocked his head and grimly smiled. I hear ya, mate, he thought.

She turned back to the TV, and Seth wondered how she got on with what she did for a living.

Through years of security and door work, he'd known a few hookers, even counted a couple as friends. Some were rough as guts, some were drop-dead glamorous, but they all preferred their regulars: married men, shy singletons, time-poor professionals – fellas with respect, and each one a known quantity.

Now he remembered the Cairns working girl he'd met two years ago – his young ex-girlfriend's housemate.

"Hey, Evelyn. Do you know a girl named Ella? Skinny, pale, dark make-up and clothes, dark painted fingernails, too. Works out of the clubs and bars."

"Why should I know her?"

"She's a . . . a working girl."

Evelyn looked at Seth, disdain deep in her eyes.

"I'm not like that. I get booked. There's always a car for me. And now Hansen takes care of everything. Sorry."

"Oh," said Seth, feeling unreasonably silly in the face of this north Queensland girl just out of her teens.

Before he could hide his discomfort, she saw it, and she hit him with a brilliant smile that glowed with movie-star power.

No smirk at besting him; it was a dismissal of his gaffe, her smile saying that she didn't care and neither should he. Its compassion and grace bowled him over.

Now he saw why she was chauffeured, why she had nice clothes, and diamonds in her ears.

What she possessed was a kind of magic, a cosmos away from the animal crassness of sex and its utterly finite flare of orgasm. She had something far more durable than that, something rare and timeless.

"I better go," he said. "You'll be right with him?"

"I'll look. He'll be sleeping. Thank you, Kelly."

Seth nodded, got up. At the door, he looked back and saw her quietly go into the master bedroom. Hansen was lucky to have her around.

Stepping out into the hallway, he smelt bush tobacco and coconut oil, and a long, sinewy arm crushed around his throat like a bony python. A rock of a fist slammed into his ribs, a knee speared his thigh, and he fell forwards.

Going with it, his hundred-plus kilos tore the arm from his throat. Another punch crashed into his side. Before his knees hit carpet, he pumped raw energy into his thighs. Blasting up like a Saturn V rocket, his skull just caught the tip of his attacker's jaw.

He instinctively jumped back into the doorway. Hansen drunk in bed was a sitting duck, with young Evelyn awful collateral.

The door pushed against him, automatically closing, and he heard the solid click as it locked. Now it was just him and his assailant, face to face in the midnight hallway of a five-star hotel.

God knows who might have it in for Hansen. Seth had no doubt he'd put noses out of joint in his time, broken a few too, but the man standing there looked like he'd dished out a flogging or two to the Devil himself.

Mid-thirties, tall, rugged, and lean, with straight hair

and dark skin, he looked like he'd been born everywhere; his features a mix of Rangoon, Honiara, Port Moresby, and Kupang, with a dozen tropical ports in between.

But on his face as its defining characteristic, was the remorselessness of someone schooled in the hardest of knocks, his cold, dead eyes revealing him as a participant in pitiless things.

This was a bloke who'd react to violence and death not with a shudder, but with a shrug. Seth had met some bad bastards in his time, but right now he was looking at real trouble.

Though it must have hurt, the tall, dark man didn't even rub his jaw, and he slid in, moray eel quick, telegraphing strong punches. Seth blocked with his forearms, bone impacting bone, electric shocks of pain going up his arms. Jesus, the skinny bastard hit hard.

Punching back, Seth bulled out into the hallway, and they silently exchanged blows. In Seth's experience, most one-on-one fights didn't last too long. He usually put blokes down, scared them off, or, now and then, beat a retreat. But that wasn't going to happen here.

The same thought must have occurred to his attacker, and they paused, chests heaving, breathing hard. Seth felt his scalp tingle and the hair on his arms and neck bristle.

This didn't seem real. The man looked as if he'd stepped through a portal from another era, his long hair shining with oil, his eyes a bloodshot sepia, and his teeth stained red from betel nut.

On the new carpet, with flowers on a side table serene in the soft light and piped muzak drifting up from the lifts, the nightmare figure made a complete mockery of this soft, plush place.

"What the hell, man?" said Seth.

Stepping aside, the man threw out a hand towards the lifts. *Just go*, said his eyes.

Three things went through Seth's head. Money, Hansen, and Evelyn. One of them made him shake his head.

The man shrugged and leapt forward unbelievably fast, fingers clawing wildly. Punching the slashing hands away, Seth dodged, weaved, acutely aware of losing an eye. Now by the door of the suite across the hall, he turned and took the offensive, throwing full-throttle punches.

But the bastard didn't let up, his shoulders twisting to absorb blows, one grasping hand at Seth's eyes, the other landing hits to his ribs and guts. Seth thudded against the door, and he thought to yell through it for help. But what if the guest got hurt? Or if Evelyn heard him and opened her door? He couldn't risk it.

In a flurry of punches and talon-like fingers, he got a hold of a slim wrist and wrenched hard. They smashed together chest-to-chest, and it seemed to throw the tall, dark man, his long reach now nullified.

Dropping one shoulder, Seth hooked hard and landed a gut-buster. The bastard didn't flinch. Seth now felt air-conditioning flow onto his neck. From behind him came a masculine grunt of shock.

His attacker's eyes flashed to the doorway, and Seth put a fist into his right eye – hard, but the freaky bastard absorbed it with a shake of his head and punched back, his knuckles rimmed with rings of silver and brass.

"Jesus!" came a voice from the doorway.

Blocking punches left, right, and every bloody where, Seth managed to put a solid jab into a hard rack of ribs. Connecting with an audible crack, it also produced a yelp of pain, the first noise this scary bastard had made.

Feeling a rush of dominating power, he kicked the man in the leg, pounded in another good rib shot, and thank bloody Christ, the bastard fell back.

With textbook precision, Seth began hammering him in a rhythm of feinting, blocking, and attacking. It was like the drums and bass of a red-hot rhythm section. Whack, whack, boof, boof – whack, whack boof. It was hard-knuckle poetry. The biff as the biff should be.

With a frustrated grunt, the bastard turned and ran, his long arms and legs loose, like he was flowing through air. Seth watched him go, and down by the lifts he vanished from view.

Sucking in air, heart pounding, he rubbed his ribs, the light in the hallway fizzing around him.

"Christ, you know how to fight," said the voice from the doorway, an American accent now evident.

Seth turned and saw a white-haired bloke in his late fifties.

"You in suite two, huh?" said the Yank. "I saw you and the young lady bring the old fellow home just before."

Seth recognised him now.

The man shook his head in admiration.

"You wanna drink?"

"I wouldn't say no, Mr. Marvin," said Seth.

Think You're a Good Guy

The next morning he slept in, waking up to bruises and a hangover. It was like he'd reverted to his teens, mixing it up with bottles and fists.

He also felt incredulous. Last night had been something else. First fighting that freaky bastard, then getting on the grog with Lee, as he'd insisted on being called.

Seth had met a few rock stars before, but this was his first movie star. The bloke had been alright, easy to talk to, and funny too.

After calling the desk and hearing that security had just chased a man off the premises, the actor poured them a drink. They had an eye-to-eye toast, and Lee grilled him about the fight, his eyebrows jumping like fuzzy white caterpillars when Seth mentioned client confidentiality.

He was most intrigued to meet a private investigator in Cairns, declaring, "There's a movie in that." No fool, he quickly surmised that Seth's client had 'some history chasing his ass.' He advised Seth to look out for himself, and that no amount of money was worth taking another man's punches for, unless that was what you'd signed up for, and as a private dick, he hadn't.

Not sure about the dick part, Seth had politely nodded and accepted another avalanche of scotch on his rocks.

When he finally called time – he had an early start going fishing – Mr. Marvin called security to escort Seth to his car. He'd also be reporting the fight because the Kamslers were like family to him. Seth would have preferred to have let it slide, but he wasn't going to argue with the leader of The Dirty Dozen.

He got out of bed now, made the bloody thing, and took a beach run and a cold shower to tear the cobwebs off.

He didn't call Hansen. After breakfast, he just went in.

Entering the foyer, he saw blondie Simon, who waved him over to the front desk. With sparkling eyes, he looked Seth over like the second in a boxing ring.

"Well, I suspected you might be a bit of a tough guy, but what on earth happened here last night?" he said.

"Some idiot lurking about. Opportunist thief, I'd say."

"I bet you gave him what for."

"Something like that."

Simon's grin faded. "Head of security wants a word with you."

"Sure. I'm happy to accept his apology."

Simon's grin came back.

The head of security, a bloke in his fifties, was polite but undoubtedly tough. When they sat down for a chat on a sofa in the lobby, Seth recognised him as an ex-copper from Gordonvale and Edmonton way, a ranking sergeant if he remembered rightly.

Quickly establishing that the old sarge knew Uncle Don broke the ice, and Seth gave him a concise run-down of what had happened.

"A private investigator?" said the bloke.

Seth passed him a card. "My rates are reasonable," he said. "If the hotel needs something looked into sometime . . . or a guest, maybe?"

The security honcho ignored this. "You on your way up to him now?"

"Yep," said Seth. "You've spoken to him?"

"No, but I'll ring the police back. They'll send someone over to interview you both."

Seth didn't much dig that, but he nodded amiably.

"We'll leave Mr. Marvin out of this," said the ex-sarge.

"Of course." Seth looked pointedly at his business card in the chief's hand. Familiar with the old quid pro quo, he gave Seth a brusque nod and pocketed the card.

Going up in the lift, Seth wondered what Hansen would have to say about the tall, dark man. The truth, hopefully.

Evelyn answered the door, her smile innocent of what had happened last night. Hansen was out on the balcony, drinking coffee, smoking, and talking loudly on the phone. Evelyn sat down and watched TV. Seth joined her, and stood there watching something about the Space Shuttle.

"Did I tell you to come over this morning?"

Hansen stood at the balcony door, the tone of his voice pitched between inquiry and admonishment.

He can't remember, thought Seth. He's trowelling on the bluster to save face. Nice and calm, he walked over.

"Let's go outside," he said. Hansen didn't move, and his body seemed to expand and grow more solid. Seth flashed on this as a tactic used to monster recalcitrant crew.

"A tall, dark fella," said Seth quietly. "Two scars here."

He touched a cheekbone, then raised his right fist. "And

199

three rings. Two silver, one brass."

Recognition, and fear, flashed across Hansen's face.

"Sweetie," he called to Evelyn. "Go and watch television in your room." Turning quickly, he went back out on the balcony and snatched out a smoke from the pack on the table. Seth let him take a few drags and lower himself into a chair before he went outside.

Hansen softly swore. "I didn't think he'd try and get into the country. He's got outstanding warrants here. Serious ones."

Seth wanted to give the old bastard a real serve. Instead, he leant against the balustrade and let the breeze cool his head. Head down, Hansen kept smoking. Then he looked up with soft grey eyes. "What happened?"

"This . . . mate of yours ambushed me outside the suite last night after you'd gone beddy-byes. He wanted to get in, but I stopped him. It wasn't exactly easy."

Hansen sat silent and expressionless. Seth hoped he was thinking about Evelyn. But when he looked at Seth, there was nothing like remorse on his big, ugly face.

"Seeto," he said. "Eddie Seeto. They call him Sunshine. Or Masta Kilman."

His accent had thickened with the inflections of pidgin English.

"Worked for me. Sorted out labour problems and crew trouble. Caught and punished thieves. I gave him a good wage, a bit of respect, and it straightened him out."

"Straightened him out?"

"He was a bad boy."

"Was?"

Hansen's short laugh was mirthless.

"It's all changing now, but it's a very different world up there, son. Rough and tumble doesn't really do it justice. Lawyers mean fuck-all at the end of a fever-coast jetty. Police? A couple got eaten not so long ago. Sunshine was sometimes the only way I had to protect my business."

"So, now this evil bastard's gunning for you."

Hansen made an unhappy sound, shrugged.

"You're playing with a young woman's life," said Seth. "Not to mention mine. You think that's okay?"

Hansen stared at him. Seth stared back.

The old bastard took a deep, rueful breath.

"I didn't think he'd come to Australia. He's chalked up a whole heap of trouble here."

"While he was working for you."

Rubbing the bridge of his nose, Hansen looked Seth up and down. "Any damage?"

Seth shook his head. Hansen nodded appreciatively.

"Don't you have something to say to me?" said Seth.

Hansen stared. Seth waited, his eyelids sinking, his lips slowly pursing.

"Like what?" said Hansen.

Fuck you, thought Seth. If I don't hear it in the next few seconds, I'm gone.

"What, what? Like sorry?"

Seth dug the note of panic in Hansen's voice. He shook his head. Hansen stared some more, then got it.

"Thank you. Thank you, Kelly."

"You're welcome," said Seth. "Now, we have to talk to the cops. Hotel security called them."

"Yeah, yeah," said Hansen in total agreement, but Seth could see the gears spinning in his head.

"What?" he said. Hansen looked pained.

"Problem is, the way things work, it might be days or weeks until he's arrested. Up there, I'd get things made priority one by dishing out a good wack of cash-cash."

Hansen looked at Seth. "You know any Cairns boys in blue who might be of help in that way?"

Funnily enough, Seth did, but he sure as hell wasn't going down that road, and he shook his head.

But Cairns was a small town, and lo and bloody behold, the very same coppers that had come to mind now arrived to interview him and Hansen. Due to some serious shit earlier this year, they recognised him straight away.

"Kelly," said the detective with the big sideburns. His partner, a pale fella who looked like a maggot in clothes, gave Seth a nod of familiarity that was closer to a twitch.

Hansen watched this closely, and Seth saw him putting two and two and bloody two together.

The Ds identified themselves to Hansen as they looked around at the suite, the furnishings, décor, and the closed bedroom door with the TV on behind it. Sideburns sniffed the perfume in the air. "Nice," he said.

"Captain Hansen," the Maggot began, but Hansen went to the balcony, gesturing for the Ds to follow.

"Smoke," he said.

"Good idea," said Sideburns, pulling out a packet of Pall Mall. With a weary grimace, the Maggot followed his partner outside. Seth went and stood in the doorway.

The old skipper lit his cigarette and smoked, in no hurry

to kick things off. The Maggot took a quick look over the side, hands tight on the rail, and turned back with a giddy scowl.

"Well, this is alright," said Sideburns, looking out at the inlet. "First time at The Pacific International for us, but it won't be the last. Rich, poor, there's always crime."

"What occurred last night?" said the Maggot to Hansen.

"I was asleep." Hansen nodded at Seth. "Mr. Kelly was the person attacked."

The Maggot, evidently briefed by the security chief, said, "Yes, I know that. Was this intruder known to you?"

Hansen nodded. "One Eddie Seeto."

"Eddie who?" The Maggot pulled out a police notebook.

"Seeto," said Hansen. "Not his real name; no one knows that. He's a resident of Papua New Guinea, but I doubt he's got a passport or any sort of identification. The only thing I'd say with any certainty is that he came down here through the Torres Strait."

"What's your relationship with him?"

"I was his boss in Papua New Guinea." Hansen took a drag and exhaled, his eyes squinting against the smoke blown back by the breeze.

"And in what capacity did he work for you?"

"As muscle. He kept the crew and workers in line, saw off trouble-makers, delivered threats and bribes."

The cops stared at Hansen, poker-faced, but Seth knew the bastards were thrilled. Here was a man after their own hearts; accustomed to violence and the bending of rules.

"What's your profession, Mr. Hansen?"

"Businessman. A very successful one."

The Maggot leaned forward, the tang of lucre catching his hook of a nose. Sideburns side-eyed Seth.

"Seeto is a dangerous man," said Hansen. "He needs to be found fast, and . . . well, jailed or deported, I suppose."

"How dangerous?" said Sideburns.

"Oh, several outstanding warrants for serious assault in this country. Also attempted importation of contraband – drugs and firearms."

Like a magic trick, the Maggot was now writing in a tiny Spirax notebook nothing like the official one.

"Hell of an employee," said Sideburns.

"He always got it done," said Hansen.

"Why is he here?" said The Maggot.

Hansen pondered the question. It was bullshit, but the detectives knew what was good for them and they waited politely. Hansen finally shook his head in bemusement.

"Look, I'm a busy man. I have nine companies to run, so having an ex-employee grinding an axe outside the door of my hotel suite is a distraction I do not need."

"You've got Kelly here for him to grind his axe on," said Sideburns. "He's a capable bloke. Not much he can't, or won't do."

Seth ignored the detective. He knew what the bastard was referring to. A fella out west a little while back had got a hollow-point magnum round through the eye.

Hansen shook his head. "Unfortunately, that's not so. Mr. Kelly has his limits, and he's made them clear to me."

"Is that right?" said The Maggot, staring at Seth with anthropological interest.

"Maybe you're not paying him enough," said Sideburns.

Hansen shook his head again. "No, we tried that."

The Ds tried to get their heads around this but failed.

"So," mused the Maggot. "You want this fella found and what . . . deported or jailed?"

Hansen shrugged. "There's no Seeto family."

"No family," mused the Maggot. "No friends?"

"No. Like I said, he doesn't even have a passport."

The Maggot didn't need to look at Sideburns.

What the hell is this? thought Seth, and he gave Hansen a hard look. The bastard, suddenly busy with his coffin nail, hid behind a cloud of smoke.

The Maggot pretended overwork. "Quickly found is a nice idea, but like you, we're very busy men."

Hansen pretended outrage. "There's been an assault in Cairns' newest luxury hotel."

"Like my colleague said, it won't be the last."

With a decisive grunt, Hansen butted out his smoke, a highly inclusive smile signalling the next play.

"You gents had time to try any of the bars in the hotel?"

"It's barely eleven o'clock," said the Maggot, knee-jerk prim. Sideburns smoothed his moustache to hide a smile.

Hansen bristled with amusement.

"No, no, I didn't mean now. Look, why don't we resume this later on this afternoon? We'll have a drink. I'll have organised some . . . wherewithal for you."

The Maggot's face twitched with acquiescence, and he threw Sideburns a look that prompted their departure. Sitting there, Hansen gave them the nod, the bossman in charge and running the show.

Seth stepped away from the doorway. As the detectives

passed by, Sideburns looked at him with something like admiration. "Fuckin' amazing," he said.

When the front door of the suite closed, Seth went back outside. Hansen had an accusatory expression on his face.

"You said you didn't know any police like that."

"I'm trying hard to forget those bastards," said Seth. "It must have worked."

"Yeah? They got something on you?"

Seth shook his head. Hansen got up.

"You think you're a good guy, but you just don't know how bad you can be," he said, and he went inside.

Seth stood there thinking pretty hard. It felt like he'd heard the commission of a knock. Maybe he should step back now. But with Hansen, that would be the end of it.

Laughter wafted up from the street. The inlet glittered silver and blue. The sunshine warmed his arms, and he softly sighed. He'd survived Masta Kilman and met Mr. Marvin, and he was pulling in the dough. Life was sweet, right?

Hansen called for him, and he went inside and listened. Then he took the cheque down to the bank and cashed it.

Evelyn was still in her room when he got back, Hansen out on the balcony. He took the money from Seth, smiled.

"Wanna a beer? Coffee, some food?"

Stone-faced, Seth shook his head.

"Piss off then," said Hansen, not unkindly. "I'll ring you when I hear from them and you can come back here."

"What do you need me for later? What with my limits."

Hansen suddenly looked tired and uninterested; the big blonde man standing there an annoyance easily ditched.

"You want to keep working for me?"

Seth looked at the bastard, then nodded.

They reconvened at five-thirty. Seth had showered and changed into some smart casual gear, keen to keep things on a professional keel.

They sat outside at the Pacific International's ground floor bar on the Esplanade. Hansen ordered drinks from an efficient young waiter, pressing a fifty into his hand with instructions to keep them coming.

Hansen had changed his shirt, but he and the Ds were pongy, reeking of ciggies and BO.

"So, this Eddie Seeto fella," said Sideburns, lighting a cigarette. "You say he's dangerous."

The Maggot chased ice around his glass of Coke with a bony finger, his colourless eyes trained on Hansen.

The old skipper produced a plump envelope, and put it on the table. The detectives watched it as though it might grow legs and run out onto the Esplanade.

Seth drank his beer and checked out the joint. With its name paying homage to one of the hotels that had stood here, the 1906 Strand Bar, like the rest of the hotel, was brand new; the tiled floors gleaming, the tables and chairs all factory fresh, even the ceiling fans spotless.

Through scrolled iron rails, the Strand Bar featured a view Seth had known his whole life: the corner of Spence, Wharf, and the Esplanade. It was like the eye of Cairns.

Hansen rattled the ice in his drink. The two Ds looked at him with real interest now, obviously stirred by his ability to produce a good whack of cash-cash.

"How dangerous?" said Sideburns.

Hansen looked around at the other drinkers, then, like the player he was, he leaned in. "He's killed men."

"Is that right?" Sideburns looked like a dog smelling a bitch in heat. The Maggot slowly gulped, his Adam's apple squirming in his pale chicken neck.

"Oh, yes," said Hansen. "He put a gaff hook through a fella's eye socket one time and dragged him kicking and yelling to the ship's rail. Pitched him over the side."

Sideburns looked as spellbound as a bedtime story kid; his schooner arrested mid-air. The Maggot was rubbing his upper thighs with delicate fingers, the tip of his little pink tongue sticking out like a puppy's . . . Seth felt sick.

On the inlet, the de Havilland floatplane began its take off, the rising drone reverberating across the water. As the noise rose to a crescendo, the tables on the terrace raised their voices in competition.

The cops guzzled their drinks, eyes on Hansen. The old bastard nodded reflectively, as though weighing up the effects of what he was about to reveal on the mental constitution of the two detectives.

The howl of the Pratt and Whitney engine had not yet died away when Sideburns leaned in. "And?"

With diabolical skill, Hansen now laid out a tale of gaff hooks and crab traps, of bald-faced treachery and grisly revenge. The two detectives lapped it up.

It sure looked like they'd be happy to stay here into the night with Hansen if he kept buying the drinks and telling the stories, but a beeper going off on the Maggot's belt put paid to that. A crime, or a new bit of business, was calling.

The detectives finished their drinks and got up.

With customary ease, the Maggot took the envelope and pocketed it. Sideburns bestowed the deed a casual glance.

"Now, gentlemen." Hansen flashed a forefinger at the Maggot's bulging pocket. "I think you'll appreciate *how much* I trust you in handling this, but if you can discharge this task quickly and efficiently – there'll be a bonus."

Sideburns, in full view of the public, didn't want to look servile; he was a detective in the Queensland Police Force after all, and he briskly nodded, keeping his eyes on the sidewalk outside.

The Maggot looked down at Hansen with glowing eyes.

Oh, no, thought Seth. Please no.

But the Maggot was feeling good, and the lower half of his pallid face, like some grotesque sea creature, wriggled, then split apart in an appalling imitation of a smile.

Seth, his gorge rising, looked away.

Big League

A few days later, Stasia rang. There was a lull at work, and she was on an extended lunch break, doing banking and picking up mail. She wanted to see him. Now.

They went at it like rabbits all over his house, even on the floor, and once again in the shower. After a cuppa and a gingernut, she dressed and shot off back to work.

Stupidly, Seth felt strange. Pulling on shorts, he made another cuppa. Sitting outside, he examined the feeling with the caution of a snake-catcher in a junk-filled shed.

He felt like a pitstop, a box ticked. He felt used. It was crazy, because most blokes would be over the moon.

Closing in on the feeling, he saw in it the recognition of something deeper. Stasia coming and going like this felt just too abrupt for what they had going on. It wasn't the usual boyfriend-girlfriend malarky, and it was more than just old friends having a casual root from time to time.

They had something; he knew that, but what?

The groovers went on about having a soulmate, that special someone who yinged your yang, inducing deep feelings of cosmic connection and almost supernatural affinity. It sounded like an awful lot to hang on someone.

But there must be something real solid happening for couples to be happy together after decades. After twenty years or more, things must get stripped right back, the only dramas being nuts and bolts ones like sickness or injury. Anything else that had been a problem wouldn't matter a fly's fart anymore. Differences that had once caused heads to knock would be as forgotten as losing quarter-finalists.

Living like that – post-bullshit – would require a level of cool that he and Stasia could probably get to. But they'd never know until they'd put in the time. It would require dead-set perseverance and real bloody commitment.

It was possible. Nearly the same age, they were roughly at the same part of the journey. The older he got, the more he realised how important that was.

An on-shore breeze rustled the pandanus. He finished his cuppa. Pondering this is just pondering, he thought. The smart thing to do is to forget about it.

To help him get smart, he made a call to Laidlaw, his strange but clever friend down in Sydney.

One of the most boring things about coming back to live in far north Queensland was the dearth of good music to be bought, or more precisely, the knowledge of what was worth buying. Music papers like Ram, Rolling Stone, and Juke provided clues, but that only went so far. And the local record shops and radio stations . . . well, yeah.

He'd given Laidlaw five hundred bucks, and a couple of times a year his mate would send him up ten quality LPs. He just had to remind the freak to do it.

"What?" said Laidlaw when he picked up the phone.

A man of very few words, people said he lacked social graces, and his reclusive life made him ratty. Seth didn't care, because when Laidlaw did speak, it was like the oracle on the mountain, his enormous, ever-pulsating brain buzzing with musical wisdom. And not just some music; Laidlaw listened to it all.

Glam rock, prog rock, punk rock, jump jazz, surf pop, be-bob, blue-beat, afro, roots, psychedelia, and out-there experimental was just some of what he liked.

Laidlaw's massive record collection was ordered to a system only he understood. Lightin' Hopkins, Annette Peacock, the Clash, and Kraftwerk rubbed shoulders with Paco de Lucia, Osibisa, and Suicide. Gram Parsons, Can, and Television sat cheek-by-jowl with Fred Neil, Eno, Dollar Brand, and The Band. And he had albums from places like Appalachia and the Gilbert and Ellis Islands.

The only kinds of music that didn't get Laidlaw's stylus in the groove were opera, disco, and heavy metal, and that was fair enough.

"Hey Laidlaw, it's Seth. So, maestro – what have you got for me this time?"

On the other end of the line, Laidlaw's big sound system was playing something that sounded like detuning kettle drums in combat with packs of echoing horns.

In his oblique way, Laidlaw said, "Hey, Seth. What have you been doing lately?"

"Just working, mate. The usual stuff."

"Oh yes, looking after bands up there."

"No, I've got a business. I told you, remember?"

"Uh . . . no." Laidlaw actually had a good memory; he

wrote programmes for government computers, and could tell you who'd sung the vocals on 'The Nazz are Blue.' But the day-to-day stuff could escape him.

"I'm a private investigator, remember?"

"Oh, very cool. A tropical Travis McGee."

This baffled Seth, but the Ever-Pulsating Brain in its lair in Newtown often baffled him.

"You're talking Greek, mate. So, you got some albums for me? The last batch wasn't bad. I liked The Jam, tough bastards, and Word of Mouth was dynamite."

"Oh yes, what a line-up."

"What about the new Elvis?"

"Ahhh, it's not very rock'n'roll. He's done a track with Chet Baker. There's orchestral stuff, Tin-Pan Alley even."

"Yeah?" More bloody Greek, but he trusted his mate.

"I'll put a selection together for you," said Laidlaw.

"So, whatcha think of the Hugh Christie album?"

Laidlaw grunted unhappily.

"What?" said Seth. "It's a bit pop, but it's okay."

"Okay means mediocre. He's trying to please everyone. Is he a Frampton or a Page? This dilution of his strengths does him no favours."

"He got a number one."

"So did Sherbet."

Faced with this implacable nugget of logic, Seth shut up. Down the line, the kettle drums were being whipped with buzzing steel chains now.

"You got a theme song?" said Laidlaw.

"A theme song?"

"A private investigator – you must have a theme song."

"Jesus, Laidlaw, get real."

There was a stubborn silence.

"Ah . . . the theme from Ryan?"

"Old hat."

"Watching the Detectives?"

"Cute. Listen, I'll find something for you."

The line went dead, and Seth smiled. It had been a fairly long conversation by his mate's standards.

He'd spent many nights hanging out with Laidlaw in his sprawling flat above King Street. Sitting on the red leather lounge with his crackerjack sound system, pipes of hash, and a bottle of bourbon, they just listened without talking, album after album, sometimes going until dawn.

Putting on a shirt, he took a quick spin up to Cook and Piccone's for a few items of essential groceries, with olive oil and toilet paper at the top of the list. It saved a trip into town – and they had mango Weis bars. He bought four to restock the freezer, eating one on the way back.

He hadn't been home long when the phone rang. It was Hansen wanting him to come over. A few days had passed since he'd unleashed the two Ds on that Sunshine bastard, and Seth wondered if this had something to do with that.

I'll listen, he thought, but I'm not hunting that slice of danger. Those bastards can earn their fifteen grand.

After a shower, he pulled on some decent slacks and a clean shirt. As he put on shoes, the phone rang.

"Seth. Listen, mate, you gotta go get Don at the RSL. He's not good." It was Harry Spinks, an old cabbie mate of the family. "Dispatch just called, but I'm at Edmonton. I'm not sure another driver could get him into the cab."

"Yeah, no worries, Harry. I'll go get him," said Seth.

"Good on ya, Seth," said the cabbie. He sighed. "The war couldn't break him, but this shit –"

When he hung up, Seth tried to remember if he'd ever heard Harry swear before.

In town, he parked on the Esplanade out the front of the Returned and Services League Club, where those who'd served in the military, and their guests, could have a yarn over a beer. Getting out of the Pig, he heard the old bloke yelling.

"This town's going to hell! But you silly bastards don't want to admit it!" Uncle Don was pissed and angry.

Just inside the arched entranceway, an RSL manager and one of Uncle Don's mates were trying to placate the red-faced man. Shaking off calming hands, he turned to shout into the room at blokes trying to ignore him.

"You can't tell me there's no coppers on the take. And magistrates too!"

"Don, please mate. C'mon Don," said the bar manager.

"And the council and the harbour board? Those venal, conniving bastards and their crooked mates are knocking down our buildings, our bloody heritage! And you know where the money's coming from, don't you? Don't you?"

"Seth," said the bar manager with relief. "I tried to . . ."

"It's okay," said Seth, and he put his arm around Uncle Don's shoulder. The old ex-copper turned with a grimace of rage, but when he saw it was Seth, the hard tendons in his neck relaxed back into his stubbly jowls.

"Hey, mate," he said with beery breath. "These blokes are living in la-la land, I tell you. Heads in the sand!"

"Yep, you're not bloody wrong. C'mon Uncle Don." Seth steered him from the door. "I'll take you home."

In the Pig, the old bloke was silent, looking diminished and worn-out. Oh, mate, thought Seth. You have to let go of this or it's going to kill you.

Uncle Don had been a good cop, but his vocal disgust at what the mountains of money made from marijuana was doing to the north had got him railroaded out of the force two years ago. Other honest cops tried to back him, but the money pushed back hard, and those blokes got cut out of the pack to be ostracised, threatened, victimised, or fired. Now a whole crooked slab of the Queensland Police Force had become a law unto themselves.

Looking at Uncle Don slumped in the seat, Seth's heart went out to him. Unpunished injustice had eaten away at the old cop, bringing out a deeply cynical and pessimistic side that hadn't been there before. He drank more and got angry with it. This was the third time Seth had got the call from Harry Spinks to come get him.

At the little Queenslander in Manunda behind the high school, Seth helped Uncle Don into the house. Aunt Mary followed him into the bathroom, where he washed his face and brushed his teeth. They went into the bedroom. Seth heard her murmuring, then the thump of shoes hitting the floor. He waited in the kitchen. When she came out, he gave her a hug.

"Thank you, Seth," she said. "Sit with me for a minute."

They sat out on the verandah.

"So, how have you been, Seth?" said Aunt Mary. "Work keeping you busy?"

"Yeah, it's ticking along."

Auntie Mary looked tired. He gave her a good smile, and she smiled back. They both missed Mum like crazy.

"I think we should move from Cairns," she said. "Try somewhere new."

"Things here make him angry."

"That they do. What he went through with the job, and the way Cairns is changing, well, he's not happy here."

Something occurred to Seth. "Y'know, Aunt Mary, he's not shy of speaking his mind, and when he's drunk he talks about the things that made him resign. Have you had any . . . visits?"

Aunt Mary knew exactly what he meant, but she shook her head.

"No, I believe the force is done with him. He's like the man who never was. He's still got a few mates, but I doubt anyone's spoken to him."

The bell at the school rang for little lunch. Seth's tummy grumbled.

"Or he's kept it to himself." Aunt Mary's voice was soft.

"Okay," said Seth. He got the Yellow Pages from the hall table, and found the number. He wrote it down on a piece of paper, and she read it.

"Bob Loftus?"

"He's a lawyer. Anyone comes round, you call him."

"We don't have much money, Seth."

"Aunt Mary, I do. And this lawyer is up in arms about corruption. He'll work pro bono, which means . . ."

"I know what pro bono means. Well, he sounds like a good man. For a lawyer."

"He's a bulldog, Aunt Mary. He won't let it rest."

From the bedroom came the sound of snoring, and Aunt Mary smiled.

"Sounds like they'd make a good pair," she said.

He parked near the Cairns Harbour Board office and got out. Surrounded by hot car park, the horrible red brick block of a building looked like a prison block.

Out the front, a gaggle of knee-socked bastards holding briefcases were talking. They had the vibe of the blokes Uncle Don had been going off about.

Who knew where the truth lay, but Seth had no illusions that some pillars of society were bent; doing back-room deals with their developer mates, laundering dope money through property sales, and bankrolling demolitions.

And these crooks were in cahoots with the rotten mob of rogues down in Brisbane – the dodgy, long-standing state government, fronted by its bible-bashing bastard of a premier.

The really crazy thing was that none of it was a secret. In parliament the opposition hammered the government, questioning links between marijuana money and political donations, while journalists and honest cops risked their careers, maybe even their lives, spilling the beans.

The rest of the country looked upon Queensland with horrified amusement, regarding the state as hopelessly backward and corrupt. Wags called the border with New South Wales the banana curtain, and Seth had got more than a few mocking laughs in Sydney when blokes heard he was from the sunshine state.

But whatever the hell was going on in Cairns, the results were plain to see. Wonderful old buildings, the places he'd grown up with, were being knocked down all over, with bloody concrete boxes taking their place.

It was as though the bastards wanted to erase not just the structures that gave the place its character and charm, but its past too, with all of its history, good and bad. It was like they were afraid, or guilty.

He crossed the road to Anzac Park. On the park's corner was the stone and marble fountain dedicated to Dr. Koch, who had connected mozzies with malaria back in the day. Thousands had died, so he qualified as a hero around here.

Slumped against the fountain was a Murri bloke; sick, drunk, or asleep, it was hard to tell.

"You alright, mate?" said Seth. The bloke's eyes flew open. He didn't look sick or drunk now.

"You wanna be careful." Seth nodded in the direction of the Cairns watchhouse, one short block away. "Cops just up there."

"Fuck the cops," said the bloke.

You couldn't really add much to that, so Seth crossed the road to the hotel. He looked, but Simon wasn't on, and he took the lift to the second floor. Sauntering down the hallway, he wondered what Hansen had for him today. Enjoying the anticipation, he knocked on the door. Thirty seconds passed before Evelyn opened up.

"Hey Evelyn, how are you?" said Seth.

"I'm good, thank you," she said sweetly, but there was a warning in her face. Without elaboration, she turned and went to the lounge suite.

Hansen was outside on the balcony, reading a sheet of paper. Rather you than me, thought Seth, reaching for a chair. As he pulled it out, Hansen sharply said, "Oi."

Seth paused, unsure, standing there like a kid in the headmaster's office. Hansen's eyes flicked up at him, hard as battleship steel.

"You wear that nice watch for show?" he said.

Seth let go of the chair. "What's the problem?"

"You're late. Nearly an hour late."

"Okay. Well, I'm sorry. Something came up."

"What – your cock came up? A beer bottle came up? Listen, when you tell me you're coming here, I expect you to be here quick smart. You're getting good money off me. You getting sick of that?"

Here was the hard-as-teak skipper, the righteous bully – and it pissed Seth off. He shook his head, but didn't hide how he felt. Hansen's nostrils widened, his eyes flashed. The page he held fluttered to the table.

"Something important came up," said Seth. "If you'd told me to rush over, I would have rung and told you."

"What was so important?"

Seth tried to lose the frown.

"I had to get my uncle from the RSL. He needed me."

Hansen stared at him, breath whistling through his big, broken beak. He sagged back in the chair, took a cigarette and lit it.

"RSL," said Hansen. "He was in the war?"

"Yep."

"Where did he serve?"

"Papua New Guinea. Borneo."

Hansen nodded slowly, gestured at the chair.

"Take a seat, Seth."

Seth did, thinking this was the first time Hansen had used his name.

The older man nodded in reflection, his eyes on the inlet. When he spoke, his voice was almost reverent.

"I was in the navy. Supply convoys, invasion support, patrols. I suffered Savo Island. Hell in paradise. I thought of my father that night."

He looked at Seth. "Your father serve too?"

Seth nodded.

"He ever talk about it?"

"Not really. I heard stuff on fishing trips with his mates and Uncle Don. Us kids were supposed to be asleep, but I'd sneak over and listen. They'd be drunk by then."

Hansen nodded. In the silence, memories raged behind his eyes. Seth waited respectfully. What those blokes had gone through defied comprehension.

"Okay," said Hansen. "We're off to a meeting tomorrow. Bring a hat and sunglasses. We'll be out on the reef."

"The reef?" Seth didn't hide his surprise. Hansen's eyebrows flew up in piercing query.

"Something wrong?"

"No. I'm just wondering what I'll be doing."

"Keeping your bloody eyes open. You might see things that escape me. You can handle that, right?"

"Sure," said Seth, suddenly pleased to be in the dark.

It was bullshit; he knew that, but mixing it with fellas like Hansen, and Burns for that matter, made him feel like he was playing in the big league.

"Time for a drink," said Hansen.

You're paying me, thought Seth.

They sat inside, the air-con trumping the view, Hansen smoking at the dining table. Comfy on the lounge, Evelyn watched TV, glossy fashion magazines at her side, a tall Coke and ice on the coffee table in front of her.

Seth drank Crownies, Hansen Glenfiddich. The bottle was already half empty, but a fresh one sat on the bar.

As usual, Hansen spun tales from his life, tonight's theme about always being on guard. When he told Seth about a salvage job in the Loyalty Islands where his long-time partner in Noumea had stiffed him big-time over fuel – the Frog bastard had a mate who ran the bowsers at the wharf – Seth thought of the old bloke at McKenzie Street. He'd been Hansen's mate. For twenty-seven years.

It was as cryptic as hell, but he was getting the feeling that Hansen was trying to ask him something, and it felt almost like a plea. He couldn't work it out, but it felt like the door into the man had opened a little wider.

But, Jesus, he could drink. By the time Seth had drunk his third Crown Lager, Hansen was nearly finished with his sixth big scotch, the new bottle of Glenfiddich already breached.

Seth watched him, thinking how grey he looked, and an unaccountable feeling of compassion and concern for the old bastard washed through him.

"Hey, um . . . Hansen. What's with the thirst?"

Hansen reared back, his hands against his chest in an imitation of an old auntie's shock, the frown on his face not without humour.

"You a doctor now?" he barked.

"No, but . . ."

"Then stow it."

Seth unhappily smiled, the feeling still strong.

"What? You worried that your meal ticket's gonna die on you?" said Hansen.

"No, it's just . . . it doesn't matter."

It wasn't the money, it was the man.

Hansen lit a cigarette and blew a plume of smoke at Seth, who turned in his chair to avoid it.

"Hey, sweetie," Hansen called out to Evelyn. "Come and talk to us. It's getting maudlin over here."

Evelyn came over, her painted toenails vivid against her skin. "Maud Lynn?" she said, "She doesn't sound like a girl you want to know."

Hansen stared at her, then roared with delight. Seth laughed too, blinded by the girl's winner of a smile.

She put a slim arm around Hanson's neck. The old man put his cheek against her hip, and inhaled deeply. Seth looked away, embarrassed at what he saw in Hansen's eyes. Considering the circumstances, it seemed a bit sad and pathetic.

They got room service for tea: rib-steaks for them, fish and chips for Evelyn, chocolate mousse for everyone.

Evelyn ate in front of the TV, plate on her knees, using her knife and fork down to the last chip.

When Hansen had finished eating, she softly called, the tone of her voice somewhere between a reminder and a command. "Hansen."

Without acknowledgement, Hansen spilled some pills

from a brown bottle into his hand. Draining his glass, he washed them down.

"Heart?" said Seth.

"Guts, nuts, eyes – you name it," said Hansen. "See, I've eaten every kind of thing. Curries, chillies, bush meat. I've had every bloody malady – dengue, typhoid, malaria. And I've screwed around like a wild pig. Been treated by every clap doctor from Penang to Pago Pago. You only live once, son, so don't waste any time."

The old skipper regarded Seth. "You take a drink, but you don't smoke."

"Ah . . . I do," said Seth, wondering what Hansen would make of this. "But only marijuana."

Hansen nodded. "The old wacky baccy, hey. I first saw the boys smoking it before the war – Lascars, Singhalese. Never minded it on my crew. Same as grog. Whoop it up all you like on land, but don't you fall down a ladder or shirk your duties back on my ship."

"You smoke it?" ventured Seth.

"Why? You got some?"

"Ah, not on me."

Hansen laughed at this, a great bubbling chesty sound. His amused eyes lingered on Seth, then he looked across at Evelyn.

She'd turned down the TV and was looking through a pink vinyl bag that rattled with music tapes. With a sweet smile for them, she chose one and loaded it into a portable Sanyo cassette player.

"She's good," said Hansen. "Never plays it too loud."

A song began playing – a sax-led rocker, the vocals

undoubtedly Joan Armatrading. Though Seth wasn't a big fan, the track wasn't bad, and he began nodding along.

The old skipper looked at him, and the indulgence left his face. A bit self-consciously now, Seth kept grooving.

With a flicker of scorn in his eyes, Hansen took a hit of scotch. "You like your music, hey?"

"Oh yeah. I hardly watch TV, but I listen to my albums."

Hansen nodded, but he didn't get it.

"I've got nearly three hundred," said Seth. "I copy the LPs onto cassette so I can play 'em in my truck."

"Yeah? What's wrong with the radio?"

Seth laughed. "Up here? You're kidding."

This time Hansen didn't even pretend to understand.

Essential Unimportance

The next day he met Hansen outside the hotel. The sky was a knockout blue, the air sparkling like champers.

He'd brought a small canvas bag; inside it a bush hat, a water canteen, and the Tascos. Wearing Wayfarers and a pair of canvas reef shoes, he was ready for hours on the water. Hansen wore a cheap terry-towelling hat, a pair of expensive-looking sunglasses, and a frown. He grunted in greeting, and in silence they walked from the hotel to the jetties on the inlet.

At the BP fuel station by the water, a scruffy old boatie emerged from the twenty-cent showers. He looked like he'd been carved from mahogany, marinated in rum, then boiled in saltwater. In the car park, a couple of fellas living out of their van were boiling up a billy on a gas bottle.

They passed boat after boat walking out along the jetty, but when Hansen stopped at the De Havilland floatplane moored at the end, Seth began wondering what the score was today.

The pilot was called Roger, and he looked spiffy in his uniform of tailored blue shorts, white short-sleeved shirt, and a peaked flight captain's hat. Instead of the usual polished shoes of a pilot, he wore scuffed Dunlop Volleys.

Hansen and Roger conferred. Reefs got mentioned, but no destination. When Seth asked Hansen where they were going, he got a cryptic grunt. Relax, he told himself. You're getting paid to go on an aeroplane ride on a beautiful day.

Heaving himself up the steps on the float strut, Hansen settled into the passenger seat up front. Ducking his head, Seth got in and sat on the bench seat down the back.

Roger hopped into the cabin, a coil of yellow nylon rope in hand. Giving Seth a cheery smile, he secured the door, and went through his pre-flight; flicking switches, briskly writing in a log, and muttering into his headset mike; the unseen airport control tower two kilometres to the north.

With a chugging cough, the radial engine came to life, and within seconds it was hard to imagine life without its clamouring roar. Roger goosed the throttle and taxied out towards Trinity Bay. The revs built, the plane picking up speed, and suddenly they were off the water, the yacht and boat-dotted expanse of the inlet unfolding behind them.

Along the Esplanade, Seth saw the buildings that had all opened up in the last few months: the ten stories of the Lyons, conference rooms and all; the Aquarius, its sixteen floors shadowing the RSL next door, and Hansen's hotel, the Pacific International. Among the tin roofs of Cairns, the towers looked like brash intruders.

They gained altitude, Cape Grafton falling away, and after five minutes of climbing they levelled out, Seth guessing at about three thousand feet.

Henry was right: the unpressurised plane was bloody noisy, its sonorous drone ever-expanding, filling the skull with an endless machine roar.

If the soundtrack was duff, the visuals made up for it. A line of little fluffy clouds were sailing out over the Coral Sea, the ocean and sky stretching all around them.

It was calm down there with no windblown flecks of white, just a slowly moving lace of waves breaking on long lines of reef. Immense and gorgeous, the view filled Seth with a sense of security and peace.

The world, with its Middle East slaughter and oil-rigs sinking, and Poms and Argies in the Falklands like two bald men fighting for a comb could all go to hell in a handcart for all he cared.

Out here amongst it all, it was God's own country, and you could feel an eternal power that would long outlive the schemes and machinations of homo sap.

Sure, he loved humanity, but he was under no illusions as to its essential unimportance. You didn't need a degree in philosophy to know that. A tab of good acid pulled the curtains back on that bullshit real quick.

They turned and flew north. The hazy green of the coast unfolded on the left, and he checked it out, engaged by this rare view: the bump of Port Douglas sticking out into the bay, the silvery notch of the Daintree River mouth, the King Kong mass of Thornton's Peak capped with white cloud, and out west, the Windsor Tablelands nudging the sky. Somewhere there, unseen but lurking, was the crop.

Moving across the seat, he looked down at the coral complexes of the inside edge of the Great Barrier Reef. He recognised some from charts he'd used fishing and diving: Pickersgill Reef and Endeavour Reef where Captain Cook had come a gutser, and Egret, Boulder, and Lark. Seeing the familiar shapes from up in the sky was really cool, and that big, omniscient feeling returned.

Time slipped by as they flew north, the numbing engine roar stupendous. Hansen leant over to Roger. They yelled over the noise, and the De Havilland banked and began losing altitude. Hansen started looking out his window. Moving back across the seat, Seth joined him in scanning the surface of the sea.

They got lower and lower, and he saw amongst reef and ocean the glimmer of a tiny sand cay: a hundred metres long, maybe sixty metres wide. Just out from it, anchored in the deep blue of a channel, was a fishing trawler.

They circled the cay. Seth craned his neck, saw nobody on the trawler's deck or in its dinghy. After two low passes looking for coral bommie heads that might tear the floats off and fling the plane into a somersault, Roger brought the de Havilland down onto the water.

Beneath the surface, coral flashed by, a filigreed pattern of plates and branches. As they slowed, Seth saw a startled eagle ray break from the surface like a big spotted bird, its winglike fins flapping in mid-air, before splashing down into its cool, submarine world.

Taxiing in towards the cay, Roger cut the engines five metres out, and worked a lever to raise the float rudders. There was a moment of blessed quiet, a hiss as the De Havilland ran up onto pulverised coral sand, and the real silence began.

The absence of noise was breathtaking, almost loud in itself. Seth stretched, eager to get out and stand. Roger got out the side door by his seat onto the float, feet thumping as he went along it. Cracking the door, Seth climbed out and stood on the float, grateful to extend his legs.

On the beach, the pilot sank a small claw anchor into the sand, its end secured by the nylon rope to the plane.

Grunting and farting, Hansen exited and deftly walked along the float to hop down onto the sand. Seth joined him, and they stared up the sweep of sand at the trawler.

The enormous silence was only broken by the sound of the flat sea gently breaking on the coral sand beach. The sky was a blue hemisphere around them, and without the sunglasses they wore, the sunlight bouncing off the pure white sand would have been difficult to take.

Hansen reached into his pocket, pulled his smokes out. He lit one, the smoke slowly rising. Jeez, it's still, thought Seth. It feels like everything's frozen, like we're stuck in a postcard.

Roger came over, pulled a packet of Pall Mall from his shirt pocket and lit up. Out on the trawler there was no movement, and for a creepy moment Seth had the vibe it was a ghost ship; abandoned, or strewn with sun-dried cadavers.

Sweat began to bead on Hansen's thick neck. Seth took the floppy hat from the bag at his waist and put it on.

"They know you're coming, right?" said Roger.

"I spoke to that boat on the HF yesterday," said Hansen.

Roger blew smoke from his nose, nodded like he knew what was going on. His peaked hat looked hot on his head.

The sound of an outboard motor starting came across the blue slot of the channel.

Roger grinned. "There you go. I'll sit in the plane, hey?"

Hansen shrugged, and the pilot walked back to the de Havilland. Seth took out his canteen. The trawler's tinny came out fast from behind the boat. Seth took a swig and held out the canteen. Hansen shook his head.

"Alright," he murmured. "Let's be done with this."

The sun flashed on the tinny, three figures sitting in it. Coming in fast, it headed across the channel. Making no deviation towards the floatplane, it would hit the shore thirty metres away.

Hansen, already done with his smoke, threw it to lay smoking on the pristine sand. Seth frowned. He put the canteen in his bag, looked back at the de Havilland. Roger was hidden in the cool gloom of the cabin.

Hansen began walking. Seth fell in beside him. The outboard engine changed pitch, going a little faster. Seth tried to make out the people sitting in the dinghy.

A renegade cloud moved across the sun, and with the glare suddenly gone, Seth saw Eddie Seeto in the bow of the dinghy, holding what looked like an M1 carbine.

"Shit," said Seth.

"There are people in PNG I can't protect anymore," said Hansen. "Good people. Things changed, so I have to give him something to leave them alone."

"Jesus, Hansen. What the hell did you do to piss him off so badly?"

Hansen sighed heavily. "After nearly twenty years, I left him behind. I paid him, but . . . apparently not enough."

"Why didn't you tell those Cairns Ds to be here? Or the bloody Navy?"

"If he doesn't get back up there by Monday, his rascals

will do those good people in. He told me that yesterday."

"Why'd you have to bring me for?" said Seth, despising the dread in his voice.

"To keep an eye on me. Bear witness. Moral support."

"Moral support? He's got a semi-automatic rifle!"

The outboard went silent and the tinnie came sailing in, a perfect little wave at its bow.

"Look, he knows it takes three days to get back to PNG," said Hansen. "And he knows the plane's got a radio. It's a stand-off for both of us. He won't try anything crazy."

"Hansen!" Roger yelled from the plane in shock. He'd seen the M1.

"Stay off the radio!" Hansen yelled back, his voice calm. "This'll take five minutes."

Hansen pulled a chamois bag from his pocket. Seth heard the click of hard plastic. Jesus – those unbelievable opals!

Sunshine jumped from the tinny as it hit the beach, and ran a few paces towards them.

"Eddie!" yelled Hansen.

Raising the carbine, Sunshine sighted down its barrel. Hansen began to walk forward. Seth took a big breath, did the same. Ka-pow! Sand jumped near his right foot – ka-pow! – a second round impacted by his left.

He threw himself to the hot, gritty whiteness. He didn't know if these were warning shots, or if Sunshine was just getting his aim in, but the .30 calibre carbine could make holes in a bloke real bloody fast.

The gunshots lingered; false echoes evaporating under the stark blue sky. Hansen, standing next to him, sighed.

Sunshine, the carbine still against his cheek, motioned Hansen forward with the long fingers of one hand. Re-aiming the gun at Seth, he shook his head.

"Hansen," said Seth. "Wait a sec."

The other two blokes were out of the dinghy, neither armed, and they walked to stand beside Sunshine.

There was the snick of a lighter, the smell of smoke, and Hansen walked towards the men, cigarette in mouth, his fist wrapped around the chamois bag.

With a brittle hiss, a small wave lapped against the long flank of the cay, moving tiny fragments of bleached coral, the water's edge less than a metre from where Seth lay. A moment of silence, and the lazy sound came again.

Amplified out here, crystal clear, the inhalations and exhalations of the sea were a sound from the beginning of time. In different circumstances, say with a lovely, naked woman next to him, Seth would have found this delicate chinkling relaxing.

But here, watching Hansen lumbering towards that scary bastard, it was sepulchral: the sound of bones; the coral polyps once magnificently pulsing with colour now dead and ground to bleached-out fragments.

Staying flat on the sand, Seth inched his hand into his bag. He got the Tasco binoculars out and slowly pulled them through the sand to his head.

"Hey, hey!" yelled Roger. "What the fuck's going on?"

"Just stay in the plane," Seth yelled back. "He'll give him something and we're out of here."

"He told me to keep my mouth shut, but this is nuts. If anything happens I'm taking off and radioing it in."

"The bastard with the gun knows that too. It's gonna be cool, mate. Just a couple of tough blokes taking it outside. A few more minutes and we're gone. Okay?"

Roger let out an affirmative moan.

Hansen came up to Sunshine and stopped. The tall, dark man lowered the M1, but kept it pointed towards Hansen. Seth put the binoculars to his eyes, focused in.

Sunshine was smiling like a resort island host. His two mates – one brown, one white, both hard-muscled lumps of trouble – also looked tickled to see the old skipper.

Sunshine spoke, his face now expressionless. Then he listened carefully to Hansen's reply. Seth couldn't make out any of the words, but their voices sounded reasonable and calm.

Hansen held out the chamois bag. Sunshine pocketed it without comment, and began talking again, the bastard looking pleased with himself now. Yep, a fortune in opals could do that to a bloke, thought Seth, completely blown away by what had just happened.

There was a burst of laughter from Sunshine – sweet they were done – and he put the M1 to Hansen's head.

Seth's gut swooped and he closed his eyes. Coral sand hissed and tinkled, but no gunshot came.

Opening his eyes, he saw the carbine still at Hansen's head. All the fun had left Masta Kilman's face. His mates had moved in closer and were intently watching Hansen. With harsh command, Sunshine's voice rang out. Hansen got down on his knees.

This time Seth didn't look away. Sunshine handed the carbine to a mate, undid his pants, and pulled out his old fella. A stream of liquid glittered, splashing onto Hansen's head. Laughter filled the air, the trawler boys cracking up.

As he pissed on his old boss, Sunshine looked over with a broad smile. With his free hand, he pointed at Seth, then at Hansen; the insinuation being that this was something that Seth would also have to do one day.

Spraying a final burst off Hansen's head, Sunshine put it away and took the M1 back. Turning to Seth, he raised it, and pow! pow! pow! pow! Coral sand spurted on either side of Seth's shoulders, peppering him with sand.

The bastard was being a bastard, but Seth was more than thankful that he knew how to shoot.

The echoes died off. He took a peek and saw the cheeky prick waving bye-bye. Leaning down for a final word to Hansen, he led his boys back to the tinnie.

Seth rolled onto his back, sat up, and yelled at the plane.

"Roger! No radio! I'm okay, Hansen's okay!"

The pilot appeared in the doorway. Seth pointed at him.

"No radio! People in PNG will die if that bastard doesn't make it back there. You understand!"

Roger, looking very pale, nodded.

The outboard of the dinghy kicked in. Seth turned to see it pull away, nobody giving a shit about looking back.

Watching Eddie Seeto, his dark hair flying in the air, Seth felt no especial hate for him. Sure, he'd not hesitate a second killing him if he had to, but he'd feel nothing more than the primeval triumph at just staying alive. But he sure as hell never wanted to see the bastard again.

He got up and carefully brushed sand off the Tascos. Slipping them back in the case, he looked up the beach.

Hansen was standing now. As Seth strode over to him, the old skipper had zero emotion on his face.

Looking down at his soaking pants, he said, "None of that's mine."

Like Us

It was a hell of a way to make a buck, but Seth wouldn't have missed it for the world. One day, he'd tell his mates about it. Jaws would drop, eyes would pop, and there'd be more than a few 'no fuckin' ways.'

I couldn't believe it, he'd say. On a scrap of sand on the edge of the world, and this stone-cold killer with an M1 is about to get handed half a mill in opals. He'd take a hit on the joint and let the wide-screen magnitude of it all sink in, then say – "And an hour earlier I'd been watering my hibiscus!"

Back at the plane, Hansen had chucked the contents of his pockets on the sand and stripped to his jocks. Sitting in the shallow water, he washed his face and clothes.

The tinny got behind the trawler before Roger appeared in the doorway. When Hansen got into the plane, dripping with saltwater, the pilot started whinging.

Hansen shut him up; his voice nasty, the offer sweet.

"I'll double your fuckin' money, alright?"

On the way back, the noise of the plane was even louder. It still looked beautiful down there, but Seth now saw the dirty history submerged beneath the endless glitter.

Back in Cairns on the jetty, with Hansen and Roger in a monetary huddle, Seth had looked around at the moored boats, with the yachties pottering about and kids fishing, everything looking sweet and dandy under a pacific sky.

Then Hansen had strode right past, his jaw set, his eyes straight ahead. When Seth caught up, he'd waved him off, snapping, "You're knocked off for today."

That stopped Seth dead in his tracks, and he'd watched Hansen stomp off up the jetty. Yeah, it was a hell of a way to make a buck.

A hell of a lot of bucks, actually. Checking the business account the next day, he saw that twenty grand had been deposited in it. Holey moley. He hadn't expected that, but it was damn good to see – a proper acknowledgement that he'd put his life on the line at there.

The money got Dad more than curious. Seth explained in a roundabout way that it was a bonus for preventing Hansen from getting into some serious trouble, and that his role with this client had changed. His father made that musing sound of his.

"It's like what I did in Sydney, Dad. Playing minder to the bands, but just . . . better paid."

"Why does a businessman need a minder?"

"Well, he's narked off a few blokes off over the years."

"What – enough to get physical?"

"Well, yeah, and he drinks a bit, too. I've had to bring him back to his hotel."

"He sounds like that son of Michael Christie you had to babysit over Christmas."

"Exactly, Dad."

"So, ocelots all around?"

"We'll take them with us to Fiji."

As they laughed, Seth felt a weight lift off his shoulders. Not only did he have real trouble money now, he also had the space to consider his future.

Hansen rang at the end of the week, suggesting dinner at the hotel. Evelyn was with him when they met at The Waterfront, the swank restaurant on the ground floor. There were many old photos and historic items, and a one third-sized replica of a sailing ship's bow in the dining room.

"Look at that," said Hansen, pointing out a framed old document. It was a ship's master certificate.

"Joseph Conrad's," said Hansen. "He lived it all before he wrote it. Like us."

Over dinner, Hansen was genial, but it was plain that their little jaunt to the reef was not something he'd ever mention again. Seth also felt a new vibe with him.

The sense of antagonism, and of being tested, was gone. Even the piss-taking felt friendly. Evelyn, silent and softly smiling, felt it too. When she dabbed a crumb of food from Hansen's beard with her napkin, they all smiled like idiots in some dicky TV show.

Things had changed, and he began to have dinner with Hansen and Evelyn every few days. There was no mention of work, but he knew what he was there for.

Near dusk he'd rock up, and after a drink in the suite they'd head out: Hansen in his island print shirts, Evelyn in strapless dresses, nice shoes, and makeup, and Seth happy to have the chance to wear some of his nice threads.

Usually keeping it in-house, they'd start at the Pacific Harbour Bar with its inlet view, before heading down to The Waterfront restaurant, where Mr. Kamsler himself might stop by and spend a few minutes chatting.

After dinner, Evelyn would retire to the suite, and Seth and Hansen would hit the cosy Gallery Bar, where the old skipper would inevitably hold court.

It would usually start with some bloke on his own, or an amiable couple, and before long Hansen would have the whole place listening to him.

From a rundown of current weather conditions to an analysis of astral navigation, he'd move on to tales of the decadent, pre-war ports of south-east Asia or of battling big seas while pulling off dangerous but lucrative salvage jobs on remote Pacific reefs.

He should be filmed, thought Seth. Not just as a record of a time nearly gone but as pure entertainment: for here were real-life adventure tales of derring-do, deftly spun with outrageous anecdote, pirate humour, and hard-won insight. He felt bloody lucky being there.

On other nights, they'd go across the road to Tawny's, or they'd taxi it the few blocks north to the other Kamsler hotel, the Tradewinds, and spend three or four hours at The Outrigger, enjoying the superlative food and service.

There were probably another half a dozen or so places around town worth eating at, but Hansen wasn't much interested in trying them. He could be a crude bastard at times, but he knew quality when it hit his mouth.

They caught music at Dukes, Hansen instructing him to look out for gigs with the pianist and singer they'd seen, and those nights were sweet. With low lights and quality drinks, people in their upmarket clothes digging the silky smooth vibe, it felt grown-up, even big city.

Then one Tuesday, Seth was in town getting a bit of cash out, when he saw that his retainer hadn't gone in. In case of a clerical error, he gave it a couple of days, but there was still no money from Hansen in the account.

Leaving the bank, he went to a milk bar and got a mango Weis bar. On the pavement, he ate it and had a think.

Getting paid to eat and drink and listen to stories was a lurk; truly money for nothing, but wasn't he Hansen's minder now? With possibly other Eddie Sunshines about, wasn't it worth keeping him on a retainer?

Ringing up Hansen to find out what the story was didn't feel right, though. This sort of thing was better broached man-to-man over a drink or two.

Unease fluttered as he realised he hadn't got the call for dinner in the last few days. There was a tap in an alleyway up ahead, and he washed his hands, then walked the block to the Pacific International.

Simon was on and they exchanged greetings.

"He's not here," said Simon, "Checked out Monday."

Unaccountably, Seth felt a pang of loss.

"Yeah, I know," he lied. "I was just passing, so I thought I'd pop in and say hello."

"Oh, hello," said Simon.

"Hey, listen." Seth took out his wallet. "You wanna do a bit of business with me?"

"Ooo, what's on your mind?"

Seth gave Simon a business card.

"Oh, I see. Mr. Marvin said you were a private dick."

Seth leant in. "What's this . . . this dick thing?"

In a swirl of cologne, Simon leant in too. "Dick thing?"

"Yeah . . . this private dick thing."

The receptionist pealed with laughter.

"A private dick is a private eye, Seth. Humphrey Bogart. Old movies. It's American."

Somewhat illuminated, Seth straightened up.

"So, this bit of business with me?" said Simon.

"I might need my own private eye in the hotel at times."

"What does that entail?"

"Just information," said Seth. "When a guest comes and goes, the length of their stay. That sort of thing."

"Nothing illegal?"

"Nothing illegal."

"Damn."

Seth laughed. "So . . . when's he back?"

The receptionist's eyes took on a snakish cast.

"Don't you know? I thought he was your client."

Seth took a ten from his wallet. Simon smiled.

"He's back on the eighteenth of next month."

Seth slid the money forward. The receptionist raised a hand. "Introductory offer. On the house."

Like an all-knowing god, Hansen rang that night.

"I'm in Sydney for a month or so. There are some things I can't pay to avoid."

"So, I'm not on a retainer anymore?"

There was a sound of derision. "Money, money, money. You ever dream of a time when you're beyond it?"

"It won't be on this planet," said Seth.

Hansen laughed. "I'll see you when I get back."

"OK, but I might have a client, so . . ."

"Whatever," said Hansen, hanging up.

In the kitchen, Seth stared into the fridge. Grabbing a beer, he sat out the back and glared at the starry night.

He felt mucked around, played with. And he'd gone the sook over the bastard today. Don't get mixed up here, he told himself. He's a client, not a mate.

Work kept on not rolling in, and with time on his hands, he went and made amends.

Outside Uncle Owen's, he waited late one afternoon for the pink two-door Corolla that Jeffyman drove to pull up. When it did, he took a couple of coldies from a little Esky, popped the crowns, and went over.

Jeffyman sat there grinning with undiluted pleasure at seeing a mate offering him a knock-off beer before he'd even got out of his car.

"Talk about service," he laughed.

Leaning against the Corolla, they drank beer; Jeffyman sighing at his first big swallow, Seth pleased that things were cool between them again. Jeffyman was good that way. He might get angry fast, but he'd move on fast, too, without grudge or bullshit. Just like a real mate.

Jeffyman told him about his new job wiring up offices on Sheridan Street, and Seth almost told him about the trip out on the reef. But it would be better with a joint and a few nips of rum. After another beer, they parted, with pencilled-in plans to catch a band when they next went out.

On a roll, he made dinner at Uncle Don's, knocking up a veal stroganoff and rice that Aunt Mary said was as good as Mum's. Uncle Don looked okay. He'd been with Dad on the farm helping with the gardens, and they'd even gone fishing off Kurrimine Beach a couple of times.

Inspired by this, Seth drove down and helped Dad redo the back terraces, a job they'd been talking about for ages. The railway sleepers were okay, but the flitchers, always a stop-gap measure, were just about rotted out.

At the Mulgrave River, they collected trailer loads of dark river stones. With Seth mixing the mortar and Dad working the string line, they set to work and made some groovy new garden beds.

Using up the last of the mix, Seth trowelled it over a corner. Picking up a twig, he scratched his name and the date into it. Dad took the stick and did the same.

Looking at their names, Seth felt both the presence and absence of Mum and Alex. He knew his father felt it too. Huge guilt and bone-deep grief swamped him, and that fatal moment replayed in his head.

Popping in on Mum at the farm, Dad down in Brisbane for a couple of weeks. Alex inside when he arrived, a tarp-covered load in the tray of his ute. Curious, going over, leaning down. The smell of something familiar. Loosening the tarp on one side, pulling it open, looking in. Plastic and tape-sealed bags. Jesus, Alex had like twenty pounds of dope there.

If only you'd stood up to him and followed through with the threat to tell Mum about the dope. They wouldn't have gone to the Tablelands, and they wouldn't have –

Dad chuckled, the sound chasing the darkness away.

"Hang on," he said. "I've got an idea."

Darting off to the shed, he returned with a handful of glittering things. "Come on," he said, "before it sets."

A few minutes later, two mirror shard and brass lug nut flowers were set into the cement next to the names.

"Very hippy," said Seth, loving his father like crazy.

"Never too late to change your spots, son."

Dad went and put the kettle on. As Seth cleaned up, he heard the phone ring. He hosed down the wheelbarrow, washed and dried the tools, and put everything away.

Up at the house, Dad was on the back steps, smiling like a country kid at the Cairns show. The phone call must be good news, maybe even a job.

Dad laughed now. Seth grinned in anticipation.

"What?" he said, coming to the foot of the steps.

"Guess who's moving up here?"

Seth's smile exploded. From the joy in Dad's voice, he knew just who.

Made of Purple Glass

"Uncle Seth! Uncle Seth!"

The little girl ran down the steps of the house at Palm Cove, her cries setting off a couple of top-knot doves, their feathers sounding the alarm as they flew away.

Overjoyed at her glee, Seth flung the little screamer up into the air and caught her in his arms. She wriggled as he rubbed her face with his nose, her hair flying everywhere.

"I missed you," said Sophie, and she bestowed a serious kiss on his forehead. He held her close, feeling her heart beating against his bicep. Slinging her onto his hip, he turned and looked at Lou standing on the front steps.

She smiled at him. He hadn't seen her in close to a year. Though she'd finished her degree at Lismore, she was still studying, a career in psychology in her sights.

After Alex died, Lou rented out the house, picking a top tenant; a TAA aero mechanic and his family. They loved the place and had kept it in good order over the years.

Bought with the dope money, it was where Sophie was supposed to grow up. But like Seth, Lou had left right after the funeral, and Sophie had gone from burbling toddler to primary school princess in the bosom of Lou's family down south.

Over the last couple of years, Lou began reconnecting with far north Queensland, making an annual trip to see friends, and her Kelly family. Each time Seth had offered his place, but Lou was happy staying with mates, or at the farm with Dad.

They'd always got on, Dad absolutely stoked to see her, and his one and only grandchild. They'd stay for a week or so, and it would thrill the old bloke no end.

Sophie loved Dad too, and they gardened together. He had knocked up a kid-sized rake for her, and they'd potter about having raves about the trees and worms, and the big golden orb spider who lived by the shed.

When they stayed with Dad, Seth had driven down, and it had been wonderful. Even better – Sophie had slept over with him at Cinderella Street. Twice.

He'd shown her how to fish and find pipis in the sand, and she'd learnt how to put a record on: with clean hands, and without touching any grooves, keeping it real steady as the needle touched the platter.

She liked the Mentals and Boris the Spider by The Who, even a bit of Hawkwind. Seth loved how she called out for more volume if she liked a track. What a girl.

Two years ago, they'd all camped for a week with the Knuckeys at Ella Bay, and he'd thrilled Sophie with the burning ball. Under his close supervision, she'd been allowed to kick it flaming along the beach. Her screams of delight had nearly burst his eardrums. His heart too.

"Uncle Seth," whispered Sophie, her eyes looking out from under her fringe at her mum. "Am I staying with you sometimes?"

Seth nodded slowly, making big, you-sure-are eyes, and she giggled into his head. Glowing with happiness, he went up the steps and gave Lou a peck on the cheek. For a wonderful second, they were all very close.

"Cuppa?" said Lou. Seth beamed, and nodded.

As they went inside, Sophie began squirming, and he let her down. With a shout of glee, she ran up the hall, feet thumping on the wooden floor. With a grin, he watched her. When he turned back, he saw Lou look away and go quickly go into the kitchen. With his head suddenly light, he followed her into the bright, breezy room.

A builder mate of Alex's had knocked two rooms into one, installing the open-plan kitchen with the view of the sea that Lou had wanted. As she filled the jug, Seth leant against a shiny new stove and looked around.

On the counter: the keys to the Honda Civic in the car port; a soft leather handbag; and a carved wooden bowl cradling a hand of ladyfinger bananas and a bombshell of a pawpaw. A bright one-piece swimsuit was draped over one of the modern chrome and wood stools at the counter.

Lou reached to get mugs from a shelf, her t-shirt riding up off her hips. Seth quickly came off the stove and went into the living room.

It smelt faintly of incense and nice perfume, the sea breeze bringing a tang of salt. Some of the old furniture was still here; the dining setting the wood-working wizard at Daintree had made, looking a little scratched but still solid. Through the French windows on the long verandah, he could see the planters' chairs he and Alex had salvaged from a ruined Queenslander off Syndicate Road.

A big Dr. Seuss book and an interior design magazine lay on a new lounge suite; the slew of big-eyed dolls, paper cocktail umbrellas, and bright plastic jewellery scattered across them were signs of serious play.

A vase of white hibiscus shimmered on the dining table, beside it a ceramic bowl filled with seashells and glossy black burny beans, and a little four-sided bottle made of purple glass. Turning from the table, Seth looked up the hall to the master bedroom.

They drank their cuppas sitting on the front stairs: the sun behind the house, and the beach almonds and Queen of the Seas across the road cooing with top-knots. Sophie flew up and down the verandah in imitation of the big jet plane that had brought her to Cairns.

With succinct questions, Lou got the drum on Seth's life since they'd last connected. Heavy shit had gone down, desperate moments with dangerous men; death close and grinning in his face. He'd also found another depth to the tragedy his family had endured, another rampart of regret to surmount. But he wasn't telling Lou any of that.

Cherry-picking the crazy fun stuff, he told her about the tiger shark last year and the strange creature he'd seen up in Malaan, and, of course, Kelly Investigations.

Unlike just about everyone else, she didn't take the piss. She asked questions, and made some suggestions about finding more clients that made good sense.

Then she brought him up to speed with her plans. She was back for maybe a year, and was keen to fix up the house with renovations, garden beds, and a covered deck out the back. She wanted everything tip-top so it could be put on the market. Or not. She wasn't sure yet.

Seth nodded encouragingly through his dismay.

Lou put a hand on his arm, and her eyes lit up for him. Sophie would go to primary school at Machans. He could collect her on a Friday. They'd have weekends together.

He liked that. Time with Sophie was great. And he'd be good family, too, so Lou could have some time to herself, even go out with her girlfriends for a dance and a drink.

Now something nasty wriggled in his head. Lou would meet a fella out dancing. He'd stay the night and one day move in, and he'd make Sophie breakfast and comfort her when something went bump in the night.

Smiling at Lou, he tore himself away from this slimy thought and faced what was really crumbling his biscuit – the idea of selling the house. He'd put up close to half the money, loaning his brother a big chunk of the profits from a crop. Alex had just about pleaded with him, saying that for the price, it was an opportunity too good to miss, and that it would help him and Lou get started as a family.

It had been a good idea then, and it was a good idea now. Sophie should grow up here, by the sea, up in the north, and in his life. It was her house, really.

The funny thing was, though, none of this was on paper. Only Alex had known about the money.

"I'm going to do a master's," said Lou.

"Oh, wow," said Seth.

"With that sort of qualification I could set up a practice in Brisbane, the Gold Coast, wherever."

"That's great, Lou."

He pushed away his irritation and the sense of Lou as a carpetbagger only up here to make some bucks out of the house. He wasn't going to say anything right now. She said a year, and things could change in a year.

They had tea together, sitting on the verandah as the sky went pink over the sea. There was melaleuca swamp along the back boundary, but no mozzies. Lou had got the place sprayed before she'd come up.

They ate in happy silence, Sophie singing to herself at times, the insects and frogs providing a backing track. While Lou showered her, Seth tuned in the stereo and TV.

A sparkly but sleepy Sophie came out for a goodnight kiss, the promise of tomorrow making them both smile.

While Lou put her to bed, Seth sat on the verandah with a beer. On the empty street, an Atlas moth as big as a bird fluttered about before settling on a big timber power pole, its wingtips showing on both sides. Seth toasted it.

Looking up the verandah, he saw that the stuff he and Alex had collected fishing and diving was all still there. The rope-woven glass fishing buoys, the giant clamshells, and something never credibly identified – a lump of metal corroded inside a chunk of coral rock. The aero mechanic must have dug the maritime vibes.

Like the farm, the house held memories. He'd visited infrequently, never feeling relaxed. Seeing his brother always made that black box of bad stuff inside him grow heavier.

As he thought of all the darkness caught inside him, the lid of the box flipped open, and he was back at Cairns Base Hospital six years ago, his jaw wired together and his head pounding from the awful bashing he'd got from Alex up in Kuranda.

Lying there doped up in a filthy nest of pain, thinking about leaving Cairns. Alex and Lou suddenly there in the room, coming up to his bed. Lou smiling faintly at Seth to show she was okay, Alex putting a stack of new bike and shooting magazines on the bed, pulling up chairs, talking a mile a minute, loudly filling the room with his bonhomie and bullshit.

Seth looking at Lou, searching for marks, seeing the truth but wanting to hear it from his brother. Writing on the pad, pushing it at Alex, who read it and recoiled, his voice righteous. "No way, mate."

Seth felt shame, apology, but saw none on his brother's face. It was like nothing had happened, Alex grinning, the tough guy's tough guy, his vibe – boys will be boys, blood's thicker than water. Seth blinking, fighting that rough status quo – and his love for his brother.

Alex, his tone wise and lenient, exonerating everybody with a post-mortem of the raid. Then lauding Seth for keeping Lou out of jail, and calling her Lulu and Luluwa; private lovers' names, the exclusion made clear. Winning a smile from her, he amplified it on his own face and gave it to Seth. Charm overdrive, grand forgiveness – they were a family again.

But when they left, Seth in a mess of emotion and pain, Alex had ducked back in, that killer smile lighting his face, his eyes gleaming with emotion. As he came up to the bed, Seth felt a rush of love, and a desperately wanted forgiveness from his brother took hold of him.

Alex leaned in, his voice low. 'Go anywhere near her again and I'll fuckin' kill you.'

"How's your beer?" said Lou from the kitchen. The lid on the black box slammed shut. He turned and smiled.

"I'm good, Lou."

Solid Quietude

It was better than cool: Sophie and Lou living just north of him. Having the little groover in his life was the best thing in a long time. Knowing she was around made him wake up with a smile and go to sleep with one.

As planned, Sophie enrolled at Machans Primary, and he felt pretty excited the first time he went to pick her up.

As kids came out, he saw Sophie talking to someone he knew, Sunny, who worked as a teacher's aide. Seeing him waiting, she smiled, and the unease he'd felt at seeing her ebbed away.

Nearly half his age again, Sunny lived in a little cottage on the esplanade at Machans. Part bushie, part hippie, she was an avid gardener who liked a smoke and a chat, and was hopefully still a friend.

Earlier in the year, he'd mucked it up with her. She'd overreacted and there'd been . . . a clash. Now they were attempting to renew their friendship, putting in the time for a chat when they bumped into each other outside the post office or store.

It had been mutual bloody awkwardness at first, but by exchanging apologies they'd got to a level of semi-relaxed dignity. They might not ever be tight, but he sure wasn't having any bad vibes with her. She was too cool for that.

"This is my Uncle Seth," proclaimed Sophie. "He's tall."

"Hello, Uncle Seth." Sunny had a twinkle in her eyes. He grinned foolishly. "Hey Sunny."

"You know each other," said Sophie.

Seth smiled at the smarty-pants. "Yeah, we do."

"Why? You don't have any kids."

"Oh, Machans is small. You meet everyone eventually." Smiling, Sunny waited.

"My brother's wife is back in town," he said.

Compassion touched her eyes. She knew about Alex.

"Well, that's great that you two can get to hang out. Isn't it Sophie?" she said.

The little girl whooped in affirmation, thrust her hand into Seth's. "He's taking me to the beach."

Seth paused, the little girl pulling on his hand.

"Hey, this is cool . . . you being here, Sunny," he said. "She gets to hang out with you. It's wonderful."

Appreciation warmed Sunny's face, and they shared a good smile.

Twenty-five minutes later, Sophie was running along Ellis Beach like a jet plane, making a roaring sound with her arms spread. Seth soared along beside her, making his own aeronautical sounds, and, man, it was fun.

Before long, he was spending just about every weekend with Sophie, picking her up on a Friday and dropping her back on Sunday. There were a string of beaches from his place north, and soon Sophie knew them all.

On Oak Beach they looked for crystals, six-sided points of clear and smokey quartz washed down from the coastal range. Overhead, a pair of sea eagles circled, occasionally swooping down to claim a fish they were stalking. Sophie loved it, bottling up her squeal of excitement so as not to scare the birds away from their dinner.

Yorkeys Knob and Trinity were cool too, but Ellis Beach became a favourite. After paddling in the creek mouth by the cabins, they'd take a freshwater dip in the creek-fed pool behind the café car park, Seth piggybacking her over the rocks to get there.

After the swim they'd have an ice-block at the café. He'd make a show of getting their mango Weis bars from the freezer. Savouring his with gusto made her laugh, but, smart girl, she also saw how deadly serious he was.

Lou hadn't changed that much. She didn't smoke dope anymore, not that she did much back then, but she liked a couple of drinks with dinner, sometimes a few more.

That sense of self-possession had deepened. Never one for small talk, she was content not saying anything if there was nothing to say. He didn't mind that, as they did things instead. Like gardening.

Compact and capable, with her brown hair pulled back in a girlish ponytail, Lou made a no-nonsense work-mate. They put in gardenia bushes out the front, pulling out the big stands of ginger going wild. The Bougainvillea taking over the garage got the big prune, and a geriatric she-oak, its top blown off, came out stump and all.

They laid garden beds in along the northern side of the house, planted ornamentals, and replaced a whole heap of dud pickets along the fence line. They made drains and culverts, and put in a stack of bromeliads. They also began collecting plants for when the back deck was built. There were dozens of gardening jobs to do, and he put in some long hours.

Helping out was a good family thing to do, but it was a real kick being around Lou. Her solid quietude gave him a comfort he hadn't expected. Their shared tragedy, though unmentioned, was sublimated into the day-to-day stuff they were doing. It felt natural and healing, and he wasn't ashamed to admit that he needed a bit of that.

He was pleased that they didn't talk about him. There was nothing to say, and only he knew the truth, and he wasn't telling anyone – not Lou, not Dad. It was just another horrible secret locked away in the black box.

Lou looked great, a clean-cut mix of a tomboy and the girl-next door, moving with a sweet physicality that had always attracted blokes. Fit and bright, she looked *on*, turned up, but relaxed with it.

Careful not to get caught, he rationed himself to an occasional sly peek of appreciation. Lou, in her focused way, wouldn't have noticed anyhow.

A few times a week they'd all eat tea together, usually after gardening. Sitting out on the verandah, laughing and eating, with the waves on the beach and the warm velvet night around them, soon felt like the most natural thing in the world.

Being part of something bigger than himself made him understand why blokes got wrapped up in being family men. Once synonymous with surrender to straightdom, it felt like something really worthy now, and the house at Palm Cove began to feel like a home.

In daylight hours, it was busy. Sheets of roofing tin were replaced, and a new toilet and laundry got built out the back. Six stumps, the front window sills, and a back door were replaced, and the postholes for the deck were dug.

The interior was going to be repainted, and the floors sanded and polished. When this all happened, Lou and Sophie would go and stay with Dad and friends, and Seth would keep an eye on the place.

Totally efficient, Lou found tradesmen, got quotes, and set it all in motion. Seth had offered his help, even happy to provide some money saving labour, but aside from the gardening there was nothing she wanted him to do.

Some blokes might have been a bit put out by a woman being in control, but Seth was relieved. Manual labour, tools, all of that, was profoundly boring, sweaty, and dirty.

With all the work, a few bucks were being spent, that's for sure, and he wondered how Lou, a single mum without an income, was paying for it. He guessed her family, or an inheritance, maybe even savings.

One night, with Sophie asleep, and Lou on a third glass of wine, he brought it up.

Taking a good hit of plonk, Lou smiled.

"I suppose I can tell you. There's nobody else I can."

Seth got it right away. It was pretty obvious, really.

"Alex had money hidden away. A lot," said Lou.

The thirty grand he'd given Alex flashed through his head, and he felt a flash of hate. Jesus, his brother's selfish rat cunning was astounding.

"Well, that was good of him. He used to spend it fast."

"Oh, I had to find it. He never told me about it."

She didn't seem too upset, but anger lit up the inside of Seth's skull.

"He'd been up in the garage roof for no obvious reason, and when I asked him why, I got brushed off in this funny way. So after the funeral, I got the stepladder and spent a mucky half hour crawling around up there and found it."

"Good work, Lou," Seth toasted her.

"I put half of it away for Sophie, for university, study, whatever education she wants to do after high school."

"That's smart, Lou. Very cool."

"And you? You're alright for money?" she said.

"Yeah, yeah, I'm fine."

Smiling reflectively at him, she stroked her arm.

"You're a survivor, aren't you?"

Without thinking, he said, "I'm still here."

Her hand stopped, her smile unfaltering.

Embarrassed, he drank beer, thinking about how he'd mulled over giving her money. The business account had filled up nicely, and Dad would be right up for helping two people he loved dearly. And he still had money coming from Burns. But with Alex's sneaky stash now revealed, it didn't matter anymore. I suppose that's something I can thank the bastard for, he thought.

Then his own bright fiscal future called, Burns ringing from what sounded like Mareeba, the twang of Dusty or Merl and the crack of a pool ball break in the background. He was coming to Cairns tonight, and they'd go and see the 'cousins' early next morning. The cousins were doing fine, but Burns wanted uncle to have a cuppa with them.

Seth had been following the weather on ABC radio and TV, checking the synoptics in the paper, and even ringing a mate up in Julatten, and it looked like there'd been some rain up there. Maybe enough to keep the creek running so that the plants could reach peak form.

Driving up the next day, a cheery Burns confirmed it. They'd got handy rain, and the plants were looking like show winners, he said. He wasn't telling lies.

As they walked through what was now a forest of plants, many over two metres high, Seth was happily impressed. Burns buzzed with enthusiasm, constantly touching the plants, running his hands through leaves, softly squeezing heads and sniffing his fingers.

Seth had to laugh. Burns had been hooked completely by the horticultural process and was compelled to give it his best shot. Strutting along like a rooster in a cowdy hat, he was fairly glowing with pride at his prowess.

Seth knew that growing things well could make a bloke feel good, but what made this a real hoot was that it was a drug squad detective doing it.

As instructed, they'd been cutting off the shade leaves, shaping each branch ever closer to the end product. Some plants were better than others; they might produce a good pound, the weedier ones closer to half that.

"Look at this," said Burns with a grin, and he led Seth down the far end of the crop. A few metres into the scrub was a structure of branches, canvas, and camo netting.

In its shade, Rockjaw was looking at Seth through the scope of a rifle. Fully bearded now, he wore a bush hat. As soon as Seth saw him, he lowered the rifle.

Behind him, cigarette smoke betrayed Silent Smoker, his own attempt at manly hairiness downright disturbing. The idiot was reclining in a nest of beer cartons, his pistol laying on his chest. You wankers, thought Seth.

"The boys like it down here. Maybe too much. I reckon they're going feral on me," said Burns.

"We'll go feral on anyone sniffing around here, I can tell you that," said Rockjaw, his sunnies trained on Seth.

"Groaoowww!" Burns shook his head like a dog with its teeth in something. "You get 'em!"

As they walked back through the thick, pungent rows, Seth just knew the bastard was looking through the rifle scope at him.

"That's a stupid idea," he said.

Burns looked at him. "What's a stupid idea?"

"That little set-up they've got back there."

"Aw c'mon, mate. It hot and not much fun out here."

"Yeah, I know all about it. But it's bullshit. A static position like that is not only a target, it also gets you thinking the whole world revolves around your little hideout. Big mistake."

All ears, Burns watched Seth as they walked.

"We just dealt with it. You find the different places that get the breeze and shade throughout the day and move between them, quietly, slowly, looking at the area from every angle. When you feel like you know every square inch of it – that's when you'll see what shouldn't be there."

"You learnt that growing marijuana?"

"Yeah, and from a mate who went on long-range patrols in Southeast Asia."

As soon as he said it, Seth knew it was a mistake.

Stopping quickly, Burns blocked his way.

"Those fellas from Cape Tribulation?"

Seth knew just who he meant, the papers had been full of it, but the detective was barking up the wrong tree.

"Nah, a bloke in Sydney," he lied. "Mixes bands at gigs nowadays."

"You know a lot of people, don't you?" said Burns.

Seth shrugged. Burns looked at him seriously.

"That's really worth something," he said.

Though he'd been living a life of duplicity since his late teens, Seth had never been that cool with it. Unlike Alex, who saw it all as a big game to be played with manic relish.

Outside underage drinking and spins in hot cars, it was the illegality of marijuana that had driven his double life. In itself, dope was harmless, no matter what the straight world said. But the lies, black money, and illegal firearms were the inevitable spin-offs of growing it – forced upon him by laws that he knew one day would be gone.

For years, day in and day out, he'd played double man, lying to family and friends while all around him everyday citizens did everyday things. Most people had no idea.

Moving between the straight and bent worlds required one's wits and a bit of mental resilience. Things might get heavy and out of control, but those two worlds must never meet. He'd got clever at moving from one to the other, but now it was starting to feel downright freaky.

To come from a world of dangerous blokes stinking of violence to the sweet feminine energy of Lou and Sophie was a real jolt, the disconnect making him queasy.

One Saturday, he took Sophie fishing at Kewarra Beach. She got bored when nothing took the bait, so they walked along the beach to Taylor Point. He was so pleased to see her watching the sea for something to appear. Just like me as a kid, he thought: two souls just the same.

She saw the dolphin first, excitedly running down to the water. He followed, feeling a rush of pride at her clear-sighted connection with the world. Watching the dolphin surface at intervals, she yelled out hello each time, and he joined in.

When the fun had swum past, they continued walking, their footsteps squeaking on the sand. Coming towards the point, they saw a fishing camp under the sheoaks: canvas tarps, driftwood poles, a battered tinny with an outboard, and a clutch of twenty-litre drums. A couple of blokes sat smoking, mending nets. Behind the camp, a woman moved through stands of pandanus.

"Who are they?" said Sophie as they went past.

"Just people. Fishermen, probably. Between boats."

"Don't they have homes?"

"Maybe, or they could be travelling around camping."

The north was dotted with people living rough like this. It had always been.

"What about if it rains? They'll get wet."

"They've got tarps. They know what they're doing."

"I have a home," said Sophie, looking perturbed.

"You've got two. One at Cinderella Street with me and one at Palm Cove with your mum. You're a lucky girl."

On the point, they sat on warm rocks, the sea foaming

near their feet. Sophie looked at him. She looked worried, obviously still concerned about the people in the camp.

"What happened to Daddy?" she said.

Seth hid his surprise. What was this? Sophie knew that Alex had died in a car accident when she was still a baby.

"What do you mean, sweetie?"

"He was never around."

Too young to remember, she was repeating something she'd heard from Lou. He felt sorrow, and relief.

It was a blessing she'd been too young to know. Things had got real crazy that last year, his brother going off the rails big time.

After setting up the house, Alex got back into it with the boys – and girls. Besides the rooting around, he smoked bongs, snorted speed, and if there was acid around, he'd take it too – all while smoking thirty Rothmans a day and sinking a boatload of grog.

Seth had been busy working doors, growing dope, and being a boyfriend, or friend in need, and he hardly saw his brother. When they did have a drink, the past made it claustrophobic, and talk would die.

Alex had done a lot of bad shit, things that had put him right off, but he always made it feel like it was Seth who'd buggered things up between them.

One time, to his shock, his brother brought it up.

Alex red-faced, drunk as, tripping too. The National on a Friday night full of hard-cases, fishermen, crims, and apprentice arseholes, the Aztecs blasting on the jukebox, Lobby Loyde smashing out the solo.

I never asked you said Alex. How was it? How was

what? he said. Lou, said Alex. Nice aye? Tight too.

Guts rolling in dismay, he looked away, saw some fella in a cut-off shirt vomiting over a bar stool.

You little cunt, wanting what I had. Couldn't keep your dirty paws off her. Alex grinning like it was a joke, his eyes acid mad.

You nearly broke us up. She wouldn't let me near her for ages. No kisses, nothing. She took off to Ballina for two fuckin' months and I had to go down and fucking beg. Beg! And I hadn't done a thing. It was you. My own fuckin' brother.

He tried to keep clear of his brother after that. He heard the stories, and it was clear that Alex's carousing wasn't a last hurrah before settling down. Nah, this was an extra life adjacent to the one he had with Lou and Sophie. He'd just strapped it on or something.

It went downhill fast, Alex falling back in with the Mac brothers, two of the nastiest bastards in the far north by then. Instead of just leaving them in his past, he'd tried second-time lucky.

"Maybe he was busy," he said to Sophie.

The little girl's face flickered with doubt. She knew she was getting the run around. With anger grating inside, he fired up a smile, and leant down. "You okay, sweetie?"

She looked at the rocks by their feet. "They're listening to us."

A scattering of tiny crabs had appeared. Seth laughed cheerfully, hopped up and brushed sand from his hands.

"Let's go back, hey? We'll get a mango Weis bar."

Sophie got down from the rocks, looking at the crabs,

and whispered, "I hope they didn't hear what we said."

Walking back, with Sophie looking out for the dolphin, he tried not to let the past spoil the moment.

A few days later, something else came slinking in from the past – something he didn't mind at all.

Taking a break from gardening and drinking ice water, he snuck a look at Lou, checking out her full, damp t-shirt, her smooth legs smudged with dirt. She caught his look and smiled.

Keeping his cool, he floated a placid smile back. Her eyes changed, and he saw the zing of lust. Stunned, his heart accelerated from zero to a hundred in a second.

Teetering on the brink, they looked at each other. He wanted it very much, but he kept very still, willing her to make the first move.

And she did, stumbling in her haste, and they kissed, her gorgeousness moulding into him, her hands taking hold of his waist. As bliss blew the top of his head off, she jumped away from him and ran into the house.

He nearly fell over – she'd been right there in his arms! Throwing his head back, he breathed deeply instead of roaring loudly. Lady's prerogative, but damn, it had felt so right, and she knew it too.

Staring at the sky, crazy thoughts whirled through his head of a future solid and inconceivably sweet.

Giving it a few minutes, he went around the front, and on the verandah made his footfall deliberately loud. At the front door, he paused.

"Coo-ee," he called out in the voice of a gumnut baby,

wanting to keep it light. Lou appeared from the bathroom, came down the hall. She looked distressed – not her style at all. "I'm sorry, Seth."

Seth waited, but she didn't have any more. She tried to smile, making a mess of it, obviously in a real stew. So was he, but he popped out a goodie of a smile.

"It's all cool, Lou. Just, y'know . . . a near-hit."

Her smile began to stabilise.

"Like a meteorite and a spaceship. That's us."

It was nice saying 'us.'

She came up, looking so grateful it hurt. Seth stayed put at the doorway, a clumsy smile on his face. Oh, baby, he thought, we really clicked just then.

Back in control, Lou gave it to him straight.

"Let's just keep it family, hey?"

He wished it wasn't so, but he could only agree.

It was cool between them after that; no problems there. They worked in the garden and hung out like nothing had happened. In her switched-on, forthright way, Lou had quickly moved on, and he really dug that.

It wasn't surprising really, but more of their shared past appeared – this time not so nice.

Late one afternoon he got a call from Lou asking if he could come over.

"The back deck is finished," she said. "But the builder's handed me a new invoice that's hundreds of dollars more than what I've already paid. He's talking like he wants something else in payment."

Seth blinked, a sudden salty taste in his mouth.

"I'll be right over. Keep him outside."

He drove too fast, overtaking car after car. Lou met him at the front door, looking unfussed.

She handed him an invoice. "I've paid this one." Seth read the total, and smiled reassuringly. "I'll fix this."

Out on the new deck, the tradie stood with one boot on his tool box, a thwarted frown smearing his face at the sight of Seth. "You said he was dead," he said to Lou.

"This is his brother," said Lou.

"Ohhh, I see." The tradie gave them a slimy grin.

"Let's have a look," said Seth, gesturing for the invoice the bastard was holding.

"Nah, mate – this business is with the lady."

Seth went in fast, plucked the invoice from the prick's fingers, and stood right next to him – real close. Suddenly getting the vibe, the tradie stumbled back off his tool box.

Seth compared invoices. The new one was five hundred bucks more.

"She's paid," he said. "End of story."

"The price of timber, mate. With all the building going on at the moment, it went up," said the tradie.

"By what percent?" Seth shook the invoices.

"Aye?"

"By what fucking percent?"

"Ah . . . nearly fifteen I think."

Seth snarled in disgust, his voice rising. "You can't even remember what you wrote! C'mon, let's go."

Grabbing the scammy shit's toolbox, he quickly went up the side of the house. The bastard followed, baying for his property. Out the front, Seth banged the toolbox down on the tray of the fella's ute.

Red-faced, the tradie attempted to re-stoke his bogus claim, but Seth screwed up the new invoice and pegged it at the prick's head.

"Account closed," he said. "Now piss off. You show your tiny head around here again, and I'll –"

With a wild roar he jumped forward, fists clenched. The tradie ran around his ute, scrambled in and slammed the door, and peered fearfully out like a tourist in a big game safari park. In stern command, Seth pointed up the street. From the corner of his eye, he saw Lou watching from the front door of the house.

With a stream of muffled swearing, the tradie drove off, Seth smiling meanly in farewell. When he turned back to the house, Lou was gone.

Then he saw Sophie, her face pale behind the glass of the front bedroom window. The bewilderment in her eyes punched him in the heart. Jesus! She must have seen what had just happened, summoned to the window by the tradie's cries of outrage.

Shame hit him. He'd forgotten that she'd be here. But he hadn't touched the bloke. He'd roared and capered about, that's all, and that might look like fun to a six-year-old. So, he roared and capered about like the big sillies did on Playschool, and thank God, she was laughing at him now. He threw her an extravagant wave and she gave him a goofy wave back. With a final roar and caper, he blew her a kiss and went back out to the deck.

Lou was examining the finished work, silently checking out joins and screwheads. She was pretty engrossed, and Seth gave it some attention too. It looked pretty good.

"What?" he said after a bit. "That's what you wanted, right? Puff up the feathers, show some teeth?"

"Yeah, it was," she said. "Thanks."

Her eyes lingered on him in uneasy contemplation.

"What?" said Seth.

"You looked just like him,"

Men Got Eaten

"Kelly, I've got a bloke here you need to meet."

Hansen's smokey voice on the phone line lit up a smile on Seth's face. The old bastard was back.

"And bring a pry bar. Buy one if you have to."

"A pry bar?"

"Leave it in your vehicle when you come up. We'll go for a drive after that."

"Why a pry bar?"

"To do some prying with."

Hansen's mate was a smooth bloke with a gold Cartier watch, tailored slacks, a nice silk shirt, and what looked like Bass loafers on his feet. Mid-fifties, office pale, he had the hard-nosed look of a man who spent his days around serious money. With sharp eyes, he took in Seth's pressed chinos and freshly shined shoes.

"Gus Reynolds, Seth Kelly," said Hansen.

Reynolds smiled as he stuck out a hand, his teeth more than perfect.

"So, you're the fella who caught Dean Meadows with his hand in the till. And damn quick about it too, I hear."

Seth nodded as they shook.

"You have a card?" said Reynolds.

Seth handed one over. "What do you do, Gus?"

"I'm a lawyer."

"My lawyer," said Hansen. "The buck stops with him."

"But not with Meadows it seemed," said Seth.

Reynolds laughed, the old skipper a beat later.

"You're a funny man," said the lawyer.

"Gus is my earthly representative," said Hansen. "What he says goes."

Seth nodded at the lawyer to show he got it. Reynolds knew about the important stuff in Hansen's life. If the shit hit and broke the fan – this was the bloke who'd fix it.

With a return nod of confirmation, the lawyer slipped Seth's card into a slim wallet.

"Never know when I might need a good investigator," he said. "I'm in Sydney, but you'll travel?"

Seth nodded, and Hansen laughed mirthlessly.

"Hold on a sec, Gus – he's working for me."

"Jake, you're a businessman putting his affairs in order, and one day it will be done. Your needs are finite. I'm a lawyer – my needs are infinite."

They had a drink, and Seth got the drum. Reynolds was taking a well-earned holiday, booked into an island resort for a week of swimming and diving. He used to be fit, and tanned, but . . . well, he was hugely busy nowadays, what with Kerry Packer and those Western Australians digging stuff up. Thank God it paid so well, hey?

Seth was impressed, but he maintained a professional demeanour, looking relaxed but engaged.

Pretending exhaustion, Reynolds nodded at Hansen.

"But I had a bit of business with him first."

Over the last few days, the lawyer explained, he and Hansen had been working, and eating and drinking, even having what sounded like a party in the suite. He sighed happily, and turned his attention back onto Seth.

"You been to Sydney, Seth? Any big city?"

"Yeah, I know Sydney. Worked doors in Potts Point and the Cross, then armoured cars for Wormald and security at night for rock bands. Saw a lot of banks and clubs."

Reynolds looked impressed. "That's excellent. So you know how to handle the rough stuff."

"I'm a private investigator now," said Seth.

The lawyer smiled graciously. "Of course."

They talked about Sydney a bit over a second drink, and then Reynolds checked his Cartier watch. With a chuckle, he slapped Hansen on the back. "It's massage time again."

When he shook hands with Seth, his eyes honed in. "It's good to meet you, mate. We'll definitely catch up again."

With an explosion of knowing guffaws, Hansen saw his lawyer out, then went into his room.

Seth finished his beer, wondering what sort of work Gus Reynolds would have for him. It would be well paid, that's for sure. Real big league stuff.

Hansen came back out, his wet hair combed back in a frozen grey wave. "Okay, let's go to the airport," he said.

Down at reception, Simon was checking in a small group. Hansen went up to the counter, and stood next to them. In the midst of what he was doing, but so smooth that no one noticed, Simon hooked an envelope from the guest mail slots and manifested it by Hansen's hand.

Out on Spence Street, Hansen shook the envelope with appreciation. "A good kid. You'd be happy to have him on your crew."

At the airport, Seth parked as instructed by the freight sheds. Hansen showed the bloke on the counter some I.D, and signed a docket. They waited, listening to the bellow of a plane taking off. As the roar died away, a bloke came out with a small timber crate on a trolley.

"You'll be right with that," Hansen told Seth. Grabbing the crate by its rope handles, he had to agree. At the Pig, he put the crate between the bench seats in the back while Hansen did battle with the seat-belt.

When he got in, Hansen said, "McKenzie Street."

They didn't go into the house at first. Seth stood on the path, the crate and the pry-bar at his feet, while Hanson strode about letting off satisfied grunts as he inspected the trees and garden.

"I've spent a lifetime at sea," he said. "But I know how a garden should look. And the cleaning and maintenance. They're all doing a good job. They're a good family."

Inside, Seth took in the heady smell of the house again. In a corner of the landing, he saw a cast-iron boot scraper in the shape of a buxom mermaid holding up a seashell. On the built-in corner shelves above it sat two old leather binocular cases.

Going further in, he was absolutely stoked at what he saw. What he'd glimpsed that night hadn't really prepared him for the inspired interior of this old timber house.

Following Hansen, he saw that a master cabinet maker and his crew had been crucial in the house's construction.

The burnished panelling of the walls was finished along the edges with inspired parquetry; the big panels framed by hand-turned runners and blackwood ledging that ran above head height along the walls. The ventilation panels crowning the high doorways were intricately jig sawed in the shapes of birds, shells, and fish.

Everywhere was detail. Windows edged with stained-glass trims, chunky brass door locks with raised patterns of dolphins around the keyholes, window sills in semi-organic shapes, and in the pressed-tin ceiling, screened air vents precisely paired and well-located.

Tripping on this manifestation of skill and downright beauty, Seth kept turning his head to check it all out.

Hansen led him into a study and pointed to the floor. Seth put the crate down and looked at a fabulous built-in writing desk, its hutch an asymmetrical maze of recesses, some lockable with the keyholes empty. It was a treasure.

Around the desk and up the wall were bookshelves, one floating right out as a trophy display. More bookshelves lined a wall, the empty shelves flush to the ceiling.

Big black bean floorboards gleamed underfoot, almost maroon in the light coming from a bay window. Beneath the curve of the windows, there was a window seat with storage doors set beneath it. The study felt like a ships' cabin, with space neither wasted nor compromised.

"Open her up," said Hansen, and Seth used the prybar to pop the crate's lid. Inside, packed in tight with wads of hessian sacking, was a wooden chest.

Slapping the desk top, Hansen said, "Up here."

The chest felt full but not heavy, nothing moving in it.

Putting it on the desk, Seth stepped back. Hansen winked at him and sat down, a key now in his hand.

Made of dark pine, the chest looked old and innocuous; nothing flash. Hansen unlocked it and raised the lid to sit back on leather straps.

"Get a seat," he said, taking a fitted wooden tray out.

Moving the other chair in the study over, Seth sat down. Hansen took an old canvas bag from the tray and spilled an unbelievably beautiful gold necklace onto the desk top; its quality of work uncanny.

Stunned, Seth laughed in unfeigned pleasure, wonder bubbling up like spring water. Hansen's face lit up with a huge smile.

"How about that?" he chortled happily. "Y'see, there are such things as pirate treasure."

They grinned at each other for a moment, then Hansen looked down at this otherworldly shimmer of perfection.

"Gold. Javanese. Majapahit, so it's five hundred or so years old. Lovely piece."

Touching it, the old skipper moved the links around, his eyes unfocused. Then he slipped the necklace into the bag and put it back in the tray. He glanced at Seth's hands.

"You don't wear rings but look at this." He took a little leather box out. Inside was a fat gold ring set with a smooth purple stone like a half-sucked lolly.

"Also twenty-two carat, and set with Indian amethyst. Here, cast your eyes over it."

Taking the ring, Seth checked it out. Cast in gold, its shoulders and shank were decorated with ecclesiastical imagery; a shepherd's crook, a cross-topped sceptre, and a monkey with a lewd grin, its old fella halfway up a busty nun. Though not a churchie by a long stretch, Seth felt a spurt of shock. Hansen laughed.

"Made by a Malabar goldsmith for a lapsed English or French merchant, I'd say."

Though he wanted to examine every object that Hansen produced from the chest, the ring was the last thing he got to touch. With laconic commentary, the show and tell was a swift affair; everything held up for a moment, then put away, as though *ninjas* and *raskols* were about to come bursting in through the window.

"This is the handiwork of man," said Hansen, removing a handful of pig tusks from an oil-skin packet. Yellowing and acutely edged, each one spiralled around to at least a double circle.

"They knock the upper canines out, so the tusk curls through the gap." He held up one with three turns. "Very rare. A nice bit of dowry for a lovely young wife. Or better yet, some grease for a timber or fishing concession."

A woven pandanus box contained six golden cowries.

"I've had dozens pass through my hands, but these are flawless. Truly flawless."

Carefully opening a roll of tapa cloth, Hansen revealed four wooden implements, none longer than twenty-five centimetres. Beautifully carved, each one ended in four sharp prongs. One was long and slender, another squat. Very old and very dark, they seemed to swallow the light.

Feeling an involuntary shiver, Seth moved back in his chair. Looking at the forks, Hansen grunted in agreement.

"A lot of men got eaten with these."

When he rerolled the tapa around the implements, the sunlight outside seemed to go up a notch.

Hansen laid out a strange-looking dagger, its blade gold damascened, the flanged sides of the H-shaped horizontal grip finely ornamented in silver, the knuckle guard in the shape of a gorgeous flower. The work in it was incredible.

"Mughal katar," said Hansen, and he put it away.

Seth felt something subtle but colossal growing around him. It was as if the study, with its massed polished wood, had become a nexus of worlds, eras, and cultures. Energy had been conjured up by the objects in the chest, each one humming with longevity and import, and the house, with its undoubted history and vibe, was like a conducting rod.

In this prism of time, Seth heard a hundred whispered stories become one. And the sound of the sea outside the windows wasn't just impossible, but loud too. It didn't feel like nineteen-eighty-two in here anymore.

The flow of marvels continued: eight perfect pearls as big and black as olives; a glass tumbler etched with egrets that Hansen said was six hundred years old; a tobacco tin full of gold silkworms cast in one hundred BC.

Hansen now produced a silver box shimmering with a fine hammered design. Opening it, he gave Seth a glimpse of what lay inside – a small human skull cradled on red material. Or was it two skulls? Wait a sec – the skull had multiple eye holes! Raising an eyebrow like the Dr. Spock bloke did on his mysteries of the world TV show, Hansen snapped the lid shut.

Exchanging the silver box for a tortoise shell case, Hansen took out four slim bones: each one curved and finely carved with flowers and half-clothed women.

"Baculum dildos," he said. "Made by deep sea Japanese fishermen for their wives. Or to sell to brothels."

"Baculum?"

"The bone from the cock of a dolphin."

"Right," said Seth. That was a new one.

Then suddenly it was over, the bottom inserts not even seeing the light of day. Hansen shut the lid of the chest and patted it. "Part of my seven seas collection," he said. Locking the chest, he sat back.

Overwhelmed by the wonders he'd seen, Seth whistled. "Shouldn't it be in a bank vault?" he said.

"Yeah, yeah, it will soon enough."

"You got anything like those opals in there?" said Seth.

Hansen raised an eyebrow.

"Why? You going to pull a Meadows on me?"

Seth didn't like that. "That's a shitty thing to say."

Hansen laughed at the hurt on Seth's face.

"I must have had two thousand men sail under me over the years," he said. "Don't worry, I can see what a bloke is made of pretty damn quick."

"So why'd you employ Meadows as an accountant?"

"I knew it would be chicken feed with him. Small man, small dreams."

Really? thought Seth. The Bramston Beach shack and its planned renovations weren't exactly chicken feed.

"He took you, though. Ripped you off," he said.

A smile cruised Hansen's face.

"Accountants are useful. And if you have something on them, it brushes up their creative instincts."

Well, how about that, thought Seth. He must be getting pretty relaxed with me to admit he's cooking the books.

"You go and check up on him?" grinned Hansen. "Make sure I hadn't chucked him into the sea?"

Seth said nothing. But he had.

"You check on Mrs. Meadows too? She's a real nice sort, isn't that what you said?"

"Oh, come on, Hansen."

"What? Because she's married? He's got fanny on tap at his love shack down the coast."

And you've got yours in a five-star hotel, thought Seth.

"Can we keep it professional?" he said.

"Bit of a wowser, are you, son?"

Seth said nothing, trying not to feel upset that Hansen was back to being a prick again.

The old bastard nodded at the door.

"Step outside and close the door."

Seth obliged and stood in the hall. The house felt very still. From behind the door came a thump and a sliding sound. After a bit, another thump, and more sliding. Then silence.

Hansen called him back in. "Okay, we're done," he said, indicating that Seth should take the empty crate.

The chest was nowhere to be seen. It was as though the study had swallowed it. Seth looked around at the walls, inlays, and panels. With the desk and the bookshelves, the room fitted together like a jigsaw, with every join flush or sealed with timber beading.

"You'd need an x-ray machine to find it," said Hansen.

They went back through the house, Seth slowing to look

at the framed old engravings on the walls of the long front room, marvellous images from early Pacific expeditions.

"Want to look after this house for me?" said Hansen as he locked the front door.

Seth laughed. It was a beautiful house, but it felt like a lot of responsibility. He'd be basically security, and that would tie him down.

"I'd love to, but I've got my joint."

Hansen went past him down the stairs.

"Like this?" he said.

"No, mine's fibro and concrete block, two bedrooms on the beach. Nothing fancy, but it does me."

Seth had said that last sentence a dozen times, but now he felt a squiggle of envy, and the house at Palm Cove flashed through his head.

Hansen walked on and opened the gate.

Feeling like he'd made a mistake, Seth went down the stairs and took a last look at the place, still flying on what he'd seen, and felt.

The house had the depth of a museum, the richness of an art gallery, and, strangely, the reverent feeling of a church. Just an old house near the seawall and the mud of Trinity Bay – it felt like *mana* central in there.

While Hansen got into the Pig, Seth put the crate in the back. When he got behind the wheel, he asked Hansen how long he'd owned the house.

"First one I bought. Back in fifty-one."

"Lots of people would like to rent it," said Seth.

"Needs the right person."

"So the old bloke with the stiletto, wasn't it?"

Hansen was unamused. "Loyalty, see? It's a very shabby state of affairs when someone you've trusted turns on you. And not just someone you're paying, either."

"So, it's just going to sit here?"

"Suppose so. I might sell it."

That saddened Seth. If some arsehole bought it, he'd knock it down and put up concrete flats.

"What are you looking all cow-eyed about?" said Hansen.

He waited as Seth shook his head a few times and tried to find the words.

"It's just . . . so beautiful. It's pure bloody class."

Like a stone idol, Hansen sat without expression.

"Nineteen fifty-one," said Seth. "Must have cost you all your savings."

Hansen grunted with derision, and the deeply cynical sound prompted an image in Seth's head: Sunshine firing the M1 at him with elite skill, his conquering power once directed by Hansen.

My God, thought Seth. With his help and the help of other killers, what had Hansen seized for his own?

An untold treasure of land, gold, and copra. An ocean of shells, fish, and pearls. A mountain of salvaged steel, copper, and diesel fuel. All taken, with the truth of its getting menaced into silence or sunk fathoms deep.

Finder's fucking keepers, Hansen had got stuck right in, tearing off and gulping down whatever he wanted, taking the prime cuts off his fellow man.

On a wide-open frontier, across oceans and decades, he'd run amok, applying that age-old formula for success: brute force plus money.

And the shipping agents and customs officers, police, lawyers, and accountants made it all legit in the end, with the land titles and ledgers, the rubber stamps, certificates and licences as unassailable evidence of an empire's right to be.

In that busted old face, Hansen's eyes were cold and hard. He knew what Seth was thinking.

Absolving himself with a shrug, he began fumbling with the seat-belt.

"I can't claim to have always been on the straight and narrow," he said, "But I never took water from a thirsty man."

Dominance and Control

A perfect northern winter arrived; the days cooler, the nights clear. It was one of the best times of the year, a few lovely months before the humidity and rain set in. This was when they took all those postcard shots, and when people fell in love – before the sheets got dank and mould grew on camera lenses.

With his retainer back online, Seth resumed the role of minder and drinking companion. It was still a heap of fun, but without any actual work, it was bloody predictable.

One night at dinner, he asked Hansen in a roundabout way if there was something a little more exciting in the works for him. He got a quizzical look.

"My company no fun anymore?" Hansen's voice had a veneer of humour, but Seth saw his question had touched a nerve. He ordered crayfish and didn't mention it again.

He endeavoured to catch up with Stasia, and they had dinner a few times, once going back to his place for some funky monkey, but she always looked tired. And drank too fast. On weekends, she didn't want to make plans, and that was fine. With Sophie and Lou in his life, he pulled right back and gave Stasia her space.

When she came down with what seemed like an endless cold, snuffling down the phone like Tom Waits' sister, she kept working, and Seth got browned-off at her brother for going along with it.

The following week, Burns rang, suggesting they meet at The Outrigger's bar at seven. Seth was cool with that. Like Tawny's, it wasn't cheap, so the odds of being seen by a mate there early in the evening were pretty low.

Burns was leaning against the bar, when Seth arrived. In a shirt opened halfway down his chest, fitted tan slacks and brown dress shoes, he was talking to a woman, her pale skin and hibiscus-print dress marking her as fresh off the plane. She had a dated haircut, quality jewellery, and at least fifteen years on Burns.

"Ah, here he is," said Burns expansively as Seth joined them. "Thelma – meet my brother. Barry, this is Thelma. Thelma's up from Ballarat on a well-deserved holiday."

Smiling at the woman, Seth shook her hand, Burn's grin burning in the background.

"Hello Barry, lovely to meet you," said Thelma, her eyes glowing at the sight of another well-dressed and capable looking man.

"Yeah, Barry grows things," said Burns. "What do you call yourself, Baz? An arborist? Horticulturalist?"

"You all right for a drink, Thelma?" said Seth, turning to catch the barman's eye.

"I'm fine," said Thelma. "But it's a good job you turned up. Andy lost his wallet, and I had to buy him a drink."

Grinning like a bastard, Burns tried to look sheepish.

"Yeah, I can't work out how."

Seth took refuge in ordering a rum and coke.

"So you grow things, Barry? Is there good money in it?" said Thelma when he turned back. Burns made a noise of stifled glee.

"Um, yeah, it's okay," said Seth. The woman's perfume was strident in his nose, the stupid game getting up it too.

"Do you do flowers?"

Smiling pleasantly, Seth shook his head. "No, I don't."

With her drink in both hands, Thelma watched him, deference in her eyes as she waited for him as the bloke to steer the conversation.

She was also looking at his height, his wide shoulders, his blonde hair and blue eyes.

Burns put a gentle hand on her bare, white shoulder.

"What about this, Thelma? After this drink, let's all go up to your room, and we'll give you the fucking you want."

Her mouth fell open in shock.

"Jesus, Burns," said Seth.

"From both ends," said Burns. "Sound nice?"

As she stared at him, crazy realisation dawned in her eyes. Getting the result he'd wanted, Burns sniggered.

"Whoa. Thelma, listen," said Seth, depositing his drink on the bar. He hopped in beside Burns, threw one big arm around him, and trapped his arms.

"My name's not Barry and I'm not his brother," he said. With his free hand, he snatched out the detective's wallet and threw it on the bar.

"He's a bullshit artist. He's playing games with you."

His hard-muscled body unresisting, Burns convulsed in

laughter against him. The woman's face fell apart, dismay and humiliation replacing her shocked desire.

"You horrible, awful men," she said in a choked voice. Banging down her glass, she hurried away.

With a shove, Seth let go of Burns. The bastard regained his balance, still laughing his head off.

Shaking his head darkly, Seth knocked down half his drink. People were looking at them; the barman with hard eyes. Yeah, two smooth-looking blokes being rude to an older lady, thought Seth. Real bloody nice.

Burns stopped laughing, wiped his eyes. Seth tried to ignore his idiot schoolboy grin.

"Well, bugger you," said Burns. "I'm not taking you out undercover again."

"What is wrong with you, man?" said Seth.

"C'mon, it was a joke. No one got hurt."

"I think she did."

"Only because you ruined it."

"What? You'd have gone through with it?"

"Yeah, why not? She wanted to."

Seth stared at the bullshit sincerity on Burn's face and flashed on his brother. Alex had suggested the same thing, just about the last thing Seth wanted to do. And who the hell could get barred-up with another bloke in the room? It was weird then, and it was weird now.

"Don't pull shit like that on me again," said Seth.

"Okay," said Burns reasonably.

They had another drink. Burns said tomorrow was just a day trip. As he talked, Seth saw the woman's face again, her jack-pot excitement turning to awful mortification.

Though the food here was better than good, he fobbed off eating, bodging up a prior dinner date as his excuse.

"Chickybabe?" leered Burns.

It was easier to agree.

At dawn, Burns collected him from Cinderella Street, and made a show of checking Seth's neck for love-bites. Still pissed off about the woman, Seth stuck it up him.

"What are you so bloody interested in my sex life for? Y'know, after last night, I'm starting to wonder if you haven't got a bit of the arse-bandit in you."

That shut him up. Giving it an extra pump, Seth started belting out that old Supernaut song, I Like It Both Ways.

It took nearly a minute, but a grin began to tickle Burns' mouth. Seth punched his arm, hard enough to make him swerve, before madly correcting again.

"What the fuck!" yelled Burns.

Yeah, I'll give you crazy, thought Seth.

"Slow down!" he yelled back at Burns. "This is Machans Beach, not bloody Mount Panorama."

Yeah, let's pull over and have a punch on, he thought.

But with his eyes gleaming and an odd smile on his face, Burns sucked it up, happy to be on the receiving end. Like it both ways, indeed.

Animated now, he said he wanted an estimate on how far off harvesting was. Seth shrugged, made some Italian hands. Maybe a month. Fingers crossed.

As they drove up the range, Burns began talking about the Cairns dope scene with some familiarity, dropping the names of some players. Seth listened to his performative display, wondering why Burns was letting him know that Andy was out and about and working it.

In a casual trawl for information, Burns also chucked in some dots he'd connected, any reaction or answer grist for his mill. Seth lied or just shrugged in ignorance, leaving the detective's assumptions unanswered.

Some kind of game was going on here, but for the life of him, Seth couldn't see what it was. *I show the bastard how to grow a crop, I get paid, and that's it.* For Burns to think he was still part of, or interested in, the far northern dope scene was stupid. And the bloke wasn't stupid.

Maybe he should ask him what the hell he was on about, but it felt like he'd get sucked into more bullshit, and more questions. Half listening to the D, he watched the country go by, thankful when they finally bumped into the camp.

In the big clearing, what he saw made him happy: this visit was the penultimate one. The plants were nearly there, the branches packed with fat, purple-haired heads. Using the hokey jargon that he liked, Seth told Burns that for optimum yield, there was another month in it.

Burns wanted to know how much product was likely. Seth roughly estimated that after the drying and cleaning, there could be something close to five hundred pounds of primo dope.

Walking with his arms out, his fingertips brushing at the bushes as he passed, Burns chuckled and said, "Five hundred? I bet it's more."

Through the tall, green plants came voices. Burns made for them, Seth in tow, and they came to a row where the Barrys were pruning.

"So what do you think of our work?" said Burns to Seth, his voice rising.

Silent Smoker turned to hear Seth's reply. With his weird beard, cowboy boots, and skinny legs, he looked like a Walsh River freak. Rockjaw ignored them.

"Pretty good," said Seth. "You've done real well."

Chuckling with delight, Burns feinted blows into Silent Smoker's ribs, who grinned through a mask of smoke.

"Hear that?" Burns yelled at Rockjaw, who frowned and turned away.

"Mate, come here!" Fully excited, Burns waved Rockjaw over. The cop came over like a bull with its nuts caught in barbed wire.

"Tell him what you said," said Burns to Seth. This was more classic Burns bullshit, but, it had to be said, they'd done a good job.

"You blokes have done a real good job," he said.

"*Fuck* you," said Rockjaw, and he walked away.

With a suppressed chortle, Burns shrugged, raising his hands in a 'what can you do' gesture. Seth felt himself being pushed towards that cock fighting ring.

Once again, the disconnect hit hard. He was waiting to pay at Gerhards, the new deli in Earlville, with the smell of cheese and fresh bread filling the air. In the line ahead of him were two young women. Short-haired, fresh-faced, in sleeveless blouses, loose Asian pants, and sandals, they were talking about butterflies. They were real sweet girls.

Amongst all this niceness, Seth flashed on the Barrys: filthy, pig-mean, and gunned-up, men steeped in menace and brutish machismo. His involuntary grunt of disgust made one of the women look around at him.

"You right there?" she said, a wary look in her eye.

Seth smiled most apologetically. "Oh, I'm sorry, I just remembered something."

She turned back to her friend, and they waited silently, the butterflies now gone.

He cringed inside. He'd sounded like a meathead, and freaking women out was something he tried hard to avoid. Though he cultivated a personable demeanour around the opposite sex, he couldn't hide the way he looked – big and fit, his lumpy knuckles, recently scarred ear, and nicked eyebrow betraying a violent past. Luckily, his good Kelly genes kept him from looking like a total ape.

Though he wasn't about to take up macramé, keeping his own masculine energy in check was something he took seriously. Working doors in the clubs had helped, and a savvy bloke at Bob James Security in Sydney had told him about the fine line between dominance and control.

One was about the well-being of others, directing them if need be; the other was about pushing a personal agenda.

But who could be perfect all the time? A month later, he crossed that line – with Lou, and it moved things to a place he worried they might never come back from.

Following the girls in Lou's Honda Civic, they'd gone to visit a friend of hers: Ellen, a single mum with a two-year-old girl, who had just moved into a newly built house near Caravonica. Beyond it being an excuse to spend time with the girls, he was going to be Mr. Handyman and put up a clothes line for Ellen in her laundry.

There were house blocks cleared on either side of her place, a shit show of red dirt and noxious weeds, with piles of ripped up trees dumped at the rainforest's edge.

Dead centre in a yellowing lawn, with the bush a green wall along one side, the house was breeze-starved, hot and airless. Good money would vanish into thin air every day running the ceiling fans.

With the girls in the lounge chatting and playing with bubba, and Sophie uninterested in being his offsider or the keeper of the tools, he started work in the laundry.

With the back door wide open for air, he took his time, measuring and cutting the clothes line, and looking for cup screws in the tin of bits he'd bought. Applying the gimlet to the first of the two pencil crosses he'd made, he heard a familiar sound.

Looking through the doorway, he saw Sophie running towards the bush, swooping with the model plane he'd got for her. That wasn't cool. Ticks, bugs, and snakes hung around the forest fringe. Even cassowaries.

Nipping out the door, he briskly walked over. Sophie's imaginary flight was headed for the weeds on the edge.

"Hey, Sophie," he called. Ignoring him, she zoomed into a sunlit gap, and weaved between metre high shrubs, their heart-shaped leaves chewed by insects. Seth's gut did a somersault as horror spiked through him.

The shrubs were young stinging trees, every surface covered with tiny toxin-filled hairs. Just brushing against a leaf caused excruciating, mind-cracking pain. He knew this from bitter experience, lucky to have had only the tiniest bit of skin in the game.

This pain was more than awful, electric in its intensity, and the silica-tipped hairs went under the skin and were almost impossible to pull out. And it hurt like the Devil's buggery for weeks on end.

As a warning, Dad had freaked them out as kids with a story about a bloke he'd trained with in the war near the Barron River. Doing a Tarzan, the fella had swung over a creek on a vine. It broke and he fell into a stinging tree. They had to tie him to his hospital bed for three weeks.

Even worse, this same bloke knew of an officer who'd been badly stung. The poor bastard had shot himself.

Sophie, in shorts and a sleeveless top, and with her face at leaf height, was running into absolute disaster.

Keeping the fear out of his voice, he called out in a mischievous tone that he knew would grab her attention.

"Heyyy, Sophie. You wanna play a game?"

The plane came to a halt.

"You can't move. Not an inch. If you move, you've lost."

Hooked, Sophie stopped.

"Starting now."

She froze.

"Don't you move," said Seth, a big conspiratorial smile on his face as he strode up. Sophie giggled.

"Hey! No giggling. Don't move a muscle or you lose."

Super serious now; she didn't like losing.

Now at the edge of the bush, he saw that he couldn't fit in amongst the stinging trees to get to her. He was too big.

Should he tell her about the stinging trees? But what if she got scared or confused and made the wrong move? Or touched a leaf just to see? No, they'd play the game.

"Okay, you have to copy what I do exactly. When I move a step, you have to move the very same step. Yeah?"

The little girl, completely agog, nodded eagerly.

"Okay, here we go!" He drew his elbows in and held his arms in front of his chest. Sophie quickly did the same, her eyes saying, 'This is easy.'

He made a tiny move to the right. She took a tiny move. "Pretty good," he said. "Okay, we're going to do this one step at a time. The winner gets to go to the movies."

Sophie nodded, eyes alight with the challenge. Loving her so much, he stepped forward, gauging how close she would come to the nearest leaf. She followed perfectly.

Turning slowly on the spot, he moved half a step to the left. Once more, her move was exact. They exchanged big grins.

"Sophie!" Lou's voice rang out, bright and pleasant, but loud. Sophie began to turn.

"Oi!" said Seth, holding up an admonishing finger, his eyes glowing with a collusive cheekiness that said – *it's you and me hiding from Mum*. She loved it.

"Come on." His voice was focused, grown-up. She loved that too, that their mission together was deadly serious.

Watching like a hawk as the little girl watched him, he took another step that she copied. But he'd cut it fine; a fuzzy green heart was now less than ten centimetres from her arm. He thanked the stars there was no breeze.

"Sophie? Where are you?" There was real alarm in Lou's voice now. Sophie grinned like a thief.

"Okay, we go like this, and then this." He took a step, then another, and the little darling was right on it.

"Look," he said, refocusing her attention on him. "We step this way, and then this way."

She was at the last stinging tree, now, and he wanted to run and grab her. But trusting her, he played it safe, and she copied his last moves away from the tree to a T.

"Nowwww." He threw out his arms. "Give me a hug!"

With a squeal, Sophie ran to him, and he swept her up with incredible relief. Squeezing her close, he kissed her.

"I won!" she yelled.

"Well, you two are having all the fun." Lou was standing next to them. Sophie gave Seth a little head-shake – their game still a secret – and then she wiggled around trying to look at her mum. "I'm thirsty," she said.

"Okay, let's get a drink," said Lou. "Some apple juice?"

Seth reluctantly put her down.

"Lou, when Sophie's got her drink, can you come and see me for a minute." He kept his voice level, even smiled. Innocent, sweet, Lou smiled back, but his anger kept her loveliness at bay.

In the laundry, he tried not to dig his fingernails into the palms of his hands as the image of Sophie screaming in endless pain flashed through his skull.

Lou came in. "Everything alright?"

"No. No, it's not."

"Oh, gosh, what's up, Seth?"

Lou smiled at him, completely ignorant of what had just happened.

"Why did you let her run off?" He glared down at her, blood thumping in his ears. "Jesus, Lou, I found her in a clump of fucking stinging trees over there."

"Oh, shit." Lou didn't look as shocked or guilty as she should have.

"Did you hear what I said?" Anger thickened his words. Lou's face went blank. "Yes, I did. But she's okay."

"No thanks to you!"

"Seth, she ran off. She was gone a minute. A minute. I immediately came looking for her."

"That's long enough. You know the pain from a stinging tree is unbelievable? Like really unbelievable."

Totally steaming, he had to consciously lower his voice. "Yes, I know. Alex told me about it."

"Fuck Alex!" He saw spittle fly.

Lou stepped back. "We should stop now."

"No, no, don't cut me off. She nearly got badly hurt."

"But she didn't. It was bad luck she ran so quickly into the worst place she could have. But it was good luck she didn't get hurt."

"And why was that?"

"Because she didn't. Because you got her. I don't know what to say, Seth. Bad things happen, but until they do, I'm not freaking out about it."

"That's a cop out."

"Let's just stop now. You're angry."

His voice rose again. "Of course I'm . . ."

Sophie was standing in the doorway holding a plastic cup. Seth's heart plummeted at the sight of her face.

"Why are you yelling at mummy?"

Lou threw Seth a look of sorrow that took a cricket bat to his heart. She turned and crouched down by Sophie.

"We were talking and Uncle Seth got a bit excited. Like

you do sometimes. A big yell – and it's all over."

Sophie stared over her mother's head at him, and he managed a sickly smile. Unsmiling, she kept staring. Then she came to a decision, and her eyes went to Lou.

"It's not Uncle Seth's fault, mummy. We were playing a game and I was keeping quiet."

Emotions roiled in Seth's chest: anger, love, pride, and guilt, crashing about like drunks at a party.

Lou stood and ushered Sophie out the door.

"Come on, sweetheart. Uncle Seth's got his job to do."

Reeling inside, Seth watched them go down the hall, and a bad intimation rose like poison in him.

Sure enough, as they were leaving, Lou, all smiles, said very reasonably. "Let's take a break for a bit, Seth. I'll ring you, okay?"

Dumbly, he had to agree.

A Hungry Woman

"What do you call this, hey?" demanded Stasia, hitting his bare arse with a floppy stick of celery. "It's gone soft! You can't feed a girl that!"

They were both nude and freshly showered, with three drinks and a joint under their proverbial belts. It was a Sunday afternoon, and they'd just spent a couple of hours playing at six kinds of naughty. They could easily make it seven, but it was time to eat.

Hooting in fear, Seth scampered out to the barbecue. Stasia chased after him, yee-har-ing as she pummelled his arse with her vegetative crop.

He took his punishment, as he quickly deposited a plate of marinated lamb chops on the wrought-iron table next to the smoking hot barbecue. He spun around, shaking his hips to make his old fella spin like a propeller. As Stasia came to a wide-eyed, screeching halt, he stepped close to the grill plate, the sizzling steel right by his groin.

"I'm warning you!" he yelled dramatically. "If you don't stop that – the old fella gets it."

Stasia snorted with laughter, pretended alarm.

"Oh, no – not the old fella!"

Seth slowly leant forward, staring with brutal intent as he inched his pink bit towards the scorching metal.

Stasia's laughter hit an incredulous pitch. "Seth!"

He pointed a stern finger at the garden.

"Go on. In the bushes."

She bit her bottom lip in glee at his threat, and with a curve-shaking wiggle of defeat, flung the stick of celery away. Things were warming up, but he didn't move.

"It's still there!" cried Stasia.

"It needs rescuing. You have to help me."

Yelling in triumph, Stasia dashed over and took matters into her own hands.

"Jesus, Seth," she said, "It's got a bit warm."

He let her push him away from the barbecue, and they hugged, Renée Geyer smouldering on the stereo inside.

She looked up at him with serious eyes, and the concern in them threw a deep shadow over him.

"What, babe? What?"

She took a deep breath, but didn't speak.

"What?" His voice cracked.

"Could it have . . . self-combusted from the heat and just gone up in flames?"

"Gone up in flames?"

"Yeah, your old fella."

With a squeeze of exhibit A, Stasia yelled with laughter. Beaming like Buddha, Seth roared happily, and lifted the cheeky girl up so he could plunge his face into the honest-to-God nirvana of her chest.

The laughing and roaring made a hell of a din, and a pair of pee-wees on the lawn flew away screeching. Grappling, and staggering about, Seth's thigh connected with a chair, and the sound of its fall brought the horseplay to an end.

Seth put her down and kissed her head. Standing there, their breathing slowing, Stasia looked over his shoulder at the windows of the house next door.

"Your neighbour's no prude, is he?" she said. "Because he'll have copped an eyeful of everything. Boy's bits, girl's bits – the whole nuddy shebang."

"Nah, Rod's cool, but he's out on the mines the next two weeks. I wouldn't be out here bare-arse if he wasn't."

"Is that right? Not even on your own?"

"Only to hang out a towel or take a leak. I check first."

"Mr. Considerate."

"Hey, what's going on?" Stasia was looking down. All that plunging into nirvana had got his blood flowing, and he began to stroke her glorious curves.

"The phoenix," he said. "Rising from the ashes."

Stasia laughed, pushed him away. "Nah, I'm hungry."

"A hungry woman is sexy."

"You're just saying that because you like cooking."

"I like it all."

"I wouldn't have it any other way. Another drink?"

"You finished making the salad?"

"Fuck the salad."

"I'd love a drink."

Stasia gestured at Exhibit A.

"You want to let the air out of that, Captain Phoenix, or you really will burn it."

Seth snapped off a salute and watched her go into the house. This was good mucking about and having a laugh, because she was looking a bit drawn lately, the darkness under her eyes not kohl.

"Heyyy! Hello, Seth?" Over the music came the sound of a female voice in the carport. He panicked. Hells bells! Caught nude and barred up too.

Quickly hopping behind the barbecue, he saw Sunny come out of the carport towards him. He manoeuvred to keep his lower half hidden, but not too close to the heat. Damn it to buggery, if only he'd brought a tea towel.

Sunny came across the back lawn, her eyes taking in the lamb-chops, her smile uncertain, and Seth saw how brave she was coming to see him.

"Hey, Seth. I went for a walk to the river mouth and as I came back along the street I heard the music. Sounds like Renée, so who could resist, hey?"

Suntanned, her auburn hair a wild mop, Sunny was barefoot and braless, wearing nothing but old shorts and a singlet. There were beads of sweat on her upper lip and sand on her feet. She looked great.

Now Stasia came out of the house, still nude, a finger held up in question. Neither she nor Sunny could see each other, as the wall of canna lilies screened the carport from the porch.

Seth opened his mouth, but words failed him. The sight of them together like this was captivating.

"Seth, where is the . . ." Stasia saw Sunny now, and she laughed in surprise, too much of a groover to care about being naked. Besides, Sunny had been a friend for years.

But Sunny's dismay betrayed her. "Ah, shit, I'm sorry, Stasia. Sorry, I didn't know."

As she turned to go, Seth felt regret and relief collide in his belly, and his knees went weak.

"No, don't go!" said Stasia. "Stay, Sunny. Seriously. I'll put something on and make us a drink, okay?"

Without waiting for a response, she turned and scooted back into the house. Sunny shot Seth an embarrassed look, and his heart went out to her. He gave a welcoming smile while his hands made a casual screen down there.

Gosh, he thought. Getting startled should have knocked the phoenix on the head, but for some reason it appeared to have the opposite effect.

Some reason? Don't bullshit yourself. You're zinging on two very cool and sexy women, still on a horny high from the last few hours, and your filthy little mind is running a preview of what you'd like to happen. No. You're a lucky bastard to just be standing here, so leave it at that.

"Hey, Sunny," he said, putting a note of command into his voice. "Why don't you go in and give Stasia a hand with the drinks? I'll put the meat on."

It sounded as fake as a TV ad, and Sunny smelt a rat. She took in his stance with his hands down there, and her eyebrows shot up as she let out an incredulous laugh. For all his handiwork, she'd seen the risen bird.

Pretending to be shocked, she came around the cannas, still laughing, and went into the house. Seth now raced across the lawn to where a towel hung on the clothes line.

They ate outside on the back table, three pairs of shorts and two singlets between them. Seth concentrated on the lamb chops and potato salad. A green salad would have been good, but Stasia was beyond that. She'd made them all drinks though: vodka, soda, lime, and mandarin juice.

When they were done, Seth cleared the table and put on some Rufus and Chaka Khan, a worthy selection after Renée. Stasia and Sunny hadn't seen each other for a while, so he left them to it and got into the dishes. When he was done, he got a nice head his mate Rockwell Pete had grown, broke it up into a bowl and took it outside.

Sunny and Stasia were shoulder to shoulder, bare arm against bare arm, their unruly hair touching as they raved. While Sunny rolled a joint, Seth cleaned the barbie, and Stasia made fresh drinks. They smoked the joint so bloody quick, Sunny had to roll another.

While they smoked it, Stasia gave them a lecture on where society was at: blokes chasing money appeared to be at the root of most evil. She was funny, but angry too. Sunny, looking a bit loaded now, sat drinking, her eyes glued on her friend.

Seth didn't say much, content to listen, and he realised he'd never seen Stasia this out-of-it before. Sure, she got wild at parties, but she always paced her drinking.

"If we were given half the chances that men got, we'd still have to be twice as good," said Stasia. "I'm lucky to have a brother who'll give a girl a go."

"He's the lucky one, Stasia." Sunny shook the ice in her drink, spilling a bit down her front.

"I never wanted a real job," said Stasia, rubbing one eye. "Not because I don't like working, because I like working, but because of stupid blokes, present company excluded, who don't believe that you can do the job, or who fuckin' undermine you when they see you *can* do the job. How come there's not more murder in the workplace? Hey?"

"Because we're sweet," said Sunny. "Women are sweet."

"Well, that gets me feeling bitter, mate. We get walked over because, what – we're naturally nice? Fuck that!"

Sunny laughed like a pirate, began rolling a cigarette.

"Yeah, I'll have one," said Stasia. She took the tobacco from her friend. With a flourish, Sunny lit up, the front of her t-shirt bouncing wet with spilt drink.

"So, how's it going with Sophie?" she said to Seth.

"Yeah, it's great," said Seth. Stasia looked up.

"She's a real sweetie," said Sunny. "Mixes with the other kids, and just mad about planes." Sunny waved at the air above them. "She loves the flights coming over. I reckon she'll be a pilot one day."

"I reckon so, too," said Seth.

Stasia lit her rollie, blew tobacco crumbs and smoke to one side.

"Lou, hey," she said. "Always looked gorgeous. Tough too. But you'd have to be - with him as your husband."

Seth hit his drink. Sunny smoked.

"So, how is Lou?" said Stasia. "Alright?"

Wiping his mouth, Seth nodded. "Yeah, she's good."

Her eyes were just about solid black. Sunny fiddled with her pouch of tobacco. Stasia puffed on her smoke, then turned to Sunny.

"Heyyy, what about another joint?"

"Now you're talking," said Sunny.

"I want to make a toast," said Stasia. "But I don't have a drink."

"I'll make them," announced Sunny. As she collected glasses, Stasia jumped up in mock alarm.

"No, no, hold up. I want to make them my way."

They went into the house, and Seth closed his eyes. He was feeling a bit out of it himself, and – Jesus, Stasia and Sunny were sexy women.

Returning triumphantly with drinks, the girls wiggled and jostled onto the bench seat, laughing like kids. With heavy eyelids, Seth watched them jiggle about, then settle.

Smoothing her singlet across her chest, Stasia raised her glass. "A toast! A toast to my loan!"

"Good onya girl!" Sunny raised her glass, Seth too, and they clinked glasses and drank deeply.

"Yeah, I fuckin' did it," nodded Stasia grimly. She began to roll a joint. Sunny relit her cigarette and said to Stasia, "Y'know, when I first applied for a loan – for my first car, they said my wages wouldn't count."

Stasia looked up, shocked. "What? Why?"

"They said I'd get pregnant, and then where would I be?"

"You're fucking kidding."

"I wish. I never got it."

"When was that?"

"Oh, ten, twelve years ago."

"Far fuckin' out, Sunny."

"When I finished school, I couldn't get a bank account without my father coming into the bank with me. Or if you were married, your husband had to be there."

"What a mob of controlling pricks," said Stasia.

Wow, thought Seth. I had no idea.

"It's all changed now, thank God," said Sunny. "Got my loan three years ago. Paid it off March last year."

Seth raised his glass, and with a wrenching sob, Stasia

dropped the half-rolled joint, put her head in her hands, and began to cry.

Sunny gave Seth a quick hard look, saw his surprise, and put her arm around Stasia. "Oh baby. What's wrong?"

Seth was shocked. He'd seen Stasia unhappy, sad too, but he'd never seen her cry.

"I fuckin' . . . I . . ." Stasia tried to speak through sobs.

"Go, slow. It's okay," said Sunny. Stasia looked up, and the self-loathing in her eyes blew Seth away.

"I fucked up!" she wailed. "I ordered four thousand dollars' worth of concrete we didn't need. Five thousand P.S.I. that sets in two hours! I rang and rang around trying to find someone to take it, but it went off."

Drunk, stoned, and so ashamed, Stasia threw her arm around Sunny, and pressed her face in to her neck.

Crooning softly, Sunny pulled her friend close, kissed her head, and stroked her shoulder.

Flabbergasted, Seth sat there. Why didn't she tell me?

Looking at them hugging, he suddenly wished that it was him comforting Stasia.

You stupid bastard, he thought. He got up and went and hugged her, his face in Sunny's hair.

Sympathetic noises rumbled in his chest, mingling with Sunny's soothing murmuring. Stasia's sobs now began to falter, wretched laughter now coming in.

"Jeez, I'm a big sook," she said.

"No, you're not," said Seth and Sunny.

Seeds, Dirt and Sunshine

Burns rang, his voice as sunny as the weather.

"Mate, the cousins are doing great, but I think it's time for them to go now."

Pleased as, Seth rogered that, and Burns continued.

"Drive your vehicle up tomorrow. Early as you can."

That makes sense, thought Seth, pleased to be using his own wheels. By nightfall tomorrow, the site would be just a clearing in the scrub again.

The drive up was lovely. On the empty dawn highway between Kuranda and Mareeba, with the Lamb Range in ancient silhouette, long flights of white ibis trailed across the pink sky.

He thought about this next stage as he drove. Burns had a list of what they needed, with a big place to dry the dope at the top of it.

When he got to the camp, he saw that the pile of empty bottles had grown. Burns and Rockjaw were sitting under the kitchen tarp drinking tea and smoking. As he got out Burns waggled his cigarette in foppish greeting.

"You gonna take all that glass away?" said Seth.

Burns and Rockjaw looked at each other, then burst out laughing.

"Is he for fuckin' real?" said Rockjaw.

"Yes, he is," said Burns, and he looked at Seth. "And yes, the glass will be removed."

Rockjaw smirked at Burns. Seth glared at this bullshit.

"The other blokes down at the crop?" he finally said.

"No, just us this morning," said Burns. "You show us how it's done and we'll show them how it's done."

Seth hid his surprise. Fully mature now, the crop was ripe for a rip-off: there should be half a dozen blokes here.

But maybe these two bastards had automatic weapons and rucksacks full of thirty-round clips. Maybe they were looking for a gunfight, relishing the chance to blaze away at a crew of crop raiders. He wouldn't put it past them.

We used to sweat it with at least two blokes on watch, with a few bolt-action rifles and twelve-gauge shotguns as our arsenal of deterrence, thought Seth. And back in the day, that would have done the trick. But crop-watchers carried automatic weapons now, just like the fellas doing the rip-offs.

Down at the crop, parked by the wall of marijuana, was an all-wheel drive truck – a Ford Blitz V8, one of a few from the war still bombing around the north.

Close to indestructible, with a three ton payload and forty-three-inch tyres, it was perfect. Rusty khaki against the sea of green, it looked like something from a movie: Mad Max Meets Cheech and Chong. Hanging over the high sideboards of the tray, nearly to the ground, were the edges of a big tarp.

"No bags or tarps?" said Seth.

"We're taking them whole."

"We want to break them down here, remember?"

"No time, mate."

Pig-dog mean, Rockjaw stared at him.

"Someone been sniffing around?" said Seth.

"No."

Neither cop looked worried, but Seth smelt something more than plants thick with fudge-sticky heads. Shut up, he told himself. You're real close now.

With a pruning saw, he cut a plant down, getting Burns and Rockjaw to hold it as he cut. Three metres high and very sticky, it couldn't touch the ground. Dusty, dirty dope was something no bastard wanted to smoke.

Burns and Rockjaw put the plant in Blitz. When they came back, he cut down another plant, and so it went for a couple of hours. The smell of their work was intense: the air thick with the pungent vegetative odour of fresh dope, and their gloves and clothes soon became sticky.

"Fuckin' stinks," complained Rockjaw. Burns rolled up a ball of resin and flicked it at him.

"Plant that in a hippie's pocket, mate. Ding, he's done."

"This sticky shit?"

"Hash, mate, it's baby hash."

"Yeah, right, so it is. Should we be saving it?"

"Sure, if you've got village girls to roll it between their thighs like they do in Asia."

Rockjaw shook his head in disgust. "Fuckin' savages."

They took a break an hour later. Sweating but without water, Rockjaw went up to the camp. After taking a leak, Seth drank from his canteen, grateful they weren't doing this in summer like some mad-keen growers did.

He joined Burns in the shade of the truck, thinking he'd call it a day soon. Being in the proximity of all this dope was making him nervous.

"Reckon I'm done?" he said.

"Tired, mate?" said Burns.

"With the blokes here tomorrow, you should be all done by nightfall. You can ring me the next day."

"Whoa, whoa, whoa," said Burns, looking past him.

Seth turned, saw Rockjaw coming around the Blitz. He was holding a Ruger Mini-14, the rifle's barrel pointed downwards, his finger inside the trigger guard.

"No, no, no," said Burns. "Roy, no."

Rockjaw gestured with his head for Burns to step aside, but the detective stayed put, smiling like a game-show host. Breathing nice and slow, Seth felt the sweat go chilly on his neck.

"It's an alibi," said Rockjaw.

"No, it's not," said Burns, moving in front of Seth. "Get out of here," he said over his shoulder.

Seth zapped down the side of Blitz and ran around it. With the rusty bulk of the truck between him and the Mini-14, he ran for the camp, feeling no shame at zigzagging hard, the back of his head suddenly enormous.

Bursting out of the scrub into the camp, he looked back, saw no moving figure. Jumping into the Pig, he well and truly got his arse out of there.

Two days later, Burns rang. He delivered a brisk edict and hung up. Humming with trepidation, Seth met him in Mareeba outside Foxwoods' timber yard. Letting the cop overtake him further up Byrnes Street, he followed the XY Ford north.

Turning off at Bilboohra, they drove through a maze of dirt farming roads to a tobacco drying shed on some overgrown acreage. The parking turnaround out the front was empty, but Seth stayed in the Pig. Burns came over, a greasy little smile on his face.

"That bastard in there?" Seth nodded at the shed. Burns shook his head and put on a mummy voice.

"Did the man with the gun scare you?"

"You ever have a gun pointed at you?" said Seth.

"Technically, it wasn't pointing at you, and I stepped in front of it. Lay my life down for ya, mate."

"What the hell was that? He wanted to knock me?"

"Nah, nah," Burns brushing it all away with his hands. "Just being a prick. You've seen it. He gets uptight around fellas from the other side of the game. He'd never make it undercover."

Bullshit, thought Seth. Burns leant in the window, his eyes alight. "Amazing feeling, hey?"

"Feeling?"

"Having a gun on you. Time vanishes, man. All senses running full bore. The blood pumping through your veins. Goosebumps, tingles all over. I get, like, this big buzz."

"Sounds like you bar up."

Burns nodded. "Don't joke. I reckon I just about have. Always rush off for a root after something like that."

"So you and that bastard Roy point guns at each other up there as a bit of foreplay?"

Burns burst out laughing. Then frowned.

"Did I say Roy?"

"You sure did."

"Jesus, I must have got flustered."

"Flustered? That bastard was going to shoot *me*."

Burns grinned. "Not without my say so."

"Fuck you, Burns."

"No, thank you, Burns."

With a flourish, the D produced a key. He went over to the shed doors and undid a padlocked chain. Seth got out, and carefully looked around before walking to the shed.

"It will just be me from now on," said Burns. "I'll show them what you show me."

"I wouldn't have it any other way," said Seth.

Burns opened the shed doors and went in. Seth paused, listening for the wrong sounds. He thought about the ten grand. Inside the shed, lights came on, and he went in.

It stunk of dope in there. More lights came on. He saw only Burns, and against one wall, the dope plants stacked on tarps – a great, big bloody pile of them.

Burns stood by an open-faced electrical switchboard, silvered pencil marks visible on its black finish. Plugged into the switchboard were long extension cords with work lights and industrial pedestal fans. The fans would move the air around to prevent mould, and maybe even push back the big green smell a bit.

"You okay to do this?" Burns looked very serious.

"Yeah, I'm fine."

"Mate, you getting hurt is the last thing I want."

Hurt? Seth looked at the dirt floor flecked with trodden-in scads of wire. A Mini-14 kills you.

He looked at Burns, smiling as though it was cool. The cop nodded, closing the book on it, and they got to work.

It took all morning to string up long rows of wire. Then, with secateurs, Seth cut the branches off a plant and hung them to dangle over either side of a length of wire. He left a gap, hung another branch up, and Burns followed suit.

He headed off an hour before the light went. Burns had been given a detailed rundown on the drying process and the results expected, and it had all gone into his notebook.

In a week or so, Seth would come back to show him the final stage. Driving to the highway through the network of roads, he saw three blokes standing by a tractor in a field. Poker-faced, they watched him pass.

Checking his mail at Machans the next morning, he was chuffed to find a parcel – a square cardboard box. Grinning like a rat in a pantry, he went home, slit open the box and removed ten LPs. Laidlaw's selection had arrived.

As ever, half the artists were either vaguely familiar, or drew total blanks. That had been part of the original brief – 'turn me onto new stuff.'

He saw the goodies straight up. A couple of live albums: one from Beck, Bogert, and Appice, the other from Lobby Loyde, with the inclusion of G.O.D, and the vocals of the little fella from Rose Tattoo on one track making it an interesting prospect. There were new ones from The Jam and Pete Townshend, but the trendy look of the guitarist on the sleeve gave him a weird vibe. And how about that – a first solo album from Robert Plant.

Putting the new albums next to the stereo, he made a

cuppa and started with the artists he didn't know; playing two or three tracks from each album to get a feel for them.

Despite his mate's inherent taste and nose for musical bullshit, this could still be a hit or miss thing. He didn't like everything Laidlaw sent him, so there were a dozen or so duds down the back of an album stack – the unavoidable cost of expanding his musical horizons.

The rockabilly feel of The Blasters wasn't bad; it would make great driving music, and the album cover of Fiyo on the Bayou – a burning crocodile in swampland – made him chuckle. This must be a Laidlaw piss-take: tipping a wink at far north Queensland. But the record, by a mob called the Neville Brothers, was sharp, funky, and bright, swinging with horns, great harmonies, and some very cool grooves. So far, so good.

The next one didn't ring his bell. Some fella by the name of Zevon posed in a suit with a private jet on the cover. Immaculately played, overproduced, wordy, and forced, it plodded along like a cow. Now an album called Street Priest exploded from the JBL speakers, and the vibe of it completely lifted his wig.

The music was a free-jazz, hard rock, freaky, maybe Martian, onslaught of whacky guitars, intensely powerful drumming, yo-yo basslines, and bizarre atonal horns. Track two was called Sperm Walk.

It's like rock'n'roll, Jim, but not as we know it, he thought. The album was uncomfortable as hell, but he knew he was going to play it again. Maybe even a lot. There was always one aural hand grenade in a Laidlaw delivery, and this looked to be it.

The last LP was a movie soundtrack; the cover looking all nineteen-thirties, with some bloke in a hat smoking a cigarette, a woman's face framed by all the smoke. He put the needle on the groove and went to make another cuppa.

A harp shivered a long note; syrupy strings billowed. A trumpet came in, haunting and glamorous. Seth winced as he fired up the jug. Jesus, Laidlaw, this is the sort of Hollywood stuff our parents listen to.

The trumpet line repeated, insistent, elegiac. The track was well done and all, but bloody old-fashioned.

He went to the stereo, his mind turning to Beck and the boys. As he leant over the Thorens, forefinger and thumb reaching for the stylus head, a new track started, and he took his hand away.

Very different to the opener, it was weirdly percussive, filled with threatening repetitive sounds: a struck bell and woodblock footsteps, then baritone strings grunting with menace. When the lush trumpet briefly came in again, it was skewed, mutated, wrong. Seth sat down.

Quickly came a new track, a jazz piano solo, mid-tempo and relaxed. A hundred seconds later, it was over. These tracks must be short to fit movie scenes, he thought.

Now track four: strings and trumpet in ethereal unison, and an absolutely perfect piano line distilled from every love theme ever written, but cut through with the fears in every lover's heart: loss and betrayal.

As the piece faded into ominous discord, he noticed he was holding his breath. This flawless mix of romance and menace had got under his skin like an exquisite itch.

As he listened to the side again, he realised that this was

what Laidlaw had promised him – his own private eye theme. It was nothing like Ryan or Magnum P.I, though. No pounding beat, brass stabs, or wucka-wucka guitar; no cool cars, swooping choppers, or clifftop chases.

This was all shadow and evasion, sadness and lies: the black beyond the sunshine, the squirm beneath the smile.

It was a trick, alright: for all its sweetness and schmaltz, the music felt uncomfortably true to life. Laidlaw, the clever bastard, had nailed it.

He had a beer, smoked a joint, and listened to the rest of the LPs. The solo Plant was so-so, the Townshend one a stinker. The Jam had changed direction, sorta Motown and less punky, but not bad at all, while Beck and Lobby crunched and soared as good as ever.

Opening another beer, he listened to the new albums again, playing them all through. There was another joint in there and a few more beers before he called it a night. Besides a dross count of two, and one so-so, he'd scored some cool records. But it was the exhilarating bedlam of Street Priest and the naggingly weird movie soundtrack that pegged claims in his head.

The next day he taped the new LPs, making copies on metal TDK tapes to play in the Pig. As the Marantz three-head tape recorder silently did its work, he wrote up the artist, album, and song titles on the blank card inlays.

Inking out itty-bitty words with a felt-tip was always a chore, but if he focused on hammering them out letter by letter, it went faster.

Finally done, he went out to the carport and swapped them for the played-to-death tapes in the Pig.

Driving back up to the shed full of dope a week later, he ran through some of the new albums, turning Street Priest down as he got in to Bilboohra. Yeah, the farmers around here would blow a gasket hearing this.

Like he'd said he would be, Burns was alone. He looked a little gaunt, and Seth saw sheets and blankets and a cardboard box of food in the cabin of the XY ute.

Inside the shed was an upside-down forest. Against the wall lay the pile of stripped plants. Though it still overran the nostrils, the resinous stink wasn't quite so bad now.

Reaching up, Seth touched fat heads, felt them. He bent the stem of a small branch and there was an audible snap. Looking smug, Burns gave Seth his little report. The fans had been constantly moved around, and they'd checked for mould. Every branch, every day.

Good for you, thought Seth. But do I care? Putting the branch on a trestle table, he squeezed the heads, and felt some excess moisture. They could do with curing for a few weeks, even a month, but he wasn't going to tell Burns that. Not now.

He vigorously rubbed all the excess leaf off the branch with his hands, the dried sugar leaves falling in crispy sprinkles to the table top.

"You don't want that. It's the shit weed, the shake. Don't try to sell it with the heads to make up weight. Works with tourists and kids, but the blokes you're trying to sting might take a look in every bag."

With secateurs, he snipped a head from the branch. He cut off the stalk and held it up.

"This is what you sell. Far North Queensland heads."

"This is going to take ages," said Burns

Seth nodded. "It sure will."

Burns took the head. He turned it in his fingers, staring at it like it was a gold nugget. "From a seed to this," he said.

They got to it, brushing and snipping, slowly covering the table with heads. When the afternoon sun brought a golden light into the shed, Seth showed Burns how to package the dope, weighing it on scales, before stuffing it into produce bags that held ten and twenty pounds.

The sun now behind the western ranges, Seth filled a final bag. "So, are we done?" he said.

Savouring a grin, Burns nodded. Seth went to the door, and looked out. He scanned the guinea grass along the driveway, even looking in trees

Burns passed him, waving a joint. "Let's see how good my marijuana is, man."

Seth came out into the cool evening air. Burns lit up and they smoked. Seth savoured the smoke, finding nothing wanting. It tasted fine, without any musty staleness. He took note of the stone too as it came oozing in, relaxing his muscles and soothing his mind. It was good shit.

The detective's eyes glinted with stoned thought as he smoked. Seth watched him from the corner of his eye. After nearly a year, he still found it hard to reconcile the bloke with his job. He'd been a weird one, alright.

Burns flicked the cardboard filter away and fixed Seth with a jubilant smile.

"Maate! I reckon we've got ourselves something bloody good, even if I say so myself."

"Yep," said Seth. "Now I want my money. Ten grand."

Wide-eyed, Burns pursed his lips and allowed a cheeky twinkle into his eyes. You're kidding me, thought Seth.

"Look," said the detective, all sugar and fucking spice. "Right at this point there's no more operating funds left. Everything's gone on growing the crop. And like I said, you're a completely unknown entity to the powers that be. They won't be handing over any more cash. Not to me, not to you."

Seth's head grew hot. "What are you saying?"

"Hey, hey, don't arc up, mate. Look, you can wait until the sting happens and I get some money. Or I can give you ten grand's worth of dope now."

"I'm not fucking selling dope!" Seth was arced up now. He could sell it, but he didn't want to risk his licence. And, damn it, he didn't want Burns to prevail over this.

"Oooo, watch out, he's getting cranky," smirked Burns.

Doubly angry that he had got stoned with the bastard, Seth stepped forward. "Do not fuck me around," he said.

In absolute delight, Burns came in with friendly hands, going for a conciliatory squeeze of the shoulders.

Seth slapped his hands away. Burns kept it up, laughing at his discomfort, until Seth gave him a jab to the ribs. The cop jumped back.

"Ow! That fucking hurt, man."

"My money, Burns. I'm serious."

The cop rubbed his side, his eyes wide with interest.

"What? You think I'd rip you off? What for? I like you, man. You've shown me something amazing. How to turn dirt, seeds, and sunshine into lots of money."

Seth's mind raced. The detective laughed.

"Just for argument's sake, because I'm interested how you'd react. What would you do if I didn't pay you?"

Seth's stoned skull reverberated with vindication.

"Dob me in?" said Burns. "Or put me in the ground? Would you kill me for ten grand?"

Seth stared at Burns. I was right all along, he thought.

Dropping the smile, Burns frowned sincerely.

"Of course, I'm going to pay you," he said. "I've just got to sell some of it first. Okay?"

Without real options, Seth had to nod.

There's a word for it, he thought, feeling truly shat off. A word for when you don't like it, but there's nothing you can do. Screwed would do for now.

Good Faith

Seth hung up the phone and pulled a face. It was like that bouncer's truism – 'You've got more chance of being kicked when you're down.' He'd just received his second hit of fiscal adversity for the week.

Hansen was leaving town again. He'd be back, but until then there'd be no weekly retainer. With a good swag in the bank, Seth wasn't sweating it, but hanging out to get the rest of his dough off Burns was giving him shit on the liver.

He'd spotted people money in the past – hell, he'd been like Alex's bank at times, but only for mates he'd known for ages, mates like Robbie the Bomb, Mick, or Jeffyman.

As the weeks ticked by, he pondered it: Burns straight-up ripping him off. He watched the detective come and go at his hotel, and tailed him to the airport where he caught a Brisbane flight, returning two days later. Hopefully it had been a visit to the cashed-up crims on the Gold Coast.

He thought of fronting Burns, but there was bugger all he could do. As a member of the biggest gang in the state, the detective couldn't be monstered. Just like the Bobby Fuller Four had sung all those years ago – those bastards always won.

Finally, Burns rang. After telling Seth to meet him at The Crown, he hung up. It was a bit bloody boy-scout, and real dubious too. After Tawny's and The Outrigger, the pub was not a good choice. It was a raucous watering hole swimming with wastrel rats, chancers, and crims.

The horrible vehicles parked outside the old pub gave a good indication as to the clientele inside: a rust-eaten ute with two scrawny dogs chained in the back; an EH Holden full of rubbish looking close to death; and a shit-brown Datsun Bluebird with a passenger door wired shut.

Pausing outside the windows, Seth scanned the bar and saw no one he knew. None of his mates would be here in the daytime, anyway. He'd give it a whirl. In ten minutes he'd be gone.

Inside amongst the broken noses and missing teeth, stained shorts, thongs, and work pants, Burns, in faded Levi's, a wrinkled shirt, and scuffed Blundstones, looked like just another dodgy bloke having a beer.

The detective got schooners, and they stood in a corner at a tiny circular table. A wall of noise pressed in around them, blokes yelling and squawking, bragging, swearing, and laughing. Taronga Park Zoo had nothing on this.

"So, the Gold Coast's happening?" said Seth.

Burns laughed like he didn't have a debt to settle.

"All under control." He put his fist on the table. A roll of fifties peeked from it. "Show of good faith, mate."

Drinking beer, Seth cast his eye around at the heaving mob of miscreants. Before closing tonight, at least one of them would get a proper knuckle-up in the gents.

"How much good faith?"

"A thousand," said Burns.

Seth hesitated. He'd seen a crim he knew called Laurie Keats come into the front bar. Parrot, as they called him, was a loser, deservingly maligned for his feeble criminal abilities. But with a talent for ferreting things out, he'd done shitwork for Alex and the Macs back in the day.

Parrot began to order a beer, and Seth, his hand close to the table, plucked the roll of notes from the detective's hand. In the cover of his fist, he hurried the money into the front pocket of his jeans.

Burns laughed delightedly. "Wow! How fast was that? Hands of the taipan or what?"

Seth killed a smile. Burns saw that, amped up his own.

"See? I'm coming through for you, mate. Slowly, slowly, but I'm coming through. I don't want to lose you."

"No one owing me money loses me," said Seth.

"Aw, you big bastard. No, seriously. You did a fantastic job, and we had a few laughs as well. We're a team. Who knows what the future holds?"

"Nine grand," said Seth.

The detective's eyes shone. "It could be a lot more."

Seth hurried his beer. They'd gone through this before, but Burns had the look of a preacher.

"Listen, we'll do it again," he said. "You choose your Barrys this time. It'll be our thing."

Seth gave him a look of disbelief.

"I'm serious," said Burns.

"Serious conflict of interest, more like it."

Burns laughed. "No, it won't affect what I do. The boys pushing smack and speed will still feel my wrath, the big growers, too. This is just a bit of moonlighting."

Seth curbed a cynical laugh; he'd sensed this all along. Burns had reverted to who he'd first portrayed himself as – a crim eager to cash in on the marijuana bonanza in the far north.

"Besides," said Burns. "Wouldn't you like a boat? The one you really want. Or the rifle you really like. Or rifles. Or months in Thailand at a top hotel? Or, or –"

"You're a persistent bastard," said Seth, as a thirty-foot Skipjack cruiser sent a prow-wave of desire through him.

"Think about it, mate. A few years from now, you'll . . ."

A fat bloke came up to the cigarette machine next to them. Red-nosed and jowly, he jingled a handful of coins. "Fellas," he said, turning to the lit-up glass and metal box.

Packs of smokes were stacked in the vertical window of the machine; Rothmans nearly out. From one of the rows, a cockroach gazed out, its antennae flickering.

"Not the sort of roach you want to be smoking, hey?" said Burns to the fat fella. That got him an odd look. Coins clattered, a pack of smokes fell out.

"Okay," said Seth as the bloke slouched away. "If I did get back into it – why would I need you?"

"Protection."

"From who?"

"From my lot. With me you get the green light. I get a share, which I share with . . . whoever I need to."

Seth had got out of the dope business because it had got too heavy. People got killed. He knew all about it.

"It's not just your lot I'd have to worry about," he said.

Burns cocked his head as though listening to gunfire in

the scrub, a mad gleam of excitement in his eyes.

"The Mac brothers were good at that," said Seth. "You do all the work and they take all the dope."

Burns grinned, made a gun with one hand, and shot the tabletop. "We give 'em the old pow, pow, pow."

Seth laughed at this boy's own bravado.

"See, that's why I want you," said Burns.

"Mate, I don't do the old pow, pow, pow."

"Really? Gordy Mac told me otherwise."

That again, thought Seth. A desperate moment whose reverberations wouldn't die away. A dangerous man, for reasons unknown, had let the cat out of the bag, but only, it seemed, to other dangerous men.

"Gordy Mac lies in his sleep," said Seth. "If you'd gone in with him he would have ripped you off."

"He and his brother turned me down. He introduced me to you, remember?"

Gordy Mac had told Seth something very different. But then the bastard lied in his sleep.

"Who's this prick?" said Burns. Parrot was coming over, an ingratiating smile on his face. Seth stifled a groan.

"That's Parrot. Small-time crim. Been around forever."

"A mate of Gordy Mac's?"

"No one was a mate of that bastard."

Watching over the schooner's rim, Burns drank beer.

"G'day, Seth, how ya been, mate?" said Parrot, all bright and friendly. With a smarmy nod to Burns, he plonked his beer down on the table.

"Alright," said Seth out of ingrained politeness, but he had to get rid of this twit without making a fuss.

Parrot pulled out a pack of Port Royal tobacco, paused for a second in bullshit reflection, then waggled the packet proudly.

"Yeah, been treating myself, aye. Had a bit of a score."

"Nice one." Burns raised his beer. "Here's to success."

"Aw, cheers, mate."

"So, the next round's on you?" said Burns.

Parrot burbled with laughter.

"Nah, it's the other way around," he said.

"Yeah? I don't follow."

"To congratulate me. Traditional, mate."

Burns laughed, amused at this larrikin stab at dodging a round. "I gotta remember that one," he said.

Winking at Seth like they were mates, Parrot sized up Burns as the new crim on the block and stuck out a hand. "Laurie's the name. Just got into town?"

Burns shook. "Andy. Up from the Gold Coast."

"Oo, the Goldie. Bet you see a lot of bikinis there, hey?"

"Mate, we grow 'em there."

"What – bikinis?"

"Oh, yeah. In plantations, like pineapples."

Parrot stared at Burns, then roared with laughter.

"So, what do you get up to, Andy? Mate of Seth Kelly, it must be something good."

Seth copped another wink.

"Aww, a bit of this, a bit of that, but more this than that if you know what I mean," said Burns.

Digging the patter, Parrot giggled like a flying fox.

"Had a nice drive up, Andy? The Bruce alright? Not too many washouts and potholes?"

"Drive? You fuckin' joking? Think I'd waste three days bouncing my balls to mush on that excuse for a highway?"

Parrot twisted and grinned like an acid head in front of a bass bin. Straight-faced, Burns sipped his beer. The crim collected himself, and pressed on.

"So, what's it like?" he said.

"What's what like?"

"Flying."

"You remember your first fuck?"

Parrot recoiled, obviously not happy remembering that milestone, and he greased his fib with a leer. "No, I don't actually, mate. Been too many, aye."

"Well, flying's nothing like it," said Burns.

Parrot dutifully laughed, panicked incomprehension at the corners of his eyes.

"So, this your local, Laurie?" said Burns.

"One of 'em. I drink in a few pubs, aye. Like to spread my dough around. Everyone knows me. I'm an old-timer, not some blown-in from down south thinking Cairns is a virgin with her bare arse up in the air."

"I would never have thought that," said Burns.

A grand was a grand, but Seth wanted to be done with Burns now. Fortunately, something happened that put his aggravation on the back burner.

Lou rang. He apologised, and she said she completely understood. He'd had a scare, but thank God he'd been there, and she was so grateful for that. Ellen had told the landlord, and he'd pulled up the stinging trees and taken them to the dump to be ploughed in as landfill.

"Good idea," said Seth. "Even dead and dry, they stay venomous for years. Probably what killed the dinosaurs."

Lou laughed, and that was good, and it was even better picking up Sophie after school that afternoon and tearing up to Ellis Beach. They ran along the beach like mad ones, swam in the back creek, and had fish and chips at the café.

After they'd eaten, he got up, pretending to leave, but Sophie sat there, swinging her legs back and forwards.

"You're not going," she said. Feeling a tingle of glee, he said, "And why is that?"

Sophie spun around in her chair and pointed at the ice cream freezer. "Because mango Weis!"

When they got back to Palm Cove, they'd hatched a plan for the weekend. "Mummy, mummy!" yelled Sophie as she ran into the house. "Can I stay with Uncle Seth on the weekend?"

The little girl's excitement was grand, but Lou's dinkum smile was even better, and it felt like family again.

After a shower, Sophie went to bed, big kisses all round. Seth grabbed a beer and sat at the dining table with Lou. Looking at the psychology books and sheaves of written notes on the table, he whistled in awe.

"That's serious study there, Lou. Wasn't three years at uni enough?"

Lou shook her head and poured herself a glass of wine.

"Not if I want a career. It's all stepping stones. The more stepping stones you have, the further you can go."

"And where do you end up?"

"Oh, I don't know, Seth. Opening doors no one knew were there. Helping people. Changing the world."

Impressed, Seth nodded. He didn't know anybody who was in with a chance to change the world.

But he couldn't quite wrap his head around psychology. It sounded more like magic than science to him: the arcane knowledge, the special words creating their own mumbo jumbo. And all that thinking about thinking.

But if it helped people unknot the freakery of their own minds, he wasn't going to knock it. Good acid dropped on a full moon beach didn't exactly qualify as psychology, but it had helped him undo some knots.

"It's a bit like what I do," he said.

"Changing the world?" said Lou with a grin.

"No, psychology. I help people, too. Observe, research, find clues. Piece it together and make a diagnosis."

Lou sat back, and watched him with a smile.

"You're an investigator of people's minds," he said.

She laughed. "That's funny."

"We have a lot in common, Lou. We're both on the same stage in life. House, a profession, Sophie."

Lou drank some wine.

"So when you have a practice, would you take me as a patient?" he asked, trading on a cheeky smile.

In an explosion of laughter, Lou nearly spilled her wine. She rocked madly in her chair, tickled to bits.

"What? What's so funny?" he said, grinning away.

But she was off her guts laughing, and it was infectious. When he caught her eye, she really lost it, and he cracked up too. It was great, their mad laughter letting a lot go.

Wide-eyed, Sophie ran into the room.

"What's happening? What's happening?" she cried.

Seth put out his arms, and she ran to him. Laughing, he scooped her up. In his arms, she began laughing too, and it was truely wonderful, the three of them like this.

When they began to settle, Sophie asked again, "What happened? Why were you laughing?"

"Uncle Seth wants a psychological diagnosis," said Lou, and she had another little splutter.

"Is that like the tests you write out?" said Sophie.

"Yes, sweetie, a lot like that."

"Was that really such a funny thing to ask?" said Seth. Lou grinned, drank some wine.

Sophie, her face next to his, waited for an answer too.

The grin had gone when she gave her verdict. "I don't think it's a good idea with family."

Hearing the finality in her voice, he shrugged.

As if in consolation, Sophie said, "Uncle Seth can do my test, Mummy. He's clever."

The Buzz

"Twenty thousand bucks," said Robbie the Bomb, the twinkle in his eye huge. Hiding his shock, Seth waited. On the couch next to him, Ray said nothing.

Crikey, it wasn't every day a mate made you an offer like that. But Robbie the Bomb was no ordinary mate.

"Six, eight hours tops. A bit of driving and a chance to have a beer or two with your old mates afterwards."

Robbie lit a cigarette, his sharp brown eyes passing over Ray; his right-hand man chewing gum and looking out at the hedge of canna lilies, his big chin moving like a cow with its cud.

Twenty grand for six, or eight hours work?

"You blokes selling some dope?" said Seth, feeling the outlaw buzz zap him hard.

Robbie flashed him a king-pin smile. "We sure are. It's been a bumper year. Hasn't it, Ray?"

Ray nodded, his attention on the cannas.

"You water 'em much, Seth?" he said.

"Yeah, you got to, aye. At least once a week. So, when's this job?"

"Ahhh . . . now?" said Robbie, like he was proposing they go fishing.

You cunning bastard, thought Seth. You're not giving

me any time to think about it. I'm either in or out.

He laughed at this. Ray gave him a brilliant smile.

"Jesus, you blokes," said Seth.

"You said you were missing the thrills," said Robbie. "So, here's a bit of fun. Be a player again for a few hours. We go for a ride, sell some of our very best, and bring the money back alive. No sweat, no trouble, no biff, and a cool twenty in your pocket at the end of it."

Okay, this is about getting me back in with him, thought Seth. The money is a nice big taste of things to come.

"Don't you have enough boys to drive a truck?" he said.

"Boys . . . yeah, that's the problem. We're a bit short on steady hands. A couple of good blokes got banged up in Stuart Creek, a few went straight. Shit, Big Teddy moved back to South Gosford."

Ray nodded ruefully. Robbie sighed.

"Sure, we got boys, there's a couple on board today, but we need somebody real solid to drive the truck. We need you, mate."

Seth tried not to smile as the electric tingle grew. The promise of outlaw action warmed him like a big hit of overproof rum.

Scratching an eyebrow, he pretended to think about it. The boys played along; Robbie puffing on his smoke, Ray getting even more botanical.

"Yeah, alright," he said.

Robbie gave him his golden look. Ray slapped him on the shoulder and said, "Good onya, Seth. Having you on board makes a big bloody difference."

It was bullshit, but Seth loved it.

Robbie used the phone and spoke a single soft sentence. Seth took off his watch and changed into old clothes. In the FJ 60, Robbie grinned at Seth, and slapped the dash.

"After today, you'll be able to get one of these yourself."

In a serious interface of man and machine, Robbie the Bomb went hard, and an hour later they were on the Atherton Tablelands driving along Upper Barron Road. After a few kilometres, they turned off and went through a few acres of hilly paddocks. At the end of the road was a homestead, a big corrugated-iron farm machinery shed out the back.

A fella came out of the shed and hurried over. In his early twenties, he nodded in greeting at Seth, curiosity in his eyes. Seth gave him a nod back. This must be some of the new blood, he thought.

He checked out the truck, a green Bedford D, its cargo bed enclosed with tin walls and roof. It was well-used, just another Tablelands truck, but the tyres were close to new, and the licence sticker on the windscreen was only a few months old.

"She's good," said Robbie. "Serviced last week."

Seth took a closer look at the front licence plate. The screw heads had some shiny scratches. Robbie smiled at this and handed over the keys. They got in, and Seth fired her up. When he tried out all the lights, Robbie laughed.

"C'mon, mate. We're not just out of high school."

The truck handled real well going down the long rutted driveway, and Seth guessed that the suspension had been goosed. Yeah, these boys were pros.

A few minutes later, Ray and the young bloke overtook them in an olive green FJ 45, and they followed it north.

Seth and Robbie yarned about the footy; going over the State of Origin, with Mal Meninga's guts-effort play in the first game winning him man-of-the-match. And that new boy, Wally Lewis had been bloody good, too. It was a pity Queensland had lost the series.

They mulled over the international airport being built and the high rises going up in Cairns, neither that keen on the influx of people all this would bring.

"Mate, that's why I live on the Tablelands," said Robbie. "Things won't change up here. Not in my bloody lifetime, anyway."

They saw a single cop car the whole way, parked outside Coles in Mareeba, with two boys in blue standing over a Murri fella sitting on the ground. Robbie shook his head at the sight. "Poor bastard. Booked for being black."

Passing through Mount Molloy, things looked half-way green. Some recent rain had turned the brown landscape verdant and the spiky grass trees glowed with life.

"What's the dope like you're selling?" said Seth.

"Oh, mate, it's champion pot. Remind me, I'll give you some. That young bloke with Ray? He's a wizard with the weed. As good as your mate Mick ever was. He's making us good money."

"Sounds like the new blood's earning its keep."

Robbie firmly nodded. "This bloke is. He's worth his weight in gold. Wish I had a spare sister for him to marry."

"So, Evil Simon's meeting us there?" said Seth, knowing this was who Robbie had rung. As gang enforcer, he'd be watching everything like a hawk with murder on its mind.

"Yep, he'll be there by now."

"What would you have done if I'd said no?"

Robbie shrugged. "Driven the truck, I suppose."

A few kilometres north of Julatten, Seth saw Ray slow and turn into an unsealed road that disappeared into the bush. Following, Seth went light on the gas as they bumped along the road, the paddocks on either side full of lantana. The road narrowed as a forested hill rose on the right, and soon the trees were close.

There was a sunlit clearing ahead; the road wider, some established trees, and it felt like there was a shed or house up there. Ray pulled over on the edge of the sunlight. Parked beyond him was a small furniture truck, and beyond that, the gleam of another vehicle.

"Just here, mate," prompted Robbie.

In the shadows of the forested hill, Seth pulled over, branches scraping along the tin sides of the Bedford.

"Okay," said Robbie, "Stay in the truck and wait for my signal."

Ray and the young bloke got out of the car, Ray shoving something into his belt, and what the hell? The heads of both men were covered, the dark material of masks tight across their heads.

He turned to Robbie – saw him pulling a mask on. Then his mate chucked another mask onto his lap.

"Put it on, mate." Robbie picked up a pistol from his lap, a Browning Hi-Power, and checked it.

"Jesus, what the hell's that for?" said Seth.

Robbie's eyes looked out of the mask.

"It's got rough nowadays. We take precautions, mate."

Seth's scalp tingled, the buzz roared triumphantly.

Robbie got out of the truck, stuck the Hi-Power in his belt, and pointed at the mask on Seth's lap.

"Put it on, aye. If there's a fuck-up, you don't want one of these bastards sticking a screwdriver into your neck one day down the track."

"Fuck," said Seth. Robbie laughed, and walked up the track after Ray and the young bloke.

Sitting there, somewhere between fuming bloody mad and grand excitement, Seth had to remind himself: What did you expect for twenty grand? A truck full of dope was always going to be a little hairy. Even the nicest blokes lost their cool around that sort of dough.

Picking up the mask, he saw that it had been carefully sewn. The work of a girlfriend or wife? A dyed-in-the-wool member of the Upper Barron Mob, that's for sure: they all knew what their fellas did.

It felt like rayon – something light, and he slipped it on and looked around. The eyeholes were of a good size and well seamed too, and the whole thing fit well. These girls could sell them by mail-order to crims across the country.

Through the windscreen, he saw Robbie, Ray, and the young fella approach the furniture truck, before vanishing into the bush on either side of the track.

Seth sat forward, the mask tightening on his face. What were they doing? Where was Evil Simon and the buyers? It was looking like a drive-in at midday around here.

In the side-window, he saw movement on the slope next to him. Not very far away, a branch twitched and jerked, then another. With no wind about, it must be an animal – or a man. Leaning forward, he saw a head and shoulders emerge in the foliage. A bloke, and he wasn't wearing a mask.

Seth froze, grateful for the gloom around the truck. The man put a scoped rifle to his shoulder, swept the barrel past the Bedford, and aimed up the track.

Very slowly, Seth put his head back against the seat, the electric hum inside now thunderous. With sideways eyes, he watched the rifleman.

There's got to be more bastards like him, he thought. Robbie's been set up; they're going to rip us off. The big question was: would they shoot blokes to get the dope?

The way to play it began running through his head. He had to assume the rifleman could see him sitting there, so he needed to dive across the seat, open the passenger door and scarper across the road into the bush, making use of the Bedford as cover.

Then he'd raise the alarm, calling out to Robbie and the boys. After that, there'd be some bang-bang for sure.

Settled in now, the bloke on the slope repeatedly scoped the driveway, up and down, the gun barrel passing over the truck each time. After a minute, Seth got the timing of these sweeps, and he looked at the passenger door handle.

Two seconds to get across the cracked vinyl seat, two more to yank the handle and open the door. Outside, he'd drop to the ground and sprint hard. If he made his move when the barrel was pointing up the track, he'd make it out of the truck without taking a bullet.

Bang! A gunshot boomed from up ahead. The rifleman

pivoted, aiming in the direction of the shot. As he did, a masked bloke popped up right by him and slammed the butt of a shotgun into his head. Rifleman slumped into the foliage. Shotgun fella leaned over and thumped again.

Another gunshot, close, now someone running through the bush towards the truck. Through leaves and branches, Seth glimpsed a man without a mask in camo pants, his t-shirt olive drab. Turning, he fired a handgun, then ran on.

A masked man appeared on the track – Robbie aiming the Hi Power two-handed. Waving madly, Seth caught his attention and pointed to where the running man was. Robbie nodded and melted into the bush again.

Seth felt like a cat at a greyhound race. Camo pants man was close, maybe aiming to use the truck for a getaway. Opening the door, he'd make Seth his hostage driver.

Someone, likely Robbie, whistled. Seth turned and saw that shotgun bloke had vanished. Time to abandon ship. As he reached for the door handle, a thumping came down the side of the truck: bodies hitting and bouncing off tin.

Right by the bonnet, Robbie sprang onto the track, the Hi-Power aimed down the side of the truck, its muzzle uncomfortably easy to look into.

A horrible snarl joined the thumping sounds; an evil voice going, "Drop it! I'll blow your fuckin' head off!"

A man slammed up against the passenger window, his wild-eyed face staring in with venomous rage. A shotgun barrel was jammed against his head.

In his mask, Seth didn't move a muscle. He sat there in the gloom, rubbing his ear as though waiting for the traffic lights to change.

"Fuckin' drop it!" yelled the bloke with the shotgun. Seth recognised the voice. It was Evil Simon.

He also recognised the furious face pressed against the glass. Chris Burns.

Moments Like This

Stasia finished work late, ringing him around seven. At Tawny's, they started with a couple of dozen Rockefeller, Stasia drinking vodka, Seth on rum and coke. They shared mains of blackened Cajun snapper and grilled scallops in dill butter while knocking back some icy-cold champers: Mumm from France. The bubbles were vintage, but what the hell – it wasn't every week you hooked twenty grand.

When they were finished eating, Stasia watched him top up their champagne flutes. As he crunched the bottle back into the ice bucket, bits of yesterday filled his head like scenes from a movie.

Burns, Rockjaw, and six others, hands tied, faces in the dirt. Evil Simon standing over them, the shotgun muzzle floating over their heads like a butterfly. Robbie's boys transferring sacks of dope from the furniture truck to the Bedford. And gleaming in the sun – Burns' Ford XY.

Driving through sun-drenched Mareeba: Murri fellas laughing outside The Royal, a clutch of old Italian boys yarning on the sidewalk, two office lasses in tight floral dresses drinking milkshakes.

Just a far northern town going about its day, while a truckload of marijuana stolen at gunpoint from the cops cruised by at the regulation forty kilometres an hour.

The ancient monster of a shed behind the homestead at Upper Barron. Parking the truck inside next to a couple of tractors, one with a sheepskin seat cover, and a sweat-stained cowdy hat atop the mudguard, the other clotted with decades of dust and rust.

Outside, the XY doing victory laps around the shed, laughing blokes sharing out celebratory six-packs of cold beer while Robbie and Ray slapped backs.

Seth apart, drinking by the truck, with everyone's eyes flitting over him, the mob of crims playing all innocent.

The air charged with portent. Evil Simon staring, his mad eyes gleaming, Ray, as ever, benign.

They'd pranked him, a crazy, out-there monster of a prank. 'You bastards,' he said.

The full-chested roar of delight made him beam, made him damn pleased to be with them – brothers-in-arms he'd shared risk and success with.

Robbie the Bomb grinning, rolling up a first joint from the haul. 'How was that, mate? Exciting enough for ya?'

'Aww yeah, but ripping off other growers isn't your usual style.'

'Oh, I wouldn't do that.' Robbie gesturing at a young fella now causing uproarious laughter with what he was holding up – a police badge and service revolver.

'No, they were cops, mate. We ripped off the cops!'

"A dollar for your thoughts." Stasia laid a hand on his forearm.

"Sorry, I just remembered something I have to do."

She gave him a knock-out smile, but he felt like shit.

He didn't like lying to her at all. Sitting here in his nice clothes with the smooth buzz of the restaurant all around, he felt shabby and junior; no outlaw buzz kicking in now.

"You were looking uptight earlier this year," said Stasia. "I'm getting that vibe again."

Seth smiled, uneasy now. Stasia was notorious for this, sensing trouble and rooting it out. He should head it off at the pass, interrupt and order another bottle of Mumm.

"Cops and crims, as I recall," she said.

Flashing on the cash in his backyard stash, Seth used it as fuel for a great smile. It was never going to be a number one, but it was up there, gleaming with the thrill of all that dough. Stasia's eyes shot it to pieces.

"Look, it's none of my business –"

"You're right, it's not." He hated his tone as he cut her off. Evading confrontation, Stasia changed tack.

"Do you need money, Seth?" she said.

"No, I don't. Look it's all good. Honestly."

"But?"

"There's no but, Stasia."

This time she showed zero mercy. "How's your criminal life going?"

Seth laughed, quaffed some Mumm – saw Burns's face squashed against the Bedford's window.

"It used to be attractive," said Stasia. "Before we hung out in Sydney. Knowing you were heavy. The outlaw vibe, the mystery. Imagining stuff. Now it bores me to tears."

"Then don't think about it."

"I don't work that way, Seth."

"I can't help you with that."

Her eyes took aim again.

"Do you ever see an end to it?"

That was a good one. He stared back at her, then firmly nodded his head. She saw the truth in his eyes, and he felt relieved, not just because he'd had a chance to be honest, but also because that end looked like it had finally come.

Sure, he'd hassle Burns for the rest of his money, keep up the act, but in a month or so he'd stop, as though over it. Finally, his life of coppers, crims, and violence would be done, and he was more than cool with that. It felt like he'd had enough to last a lifetime over the last two years.

Now came a flash of himself at the house in Palm Cove: Sophie laughing in his lap; Lou making something to eat in the kitchen; golden sunlight flooding the verandah. It felt so natural, its simplicity like medicine.

"You ever think about having kids?" he said.

"No fucking way," said Stasia sweetly. "I'm too selfish. I'm digging my life. Being a mum's not for me, and I don't care what my mother thinks."

"Fair enough," said Seth, filing that away.

"Me playing happy families? I don't think so."

They drank their champers and leisurely looked around the room at everyone eating, drinking and talking.

"Let's drink a toast." Stasia raised her glass.

"What to?" said Seth.

"My house."

"Another one?"

"Oh, there'll be many more."

"Toasts or houses?"

"I think one house is enough right now."

They chinged flutes. A few faces turned to look.

Stasia was looking good; the rings under her eyes nearly gone and a proper sparkle in her eyes. She glowed as she raised her glass, and why not? She'd scored a real goal.

"New times coming," said Stasia. "I don't feel like a rock and roll kid not giving a rat's-arse anymore. I'm always going to walk on the wild side, because that's eternal, but I feel a whole turn of the big wheel has happened. I'll take possession of my place by Christmas."

Seth toasted her again, and she hit him with starry eyes.

"And you've got Cinderella Street. Wow, hey? Look at us. No more share houses, camps, or pokey flats anymore. We're dinkum adults now."

"Who'd have thought?" said Seth, a smile hiding what he was feeling.

Stasia was working a gold mine of concrete, and there was a chance for her to kill the pig here. She might buy more property, and with a few savvy investments, never have to work again. But she'd be plugged into a proper hard slog until then, and that saddened him.

People looking at Stasia with her motorhead gypsy style would make the obvious, mostly correct, assumptions about her. Almost thirty, sex, drugs and rock'n'roll held no mysteries for her, and she'd pretty much lived as she wanted to; footloose and fancy free.

And she couldn't help cutting through bullshit, always kicking against pricks and knocking the straight world. Conventional, she was not.

But would she be that same person after years of hardcore work, after getting used to the money and all it could buy? He really hoped so.

A tiny flash of panic came and went as he felt a sense of time slipping away.

"Fancy a joint back at Cinderella Street?" he said. "It's a nice night. We can sit on the beach."

"No, I'm not keen on the drive back. I've had too many drinks. I'll be home five minutes from here," said Stasia.

"Stay the night. Try it, you might like it."

"I will, I promise, but I want to wake up in my own bed, Seth. A shower, my herbal cuppa, and I'm into it. Dougie's there at seven, we eat breakfast and then kick goals until six or seven."

"You still getting a share for all this, right?"

"It's how I pay for my mistakes. And buy houses."

"Houses?"

"Yeah, you got me thinking."

The bottle was empty, their glasses too. Neither of them had room left for dessert, so Seth paid the bill.

Outside in the car park, the ting-ting-ting of wire yacht halyards sounded from the inlet. They stood there for a moment looking at the old town.

He felt strange. They hadn't parted company yet, but he was missing her already. Alert to his mood, Stasia put her arm around his waist.

"Everyone's rushing to get their concrete poured before the wet. As soon as the rain kicks in, it will die right off," she said. "Dougie'll handle it, and I'll come and shack up with you. We'll stay in bed stoned, just doing it."

"Doing it?"

"Lots of it." She slapped his arse. "Start praying for rain, boy."

Later in the week, the prodigal uncle rang up – Hansen telling him to come over for dinner. Seth hung up grinning, and after a shower, a shave, and a greyhound of a joint, he put on some cool gear and cruised into town.

It looked busy at reception; a group of schmick-looking people, internationals by the sound of it, were checking in. Simon immediately saw Seth. Looking over the guests' heads, he smiled and flicked a forefinger upwards. Feeling pretty damn cool, Seth gave him the thumbs-up.

In the suite, Evelyn, fresh as a new gardenia, leaned up to kiss his cheek. The old bastard was on the phone, and he glanced over, raising an eyebrow in greeting. When he was done, they had a quick drink and headed downstairs.

In the Pacific Harbour Bar, a trio played Fleetwood Mac and Billy Joel. Evelyn studied them over the edge of her glass, an amazing ring glittering on one finger.

Downstairs at The Waterfront, Hansen and Seth got the rack of lamb for a change. Evelyn had the angel hair pasta and two serves of brandy snaps. After port and cheese, they left Evelyn in the lift to go up to the suite, while they went into the Galley Bar for another drink.

A dozen men and women were drinking and smoking, in the bar and it didn't take long for Hansen to get talking with two tough-looking but well-dressed blokes. They ran a fishing business that they'd been telling everyone about.

Hansen took the wheel, and with amusing eloquence, told the bar about fishing in Papua New Guinea in the old days. One of the fishermen decided to stir Hansen, asking him if he'd left a mob of half-caste kids in his wake.

That got some blokey laughter, while the women looked

either amused or put off by this coarseness. Ditching the beginnings of a grimace, Hansen regally smiled.

"Likely six, possibly eight. I paid for the schooling of the four that I'm absolutely sure of. With the exception of one glaring failure, they've all done well. Good kids."

Slightly shocked, the bar absorbed this.

"See," said Hansen, lighting a smoke. "We whitefellas have a duty to those people up there – a debt that must be repaid."

"How's that?" The pro fisherman unconsciously shook the diver's watch on his wrist.

Silence fell; all eyes on Hansen. From the bar came the tinkle of ice. A woman sat back, her dress rustling on the leather couch.

Hansen looked around, catching everyone's eye.

"Most of you here are too young to remember the war, but without the people of Papua New Guinea, the Torres Strait, northern Australia, and the Solomon Islands, we would have lost."

This assertion produced murmurs of surprise and some masculine grunts of dissent. Hansen continued in a calm but penetrating voice.

"They worked as porters, guides, as labourers building roads and airstrips. And, we must never forget, as soldiers and sailors, too. Time and time again they came through for us. See, a nightmare had landed on their doorstep. Mechanised warfare on a massive scale, with airstrips, wharfs, and bases built in mere days. Warships filling the horizon, planes crowding the skies, the bombardment and devastation. Imagine what they must have thought."

Hansen drained his glass. With a shake of the ice cubes, he caught the barman's attention. He nodded for a fresh drink, then continued talking.

"Imagine the islanders who witnessed the Battle of Savo Island playing out across their ancestral waters. The night aflame with exploding shells and rivers of tracer, stricken ships going down. The screams of burning, drowning men destroying the *mana* of that beautiful place. I was there and it scared the living shit out of me."

"Jesus," said a bloke.

"They should have run for their lives and hidden in the deepest caves and jungle mountains. But they helped us. And often paid the ultimate price."

Hansen gratefully accepted his drink from the barman. He took a good pull on it, building the expectant silence.

"Let me tell you a story," he said.

"Why stop now," murmured a wag.

"That illustrates the debt that we owe to these people. I served in the navy in the war, and we sailed convoys of ships through Torres Strait, bringing essential supplies and equipment to the East Coast. Yanks, Poms, Aussies, Islanders, Lascars – all of us running the course from Tucker Buoy to Bramble Cay."

"Know it well," said one of the fishermen.

"Good for you," said Hansen. "But we were under radio silence, on a war footing, with every man jack straining his eyeballs looking for periscopes and torpedo wakes. Now, the Straits ain't easy to navigate, even with charts and depth gauges. Especially for fellas from Southampton and San Diego. We needed pilots with local knowledge.

"But most of them were already on ships, so waiting at Bramble Cay on our way back for a pilot to turn up wasted time we didn't have. So we'd steam on to Stephen Island, as we knew it then, and the skipper would blow the siren, and out they would come."

Hansen paused, working his drink.

"Who? Out came who?" said the fisherman.

"Women rowing dinghies," said Hansen. "Who knew the waters like their husbands, brothers and fathers did. Coming alongside a great cruiser in a little speck of a boat, one of those women would come onboard – and guide our convoy through the Strait."

"Oh, my gosh," said a woman. Hansen smiled at her.

"So, remember that next Anzac Day. Remember it when you see an old Murri or Islander bloke. And that old lady fishing off the seawall down there? She might have saved many a life in desperate times."

In the pin-drop silence, Hansen finished his drink and got to his feet, everyone staring at him, everyone thinking hard. He nodded at Seth. "Nightcap?"

Up in the suite, Seth watched him pour a whopper of a scotch, and quickly drink half of it. Something was eating the bloke alive and he was trying to drown it with top-shelf liquor. A weird realisation now came to Seth: Maybe getting it all wasn't such a good thing.

The following evening, Hansen rang again, and Seth showered, got dressed, and went over. Barefoot and half-drunk, Hansen was fired up by a story he'd seen on TV. The bloody Space Shuttle was going to release a satellite into orbit, like it was giving birth! While they discussed it, they had a drink. Over on the lounge, Evelyn watched TV.

Hansen, in full flow, said that he'd like to go into space. Nodding, beer in hand, Seth glanced at the room service menu on the table. It was a Sunday, so it would be a new one. Or newish. They rotated them every fortnight.

He glanced at the TV, the Countdown theme catching his ear. Evelyn was leaning forward, like a million kids across the country were doing right now.

Talking about strange lights in the sky now, Hansen told him what he'd seen over the Western Pacific.

"I'm not one for man from Mars stuff, but when you see a light drop down from high above and zip off over the horizon quicker than a fighter jet – well, that's when you know science doesn't have all the answers."

"Unless it's science we don't know about," said Seth, remembering something Laidlaw had told him. Hansen stopped mid-flow, a scowl claiming his face.

"The SR-71," said Seth. "Mach three. Altitude of eighty-thousand feet."

Mouth open, frown deepening, Hansen stared at him. Seth nodded in confirmation of what he'd heard, trying to remember the rest. Shaking his head as though clearing it, Hansen went on.

"Then one clear night, a thousand nautical miles from the nearest terrestrial shithouse, the whole crew, except the bosun who was in the heads with a dose of the slippery guts, see this great big light –"

The old skipper stopped and turned to Evelyn. A song on Countdown had made her turn it up – a stripped-back groove with strange muttering percussion like a log drum. Jumping up, she began to shimmy and dance. With her slim hips moving and her bare feet skipping through the plush carpet, she looked the perfect pop star.

An obliging smile softened Hansen's rough old face. Turning back, he shrugged happily; it was an interruption he was pleased to indulge.

Evelyn began singing along – something about partying like it was 1999. Hansen turned back, and he and Seth watched the video clip.

The band were dead-pan stylishly sleazy, definitely no teenybopper act: all crotches, bare chests, leather pants, and rising-sun headbands; two sex-soaked women going cheek-to-cheek and body-to-body at a keyboard.

Hansen's mouth was open. Seth wondered if he'd ever really watched Countdown, or checked out the latest crop of stage looks in music magazines.

The singer filled the screen: some skinny motherfucker with a high voice, dressed in a glittering purple frock coat and high-heeled boots. With his black eyeliner and head of cascading ringlets, he looked prettier than a lot of girls. Evelyn, boogieing away, was captivated.

Hansen turned away in bewilderment, said something about 'another bloody planet.' An image flashed through Seth's head of a Tyrannosaurus rex looking up as a purple meteorite came crashing down.

The song ended. Evelyn turned the volume down, then darted a look at Hansen, who was waiting with a dumbly valiant smile. Her eyes shone at this. Seth looked away. It was beautiful, and sad, and none of his bloody business.

Later, as Omar Sharif and Julie Christie gazed into each other's eyes on the box, a spellbound Evelyn eating room service fish and chips as she watched, there was a heavy knocking on the door.

"Get that, willya, son?" said Hansen to Seth.

On the lounge, Evelyn sat frozen, the chip on her fork at her lips, the TV flicker in her startled eyes. Seth smiled reassuringly at her as he went over and opened the door.

A sour-faced bloke in his sixties stood there, unfeasibly dressed as a trendy fella half his age, nothing working on his portly frame.

"Oho, Hansen must be doing poorly if he needs you," he scoffed. Seth waited for more, and there was.

"You tell that little bitch to get her skinny arse out here," said the pretend young fella.

This warmed-up turd must be Evelyn's pimp, thought Seth, now recognising the bastard. He was an old time Cairns crook who'd made his start selling stolen US army surplus at the war's end. Now, as well as dodgy land deals, he ran hookers around town.

"Ah, you're the bloke who fleeced Uncle Sam. You must have sucked a Yank quartermaster's cock or two in your time," said Seth.

"You cheeky little bastard," said the pimp.

"Little?" said Seth, coming out of the doorway. He had six inches on the prick and the prick backed away.

"You tell him he can't just hog her like that."

"I'm asking you to leave the premises," said Seth in a tone of voice he'd used a thousand times before.

"I'll fuckin' have *you* leave town," said the pimp.

"Kelly." Hansen's voice rumbled in his ear, and a big, scarred paw pushed him out of the way.

Seth kept his eye on the pimp as Hansen bumped past into the hall way. His heavy arm flashed, and something small and yellow bounced off the pimp's head and hit the floor. The pimp yelled in shock and anger, but shut right up when he saw what was on the deep blue carpet: a roll of fifties, tight in a rubber band.

In reflex, he snatched the money up, his gut and age producing a nasty fart. He turned and yelled at Hansen. "You can't just buy her! This ain't the old days anymore."

Suddenly breaking into a run, Hansen stampeded the pimp down the hall. Surprisingly fast, he caught up and knocked the man to the ground, the roll of cash flying from his fingers. Coming to a halt over him, Hansen went to kick the sprawling pimp in the head.

"Hansen!" yelled Seth. "No!"

The old skipper heeded his command and stood there. But as the pimp slowly got to his hands and knees, his arse in the air, Hansen kicked him in the balls. He pulled back on it a lot, but it still must have hurt like hell.

With a sickening sound, the pimp collapsed to the floor. Seth began to let the door close behind him. He'd grab Hansen now, restrain him. But the old skipper was done, and he leant down and picked up the roll of money.

Like a squashed crab, the pimp began to scrabble along the floor. Then with a cry of anguish, he pulled himself to his feet and limped off down the hall.

Walking back to the suite, Hansen had a nasty smile on his dial. By himself and somewhere else, he might have spayed the bastard. With something like pride lighting his eyes, he barged into the doorway, slapping Seth on the back like they'd just scored a try together.

Inside the suite, Hansen kept beaming, charged right up on the rush of the biff. He'd kicked a bloke's arse, and even better – Seth had seen him do it.

"It's for moments like this that I pay you, son," he said.

An End To It

Overdue for a catch-up with Jeffyman, he left a message with Uncle Owen. The next day, his mate rang him from the Redlynch pub. With an unexpected early finish, he'd arranged to pick up Uncle Owen after he'd finished work. They could squeeze in a few beers now.

Inside the pub, Jeffyman was just buying them a round; his sense of timing bloody esoteric. Leaning against the bar, drinking a beer with his mate, Seth was happy listening to him talk about his future employment prospects.

"Mate, I'll be wiring up the whole town soon. Maybe down the coast, too. They started fixing up the resort on Dunk Island. Full refurbishment for a hundred and sixty rooms. Lot of work there. Good money too."

"How about some outside lights at my place?" said Seth. "Light up the garden."

"Aye? Whatcha gonna look at in your garden at night?"

"Sitting on the back porch, it looks nice."

"Jeez, what's wrong with playing a record or just going to sleep?"

"Ladies like it. You can see the flowers and pretty green leaves. It's romantic."

"Sounds like a moth trap."

"Sexier than moths."

"I knew this woman they called the Moth. If you were up late, she'd spot your light. Next thing – tap, tap, tap – she'd be at the window. Fully scare you. Or she'd come right in if the door was open."

"Not a good thing?" said Seth.

"Nah, she was trouble. Drunk and angry by that time of night, pub finished, bridges burnt, she'd be looking for a drink, a root, or a fight. Or all three. Blokes would run and hide."

They both laughed, but something knocked the smile off Jeffyman's face.

"Here, look, look," he hissed. "Here's that bullyman, the plainclothes bastard who came to your place last year."

Remembering that day with Jeffyman, Seth turned.

Chris Burns, looking as smooth as a bridegroom's dog, sat down on a stool next to them. In some nice clothes, he wasn't Andy today. He gave Seth an effigy of a smile.

"I need to talk to you. Now."

"Sure, fire away," said Seth, dismayed to see him, and wondering how he'd turned up here.

"Let's take it outside," said Burns, throwing Jeffyman a blank look. The Murri man stared back contemptuously. Burns eyeballed him, then refocused on Seth.

"It's very important. Let's go."

"Hold on, I haven't finished my beer," said Seth. "Why don't you have one?"

"No, I said let's go." Burns looked ready to burst.

Bugger you, thought Seth. With a smile he picked up his beer and drank.

Burns jabbed a finger into his leg. "Let's go."

Jeffyman was angry enough now to speak.

"You working or just hassling my mate in your spare time?"

"Who do you think I am?" Burns said to Jeffyman.

"You're supposed to be a cop, aren't you?"

"You told him?" Burns gave Seth an incredulous look. "This bloody . . . whatchamacalluit."

"Fuck you, Jack," said Jeffyman.

"You better watch your mouth," said Burns.

"Or what?"

"Or I'll arrest your cheeky black arse."

"Pull your head in, Burns," said Seth.

"Burns?" said Jeffyman. "Burns in hell more like it."

Blokes still rabbiting away began turning to look, the smell of trouble catching on through the haze of smoke.

"You keep that up, little man," said Burns to Jeffyman. "And you'll wish it *was* the Devil you're talking to."

A bloke guffawed loudly at this guff, and fellas began looking at Burns, a hoarse voice saying, "The fancy pants said he's going to arrest the Murri fella."

"Arrest him? What, is he a cop?" said another voice.

"What for? He's not even drunk," said another.

Men began moving in, the word 'cop' going around the front bar. Burns and Jeffyman sat with eyes locked. He's going to push it with Jeffy, Seth thought.

"You a cop, mate?" said a brawny bloke to Burns. Three bikers joined the semi-circle, craning their heads to get a good squiz at this potential problem down the road.

Burns ignored the question, kept staring, but it wasn't easy to vibe Jeffyman out.

"He's pretty flash for a copper, isn't he?" said a bloke. "Can't be working undercover, hey? Looks like a heifer in a bull paddock in here."

That got a laugh, but more than a few blokes didn't look pleased to see a plain-clothes cop in their pub – especially one dressed as though he'd never done a real day's work in his life.

Cued by the comedian, fellas now looked Burns up and down, from his coiffured head to his Hush Puppy shoes. A huge, bearded bloke at the bar leant over, and took a few loud sniffs above Burns' head.

"Mmmm, nice. Fairy piss."

"Fuckin' pig," said someone with feeling. Maybe they'd been busted or even bashed by the cops.

Blokes moved in closer. Feeling the change of mood, Burns turned and gave everyone a tight smile.

"Ah yuck, is that dogshit on his shoe?" said a larrikin voice. The cop's head jerked down to look, and someone spat a big glob of phlegm onto a Hush Puppy.

Burns' head shot back up, his face glossy with anger. He looked at the smiling faces around him. It could have been any of the six closest blokes, and his look of impotent rage made the crowd around him erupt with laughter, with Jeffyman the loudest.

"G'orn, piss off," said the hairy man-mountain, and other voices rumbled with menace amongst the jeers.

Burns didn't waste another second on them. Ignoring Jeffyman too, he got up and pushed through the throng.

But the look he shot Seth held the promise of something bad to come. No way, thought Seth. There's no way.

The pub now settled, and the noise level went back up to loud. Seth was grateful when his mate just turned to the bar and got them another round. But when he took the beer with a nod of thanks, Jeffyman put him in the spot.

"What's the story with the bullyman? What's he want?"

"He's heard about me and thinks I can help him with what's what and who's who. I'm telling him nothing, but I thought he could be helpful one day. For the business."

"Business?"

"Kelly Investigations."

Jeffyman drank some beer. "You thought," he said.

"Yeah, well, he's turned into a right pain in the arse."

Jeffyman snorted. "Don't tell me you're surprised? You ever meet one who wasn't?"

Seth busied himself with his schooner of beer, nodding like it was all finished with now.

"Yeah, after that show, I'm done with the bastard."

"Or you'll get done by him," said Jeffyman darkly.

"So," said Seth brightly, "Dunk Island, hey?"

Jeffyman nodded, drank from his schooner, then began explaining how he was going to juggle work and family to score himself the job. Grateful for the distraction, Seth drank and listened, chucking in the occasional comment.

When Uncle Owen arrived, Seth made room for him at the bar, but he had no time for knock-off beers today.

Nodding at Seth in greeting, he gestured impatiently at his nephew. "C'mon, let's go."

Never a man to muck-around, Uncle Owen headed back out the door. Jeffyman finished his beer and slapped Seth on the arm. "Big family do on tonight."

"Better shoot, man," said Seth.

His mate gone, Seth stood by a window and had one more for the road and tried to empty his mind of paranoid thoughts. But the din of voices and the clink of glass kept intruding, and he went over it all again.

Burns had only had seconds to look at him before Evil Simon dragged him away. The mask had covered his hair as well as his face. He'd left his watch at home, and the clothes and shoes he'd worn had been burnt.

No, he knew what Burns wanted: for him to help find his dope and take an active part in retrieving it.

Outside, he looked around for the blue Ford Fiesta that Burns usually drove around Cairns. It wasn't there and he went home, his eye on the rear-view mirror.

An hour later, a car pulled up outside his house.

He went to the front door fast, saw the blue Ford and Burns running up. The cop looked close to detonation.

Bare-chested, Seth filled the doorway.

"Are you following me?" he said. Burns shook his head, began snarling. Seth talked right over him.

"What were you doing at The Redlynch, then? Coming in and giving my mate grief like that?" He needed the bastard on the back foot.

"I was fuckin' passing by!" yelled Burns.

"What, going to a wedding?" Seth nodded at his clothes.

"It's none of your fucking business. Now listen –"

"Don't do that again." Seth pointed a stern finger.

Burns lost it. "Will you shut the fuck up!"

"Where's my nine grand?" said Seth.

Beyond speech, Burns sucked air.

"It's been nearly six weeks. I want my money!"

The detective looked around, smoke just about coming off him. Seth made a loud sound of irritated complaint. Burns turned and fixed him with a truly evil stare, like he wanted to drill right into Seth's skull to get the truth.

Pulling out a pack of cigarettes, he lit one, his eyes never leaving Seth's face. The manic fire in them was spooky.

"What's going on?" said Seth, "What's with this weirdo shit? Where's my money?"

Burns' gaze was unwavering, heavy with accusation, suspicion sticking out from his forehead like a horn.

Stick it up him, thought Seth. Push back hard. The nine grand made it easier; he had something to run decoy with, and he let rip with some righteous anger.

"Jesus, Burns! You're gonna rip me off, aren't you? You got some bullshit you're going to lay on me now, but the end result is that I don't get my money! Am I right? Hey?"

Burns broke eye contact, dragged on his smoke. Seth's soaring unease levelled out. The bastard was still super suspicious, but he hadn't broken through.

"Fuck you," said Seth. "You *are* going to stiff me."

The cop exhaled. He looked haggard now.

"The dope got ripped off," he said.

Seth stared, giving it a few beats, then let loose.

"Ripped off! Are you fucking kidding me! You blokes are cops, aren't you?"

"They set us up. They had men in the bush waiting."

"Nah, nah, nah! C'mon, man, you're shitting me."

About to ramp up the bogus rage, Seth saw something close to grief in Burns' eyes. After all the games the joker had played, and all the crazy shit he'd pulled, things had finally got personal for him.

"I grew that marijuana. Months and months of work, and care. It was really good and they . . . they just took it."

"The Gold Coast mob?" said Seth.

Burns shook his head.

"Jesus," said Seth, like he believed it now.

The detective threw his smoke down and came in close with eyes so grim you'd think he'd never cracked a smile in his whole life. Seth got ready to block punches.

"They're local boys, I'm sure of it," said Burns. "You're going to help me find them."

"Aye? No, that won't work. No one's gonna talk to me."

"Mate, you *are* going to do this."

"Or what? I don't get my nine grand?"

"Oh, that's just the start of it. I'll have your investigator and gun licences revoked."

"Bullshit, you can't . . ."

"I'll tell all of Cairns what you've been up to with me. I'll bust your druggie mates. Marty and his best mate Peter Rockwell, yeah? I'll tell 'em you've been my dog, that you gave them up. I'll shit in your nest so long and hard you'll need a mask and snorkel. If you don't get onboard with getting my dope back, you're finished up here."

Seth stared with anger, nothing feigned now. From the moment the bastard had walked into the Redlynch pub, he knew there'd be some pressure – but not like this.

Burns tried a wink now, but it was all wrong – a slippery tic of a thing. Going for a triumphant grin, he produced a leer of cocky desperation instead.

Seth now saw that the detective was desperate, his ever-present cool deserting him. It was scary to see.

This dread, and the need to warn his mates, made him nod in grudging acquiescence. He really hated giving in to Burns's monstering, but how things might be in a few days' time was another story.

Grinning like a metho-drinker, Burns tried to slap his back, saying, "You ring me, mate."

Seth ducked the hand and left him there.

Inside he waited until the blue Ford had driven off. He took a shower, but the stink of menace overpowered the Palmolive Gold. Between Burns and Robbie the Bomb, his life had become a slippery slide into a drop toilet.

A week went by. He heard nothing from Burns, but he knew it wouldn't last. When Burns did make contact, he'd say he was asking around and getting no results.

He caught up with Marty and Rockwell Pete, gave them a description of Burns, and told them to spread the word. Grateful for the heads-up, the boys weren't at all curious where the info had come from: Seth was an old mate, and that was enough.

Dinner with Hansen and Evelyn every two or three days provided some distraction, but the old skipper would get so drunk. Not every time, but enough for it to be a worry.

He'd be talking away, and his words would start to slur and fade out. His big, grizzled head would droop towards his chest, and Evelyn would pluck the cigarette from his hand. Then, in unspoken routine, they would wrangle him home.

Luckily, Simon worked a lot of nights, and he'd zip out from reception, a smile almost hiding his concern, and help them manhandle Hansen into the lift.

In the sweatbox accommodation of the Barbary Coast pubs or in the hallways of Hides Hotel, nobody would give a tenth of a shit at this sort of public drunkenness – it ran in Cairns' blood, but in this glitzy new hotel it was more than embarrassing.

Simon in his sleek suit and tie, Evelyn in a shimmering dress and high heels, Seth looking good too. Chandeliers, mirrored walls, and polished marble floors – and Hansen, with spittle in his beard and his legs giving out. Like a throwback to an uncouth era, he was a man out of time.

Seth began to cut down on going out with them, making excuses. Hansen, on hearing that he wasn't available, would hang up without a word. But he'd always ring a few days later, and Seth, feeling guilty, would head over.

One night, as they waited at the lifts after dinner at The Waterfront, everybody still pretty lively and happy to have a last drink in the suite, Seth had a great idea – something he reckoned Hansen would dig.

"I'll see you up there," he said. "I'm just going to get something from my truck."

It didn't take long, and when Evelyn opened the door, she was laughing. Hansen sitting at the dining table was laughing too.

"So, what did you get?" he said to Seth. "Some of that wacky baccy?"

"Wacky baccy?" said Evelyn.

"Marijuana. He likes to smoke it."

Evelyn tried not to pull a face.

"No, no," said Seth, and he held up a music cassette.

Hansen snorted. "Some of your rock and roll?"

Seth happily shook his head. With a wink at Evelyn, he went to the Sanyo tape player, popped the cassette in, and hit play. Putting the homemade cover of the tape on the table for Hansen to check out, he went over to the lounge.

He sat down, and that mournful but somehow hopeful trumpet resonated through the room. Now the strings sounded, syrupy-sweet but off, as though fermented in all that this hard old life could offer.

Evelyn settled next to Seth and, surely bored by the old-fashioned music, began flipping through a glossy fashion magazine, her face serene, her pose sublime. Pausing on pages, her fingers touched the photographs as though she might bring the models to life.

Picking up a folder from the table, Hansen opened it but didn't read. With his head slightly tilted, he listened. Seth had to smile. Turning someone on to music was the best thing.

A torpor filled the room as the side played through. The tracks really sounded like scenes in a film, and Seth had the urge to see the movie of the album now. It looked old, so he'd have to go to one of those cinemas in Sydney that showed the classics. He'd smoke some hash with Laidlaw first, and they'd have a rave about it afterwards.

It felt like he was in a movie right now, sitting in a suite in a luxury hotel on the edge of the world with these two characters: an old king and a young queen. They seemed so alike. Pragmatic and tough, they knew a bitter truth:

that life was tough and you did what you had to. The only real difference between them was that Hansen had made it to the top of a big pile of money.

But Seth knew that Evelyn would do the same one day, sublimating her face, body, and emotions to rise, and rise higher still. Her beauty, coming from deep inside like a hidden seam of gold, would never fade. The more worldly she got, the more refined she'd get, with every physical and mental tool at her disposal utilised.

A grunt of rage interrupted his musing. With explosive speed Hansen leapt to his feet, throwing Seth an intense look. It pretended to be a smile, but it couldn't hide the anger and betrayal.

Cassette cover in hand, he strode over to the Sanyo and madly jabbed at the buttons. The piano and strings fast-forwarded in shrill panic, and Evelyn cried out in alarm.

"Hansen, no! Not like that."

The horrid din abruptly stopped, and with a loud clack, the player door sprung open. Hansen turned, shoving the cassette into its case, and stomped up to Seth.

"Get up." His awful smile pulsed with rage. This was emotion on a level Seth hadn't seen in the man before. Flabbergasted, he got up. Hansen rammed the cassette into his front pocket.

"Very fucking funny. Now piss off!"

Seth laughed, anticipating the joke, but the old skipper grabbed his arm tightly, crushing down on the bicep, and roughly turned him towards the door.

Fully shocked now, Seth said, "What did I do?"

Through the reek of scotch and cigarettes, Hansen, still

grinning, said with absolute finality, "Piss off."

Beyond his great livid face, Seth saw Evelyn standing there, aghast at how things had suddenly gone.

Hansen jerked him forward, and what he saw in the old man's eyes – the will to take this to a no-holds-barred physical contest – shocked him anew. Dumbfounded, he let Hansen strong-arm him to the door, then push him out into the hall.

Too Much Him

And that was that it seemed. The next day he called and was told that Captain Hansen wasn't taking Mr. Kelly's calls any more. It wasn't Simon on the line, so all he could do was leave a messagen more enquiry than apology, as he didn't know what he should be apologising for.

By the end of the week it had sunk in: Hansen had left his life for good. He tried to get his head around it. They'd spent many hours together, eating, drinking, and talking like mates. So why did he turn like that?

Maybe a life lived like Hansen's eventually numbed you to people and their feelings, so that you just moved them in and out of your life like pieces on a board.

Ashamed to admit it, he felt pretty upset.

The dollars had been great, and he had got a glimpse of a world lived in the deep shade of big money. And, in the beginning at least, he'd dug the feeling of anticipation at hearing Hansen's voice summoning him.

But it was something else: a nagging sense of belonging, as though – how weird was this? – Hansen was family, like a cool big brother or a worldly uncle. Weirder still, he sensed Hansen had begun to feel the same way. He should have said . . . what? It was all too late now.

He'd felt it coming though. It had been like watching a

colossus crumble. Now he didn't have to watch anymore.

Still, it had been a good run, nearly six months, and he'd made fist-loads of cash, which had impressed Dad no end. When Seth told him, with no mention of the bizarre way it had ended, Dad accentuated the positive, telling him that he'd done very well keeping a big fish like Hansen on the line for so long.

On the back deck of the Maria again, Henry refused the money, so Seth put the fat roll of fifties on the galley table. Back outside, he dusted off his hands as though done with it, and Henry softly smiled in thanks. Mates share a win, thought Seth, especially with the fella who'd set up the try.

Silver and white in the clear blue sky, a plane rose above the mangroves, its turboprop engines yowling.

"Swearingen Metroliner," said Henry. "Pressurised."

Seth nodded and drank his tea.

"So, it went alright with him?" said Henry.

"He paid me a lot of money for not much work, but it got heavy a couple of times. Mainly, we ate and drank. In the end, he chucked me out. Like hands-on. Grabbed me and pushed me out the door. I still don't know why."

"Chucked you out?" Henry sat up. Seth told him how it had gone, and his friend looked mystified.

"Some blokes just don't like music, I suppose."

Clouds now became a daily occurrence, with the Lamb and Macalister ranges capped with white and grey. Most days there was drizzle, showers, even a few downpours. The frogs loved it, the mould too, so he made up a tea tree spray like Mum used to, and sprayed it around the house.

Though the streets were shiny with rain, Cairns seemed duller now, the feeling of same old, same old pervading, in spite of all the new buildings going up. It was back to court-work, thieves, and jealous spouses, the small lives with small problems. If he was lucky.

Now he gave it some real thought: What sort of business could he set up with the money he had squirrelled away? Something he could make a good living from.

He'd have to start off small. Big expenditures of black money would get Dad – and the tax office, wondering. He had a couple of ideas, but he needed to do some research and talk to those in the know.

One afternoon, coming out of the Shell petrol station on Sheridan Street, and thinking about his future prospects, his cogitations were interrupted by a whistle.

Turning, he saw Sideburns and the Maggot crossing the street. Sideburns, sweaty-faced, was smoking a cigarette.

"Hey, Magnum, P.I," he said, the Maggot staring hard with his mad eyes. "How's it going with Hansen? Getting lots of work?"

"How's it going with Eddie Seeto?" said Seth. "The fifteen grand you got must have turned him up fast."

The Maggot flinched in understanding. Sideburns went straight to anger. "Fuckin' smart arse."

Seth laughed, pleased to piss these pricks off.

"Actually, I had a big hand in seeing him off," he lied. "You slowcoaches should think of that money as a present from me."

Sideburns angrily flicked his cigarette away.

"You knock him?" said the Maggot.

"Put a sock in it."

"Hansen asked you to knock him, didn't he?"

Seth rolled his eyes and turned to Pig. "Bugger this, I'm off."

"What's happening with Chris Burns?" said the Maggot.

It was damn lucky they couldn't see his face. Quickly though, he turned and gave them a look of irritation.

"What? Is this another bloke I've got to find for you lazy bastards?"

The Ds watched his face like hawks, looking for the lie. Seth stuck his face forward, mocking their intensity.

"Looks like this fella's got right up your bum. Someone special, is he?" he said.

"Also calls himself Andy," said the Maggot. "Reckons he's got a lot of cannabis for sale. You know about that?"

Keeping it moving, Seth fired up more bogus irritation.

"So, it's back to this shit again. Despite zero evidence, you blokes persist in trying to make out I'm a crim who associates with crims."

"You ever get sick of lying?" said Sideburns.

"To you blokes? No."

"You hear that?" said Sideburns to the Maggot, but the little D didn't answer; his eyes were busy trying to put red-hot wires into Seth's face.

"Nah, I'm just having you boys on," said Seth. "Look, I'll admit I was a tearaway back in the day, but I got blamed for stuff I never did, and it still happens today. Like I've told you before, I left all that behind. I've got firearms and investigator's licences, and a legitimate business. I'm not blowing them to piss about with potheads."

The two Ds contemplated this. They knew shit was out there skulking around in the bush, but they couldn't get a spotlight on it. The Maggot pursed his lips in a cat's arse of defeat.

"You need to tell us if you run into him," he said. "He's dangerous."

"Yeah? How dangerous?"

The Ds exchanged glances.

"What? He's killed someone?" said Seth.

"Worse than that. He's pissed off his mates, and they're very serious blokes. About as serious as you can get. So he's desperate, and that makes him dangerous."

"I reckon I'll stay away from him," said Seth.

"You get a fix on him, and there's grand in it for you."

Seth whistled in appreciation. "What's he look like?"

The Maggot almost smiled.

"Flash bastard, real joker. Grins all the bloody time."

"Total opposite to you blokes, then."

The Maggot showed a line of sharp teeth.

"We looked into you."

"Yeah? Whatcha find?"

"Officially, just one arrest. You bashed some fella who'd raped a girl. Nearly killed the prick."

"He dropped the charges," said Seth.

"Must have got cold feet, hey?" said Sideburns.

Seth shrugged. The Maggot came closer.

"You also worked as a glorified bouncer around Cairns and managed not to put anyone in hospital again. Played by the rules and kept your nose clean. In this town, that's some achievement."

"Now I'm a licenced private investigator with top-shelf clients. Do I detect some jealousy here, boys?"

Sideburns spat on the sidewalk. The Maggot aired his teeth again.

"Officially," he said, "You were at the scene of a violent death involving a firearm earlier this year."

"You boys were right there in court," said Seth.

"Unofficially," said the Maggot, "You shot a man dead on a marijuana crop a couple of years back."

"Is that right?" said Seth. "Okay, it's been fun fellas, but I have to go."

The Maggot stepped forward. Sideburns unconsciously put his hand on the service revolver clipped to his belt.

"Listen," said the little detective, his voice ice-cold. "You don't want to fuck around with this bloke."

"Or with us," growled Sideburns.

"Why would I even know him?" said Seth.

The Maggot crowded right in, Sideburns looming at his side. "You think we don't have eyes in this shitbox of a town?"

Seth flashed on the Crown Hotel, the bar full of crims and wasters. The Maggot nodded grimly.

"You fly with the crows, you'll get shot with the crows."

The rain became more than intermittent, and the ABC said a low was forming near Karumba. Seth test-fired the gennie and made sure he had jerrycans of fuel. Silent light was always nicer, so he filled up the kerosene lanterns and trimmed their wicks. He stocked up on dry food, beer, and Tally-Ho papers, even a few bottles of rum.

The low could yet go into the Gulf, with the power supply uninterrupted, but with the wet coming up, he'd rather get prepared now. Mastering the physical world in the far north wasn't always a breeze, but with gear and a bit of foresight, most obstacles could be overcome.

It was preparing for the other stuff, the shit that people brought into your life, that was hard.

The stink of angst enveloped him as he stood looking at the two hundred and eighty-seven record albums leaning against the wall. Burns was crawling about in the back of his head like a snake.

You're a bloody idiot, he told himself.

His karma, fertilised by hubris and the desire to be Mr. Cool, had pulled a gun and shot him in the foot. Wanting to be a player again had resulted in an own goal of epic proportions. He'd played with the Devil; now the bastard wanted his pound of flesh.

He put on the private eye movie soundtrack and turned it up over the rain, but it felt disturbing, its fusion of schmaltz and grit not working right now. He took it off, closed the turntable lid, and looked around.

Here was a home, small but perfect; a space where he could play his records loud and cook a steak to perfection and – damn it to buggery!

He almost yelled. He nearly punched a wall. That rotten cop was sticking to him like a tick, sucking away his peace of mind. When would the bastard give up and leave town with his tail between his legs?

From what the Maggot had said, Burns was in trouble. His threats to smear Seth with his mates, bust them, and revoke his licences were likely just piss in the wind now. The bastard had probably been suspended.

But he still felt a bad vibe about it. Even without official sanction anymore, Burns could turn into a shit-fight. The detective's wild-card energy and his will to push it might spill into a last-ditch effort of mindless spoiling.

A rogue cop with mayhem on his mind. How on God's good earth do you prepare for that?

Staying at home didn't feel like a good strategy, and he found himself driving out of Machans. He wasn't running away; he just wasn't there. Driving through the rain to Palm Cove, the thought of taking a break from Cairns rode the turbulent waves in his head.

When he got to Lou's, he found she was thinking much the same thing. But not just a break – a total break.

"I decided I'm going to do my masters in Brisbane," she said. "I'll make the right contacts down there for when I start my practice."

"So, you're moving down . . . soon?" said Seth. Lou nodded, and Mum and Sophie flashed through his head. He tried to smile.

"Oh, Seth." Lou patted his hand. "I know. You've got so used to having Sophie around, but you can come and visit us, and we'll still come up on holiday every year."

A squall came in, rain lashing the windows. Outside, the gardenia bushes bobbed and jumped in the downpour. Water droplets burst and trailed down the glass panes.

Lou took his hand and gave him a solid smile.

"Don't be sad. You've really connected with her, and she has with you. It's a great foundation for what's to come."

Feeling unaccountably panicked, he managed a smile. Something pivotal was slipping past him here; something profound. White petals flew in and stuck to the glass.

"No, it's great, Lou," he said.

Lou smiled, her eyes commending him.

He didn't stay long, spinning a lie about visiting a mate, but he accepted her offer of a cuppa. Looking pleased with herself, Lou gave him a run-down on how her renovation timetable had gone.

Everything was completed, almost within budget, and best of all – before the wet. She'd done real well. As he congratulated her, that niggle of panic came back, as though something irretrievable was about to be lost.

It poured all afternoon and into the night. Seth guessed at least five inches by the time the ABC late news came on. There had been big totals up on the Cape, and a few rivers were on flood watch.

Around two in the morning he woke, the rain crashing down, with the sudden feeling of somebody in the house. He jumped up, ghosted out into the living room. Waiting in the dark, he felt sillier with each passing minute.

The next day he had to fix a gutter in the rain, popping over to Anton's Wrecking for a new piece. After lunch, he made up a shopping list and went into town. Lucky with parking, he darted in and out of the supermarket. At Chandler's Music Bar, he grabbed a three pack of blank cassettes, and headed for home.

Passing the Crown Hotel, he spotted his old fisherman mate Cable, standing on the corner, glowering at the rain.

He pulled in and wound down the passenger window.

"Oi!" he yelled at the old bloke, who got a fright. "You want a ride?"

Cable's face lit up, and he quickly got in. He was drunk and not at all keen on getting soaked walking home.

"You still at Portsmith?" said Seth.

"Nah, nah, got out of there. Bloody young weirdos next door. I'm up there." He pointed towards Sheridan Street.

"At Mrs. Hanahan's boarding house."

Seth knew it. One of three 'private hotels' in a row, it was a timber and fibro firetrap where a lot of old blokes ended up, every silly bastard smoking in bed. It was about three hundred metres away.

"I hate getting wet," said Cable. "Must be why I never fell in the drink or had a boat sink on me."

"Hey, Seth!" Someone was coming up to the passenger window. Chris Burns.

"Just go along with what I say," Seth said to Cable. The old bloke sniffed and nodded.

Ignoring the old fisherman, Burns stared in. He was in his rumpled Andy-wear, unshaven, wired, and wielding a wreck of a smile. He must have stunk too, because Cable, no soap-hound himself, cringed away from him.

"I was coming to see you," said Burns, flicking rain from his eyes. "To hear what you've got for me."

"Mate, you should leave town. Honestly," said Seth.

"Yeah? Why's that? Because the local Ds reckon they've put a price on my head?"

"Burns, listen, you want to keep off the street. Go back to Brisbane. Those boys are heavy bastards."

Burns cackled, spittle landing in Cable's hair.

"I was talking to those two idiots yesterday! They're just shit stirring everyone. It's bullshit to make them look big. They can talk to me whenever they bloody well want."

Seth rubbed his scarred ear. Burns frowned at him.

"I'm getting fucking soaked out here, man. You wanna hop out for a minute? Let's talk."

"Nah, I gotta drop the old bloke home."

Burns glared at Cable, who stared straight ahead.

"Where's that?"

"Over at Portsmith. I'll be half an hour, tops."

Burns stared at Seth like he knew he was lying. Seth put his hand back on the wheel and started the Pig.

"Hey," said Burns, his eyes wide, his voice suddenly rising. "Wait a second. Kelly, fuckin' wait! Wait!"

As Seth put the Pig into gear, Burns grabbed Cable. Pissed or not, the old bloke had lived many rough decades, and he slammed Burn's head up into the window frame. Burns staggered back. Seth darted a look at the side-mirror. All clear. He turned hard into Shields Street.

"Who the hell was that idiot?" said Cable. "Grabbing me like a Barbary Coast whore!"

Trying to stay cool, Seth got on to Sheridan, drove fast, pulling a U-turn to stop out the front of Mrs. Hanahan's.

"Aw, cheers," said Cable. Seth gave him the nod.

"Listen, mate," said the old fisherman. "You wanna be a bit more selective about choosing your friends."

Seth nodded, more than eager to get going. "You're not wrong. Okay, I'll seeya around."

The rain lessened as he drove home, but his anxiety

kept growing. Burns was still here, hunting for clues in the pubs. But the cool, sharp player, always a step ahead of the game, now looked like a worm squirming in the underbelly of Cairns. A crazy sick worm.

Seth had seen the crazy in his eyes just before. And with that explosion of rage, it was obvious the bloke had lost it.

Back home, he put the groceries away, locked up, and then drove back up the street. His head was buzzing, and he felt a deep current pulling him towards something he'd been too scared to name, something he felt like he'd been waiting a long time for.

North on the highway, low cloud and drizzle blotted out the range. He saw little frogs jumping on the road, and felt his heart pound.

There'd been a few this-is-it moments in his life, nearly always life or death situations with violence crowding in, but what he was thinking of doing now was very different.

He'd lose a part of himself and not be the man he was. The things that had kept his synapses buzzing would be done with, the absolute freedom and open-endedness of his life gone. But what he'd gain.

Seth didn't subscribe to any personal philosophy, but if there was one thing he knew deep in his heart, it was 'go for it.' At the Palm Cove turn-off, he did.

From the stairs, he saw Lou sitting in the front room. She saw him on the verandah, and got up and opened the door. She looked at her watch as he came inside.

"If I'd known you were coming over, I would have asked you to pick up Sophie," she said. "It's nearly time."

"Ah, sorry, Lou. It's a bit spur of the moment."

She looked at him, saw something was up, and sat back at the table. With his heart thundering, he joined her.

"What's this about, Seth? I'm not changing my mind about moving to Brisbane."

He shook his head, feeling a great swell of emotion pass through him. This is it, man. This is it.

"I'm thinking of moving to Brisbane too," he said.

Not missing a beat, Lou nodded. "Because of Sophie?"

"And you."

She let her surprise show.

"Seth, I'm not sure . . ."

"You feel something for me, don't you? That day in the garden, and that time – up in Kuranda."

"Well, yes, you're a very sexy man, Seth, but . . . it seems kind of weird. I mean, *both* brothers."

"Oh, bugger all that, Lou. It's actually pretty natural."

"Natural? How do you see that?"

"Lots of things. We care about each other, for starters."

"O-kay, and?"

"I put thirty thousand dollars into this house. I lent it to Alex. I sell my place, and with the combined cash we could get something real nice in Brisbane. Makes sense, right?"

Lou sat up in her chair.

"And bigger than all of that – Sophie is ours."

"Ours?"

"I'm her father," he said.

"You're what?"

"That afternoon after the raid, the creek at the gorge. We didn't use anything, did we? You'd been south for a bit, and you took off back down to Ballina the day after.

He told me . . . that you'd kept him at arm's length for ages. Then nine months later, Sophie was born."

The look in her eyes ran all his hope off the road.

"Seth, I was bleeding that day, remember? You thought I was hurt. I had my period that day."

His stomach dive-bombed at the memory. Lou made a sympathetic sound. He scrambled to get his head around it, then saw his mistake.

"He lied to me."

"No, he didn't."

"There was . . . someone else?"

"There was no one else. After we saw you at the hospital we went back to the house and he raped me. Twice. Then was unbelievably caring as though nothing had happened. I left that night. I've never told anyone until now."

He felt like a Mac truck had hit him.

Lou rubbed her fingers together as though bringing the feeling back into them. Her eyes were on the drizzle outside, but she wasn't one to sidestep anything.

"I came back. Stuck with him, too. I loved him so much, even though he'd been such an animal to me. A stupid part of me thought I deserved it. For what we'd done that day." She softly smiled. "I didn't think that way for long."

"I found a way to forget about it. We both did. I was pregnant and we had Sophie and life went on. Memory is elastic. You can stick it under a table like chewing gum."

He knew just what she meant.

Looking at a House & Garden magazine on the table, he felt profoundly disturbed. His brother raping Lou. Jesus. But even sicker – he wasn't that surprised.

Like so many blokes, Alex had been in perpetual battle with the opposite sex, with a fuck as the prize demanded and taken. With his macho mates, he stayed constantly on guard against the seemingly occult power of women, bagging them and running them down, with every insult and humiliation a laugh, a joke, just a bit of fun.

But it was segregation, separation – the original sin.

Unquestioningly learned, unconsciously absorbed, this status quo had been passed on through generations. Alex had been a convincing teacher. His ability to talk chicks into letting him get up them was legendary. When he held court at front-bars and parties, blokes would listen with awed delight as he regaled them with the pure filth of all the fanny he'd ripped through.

Now Lou's confirmation of his brother's rottenness was stinking up the room. He'd loved his brother – and he'd hated him. It didn't seem possible to feel such conflicting emotions until you did. She must know that.

Feeling culpable, and burning with shame, he forced himself to look up at Lou. He tried an unhappy smile, like, 'isn't this crazy what we share?' but she had something else on her mind.

"You remember a birthday party for some people called Babs and Moonie? Six or seven years ago?"

Seth stared, truly staggered. Lou watched his stunned face, then nodded in confirmation and went on.

"People said a lot of bad things about Alex, but a short while after he died, I heard he was part of a gang rape at that party. Were you there?"

Horror squirmed, memory dragged him down.

Hard fingers digging into his arm, their evil laughter freaking him out. Fully out of it on beer, rum, and sticky heads, being pulled along, the shack swaying under their weight. Liam punching him in the kidney, jokey, not too hard, Alex's arm clamped around him like a vice.

Pushed through the doorway. A musty bedroom, kero lantern-lit, hand-made timber furniture, a quilt on a bed. And a young chick, drunk and scared.

Goggling at her, dismay in his guts. Alex telling him to go first. Gordy's hard eyes willing him, Liam laughing crazily, holding the girl's head like it was a trophy.

Shocked sober, pulling away. His shirt tearing, his fist ramming into Alex's ribs. The bastard roaring at him. Liam wading in, hitting him properly now, Alex too, and under a flurry of blows, running for the door.

"You were there." Lou's eyes were bottomless.

Seth couldn't speak, the sordid truth eviscerating him.

"Oh, shit," she said. "Are you going to tell me something horrible now?"

"I didn't do anything." It was hard to get the words out.

"Nothing?"

"Nothing. I did nothing . . . to stop them."

"You watched?"

"I ran away."

Lou looked out at the greyness.

That's my speciality, he thought. Running away. A huge sob burst from his chest. He gasped for air. The past had been ripped open like the head off a boil; poison flowed.

Seth sobbed again, his diaphragm jumping painfully.

"Why are you crying?" said Lou.

He could see the terrified young woman now, her eyes and nose, the cut of her hair, her shoulders and hands, all portrait-photograph clear.

"Are you crying for yourself?" said Lou.

Seth shook his head.

"Alex?"

"Fuck, no." Tears stung his eyes, snot filled his nose. Lou sat watching him.

"Poor girl," he finally said. "Poor girl."

Lou softly sighed, and they sat there with a big ball of shame, regret, and sorrow between them. It was more than sad.

After a bit, Seth stood, went to the toilet and blew his nose. A dolphin calendar filled a wall. Emptiness howled inside him.

Bereft of thought and pulverised by shame, he drifted, standing over the bowl, and with some effort he managed to ride the guilt and gut-deep despair.

Back at the table he waited, expecting more questions, but there was really nothing more to ask. Lou didn't look particularly angry, but she sure wasn't happy. He nodded as reflectively as he could and looked out at his truck. "I might go."

Lou stood up, eyes full of compassion, and put her hand around his wrist.

"I'll always care about you, Seth, and I know you love Sophie."

"I really do."

He wanted to talk, but Lou gave him a soothing smile, and her hand tightened.

"I know Sophie's always going to have her uncle," she said. "And I hope you'll always be my friend. But you and me together, as good as it might have been?"

She didn't have to shake her head.

"There's just too much him."

Psychic Desperation

On the corner of Sheridan and Shield Streets, he stared through the disposal store's window. Boots, canteens and compasses sat displayed under pirate and Southern Cross flags. Rain drummed on the bullnose tin roof over the sidewalk, and fell in sheets off the row of awnings that ran down the length of the block. The wide concrete pavement glistened, the gutters pulsed, and on the corner a drain was backing up.

He hadn't gone home – put off by the thought of Burns there like a monster from a bad dream. And by the idea of sitting alone with the other monster, the one from his past.

In a daze, he'd driven into town, the edges of the cane-fields along the highway now long puddles; the pooling water jumping with falling rain.

An ammo box swam into focus, but he couldn't decipher the stencilled words on it. He was here to get something from the disposals. He just couldn't remember what.

Shame coursed through him like bad acid. His psychic desperation made him sick to his guts. What the hell had he been thinking? A choccie-box fantasy of a happy family was just an excuse for what he had to do on his own.

Wind gusts changed the tone of the rain on tin roofs, and it spun off gutters, blew in arcs of spray. He read the words '.303 ball' on the ammo box.

With a wrench of his mind, he faced the monster fair and square. Fuck you, Alex. *Fuck you.*

I wanted to be you. And you wanted me to be you – the bloke's bloke all the chicks wanted and who all the fellas wanted to be. But you were cruel and sly, with everything wrapped up in the best smile and the biggest laugh.

That night at Moonie and Bab's had been the beginning of the end. He knew that Alex and the Mac brothers were capable of doing bad things to women. He'd heard stories – that he'd managed to ignore. Sure, he'd seen the slaps meted out by Alex to drunk and rowdy chicks, stuff a hell of a lot tamer than what a bloke would get, but with that terrified young woman, every awful rumour became true.

After that, he kept his distance, wanting Alex to know he'd crossed the line. But when they did meet, the bastard just kept smiling and joking like nothing had happened, his eyes daring Seth to bring it up.

The rain began to falter; a gap in the convective stream coming in off the Coral Sea. It stopped, and the darkened sidewalk under the line of shop roofs resounded with the noise of rushing gutters and pattering water.

That poor girl, thought Seth. Too shocked and gutless to intervene or call for help, he'd left her to those bastards, and hidden her away in his memory like all the other bad bits of his life. Lou had brought her back.

Somehow it felt inevitable. The last couple of years had rammed that home. You couldn't hide your shit forever. It always came back to bite you on the arse.

But what happened to her? Did she end up having kids with a good fella, her pain and humiliation hidden away so that no one ever knew? Putting the horror of that night in a box and locking it tight, so she could live her life.

Or was she still running: damaged, out of it, angry and afraid; raging in fucked-up scenes, forever cursed by bad men? Or something worse.

Sorrow, abysmal and excoriating, scraped him inside. The air was thick with moisture, his cheeks were salty wet. Someone hurried past, a vague shape with a half-opened brolly. Cars hissed by on the water-rippling street.

A face stared back from the shop window: A clean-cut looking bloke out window-shopping, expressionless, but undeniably crying.

Hating his tears, he felt their catharsis nonetheless. He'd fucked up all those years ago, but he'd never stood by like that again. He'd smashed blokes to pulp. He'd do it again.

He wiped his face, cleared his throat. He should ring Rod Savage; the bloke back from the mines for the next two weeks. His neighbour could keep an eye on his place, because he didn't want to be there right now.

Turning from the window, he saw two women walking along the pavement jerk to a stop, their shocked faces staring at him. A hand gripped his shoulder, spun him about, and whack! – he took a full-on punch in the chest, and whack! – another in his ribs.

It was Uncle Owen, warrior eyes flashing with rage, and punching like Lionel Rose. Seth took a punch in the arm, then another to his head, and he turned and ran out into the street. Skidding on the wet bitumen, he nearly fell. He spun around, saw Uncle Owen still under the awning.

"Uncle Owen! What? What? What did I do?"

Even as he said it, he knew, and a terrible chasm of guilt opened under him. Uncle Owen ran to the gutter. Numb with shock, Seth readied himself to flee, but the furious man stopped and pointed a finger.

"You stay away from my nephew! You keep away from him, you criminal bastard!"

"What happened? Is he alright?"

"He is now, but no thanks to you! Your fuckin' bullyman mate grabbed him. Put a gun in his mouth!"

Seth struggled to speak. "Where? Where is he?"

"Think I'd tell you? You fuckin' stay away from him!"

Seth flashed on Jeffyman's lady up the range – Evie.

"He's in Kuranda?"

Uncle Owen could knock a bloke off his feet, probably through a wall, but he was shit at lying. When he shook his head, Seth knew where his mate was.

"I'm so sorry, Uncle Owen. I fucked up."

"I'll fuck you up," said Uncle Own, and he ran down the side of the ute into the street.

Seth fled, a near-miss taxi beeping loudly as he pelted across the soggy meridian strip. Making the other side, he threw a look behind him and saw that Uncle Owen had gone. He'd made his point – four hard-knuckled times.

Head spinning, heart pounding, Seth gasped from the punishment he'd taken. He gave it a minute before warily crossing the street and circling back around to the Pig.

He now saw how it must have gone at the Redlynch pub that day. Burns waiting outside. Watching Jeffyman leave with Uncle Owen. Following them back to Manoora.

With a grunt of pain, he got into the Pig. Starting the truck, he pulled out. He had to get up to Kuranda and find Jeffyman. It was pretty much a dead-cert he was going to get a big 'get fucked' – but he had to try and make things right between them.

It came down hard driving up the range, the steep and winding jungle road streaming with the heavy rain. The flaky greywacke rock of the road cuttings ran with water; chunks of it fallen to the roadside, and a couple of new waterfalls were fanning dirt and stones across the road.

If this keeps up, he thought, the road will get cut. Then it's a long bloody drive through the Tablelands and down the Gillies to get back to Cairns. And only if the Mulgrave River bridge hadn't gone under.

Fingers crossed, he'd quickly find Jeffyman, grovel like a bastard, and hopefully keep their friendship alive, then hurry back down the range before it got dark.

The rain was cutting the visibility right down, but aside from a couple of cars coming down, the road was empty. Driving carefully but fast, he went up over the misty green range. On the other side he crossed over the Barron. The river was well up, the mud saturated water moving along with implacable speed.

In Kuranda, Coondoo Street was pretty much empty, the fig trees on either side blurring in the rain. He had no idea where Jeffyman's lady lived, but he needed a drink before he did anything else.

Town itself wasn't much: two pubs, the RSL hall and bowling club, a post office and corner store, a few shops, and a new restaurant he'd heard was good. He'd go have a drink at the Bottom Pub first and casually ask around. It was a Murri pub, so Jeffyman might even be there having a beer.

At the corner store, some Murri kids were sheltering out front under the tin roof. There were a few parked cars there, and across the road at the Top Pub, there were a handful more.

He drove down the street to the Bottom Pub and saw a clutch of vehicles angle-parked outside. Pulling in next to them, he killed the engine. Right across the road, the whitewashed timber buildings of the police station floated in the mist.

Quickly getting out, Seth ran in under the awning of the pub. The building was nondescript: a one storey chamfer-board and tin-roofed structure, a penny-farthing bicycle chained to a roof pole, its wheels in a storm-water gutter gurgling with frothy brown water.

The pub was almost empty, but he quickly checked out the front bar, the poolroom booths, the dining room, and the gents. They were all empty.

In the front bar, he got a beer. A luminous blue painting of a naked white woman lying mysterious under a yellow moon looked down on the handful of men drinking. These blokes looked settled in; no one that keen on going back to the gloom and wetness of their shacks and bush camps.

Seth gratefully drank beer, then gingerly touched the side of his head where Uncle Owen's fist had exploded. Around him, voices kept balls of bullshit aloft, everyone talking loudly over the rain. In north Queensland Murri,

391

Yank, Aussie, and European accents, blokes raved about forest spirits, tachometers, the rain, Kathmandu, and, as ever, the cops.

Seth dug the vibe here. It was like you were somewhere, not just in another pub in the far north, and right now he was happy to be somewhere else. But the beer didn't last, and with guilt churning his guts, he went looking for his friend.

The rain had slackened a bit, and that would make his search a little easier. First, he checked the streets in town, looking for a pink two-door Corolla. The village was tiny; he was done in ten minutes. He didn't spot the car, but it could be down a bush driveway, or parked behind a shed.

Out of town, he drove to the Murri communities along the Barron River, the dwellings there little more than run-down shacks. Like something from another country, they had minimal electricity and no running water inside. It was hard to believe it was the 80s. There were lots of kids on the verandas, a few cars parked, but no pink Corolla.

When he slowed at Mantaka to scan the vehicles there, a bare-chested bloke in blue jeans on the porch of a timber shack eyeballed him through the drizzle. I'd get real short shrift asking about Jeffyman around here, he thought. Straight-looking whitefella, short hair; they'd mark me as trouble straight away.

Driving back along Myola Road, he flicked between the radio stations, listening to weather bulletins. The Barron, Daintree, and Mulgrave rivers were all rising, with major flood levels more a probability than a possibility. The rain could last for days.

Back in Kuranda he parked by the Bottom Pub again, listening as the ABC got a weather bureau johnny on the line. It looked like today had been a bit of the calm before the storm; the proper rain was tipped to kick in tonight.

A Murri bloke was standing in the shelter of the tin roof outside the pub smoking. He wore a battered cowboy hat, cowboy boots, clean blue jeans, and a nicely ironed green long-sleeved shirt buttoned at the wrists.

When Seth got out, he smelt dope. He pointedly looked across the road at the police station. The bloke laughed.

"Ahhh, don't worry about them," he said. "They took off before. Probably a smash on the highway with this rain."

The bloke was lean, fit, and lightly bearded, looking in his late twenties. With canny eyes, he held out the joint. Seth smiled in thanks. A puff right now was what he needed.

It was bush-weed, a little dry but not too bad, and they passed it back and forth in silence. When it was gone, the bloke stuck out his hand. "Tommy Green."

His hand was rough with callus, and Seth flashed on years of rope, horses, and cattle.

"Seth Kelly."

"Irish, aye. There's a mob who like a drink and a fight."

"I try and do only one of them now days."

"Same here. Yep, I come into town for a break."

"Where did you come from?"

"I'm a cowboy," said Tommy Green, as if no one could tell. "I move big mobs of cattle up the Cape."

"That's worth a few drinks."

A cruisy smile played across the cowboy's face.

"Not wrong. Cold beer, the ladies, a rock'n'roll jukebox,

pool tables. When you've been chasing cattle for a while, you take your recreational activities real serious."

Seth laughed. Tommy Green tipped his hat back on his head and unhappily smiled.

"But this rain, aye. No mob here, no ladies, no parties. Nobody down the river. Everyone's bunkered up."

"That's a bastard."

The cowboy shrugged pragmatically.

"But we need it. I've seen too much dead stock choking up dry creeks. Bones wearing skins. Birds all dead, too."

Seth nodded slowly, grateful to ponder other disasters.

"It brings us life," said the cowboy. "Grass for the stock, water for the dams. Flowers for the ladies."

They smiled at that.

"You a churchie?"

Seth shook his head.

"Yeah, me too," said Tommy Green, and he spat into the gutter. "I've seen 'em pray for rain. Truly pray for it. But Jesus and all his saints got no bloody say in it. No one has. The rain doesn't answer to nobody."

Seth had to agree.

"But when she rains, like really rains," said the cowboy, waving his hand at the drizzle. "She's a proper destroyer. Floods up fast, and there's cows drowning, fences down, bridges gone. Houses and sheds, the bitumen – it all gets washed away."

Seth nodded. He'd seen it happen.

"She can look after us, or take everything away," said the cowboy. "That's the power of it – the power of rain."

Stoned, Seth stood there speechless.

"You right there?" said Tommy Green.

"Yeah, yeah, I'm good."

"Let's have a beer, then."

In the front bar, Seth ordered them two schooners and quickly checked the place out again. Back at the bar, he hurried his beer. The cowboy watched him.

"Looks like you working," he said.

"It's a long story, but I have to find a mate. His name's Jeffery. He's a Murri bloke. Might have been here today."

"Can't help you there. I just got dropped off before. And no one's here. It's a wash-out. Worse bloody luck."

"She does that."

"She sure does."

Wild laughter erupted. A bloke leapt onto one of the heavy wood bar stools, yelling about immortality. There were clouds at the windows, mist in the doorway.

Seth finished his beer. "Thanks for the smoke, man."

"You find your mate, bring him back here for a beer."

That would be nice, he thought as he left. A few beers with a couple of good blokes on a wet day. Tommy Green would have some yarns for sure.

Walking to the Pig, he saw a car parked on the side road next to the police station: a brown Datsun with a wired-up passenger door handle. With a real bad feeling, he jogged over.

His suspicions were realised as he looked in the driver's window. Slumped back in the seat with his eyes shut was that rotten little crim, Laurie Keats.

Seth banged on the roof. Parrot jumped in shock, and he looked up like a kid caught with his hand in a lolly jar.

Cracking a dodgy smile, he yelled through smeary glass.

"Hey, mate! How you been?"

"You wanna hop out of the car?"

"Mate, what's up?"

Seth opened the door. Parrot got out, smelling like no one had emptied his cage for a while. He grinned fearfully as Seth raked him with hard eyes.

"Everything alright, mate?" said the crim.

"Did he show you his badge?"

"Who?"

"The fella with me at The Crown the other day. The cop. They're the bastards with the badges, right?"

"Mate, I wouldn't know," said Parrot reasonably. This reflexive, mongrel lying pushed Seth's jar off the shelf.

Parrot had an arm inside the car door frame. Stepping in, Seth leaned onto the door, pushing hard. The crim, his face swimming with trepidation, cringed defensively, his free hand cupping his nuts.

"Yeah, yeah, he showed me his badge!"

Seth kept up the pressure for a few more seconds, then stepped back. Parrot slid away from the door, his face a nutty rictus of relief.

"I wouldn't have done it just for money, mate. Honest. He threatened to lock me up and bash me."

With an electric cloud of dread surging through him, Seth casually put his hand on Parrot's shoulder.

"When did you start following me?"

"Ah, three days ago? But not all of Tuesday. I felt a bit crook. Bad pie or something."

"You go to Palm Cove?" said Seth.

"Ah, no. When were you there?"

"How did you find me today?"

"Aw shit, mate, the car's not too reliable, and with all this rain . . ."

"Shut up. When did you first see me today?"

"I fell asleep at Machans, and when I saw you wasn't home anymore, I looked for you in town. I saw you going north on Sheridan, and here I am."

Seth took his hand off Parrot and wiped it on his leg. He looked at the phone box across the street.

"When did you ring him?"

"Ah, not long ago . . . fifteen minutes? I was having a rest up, waiting for you to come out of the pub."

"You reckon he'll come up here?"

"It's shit weather, aye," said the crim. "But I reckon he will. Listen, is he alright?"

"Alright?"

"He's a copper, right, but he threatened to knock me! He wouldn't do that, would he?"

"Nah, that's against the law."

Taking out his wallet, Seth found a fifty. Parrot cringed as the money got stuffed into his shirt pocket.

"What do you do now?" said Seth.

"I stop following you?"

"And?"

"Keep my mouth shut?"

"That's right. I'm not a cop, so I *will* knock you."

"Oh no, you don't need to do that, mate. Honest."

"Remember, Parrot – when that bastard has gone back to Brisbane, I'll still be here."

"Oh, yes, mate, I know that."

"Now, piss off."

"Thank you, mate, thank you."

In utter turmoil, Seth went to the Pig and just stood there. At the bowls club, two lapwings stood motionless in a puddle on the green. From all around came the sound of dripping trees.

The Datsun fired up, and Parrot came bucking along muddy ruts out onto Coondoo Street. With a cheery toot of his horn, he drove off.

Mindlessly Efficient
Machines

"Faaaark," whispered Seth. He'd come that close – *that* close. He felt bleached out with horror at what he'd done.

He'd really fucked up with Jeffyman – but the girls! He got a horrible flash of Burns hurting Sophie and Lou. He fell back against the Pig. He was wailing, but his mouth was closed. Up to his arse in arrogance, he'd opened a door between the straight and bent worlds and let something very bad in.

Get in the Pig, he told himself. Move. Freaking out over what happened or what didn't happen wouldn't help now. He started the engine and quickly ran through it.

How fast would Burns make it up here? Conditions on the range road were deteriorating. It wasn't raining here, but it probably was on the coastal side of the road. Rain would slow him, and maybe a landslide or fallen tree had already cut the road. It was best to be pessimistic, though.

Forty-five minutes up from Cairns, minus the fifteen since Parrot had squawked and Burns could be here in the next half an hour. Yep, he should get the hell out of here.

A hundred metres up the street was the intersection: the Top Pub, post office, store and RSL on each corner.

Cars were coming and going at the corner store and bottle shop; the locals knew all about cut roads and no supplies.

There was a Murri kid sitting under the tree outside the store, his head turning as he watched the passing vehicles. He was a natural surveillance operative. Seth pulled up outside the store, got out, and went over to the kid.

"Hey, yubba. You been sitting here for a while?"

"You a cop?"

"Nah."

"Bullshit."

"True. I've had some real trouble with those bastards."

The kid gave him an incredulous look. Clean-shaven whitefella in unstained clothes, the tyres on his truck not even close to bald? Yeah, sure.

"You see a pink two-door Corolla around today?"

"You got a dollar?"

Seth didn't. But he had two dollars, and he handed the green note over. "Must be your lucky day, hey?"

"Not yours, but. I've seen no car like that."

The kid ran into the shop.

Copping the sting, Seth went back to the Pig. It was time to get back down the range. Heading towards the highway a hundred metres away, he saw in the rear-view mirror Jeffyman's pink Corolla pulling in at the store. Halting in the street, he saw two Murri blokes go in.

He parked under a fig tree and watched. A few minutes later the blokes got back in the Corolla and went back the way they'd come. Pulling a U-turn, he followed them into Barron Falls Road. Turning down the hill, he saw the kid, chewing hard, back at his perch on the corner.

Two kilometres out of town, the Corolla turned off at a Queenslander house. Fifty metres down the road, there was an expanse of guinea grass under a poinciana tree; next to it the double rutted mouth of someone's driveway.

Nosing through the long, wet grass, he parked behind the poinciana. It wasn't perfect, but it would do.

Waterlogged ground squelched underfoot as he walked back to the road. The air hummed with a deep bass note, a continuous rumbling coming from not far away.

The Corolla was on the driveway at the Queenslander. On the lawn, a car body sat rusting up on concrete blocks. Parked in the space under the house was a Monaro LS, its engine block hanging from chains attached to a beam.

Clustered about the car were five or six Murri blokes, none of them particularly small. One of them saw Seth.

"Look, look," he said urgently. Everybody turned to stare. "G'day," said Seth, raising a hand in greeting.

Next to the car was a table covered in tools. A transistor radio was playing I Love Rock and Roll. A kid, oblivious to the whitefella in the driveway, bobbed his head along to the monster riff.

Empty longnecks and stubbies were lined up against a retaining wall. One fella held a chrome shifting spanner and a greasy rag, another bloke a stubbie. It was a classic Australian wet day – a mob of revheads fixing things up, shooting the breeze, and drinking beer.

Two muscled-up blokes came walking out, and Seth got a good idea why Jeffyman was holed up here. These fellas, through much experience no doubt, would face down any cop and easily see off anyone else.

"What'd you want?" said one of the blokes. His face was without expression, but his eyes smouldered.

"Fuck him up," called someone from under the house. The other bloke walking up looked like he was ready and willing to act on this advice. With squeals of excitement, some kids came running out, agog at the big man drama.

"I'm looking for my mate," said Seth. He nodded at the Corolla.

"You the police?" said the first fella.

"No, no. I'm a mate of Jeffery."

Up in an open window, a woman's face appeared.

"Don't know no Jeffery," said the first fella.

"Look, mate," said Seth. "I know he's here. Can you just tell him I'm here? Please?"

"Please," said someone in a high-pitched voice. There was laughter, and the kids all grinned madly.

"You got no mates here," said the second fella, and Seth saw how badly mashed the knuckles on his right fist were, one of them just about centred on the back of his hand.

Another bloke began walking towards them.

"Fuck him up or fuck him off," he said. Other voices began singing the same song.

"I'm not looking for any trouble," said Seth. "I'm an old mate of Jeffery's. I need to see him."

"What for?"

"I need to help him."

"What? Same help he got yesterday? Fuckin' cop with a gun?" The first fella wasn't expressionless anymore. "You responsible for that? Aye? Aye?"

"Fuck him up," insisted a voice.

"You want to leave this property," said the second fella. It wasn't a request.

"I reckon he's a dog for the cops," said a revhead. "A fuckin' undercover dog."

Everyone came forward now. Seth's ribs throbbed from the hiding he'd got from Uncle Owen. It was time to go.

"Heeeeeeeeyyy!"

The piercing yell froze everyone, a couple of the blokes instinctively flinching. Kids' mouths flew open in terror, and the smallest one fled under the house.

At the top of the steps stood a stout, older woman. Grey-haired with glasses, she was frowning fit to crack a granite boulder in two.

"You!" She gave Seth a ray gun stare. "He'll see you."

"Thank you. Thank you, ma'am." Seth gratefully walked towards the steps, the mob all fiercely eyeballing him. The woman pointed down the side of the house.

"No, you go around that way."

Without breaking stride, Seth followed her directions. As he came to the corner, Jeffyman wordlessly appeared, passing him as he made for the road.

"Hey, Jeffy," said Seth, but his mate broke into a trot, one hand signalling the watching blokes to stay put.

Seth followed, oaths and jeers ringing out behind him. When he got out on the road, he saw his mate had started running in the direction of the falls. Though he tipped the scales at a hundred kilos, Seth could turn on a sprint when he had to. But Jeffyman was a rocket.

"Jeffy! Stop! Listen, man, listen!" he yelled as he began to run. Unhearing, Jeffyman picked up speed.

Conserving breath, Seth shut up and ran. He knew this was a test. If he wanted to talk to his mate, he'd have run with him until he stopped.

Barron Falls Road curved through the rainforest, trees overhanging the road. Rainwater moved in rippling arcs across the bitumen, and mist greyed out pockets of forest around them.

Over Seth's thudding boots and the slap of Jeffyman's bare feet came that constant roar: a deep throbbing that seemed to come from the earth itself. The falls, pumped up by all the rain, were not five hundred metres away.

Jeffyman wasn't slowing, and that was fine with Seth because he didn't know yet what he could say to salvage their friendship. All he could do was say sorry. But that wasn't enough. Not by a long shot.

They ran up a small hill and down around a bend. Seth now saw the drive to the house where Ulysses used to live, where Alex had bashed him unconscious. They ran past it and went up and over another hill. Oh man, thought Seth, this is turning into a marathon.

The road forked, the great rumble of the falls on the left. Jeffyman took the right fork and they ran further into the rainforest. Dripping trees joined overhead, and on either side, walls of lawyer-cane engulfed trees.

As they ran around a bend, a new sound joined the deep thunder of the falls. Ahead, a flooded creek ran through a big culvert under the road, its torrent heading for the gorge. Seth recognised the creek. He'd brought Lou here.

Jeffyman sprinted over the culvert, then, thank Christ, stopped. Seth ran up to him, and stood there gulping air.

Jeffyman ignored him, and they both just stared down the five-metre drop at the branches swaying and bouncing at the edges of the flooded creek.

Seth needed to speak, but he couldn't just yet. A stitch was knifing his ribs, his lungs felt raw.

Jeffyman turned to him, an elemental darkness in his face. Seth straightened up and saw his friend slipping away – if not already gone.

"You've been a good mate." Jeffyman's voice was thick with anger. "But you *really* fucked up."

His eyes flashed, and his voice grew louder.

"I know what cops are like. I've seen what they've done. Who they raped and bashed and murdered. I know who they protect. I see what they do to us, how they help you bastards keep us down."

Jeffyman shook his head.

"When we were growing, I knew what I was getting into. I took my chances. But I'm an electrician now! I'm legal. That bullyman stuck a gun in my mouth. Said racial shit. He threatened my family. My family! And all the time I'm thinking – why the fuck isn't this you?"

"Mate, it will be me next. Listen . . ."

"No! *Your* problem is fucking up *my* life!"

"Listen, Jeffy, that bullyman is . . ."

"But what *really* makes me wild!" yelled Jeffyman. "Is that I got used to get at you. My skin made it easy for him. Another blackfella used – then fuckin' chucked away."

"Listen, Jeffy! That cop knows I'm up here."

"What! You're fuckin' joking." Jeffyman was horrified.

"I wish I was, man. We've got to get back to the house.

You stay put inside, I'll go back to Cairns. You'll never see that bastard again, I promise you. I came up here to tell you –"

The sound of a car coming from town made them turn. A four-wheel drive Suzuki with a hire-car logo on its side came around the bend – some donkey of a tourist looking for the falls in this weather. With a final rev of speed, the vehicle pulled up a few metres away.

Seth's guts froze as the driver jumped out. Parrot must have lied, or got his timing wrong, because here was Chris Burns pointing a black revolver at them.

"I worked it out," said Burns, and he mimicked rubbing his ear. "The mask wasn't enough."

Seth groaned. "I'm sorry, Jeffy."

"Fuck your sorry," said Jeffyman.

"Okay, tell Sammy Davis Jr. to come here," said Burns, the gun muzzle moving to Jeffyman. Mist crawled across the road behind him. No one moved.

"Tell that little black bastard to come here!"

"Don't move," said Seth. "I'm gonna talk to him."

There was the scuff of bare feet, and he turned to see Jeffyman leap off the road and vanish into the leaves of a massive king fern. The great spray of fronds shook with his impact, and over the creek's rush came the sound of him crashing through branches down to the forest floor.

"The fuck!" yelled Burns. Without second thought, Seth launched himself at the king fern.

The glittering, wet forest spun past, the fat brown snake of the creek roaring on the left. He fell through the screen of fronds, instantly soaked, and smashed into the black trunk of the fern tree. Falling sideways, he snatched out at a smooth section of lawyer-cane. It slowed him for a second, then tore away, and he swung into the trunk of a big penda tree. Bouncing off it, he fell through the thick foliage and smacked into the sodden ground.

With the air knocked out of his lungs, he just lay there, thankfully hidden from the road. Over the rush of the swollen creek, he heard shouts of rage.

With a heartfelt groan, he forced himself to his feet. For as sure as snakes shat, Burns was going to come down here after him. Soaking leaf litter fell off his arms and legs, and the tiny hooks of wait-a-while vine tore at his arms as he ducked about looking for Jeffyman. In the gloom up ahead, he now saw his mate moving quickly through the jungle, and he gave chase.

Metres away, the creek rushed along incredibly fast. It was impassable; its force would snatch a man away, tumbling him over and over, before flinging him out to plunge down into the gorge, with the pulverised body eventually spat out into Trinity Bay as fish food.

He saw Jeffyman veer away from the creek to where the bush thinned out and a hill rose. Just over the hill was the cutting of the railway line; Kuranda the next stop. Metres from the track were the cliffs of the gorge.

Seth now saw his mate's plan. After crossing the creek at the railway bridge, he'd sprint down the train track, then bush-bash it through someone's block to come out on Barron Falls Road near the rev-heads' house. If they could both stay ahead of Burns and leave the railway track unseen – they'd get away.

As Seth ran, he looked over his shoulder at times. With the noise of the creek and the thunder of the falls, it was impossible to hear any pursuit, but he might just spot Burns coming through the misty rainforest.

At the hill's summit, he saw Jeffyman moving through the trees, the ground now clear of undergrowth. He let out a low crop-sitter's whistle. His mate stopped and looked back. His face was an impenetrable mask, but he didn't start running again.

Thinking hard now, Seth ran to him, his boots skidding across wet drifts of smooth black stones.

"Listen, man," he began, looking right at Jeffyman. But he slipped and fell. Throwing out a forearm, he hit the deck hard, a fat pebble pounding into the side of his head.

Things went a bit fuzzy, and when the lights came back on, he was being shaken, his mate whispering frantically in his ear, "C'mon, c'mon, man. Get up, get up."

With a rush of giddiness, he got to his feet.

"You right?" said Jeffyman. "You got knocked out."

He nodded, trying to ignore the new pain in his head.

"C'mon, let's get to the railway," said Jeffyman.

They kept moving; the gorge close now. Mist from the falls swirled in under the canopy, and the ground vibrated from the thousands of tons of water falling every second. Over the majestic din, Seth heard a sharp crack and felt his boot break through something.

Jeffyman, barefoot, froze and scanned the ground. "What the hell! There's broken glass everywhere."

Glimpsed between dark stones and ground creepers were glinting wet shards of smashed bottles, green, white,

408

and brown. An image flashed through Seth's head of Lou and him walking along the creek that dry season years ago, and how pissed off she'd been at this rubbish.

"Watch your feet," said Seth. "It's an old bottle dump. We'll have to go this way." He began to double back, away from the glass. Treading carefully, Jeffyman followed.

They made their way towards the head of the creeper-covered gully and went around it. As they headed back to the creek, Chris Burns appeared on the other side of the gully.

He saw them, and his gun flew up, two-handed and rock steady. Seth recognised the revolver now – the Smith and Wesson magnum he'd found hidden in Burns' hotel room last year. A gun for murder, alright, taken from a crim and probably untraceable.

He didn't know how good a shot Burns was, but if he could shoot like he could fight, he'd easily put a bullet in someone's head or chest from this range.

The revolver's muzzle moved down, slightly to the right, and Seth realised what Burns was going to do – shoot Jeffyman in the leg or foot, and while he writhed on the ground in agony, the bastard would use this terrible trick to find out where the dope was. Then he'd kill Jeffyman.

Seth stepped in front of his mate, glass popping under his boots. Burns grimaced with irritation, moving the gun to find a clear shot. Searching for words, Seth raised a hand, like he might stop the bullet. He felt Jeffyman brush against his legs, heard the loud click of wet stones.

The black pistol snapped down, Burns aiming at knee height, but something smacked into his gun hand. The gun fired, unbelievably loud, the bullet zipping past, and Burns yelled in astonishment and pain.

Turning at the hips, Seth saw Jeffyman spring up and throw a second stone. It hit the cop's neck. The gun swung one-handed, blind. Seth frantically bent, snatched up a stone, and got Burns a good one in his knee. With a shout, the detective nearly fell.

Seth and Jeffyman grabbed dark, wet stones, and threw them as hard and fast as they could. The cop's right arm jigged about trying to aim, stones impacting his body and face. A shot boomed, and katock! a stone bounced off his skull. Falling to his knees, Burns shouted in pain as glass cut into his legs.

Thwack, thwack! Stones peppered him. Blood ran down his face. Two fingers on his gun hand stuck out weirdly. He tried to use the pistol to push himself back up, but Seth and Jeffyman, like mindlessly efficient machines, kept up the hard rain of stones.

Losing his balance, Burns tipped forward and tumbled through a scrim of creepers, dead branches, and leaves into the hollow ground beneath him. His arms and legs flailed as he tried to stave off the inevitable, and he began screaming with dreadful awareness of what was about to happen to him.

Stones in hand, Seth and Jeffyman now watched as the detective plunged headfirst into the gully. At the centre of the little ravine, the bottles and glass were piled at least a metre deep. A bird or a small animal could easily cross it, but for anything heavier – it was a death trap.

Gravity now pulled Burns through the layers of bottles,

bursting them into razored shards as he fell. Like in some medieval punishment, he was being flayed alive.

Over his lungs-out screaming and the rush of the creek, the breaking glass sounded like bells. In a wild frenzy of smashing bottles and tearing creepers, Burns vanished.

As Seth and Jeffyman hot-footed it to the creek's edge, the cop's voice abruptly cut out. Over the rush of the creek and the subsonic boom of the falls came the strange sound of glass cascading through the rocks of the gully.

Now a torrent of brown, white, and green shards burst out into the creek. The cataract of glass suddenly flushed red, and in an explosion of crystal and crimson, Burns tumbled into view.

He still looked like a man, but only just. Big bits of him had come off the bone, and opened musculature squirted. His face looked like something in an anatomical textbook. For a gut-wrenching moment he spasmed on the blood-slick rock – then he was gone, swept away in the relentless rush of water.

Completely freaked out, Seth turned to Jeffyman. His mate stared back in shock. The look they shared held an absolute shitload: triumph and horror at what they'd just done, relief at not being killed, and the realisation that they now shared a secret to be taken to the grave.

Then Jeffyman's face changed – a shutter came down, and Seth felt an awful certainty sweep through him.

"No, hold on, mate. Listen," he began.

With eyes like hard, dark stones, Jeffyman shook his head. "We're through," he said.

Abruptly, Seth felt drained. As much as he wanted to,

he couldn't speak. He reached out his hand. Implacable, almost unseeing, Jeffyman turned away and made for the railway track.

Blown apart, Seth watched him walk into the swirling mist and out of his life.

The Power of Rain

He woke up late. The phone had been ringing at some point, but now only the crisp roar of rain filled his ears. Lying there, he felt his brain slowly uncrinkle like a scrunched-up ball of cellophane. Last night he'd drunk a bottle of rum and who the hell knows how many beers.

It had been a rough-as-guts trip coming down the range from Kuranda. There were two waterfalls across the road, and a kilometre past the water point, he'd coaxed the Pig over the dirt of the first landslide.

At home, after a few rums, he punched a big hole in the first carton of NQ lager. After that, he went next door and got on it with Rod Savage, raving into the night. Rod, bless him, knew something was up and stuck the course, just about going drink for drink with him.

Now he felt sick – and truly gutted. It was a king fuck-up. He'd lost a good mate, an old mate, because of his greed, and his pathetic fantasy of being a player.

Forcing himself up, he bounced off the bedroom wall and staggered into the kitchen. After chugging two glasses of water, he made a strong pot of tea, and drank it slowly, the mug feeling tiny in his hand.

He tried not to think about Jeffyman – and all the rest,

but the trick of jamming it away in the black box didn't work now. Sitting there, he was forced to just let it wash through him. It was awful, sapping all hope, light, and goodness from him.

Back in bed, he drifted in a hellish limbo, the black box open like a treasure chest in a Phantom comic. Except this chest had never held treasure – just the end results of his failure; the sorrow, grief, and regret accruing like the dead earth of a poisoned mine.

Outside, the rain pounded down, leaves rattling against the glass louvre windows.

At some point, the phone rang again, but he stayed put, and fell asleep. When he surfaced, it was still raining, the faint light outside somewhere between day and night. He checked his watch, saw it was nearly five thirty.

Hungry as, he made scrambled eggs and toasted the last of the bread. It was tasteless, but he ate it all. He had another cup of tea and rolled a joint.

Gratefully, mindlessly stoned, he turned on the TV and blankly watched two women in bikinis run along a sun-drenched, palm-fringed beach. It looked just like here. Except for the sunshine.

The shrill cry of the phone cut through the continuous boom of rain, and he laboriously got up and answered it.

It was Dad, but it was bloody hard to understand him; the hammering roof drowning out his words. Stoned, Seth strained to hear. Someone had rung yesterday wanting to see him. About something important. When Dad said the names, Seth got him to shout them out again.

Captain Hansen. Gus Reynolds.

He showered, shaved, and dressed. Out in the teeming dusk, Machans was empty, everybody sensibly tucked up at home. At the highway intersection, the flood height markers were a third of the way up. Coming into town, he saw drains being overwhelmed and some street corners already under.

On the deserted Esplanade, he parked by the Mulgrave Shire Chambers and raced in under the lit awnings along the front of the Pacific International. Lights were on in the 1906 Strand Bar, but its front door was shut, and the rain swept terrace was empty of tables and chairs.

Inside the hotel, Simon was at reception, his face pale and distressed. He came around the counter and put his hand on Seth's arm. "I'm sorry, I really am."

Seth looked around at the big empty foyer, the rain faint beyond the tall glass windows. He heard Hansen's voice in his head, the rasp of his breath.

"He's gone?" he said.

With a gentle squeeze, Simon nodded.

"Night before last. Collapsed and died in his room. But he wasn't alone. Evelyn was with him."

Seth felt unexpected sorrow kick him in the guts. In a mirrored column, he saw himself; his mouth downturned, his shoulders slumped.

Something tore him acutely inside: a kind of tough as guts nostalgia for a time almost gone, a time when the world had been a harder, but more wondrous place.

Hansen had epitomised that time in spades. He'd been larger than life because his life had been huge, spanning eras and oceans; the horizon burned into his retinas; the sway of the deck ingrained in his walk. Voyaging through history – dirty, raw, history – he'd seen things people wouldn't believe.

Attack ships on fire off the Guadalcanal coast. Sea beams from dolphins diving in phosphorescence water. Now all those moments were lost. Like raindrops in the ocean.

Simon, sensing his sadness, put an arm around his shoulder, and the two men stood there while foyer muzak drifted around them.

"He was something else," said Simon.

"He sure was," said Seth.

There wasn't much more to add to that, and he began to turn towards the door. Simon's arm held him.

"Wait. There's something for you," he said. "His lawyer came yesterday and left a few hours ago."

Back behind the desk, Simon put a manila envelope on the counter. Seth, more than zonked now, stared at it.

"You okay?" said Simon.

"Sorta. Had a big one last night."

"Well, that's something."

"And – Evelyn?"

"I think the police questioned her, poor thing."

Seth nodded slowly, his skull empty of thought.

"I saw her leave." Simon nodded at the envelope. "With one of those."

Seth picked it up, stood there like a dill. Simon smiled kindly, gave him a little bye-bye wave. "Go home. Sleep."

Outside, he stood in the hotel's lights, listening to the rain sizzle on the bitumen. Across the road in Anzac Park, there was movement – figures indistinct in the rain-fuzzy glow of the park kiosk's light. They'd been there forever.

On the corner he turned onto the Esplanade, right into the eye of Cairns where The Strand once stood – those first docks and jetties just a few hundred metres to the south. He walked to where the roof ended and the rain began.

Behind him was the well-lit pavement, the string of new signs hanging overhead. Modern times were here, but all around he felt the immensity of the sea, mangroves, and mountains, invisible beyond the electric wash of the city.

Now that trumpet riff came to him: behind it the sweep of bittersweet strings. Repeating in his head, it sounded eternal, like it had always been playing around here.

Slipping the envelope under his shirt, he dashed to the Pig and got in. He flicked on the light and clacked through the tapes in the console. He found the soundtrack album and read the song titles – all those itty-bitty words in felt-tip pen. Track four was called Jake and Evelyn.

He sat back, closed his eyes, the betrayal on Hansen's face that night vivid in his head. Oh man, I stuck it up him by mistake. He thought I was taking the piss. Just what Henry warned me not to do.

He opened the envelope. There was a handwritten note from Gus Reynolds informing him that he needed to sign a deed of gift to start the transfer of a property into his name – a house on a half-acre block in Cairns. At number ten McKenzie Street.

Close to mindless, he slowly drove home; the rain busy silver in the headlights, the Pig throwing up bow-waves of water. Crossing over the Barron River bridge, he sensed the great flood rushing beneath it – massive, brown, and full of secrets.

The windscreen wipers were barely keeping up now, the flooding from the cane fields across the highway. Turning off to Machans, the water was coming up to the wheel arches. In the next hour the road would be cut.

When he pulled into the carport and killed the engine, the emotion he'd been crushing down on, burst out. Tears flooded his eyes and it was like rain pouring out of him.

He'd gone through six kinds of shit in the last thirty-six hours, and he let himself fall now, right off the fucking edge. But to his complete amazement, it wasn't giving up at all – it was freedom, and this rush of liberation and release just about blew the top of his head off. If only he'd known it was this bloody simple.

Sobs of relief hammered his chest, and that black box of pain floated off into the night.

After a bit, he wiped his eyes, blew his nose, and got out into the roaring darkness. Spray blew in on his face as he turned the carport light on. At the back door, he shuffled up the four steps and unlocked the door. Reaching in, his hand feeling for the light switch, he saw in the window by the door, bright lights appear.

He turned. Cylinders of solid rain lit up, moving fast; a vehicle coming up Cinderella Street; young fellas going to the roaring mouth of the river for a look-see.

The blinding smears approached fast, then the vehicle rapidly slowed, and swung into his drive. He hurled the envelope into the house, and snapped off the light.

Rapidly locking the back door, he leapt down the steps. Skidding along the edge of the carport slab, he made for the light switch. But the vehicle was fast, and it powered right up, its high beams making him a perfect target.

His blood turned to ice. That bastard Burns had lied. This was Rockjaw and the Barrys. They knew who he was, and they'd come for their dope – and revenge.

He'd run hard now, but these mongrel cops were going to chase him out onto the thundering darkness of the beach and hunt him down like a dog.

Regret and shame smashed him. Dad. Sophie. Stasia. Lou. All of his mates. He knew what they'd think.

Another dead outlaw. Another stupid Kelly boy.

Squinting hard against the headlights, he scrabbled at the carport light switch. As he thumbed it off, the vehicle's lights and engine died.

In complete darkness, Seth blinked madly, trying to rid his eyes of the high-beam burn, his brain racing to get ahead of what was about to go down.

Over the roar of the rain he heard a car door slam, and Stasia ran laughing out of the darkness into his arms.

Author's Note

I have endeavoured to evoke a time that existed a couple of years before I lived in Far North Queensland. I have used research and the memories of older friends to recreate this era.

Far North Queensland is full of characters. Over the years, I've been lucky enough to meet a few of them. So, this is where I tell you that the 'resemblance to anyone living or deceased in this book is entirely coincidental.'

The Power of Rain is the final novel in a trilogy, but with his origin story established, Seth Kelly will return in a series of stand-alone novels.

A soundtrack to The Power of Rain

Like Seth Kelly, I love music. Here is some of the music from
the book, plus some complimentary tracks that speak of
the place and era – the times, latitude, and attitude.

Stone Cold Crazy – Queen
Me & Baby Brother – War
Miss Evil – Frijid Pink
Harbor Lights – Boz Scaggs
Fire on The Bayou – Neville Brothers
A Town Called Malice – The Jam
When I Get it Right – Joan Armatrading
The Brood – The Roach
Sandflower – Ronald Shannon Jackson
Jailanguru Pakarnu – Warumpi Band
G.O.D – Wild Cherries with Lobby Loyde
1999 – Prince
Last Nite – Larry Carlton
It's a Man's Man's World – Renée Geyer
Bustin' Out – Material & Nona Hendryx
Jake & Evelyn – Jerry Goldsmith

Acknowledgements

A huge acknowledgement to my alpha and beta readers for their invaluable feedback and error-spotting abilities. You know who you are.

Mighty big thanks to Mike Sutherst for his geographical, technical, and experiential knowledge, and for the great time location scouting.

Big love and eternal gratitude to my best friend Jan Brown for her savvy advice, continuing support, and keen eye for both facts and emotions.